THE RUNNER

If you'd like to find out more about these
and future titles, visit www.stephenleather.com.

STEPHEN LEATHER
THE RUNNER

HODDER &
STOUGHTON

First published in Great Britain in 2020 by Hodder & Stoughton
An Hachette UK company

1

Copyright © Stephen Leather 2020

The right of Stephen Leather to be identified as the Author of the Work has been
asserted by him in accordance with the Copyright, Designs and Patents Act 1988.

A CIP catalogue record for this title is available from the British Library

Hardback ISBN 9781529345155
Trade Paperback ISBN 9781529345162
eBook ISBN 9781529345179

Typeset in Plantin Light by Palimpsest Book Production Limited,
Falkirk, Stirlingshire

Printed and bound in Great Britain by Clays Ltd, Elcograf S.p.A.

Hodder & Stoughton policy is to use papers that are natural, renewable
and recyclable products and made from wood grown in sustainable forests.
The logging and manufacturing processes are expected to conform to the
environmental regulations of the country of origin.

Hodder & Stoughton Ltd
Carmelite House
50 Victoria Embankment
London EC4Y 0DZ

www.hodder.co.uk

For B.J.

CHAPTER 1

Carlos Martinez let the crowbar in his hand swing to and fro. Blood dripped onto the concrete floor and several drops splattered onto his gleaming loafers. 'Now look what you have made me do,' he growled in Spanish. He glared at the man in front of him. 'Do you have any idea how much these fucking shoes cost?'

The man mumbled incoherently. His name was Jesus Rodriguez and he was as close to death as a man could be while still breathing. He was naked, tied to a metal chair, his head slumped on his chest.

'*Chinga tu madre,*' said Martinez. 'You steal from me and this is what happens.'

One of Martinez's men was filming everything on his phone. Rodriguez wasn't being killed just for revenge or out of anger – he was being killed as a warning to others. No one stole from Martinez. No one. The video would be proof of that.

Martinez swung the crowbar again, this time against the right knee, which cracked with the sound of a snapping twig. Rodriguez grunted. His eyes were closed now. Martinez nodded at one of his men standing by the sink. The man walked over with a bucket of water and dumped it over Rodriguez. It cascaded over him and splattered over the tiled floor then ran in bloody rivulets towards a drain.

The room they were in had been designed for torture. It was windowless and soundproofed and could only be reached through a secret door in Martinez's huge wood-panelled wine cellar. The wine cellar was in the basement of his sprawling mansion on the outskirts of Mexico City, set in grounds patrolled by men with automatic weapons and surrounded by high walls topped with razor wire and covered by CCTV cameras. Not that Martinez was expecting unwanted visitors. He had dozens of judges and hundreds of cops on his payroll and he knew well in advance when any sort of operation was being mounted against him.

There were fluorescent lights in the ceiling, a large sink with taps and a hose attachment, and several drains in the white tiled floor. The walls were tiled like the floors and dotted with hooks and there were half a dozen chain pulley systems hanging from a heavy girder that ran across the ceiling. A sound system had been placed on a table against one wall. Sometimes Martinez liked to work with music blaring from massive Wharfedale speakers.

He had been beating Rodriguez for almost an hour. He'd used his bare hands at first, punching him left and right. Then he'd used a cut-throat razor to remove an ear and bolt-cutters to take off a couple of toes. Initially Rodriguez had begged for mercy but there was no mercy to be begged for. It was only ever going to end one way and nothing Rodriguez could say or do would change that. Martinez didn't care about the drugs that Rodriguez had stolen. The theft was less than one thousandth of one per cent of his monthly turnover. It was nothing. It wasn't the amount that mattered, it was the principle, and the principle was that anyone who was caught stealing from Carlos Martinez would die and die horribly. It wasn't the first time that Martinez had beaten a man to death, and it wouldn't be the last. Despite the warnings, there was always someone who thought it was worthwhile to take the risk.

Martinez walked over to a table next to the sound system. On it was a bottle of Domaine Leroy Clos de Vougeot Grand Cru, one of his favourite wines. He had half a dozen cases and each bottle cost more than two thousand dollars. He had already drunk half the bottle and he sloshed more wine into his glass. As he raised the glass to his lips, a mobile phone rang and Martinez looked around, annoyed at the interruption. The phone was in the pocket of Arturo Garcia's jacket and he grimaced apologetically. 'Sorry, Patrón,' he mumbled as he hurried out of the room.

The man who had poured water over Rodriguez started slapping his face, back and forth. When Rodriguez remained unconscious, the man turned to Martinez and shrugged. '*El esta muerto*, Patrón.'

Martinez nodded, checked that the camera was still filming, put down his glass and then brought the crowbar down on the unconscious man's head with all his might. The skull split open like a ripe melon and brain matter splattered across the floor. He raised the crowbar again and the second blow obliterated what was left of the top of the skull. Martinez stood staring at the carnage he had caused, breathing heavily. He wiped his mouth with his shirt sleeve. 'Fuck you, and fuck your family,' he said. He spat at the corpse.

Garcia reappeared. 'Patrón,' he said, holding up the phone.

'What?' shouted Martinez, and Garcia flinched.

'Patrón, it is Javier,' said Garcia. 'There is a problem in London.'

Martinez growled, tossed the bloody crowbar onto the floor and snatched the phone from Garcia's shaking hand. 'Do I have to do everything myself?' he snarled.

CHAPTER 2

Sally Page took a quick look at her Apple Watch as her feet pounded on the pavement. It was eight thirty, on the dot. There were two women ahead of her pushing toddlers in strollers, so she looked over her shoulder to check that the road behind was clear and then dropped into the gutter for four steps to overtake them. She was breathing slowly and evenly. It was just four miles from her flat in Fulham to her office in Wimbledon and she always ran, rain or shine. It was partly for the exercise, but truth be told she was pretty much addicted to running. She loved the feel of moving at speed under her own power, totally in control of her every movement.

She ran over Putney Bridge, enjoying the cool breeze that blew along the Thames. There were two bridges connecting Fulham to Putney: a road bridge with pavements either side, and a rail bridge with a pedestrian and cycle bridge that ran alongside it. The problem with the rail bridge was that cyclists seemed to regard it as their own personal bridge, seeing runners as an alien species that needed to be put in their place. They always waited until the last second to change direction if they were heading towards her, often deliberately brushing her and throwing in a volley of verbal abuse for good measure. It was just easier to run on Putney Bridge, even though it was cluttered with pedestrians first thing in the morning.

Sally always ran towards the traffic and had done ever since 22 March 2017, when a Muslim fanatic by the name of Khalid Masood had driven his car into pedestrians on the south side of Westminster Bridge, killing four people and injuring fifty more. He'd then gone on a knife rampage, murdering a policeman before being shot dead by an armed officer. From that day on Sally had taken extra care when running across Putney Bridge. The pavement was almost a foot above the road so she figured it was unlikely that a car would be able to mount the curb, but she knew that she would stand a better chance of surviving if the attack came from the front rather than the back.

She ran off the bridge and headed up Putney High Street with its trendy mix of coffee shops, restaurants and hairdressers. She passed the Odeon cinema on her left. The road became Putney Hill as it climbed south.

Even in this sedate part of the city, running wasn't without its dangers and she had to be constantly alert, especially when she was near shops. The pavements were usually fairly empty at that time of the morning but what pedestrians there were regarded runners with contempt if not outright hostility. As for motorists, they even hated each other, let alone those who travelled under their own steam. And even other runners seemed to regard her with disdain. Perhaps one in five would acknowledge her with a nod or a tight smile, but most either avoided eye contact or sneered judgementally at her baggy tracksuit bottoms and University of Reading sweatshirt.

Sally dressed for comfort while she ran, and her trainers were the only expensive item she was wearing. She had learned from experience that scrimping on running shoes was a big mistake. The ones on her feet that day were Reebok Floatride Run Fast Pro shoes. They had cost more than £150 but were worth every penny. She had two pairs – pink and green – and she alternated them. Today she was wearing green. Each shoe weighed three and a half ounces – less than her iPhone – but the underfoot platform offered plenty of support. She had her hair held back with a green scrunchie – she hadn't deliberately tried to colour-coordinate with her trainers, it was just the luck of the draw – and her face was free of make-up. It was a cool March morning and she had stopped wearing her beanie hat and fingerless gloves the previous month. By the time May came she would probably switch her tracksuit bottoms for shorts and swap the sweatshirt for a T-shirt, maybe even a vest. But everything she wore was functional rather than decorative. Running wasn't about fashion, it was about running, period. Sally had been a runner for pretty much all of her twenty-four years. Even as a toddler she had hurried everywhere, and she had started running for fun while still at primary school. At secondary school the head of physical education had tried to encourage her to run for the county but she had never been interested in running competitively. She ran for herself, and that was all there was to it.

She reached a set of traffic lights, jogging on the spot as she waited for the little green man to appear. She took another quick look at her watch. Eight thirty-six. Bang on time. The green man flicked on and she was just about to cross when a bike courier wearing black Lycra flashed by. 'Arsehole!' he shouted at the top of his voice – a bit unfair considering he was clearly running a red light.

She continued to run up Putney Hill. The road sloped up gradually but it was still the toughest part of the run and her calves began to burn. On the opposite side of the road groups of neatly dressed schoolgirls in purple uniforms gathered in groups before heading into Putney High School, while others were being dropped off, mainly by glossy women driving SUVs.

She reached the top of the hill and picked up speed. Putney Heath was to her right, bordered by the Green Man pub. There had been a pub on the site since 1700, and back in the day duellists would fortify themselves with a drink or two before heading off to the heath to fight to the death. Now that most duels were fought on social media, the pub was more commonly frequented by middle-class trendies and tourists, taking advantage of the pretty beer garden and better-than-average food. The area outside the pub was the terminus for the buses that served Putney and there were always passengers waiting at the covered bus stop.

She slowed as she crossed the road and then sped up as she headed south. Some days she ran across Putney Heath and then through Wimbledon Common, but she had hit the snooze button on her alarm clock and spent an extra ten minutes in bed that morning so she stuck to the road. She much preferred running across the common but the trails were uneven and littered with twigs and stones so it slowed her pace.

She felt the familiar burn in her calf muscles again, but she actually relished the discomfort, knowing that it was only by pushing her limits that she would improve. Her arms were powering up and down and she felt the sweat beading on her neck and back but her breathing stayed relaxed and even. She wasn't even close to being tired. Four miles was nothing; on Saturdays and Sundays she ran at least twelve and she had run the London Marathon route many times. She had never completed the marathon itself – she never wanted to run in a herd – but her solo times would always place her in the top one hundred if she had taken part.

She reached a set of traffic lights and jogged on the spot until she got the signal to cross. She ran over the A3 and now it was Wimbledon Common on her right. She raised her Apple Watch to her mouth as she ran. 'What's my heart rate?' she asked. The heart rate app kicked in and after a few seconds it gave her a reading of 125. She smiled. Not bad at all.

She skirted the common, then followed the road to the right and ran past King's College School on her left, and the stone-built Crooked Billet pub on the right. The pub was close enough to her place of work that she sometimes had lunch there, and it was where they went to celebrate promotions and birthdays.

She looked both ways, waited for an SUV with three children in the back to roar by, then jogged across the road and headed down a side street. The house was a hundred yards ahead of her and she kept the pace up until she reached the front gate, jogging on the spot as she opened it. It was a Victorian detached house with bay windows and a single garage to the right. The small front lawn had been paved over years earlier and was now used to store plastic rubbish bins. She went around to the rear of the house. The front door was only used for deliveries – everyone else used the kitchen door. A CCTV camera looked down from the roof, one of four covering the approaches to the house.

Another camera was fixed to the roof of the garage, aimed at the kitchen door. There was a metal keypad to the right of the door and she tapped in the six-digit code. The door mechanism clicked and she pushed the door open and stepped inside.

Tony Watson was staring into the fridge. She said hello but he didn't turn to look at her. 'The fridge isn't working again,' he muttered. 'It's the bloody thermostat. We'll be lucky if we don't all go down with food poisoning.' Watson was in his late twenties, tall and gangly with old acne scars peppering his cheeks. Sally figured he was probably gay but he was a private person, par for the course in their line of work, so she knew next to nothing about him. He closed the fridge door, a can of Coke in his hand. 'The bloody coffee maker's died, too.'

Sally eased past him and opened the fridge. She kept her Evian water on the second shelf down and she took out a bottle, unscrewed the top and drank half before she went through to the hallway. There were two doors to the left. In a previous life the room nearest the kitchen had been for dining and the one at the front for sitting. They were both now used as offices, and were filled with filing cabinets, desks and computers, though the worn carpets and flock wallpaper were original. The stairs were to the right and Sally headed up them. The stair carpet was worn and frayed in places and she had to be careful where she placed her feet. One of the men who worked on the upper floor, David Hansard, had taken a tumble a few months earlier and had twisted his knee badly. David was due to leave the house in a few weeks and was being cagey about where he was going.

Sally worked in what had originally been the front bedroom of the house. There was a bay window overlooking the front garden and the street beyond. Drew Mountford was already at work, blinking through his thick-lensed glasses at two screens filled with images of children being abused. Mountford had taped plastic boards to the sides of his screens so that Sally couldn't see what he was watching from her desk, and she always averted her eyes when she walked behind him. 'Morning,' he said. 'Did they tell you the coffee maker's buggered?'

'Yeah, Tony said.'

'Who do we talk to about getting a replacement?'

'Angie in Supplies, I'll call her.'

'Cheers,' said Mountford.

'Hi Fiona,' said Sally, heading over to her desk. Sally was the longest serving in the house so her desk was in the best position, facing the window.

Fiona Hyde was the newest recruit in the house, a tall brunette who had recently graduated with a first-class degree in Arabic Studies from the University of Manchester. Like Tony Watson she was fluent in Arabic and they always used the language to talk to each other, which Sally felt was both pretentious and annoying. Sally spoke reasonable French and passable German but Tony and Fiona's language skills were at a whole different level.

'I don't know how you do it,' sighed Fiona. Her desk was facing the wall. She had moved soon after she had been assigned to the house, so that she didn't have to look at Mountford's screens.

Sally sat down and unzipped her backpack. 'Saves me a fortune on bus fares,' she said. She took out her fake Prada handbag and her genuine iPhone and put them next to her keyboard. Sally pulled open the bottom drawer of her desk, took out her washbag and towel and shoved her backpack in. Then she opened the pine wardrobe between her desk and Mountford's. Most of it was filled with files but the original hanging rods were in place and she used the left-hand side to store several work outfits. There were no written rules about how they were supposed to dress in the house, but most of the staffers dressed as if they were in head office: suits, or blazers and trousers, though Fiona was a big fan of Ted Baker and Karen Millen dresses. Drew was an exception; he was close to retirement and so he had taken to turning up in a sweatshirt and cargo pants.

Sally had to make half a dozen Tube journeys that day so she chose a pair of black trousers, a dark blue shirt and a black linen jacket. There were three pairs of shoes and she took a pair of black pumps with low heels. She took her outfit, washbag and towel to the bathroom. It was small, a toilet against the far wall, a pink plastic bath with an electric shower to the right and a washbasin to the left. The grouting between the white tiles had gone grey with age and the ceiling was dotted with mould. There was a frosted window behind the sink but it wouldn't open. The only ventilation came from a plastic fan set into the glass that hadn't worked since Sally had moved into the house, two years earlier.

She closed the door, hung up her outfit and placed her washbag and towel on the lid of the toilet. She stripped off and stepped into the bath. The shower was a hit-and-miss affair; sometimes the pressure was just right and the water comfortably warm, but more often than not there was a problem, either a measly flow or the temperature ice cold or boiling hot. She took the shower head and pointed it at the tiled wall as she pressed the button to start the water. She let it run for a few seconds and then tested it. It was warm, so she fixed the head back into its holder and showered, using her own shampoo and body wash.

When she'd finished she towelled herself dry and put on her work outfit. Her hair was short enough that she never needed a dryer and a few minutes brushing was all it took to make herself presentable.

She hung her running gear in the wardrobe and put her trainers on the windowsill so that they would catch the sun. 'Shall I do a coffee run if the machine's broken?' she asked. 'I need my caffeine.'

'I'd love a latte with an extra two shots,' said Fiona. 'And a chocolate muffin.'

'You're an angel,' said Mountford, who was looking at a series of photographs of a middle-aged couple abusing what appeared to be a newborn baby. Page shuddered and averted her eyes. 'I don't know how you can look at that stuff without puking,' she said.

'Somebody's got to do it,' said Mountford. 'And it's not as if I've got a sex life to fuck with. Americano with a splash of milk,' he said.

'I'll just check my diary and then I'll head out to Costa,' said

Sally. She dropped down onto her chair and logged on to her computer, keying in a password and pressing her right thumb on a small scanner. Once she had access to the system she called up her diary and sat back as she ran through the list of the tasks she had to carry out. She was responsible for two dozen apartments and houses and she was scheduled to visit three that day. One needed gas and electricity meter readings taken, which was a nuisance because the only way to get to the gas meter was to stand on a kitchen worktop. There were Amazon deliveries scheduled for the second of the three, and she had to give the third one a quick clean.

Her social media workload was much heavier. She had several dozen Twitter accounts, all of which had to be attended to, and as many Facebook and Instagram accounts too. Plus she had six Oyster cards and a dozen shop loyalty cards, credit cards and debit cards that needed to be used. It was boring, run-of-the-mill stuff but at least she didn't have to watch child porn.

She leaned over and pressed her thumb against the reader on the front of the safe next to her desk. The locking mechanism clicked and she turned the handle to open it. Inside were dozens of padded envelopes, each with a barcode and a name and address. She flicked through the envelopes and found the three that corresponded to that day's work. She closed the safe and put the envelopes on her desk. Each envelope contained a set of keys and a thumb drive with all the information about the property. She put the envelopes into her handbag.

The Oyster cards, shop loyalty cards and credit cards were in a filing cabinet, listed alphabetically under the name of the card owner. She took out all the cards she would be using that day, slotted them into a wallet and put that into her bag too.

'Do you want a muffin or a croissant?' she asked Mountford.

'A banana chocolate muffin would go down a treat,' said Mountford. He fumbled in his pocket but Sally told him he could pay her later.

'Actually Sally, I'm going to work through lunch today,' said Fiona. 'Can you pick me up a salad or something?'

'Sure,' said Sally. A memo flashed up on her screen. One of the houses she maintained was marked as 'out of bounds', meaning she wasn't to visit until the ban was lifted. It was the large house in Hampstead, the one she was due to clean. She was only expected to check that the house was spick and span and to make sure that all the lights and taps worked, but the cancellation meant a reduced workload and she was grateful for small mercies.

She picked up her handbag and phone. 'Right, I won't be long,' she said.

Mountford waved but kept his eyes on his screens.

The smaller bedroom was being used by Mo Chowdhury and David Hansard. They always worked with their door closed and she knocked before opening. Both men were Sally's age, pretty much. Chowdhury was an IT specialist who was forever moaning that his skills were being wasted, but Hansard's degree had been in drama and he enjoyed playing different roles on Facebook and Twitter – so much so that sometimes his enthusiasm had to be reined in. 'I'm doing a coffee run, guys,' she said.

Chowdhury twisted around in his seat. He had loosened his tie and tossed it over one shoulder. His hair was unkempt as if he had just got out of bed, but Sally knew it was a look that took the best part of five minutes in front of the mirror to achieve. 'An iced cappuccino would be great, thanks,' he said.

'Costa or Starbucks?' asked Hansard, peering at one of his two screens.

'Costa,' said Sally.

'I hate Starbucks,' he said.

'That's good, because I'm going to Costa.'

'Get me a latte with an extra shot.'

'What's the magic word?'

'Now,' he said. He turned around and grinned at her. 'Sorry, I'm giving this Manchester United fan some grief. He knows fuck all about football.' He pulled his wallet out and before Sally could say that she'd catch him later he had thrust a ten pound note at her. 'I'll buy Mo his coffee too.'

'You're a star, mate,' said Chowdhury, who was looking at one of his screens. It was a Twitter page and Chowdhury had just tweeted a meme that featured a man in an orange jump suit having his head hacked off. Sally looked away and closed the door as she left.

She went quickly down the stairs and knocked on the door to the front room before opening it. There were three workstations but only one was occupied. Jane Birkett was about ten years older than Sally. She'd joined the house after five years working for an NGO in Africa and after just three months had been given a new assignment in head office, starting the following week.

Sally, on the other hand, had been in the house for two years and was no nearer getting a new posting than the day she had moved in. She was pretty sure that it was her boss, Ian Hadley, who was blocking her move. Hadley had made a clumsy pass at her in the pub about a month after he'd joined, and while she'd rejected his advances with a smile and a laugh, he'd clearly taken offence and had been cold towards her ever since. All communication between them was by email and he always referred to her as Ms Page. Sally knew that it wasn't Jane's fault that she had leap-frogged over her, but she still found it hard to smile at the woman. 'Hi Jane, I'm doing a Costa run. Can I get you anything?'

Jane looked over and grinned. 'Brilliant,' she said. 'I was thinking of going myself but I've got a dozen Facebook pages to update by lunch.'

'No problem,' said Sally. 'What do you want?'

'Decaff cappuccino,' she said. 'Low-fat milk.'

'You've got it,' said Sally, though she really couldn't see the point of decaffeinated coffee.

'And be a love and pick me up a croissant,' said Jane.

'Will do,' said Sally. Part of her wanted to point out that the calories in the croissant pretty much made a nonsense of the request for low-fat milk, but she just smiled. 'You can settle up with me when I get back.'

'It's going to rain, isn't it?' asked Jane.

Sally raised her Apple Watch to her mouth. 'What's the weather like?' she said.

'The weather's looking good today, up to nineteen degrees,' said Siri. Sally had set the voice to a male South African, and every time it spoke she pictured a tall, broad-shouldered, suntanned guy with blond hair wearing khaki shorts and carrying a large rifle. He was maybe driving a Land Rover with a dead antelope strapped across the bonnet, which she always found strange because she had been a vegetarian pretty much from birth.

'You're such a tech geek,' said Jane.

'It's a great piece of kit,' said Sally. 'It wakes me up, monitors my heart, checks on my activity levels, and reminds me what I'm supposed to be doing.'

'Sounds like my dad,' laughed Jane.

There was only one person in the back room, Afifa Farooqi. Afifa was usually the first in the house and the last out, a hard worker who always seemed to be smiling. She had been in the house for almost five months and Sally had never seen her frown, never mind get upset or angry. She had been born in Delhi but had moved to the UK when she was two years old, and had graduated with a first from either Oxford or Cambridge; Sally could never remember which. Afifa was wearing a pale blue hijab and was staring at her screens through her glasses. 'Coffee run, Afifa, the machine has died apparently,' said Sally. 'Do you want anything?'

'I'd love a caffè misto,' said Afifa.

'What's a caffè misto?' asked Sally.

'A fifty-fifty mix of fresh-brewed coffee and steamed milk.'

'Caffè misto it is,' said Sally, and closed the door.

Tony Watson was still in the kitchen. 'I'm doing a coffee run,' said Sally.

'I'd kill for an iced latte,' said Watson. He held up the can of Coke. 'I hate Coke.'

'Why did you buy it then?'

'I didn't. I just found it.'

'It had better not be Drew's, he goes apeshit when people take his stuff,' said Sally.

Watson put his hand in his pocket and took out a handful of change.

'You can pay me when I get back,' Sally said, heading for the door. She went out and walked around to the driveway, then let herself out of the gate. A woman in a red coat was standing next to a large white poodle which was trying to defecate in the gutter, and Sally couldn't help but smile at the look of concentration on the dog's face. The woman was whispering encouragement to the poodle and holding a blue plastic bag. Sally was pretty sure she made a habit of dumping the filled bags in the gutter but she had never actually caught her in the act. The woman probably wasn't breaking the law – she was clearing up after her dog, which is what the law required, but instead of taking it home she dropped the bag in the gutter when no one was watching. The woman caught Sally's smile and glared at her so she looked away. Londoners didn't react well to smiles, generally.

The sky was clear and almost cloudless but there was a nip in the air, so she walked faster to get her blood flowing. She wanted to run or at least jog but the shoes she was wearing were only really up to a fast walk.

There were only two people queuing when she got to Costa Coffee, and in less than a minute a young Polish girl with green streaks in her blonde hair was taking Sally's order. It was complex, so Sally spoke clearly and slowly, hoping that she wasn't coming across as patronising. 'So, I need eight coffees in all, with two muffins and a croissant and a salad, but I want to pay for them in four groups of two. Does that make sense?'

'Perfect sense,' said the girl, whose name tag identified her as Zofia.

Sally held up four debit cards. 'And I can just tap, right?'

Zofia smiled brightly. 'Yes, you can.'

Sally split the order into four and tapped each of the cards onto the reader. She had two Costa loyalty cards in her wallet and she handed them over. 'Put the two largest amounts on these,' she said. 'It doesn't matter which is which.'

Zofia added the points to the cards and handed them back along with the four receipts. Sally thanked her but she was already aiming her smile at the next customer. Sally stood at the end of the counter and waited for the two baristas to prepare her order. They were both guys, tall and dark haired, and they spoke to each other in what sounded like an Eastern European language. One had short curly hair and a black plastic tunnel earring about the size of a ten-pence coin in his left ear. Sally understood the attraction of tattoos and piercings, and had often thought about getting one or the other herself, but making a huge hole in your ear was mutilation rather than decoration. He turned suddenly and caught her staring at him. She blushed, but didn't look away because that would make her appear guilty. Instead she smiled. 'Jenny?' he said.

Sally nodded. Jenny was the name she had given Zofia.

'You drink a lot of coffee,' he said.

She laughed. 'It's for the office.'

He placed two coffees in front of her. His colleague put down another two, then they went back to their machines. The equipment clanked and hissed and the two baristas resumed talking to each other as they worked. When they had made all eight coffees, the guy with the ear stretcher went to the food cabinet to get the muffins, croissant and salad while his colleague placed everything in four bags to match the orders that Sally had given Zofia.

She thanked them and headed back outside. She walked quickly, two bags in each hand, her heels clicking on the pavement. Two men were manoeuvring a boxed washing machine out of a delivery van. Looking at her, one of them muttered something and they both laughed and nodded. Sally guessed that they were talking about her and she flashed them a smile as she walked by.

CHAPTER 3

S ally reached the house and held all four bags in her left hand as she opened the gate with her right. As she flicked the lock she found herself looking at a black Mitsubishi Outlander parked down the road. The driver was looking at her and holding a mobile phone to his ear. As she met the man's gaze he looked away and the hairs on the back of her neck stood up. She shivered. She kept looking at the man but he seemed relaxed enough. He was in his thirties and wearing a black bomber jacket and black jeans, and he was either bald or had a shaved head, on which was perched a pair of wraparound sunglasses. He looked for all the world like a nightclub bouncer. She shook her head at her over-reaction, pushed open the gate and walked around the side of the house. She looked up at the CCTV camera on the roof of the garage. Then she looked at the kitchen door and realised that it was open. That was against all security protocols. She hurried over and pushed it wider. Had she left it open? She could well be in real trouble if that was the case. She stepped into the kitchen and looked around. Watson wasn't there but his can of Coke was on the kitchen table.

She walked into the hallway, knocked on the first door and opened it. Tony Watson was dead on the floor, blood blossoming on his chest, his eyes wide and staring. Afifa was slumped across her keyboard, blood dripping from her chair and soaking into the carpet. Her pale blue hijab was glistening with wet blood. Her computer had been smashed and ripped apart. Sally looked around the room frantically. The three computers there had all been destroyed. The safe containing the keys and thumb drives was open and the envelopes had been taken.

Her hands were trembling and her heart was pounding. She backed out of the room. She looked to her right and realised that the door was open. She took a step towards the open door. And another. Jane Birkett was lying face down by her desk, her head in a pool of glistening blood. Sally heard footsteps on the stairs and looked to her right. Someone was coming down.

She backed away to the kitchen. She had barely reached the kitchen door when something black and metallic appeared over the banister. The Costa bags slipped from her shaking hands as she turned to run.

She heard more footsteps on the stairs but she didn't look around. She ran into the kitchen, slamming the door behind her. There was a knife block with half a dozen black-handled knives in it and for a second she thought about grabbing one to defend herself, but almost immediately realised it would be futile. Whatever weapon was coming down the stairs, it would be more than a match for a knife. She hurried over to the kitchen door and pulled it open. There was a man standing there, holding a mobile phone. It was the man from the Mitsubishi 4x4. He was as surprised as she was. He froze for a fraction of a second, stopping mid-sentence, but then he took a step back, the phone still stuck to his ear. Sally heard feet clattering on the stairs. She couldn't tell if there were two of them or three but there was definitely more than one person coming after her. She kicked out with her right foot and caught the man in front of her in the groin. The breath exploded from his mouth as he bent forward and she slapped him hard, immediately cursing her stupidity for doing it with the flat of her hand and not her fist. The blow sent him staggering to the left and knocked his sunglasses to the ground. She drew back her hand and this time punched him in the side of the head, yelping with pain as she connected. The blow grazed her knuckles but it did the trick. He was bent double now, gasping for breath. She lashed out with her foot again and caught him just below the knee. The leg buckled and the man fell to the ground, still clutching his phone. Sally sprinted along the side of the house. She reached the garden gate. The Outlander was there. Empty. She heard shouts behind her. She looked left, then right. She ran to the right. If they used the vehicle they'd have to turn it around and that would take time.

She ran at full speed and was soon panting with the effort so she slowed and took a look over her shoulder. The pavement was clear. There was a crossroads ahead of her and she ran right. A postman was pushing a cart laden with parcels. Sally ran past him. She had slowed to her regular pace, but the shoes were starting to hurt. She looked over her shoulder. Other than the postman, the road was clear. Maybe they weren't chasing her. She reached another junction and went right again. That meant she was running parallel to the road where the house was. That wasn't a good idea, she realised – now she was heading back to where the kills were. She ran back the way she had come. There was still no sign of anyone chasing her. Maybe they had left. She hurried across the junction and started jogging, her bag slapping against her side with every step. At the next crossroad she went right. There was a phone box ahead of her. She opened the door and went inside, then took out her mobile. She called Ian Hadley but the call went straight to his voicemail. 'Ian, you need to call me right back, something terrible has happened.' She wanted to say more but ended the call.

The window just above her head shattered and glass crashed around her. She ducked down. She hadn't heard the shot and had no idea which direction it had come from. There was every chance her pursuers were using silencers. She kept low as she pushed open the door and a second shot slammed into the phone, smashing the receiver into several pieces.

She shoved her phone into her bag and looked around. She knew she had to move and move fast; if she stayed in the phone box she'd be a sitting duck. But if she moved in the wrong direction she'd be walking into the line of fire. She looked up at the shattered phone. The second shot had come through the open door so that meant the shooter was ahead of her. She pushed the door hard and kept low as she rushed out, then she turned to the left and around the back of the phone box. Her phone vibrated in her bag. Was that Hadley calling back? A third shot smacked into the pavement by her foot and ricocheted away. She ran, bent double, her heart pounding. There was a young couple walking hand in hand towards her. 'Gun!' she shouted but they just frowned at her.

She kept running, expecting another shot at every second, but by the time she had covered fifty feet she realised that the shooting had stopped. She straightened up and looked around. There was no sign of the shooter. The roads were clear. She kept walking, away from the phone box. She took another quick look over her shoulder. The young couple had stopped and were looking at her. They hadn't heard the shots or seen the damage to the phone box so they probably thought she was deranged.

She turned and carried on walking, her mind racing. She took her phone out of her bag and checked the screen as she walked. It had been Hadley returning her call. He had left a voicemail message but she didn't bother listening to it and just hit redial. He answered almost immediately. 'What's going on, Sally?' he asked.

'Ian, listen to me. Someone has killed everyone in the house. Now they're after me.'

'What on earth are you talking about?'

'Just listen, will you? You need to check the house now. I'm pretty sure everyone is dead but I only saw Tom, Afifa and Jane. They shot them. Now they're trying to shoot me.'

'Sally, if this is some sort of sick joke you need to . . .'

'Ian, will you shut the fuck up!' she shouted. An elderly man in a raincoat and a flat cap gave her an admonishing stare and tutted loudly. She walked faster, taking a quick look over her shoulder. Still no sign of the shooter. Or shooters. She doubted that one man could have killed everyone in the house so there was almost certainly more than one. Plus the driver of the Outlander. 'Check the house, you'll see that I'm not joking. I'm on the street now and they've just shot at me.'

'Who?' asked Hadley. 'Who's shooting at you?'

'How the fuck would I know?' she said. 'Men with guns. Big guns.'

'Sally, you need to calm down,' said Hadley.

Sally saw a black Mitsubishi 4x4 driving down the road towards her. She didn't know if it was the same vehicle that she had seen outside the house and the sun glinting off the windscreen prevented her from seeing who was inside. 'I've got to go,' she said. 'I'll call you back.'

'Sally . . .' began Hadley, but she ended the call. The car was slowing. She turned and ran down a side street, her shoes slipping on the pavement. She thought about kicking them off but decided against it. She'd be able to run faster but only at the risk of hurting herself.

She ran by a row of terraced houses. The front door of one of them was open. She took a quick look over her shoulder. The Outlander was turning into the street. She dashed to the front door and slipped inside. A woman was standing in the kitchen and her jaw dropped when she saw Sally in her hallway. 'Who the fuck are you?' shouted the woman. She was preparing to load her washing machine and was holding a pile of dirty clothes.

Sally pushed the front door closed and raised her hands. 'I'm so, so sorry,' she said. 'Someone's chasing me.'

'Who?' the woman clasped her clothes to her chest. She was in her thirties, her dyed blonde hair tied back in a ponytail, with no make-up and dark patches under her eyes as if she hadn't had a good night's sleep.

There were three framed photographs on the wall to Sally's left, of the woman and three young children, two boys and a girl. There was no man in any of the pictures, so a single mum, either a widow or the husband had walked out. The latter was more likely, Sally decided. 'It's my boyfriend,' she said. 'My ex. He's been stalking me. Please, can I just stay here for a few minutes?'

'Is he outside?'

'He's in his car.' Sally took a step towards the woman, keeping her hands up. 'Look, I'm sorry to burst in on you, I'm not crazy, I promise. My ex is a bastard.'

The woman looked at the grazed knuckles on Sally's right hand. 'Did he do that?'

Sally nodded. 'He pushed me over.' She sniffed. 'He's always getting physical.' She licked her knuckles and forced a smile.

The woman smiled thinly. 'We've all been there, darling,' she said. She dropped the washing on the floor and walked into the hallway. 'I'll have a look outside, check if he's still there. What sort of car is he driving?'

'A black Mitsubishi 4x4,' she said. 'A big one with tinted side windows. Please don't open the door.'

'I won't, I'll check through the curtains. Don't worry.'

'Please, be careful,' said Sally. Her phone rang and she switched it off.

The woman walked into the front room and peered through the curtains, left and right. 'I don't see him,' she said.

'Thank God,' said Sally.

'Are you okay?'

Sally shook her head. 'Not really.'

'Look, why don't you have a cuppa?'

'Are you sure?'

The woman nodded and came back into the hallway. She put her hands on Sally's shoulders and smiled at her. 'Don't let the bastard grind you down,' she said.

Sally forced a smile. 'Thank you.'

The woman hugged her and patted her on the back, then took her through to the kitchen. 'You should run your hand under the tap,' she said.

Sally went over to the sink. It was full of dirty plates and dishes. She ran the tap and let the cold water play over her injured hand.

The woman switched on the kettle, then gave Sally a roll of kitchen towel. Sally tore off a piece and dabbed at her knuckles as the woman opened a cupboard, took out a first aid kit and selected a tube of Savlon. 'Put some of this on it,' she said. 'I'm Chantelle.'

'Kathy,' said Sally, the lie coming automatically. She had several prepared backstories that she could call on if necessary.

'Come on, sit down, take the weight off your feet.' Chantelle gestured for Sally to sit down at a small table. There were two toy cars and a phone with a cracked screen next to two dirty cups.

'You got kids?' asked Chantelle.

Saying she had a child would be a good way of building empathy with the woman, but it was a lie that would lead to other lies that might lead to her undoing, so she just shook her head.

'That's something,' said Chantelle. 'I've got three. Little monkeys but I love them to bits.' She applied some cream to Sally's scraped knuckles.

'They're at school?' Sally asked.

Chantelle nodded and bent down to pick up her laundry. She pushed it into the machine and set the programme. 'So what happened?' she asked as she set two mugs by the kettle and dropped a tea bag into each.

Sally took a deep breath. Her mind had been working overtime putting together a decent cover story that would keep the woman on side. 'He moved out a couple of days ago but came back today saying he wanted the stereo. I said no way, I paid for that but he said it was his money. One of my neighbours is a body-builder, a real tough guy, and he came around to see what the noise was. He told Danny – that's my ex – that he should go. He did, but when I left the flat he was waiting outside. That's when he grabbed me and I fell over. I got up and ran away and I was heading for the bus when I saw his car.'

The kettle boiled and Chantelle poured water onto the tea bags and put the mugs and a carton of milk onto the table. She sat down and looked earnestly at Sally. 'Call the cops, love.'

Even if Chantelle had known the real story, calling the police wasn't an option. MI5 always preferred to keep the police at arm's length. Once the police found out what had happened at the house, it would be in the public domain and Sally was sure that her bosses wouldn't want that. 'I can't,' she said. 'I did that once before and he went ballistic.'

'You can take out a restraining order against him.'

'He wouldn't care,' said Sally.

'Then he goes to prison.' Chantelle poured milk into her mug. She offered some to Sally and Sally nodded.

Sally forced a smile. 'For how long? A few weeks? A few months? And then what? He gets out and is madder than before.' She shook her head. 'I'm going to stay with my folks for a while. He doesn't know where they live, I'll be safe there.'

'That sounds like a plan,' said Chantelle. She poured milk into Sally's mug, then sipped her own tea. 'Men can be bastards, can't they?'

'True, that,' said Sally.

'I had three kids with mine and he still couldn't keep it in his pants. Screwed behind my back three times that I know about but I kept forgiving him, like you do. Then he made a pass at my sister. My fucking sister. He said he was just drunk, but what sort of bastard does that?'

'I'm sorry,' said Sally. 'Did he ever hurt you?'

Chantelle shook her head. 'Not physically. With him it was all head games, you know. Telling me I'm fat, telling me I'm stupid, telling me I was good for nothing. He was always doing me down. But he never laid a finger on me. Small mercies, I suppose.' She sipped her tea again. 'Men, hey?'

Sally forced a smile. 'Yeah. Can't live with them, can't live without them.'

'I'm doing okay so far,' said Chantelle. 'Me and my Rabbit.'

Sally laughed and clinked her mug against Chantelle's. 'Thank you,' she said.

'Not a problem.' She took a pack of cigarettes from her pocket and offered one to Sally.

'No thanks,' she said.

'I know, disgusting habit and I should give up but it's one of the few pleasures I've got left.' She took a cigarette out and lit it with a disposable lighter, before taking a long pull. When she blew smoke she took care to keep it away from Sally. 'So where do you work?' asked Chantelle.

'An office in Westminster,' she said. 'Accounts. Boring but it pays okay.'

'Does he know where you work? You don't want him turning up there shouting the odds.'

'He's never been,' said Sally, the lies coming more easily now. 'He was never interested in the people I work with, or my friends.'

'That's what they do,' said Chantelle. 'They isolate you then they can control you. He got rid of all my friends and tried to drive a wedge between me and my mum.'

'I'm sorry,' said Sally, and she meant it. She forced a smile, then took out her phone. 'I should go,' she said. 'I'll call an Uber.' She requested an Uber to take her to Thames House. Her driver was called Ahmed and he was driving a Prius. She stared at the screen, wondering if she was doing the right thing. She wanted to phone Hadley but she couldn't say anything while Chantelle was there.

'You're worried that he might still be out there?' asked Chantelle.

Sally looked up from her phone and nodded.

Chantelle stood up. 'I've got just the thing,' she said. She ran upstairs and after a minute or so came hurrying back, holding a long black wig and a parka with a fur lined hood. 'Wear these,' she said. 'Even if he's there he won't recognise you.'

'Are you serious?'

'My bastard husband bought me the wig for a bit of role-playing,' she said. 'It was only afterwards that I realised he wanted me to look like my sister. The parka's too small for me now. I don't think I'll ever lose the weight the twins left me with so I was going to take it to a charity shop.'

Sally reached for her bag. 'At least let me pay you.'

'Don't even think about it,' said Chantelle, holding up a hand. 'I know what you're going through and the least I can do is help. Come on, stand up.'

Sally did as she was told and Chantelle fixed the wig. She stood back and grinned. 'It looks better on you than it ever did on me,' she said.

Sally used her phone to check herself over and she smiled. She looked totally different with long black hair.

Chantelle helped her on with the parka. 'Thank you so much,' said Sally. She hugged her and thanked her again as she blinked away tears. The woman was being so damn sweet and yet pretty much everything Sally had said from the moment she had entered the house had been a lie. 'You'll be okay,' said Chantelle.

Sally looked at her phone. The Uber was less than a minute away. 'I should go,' she said.

Chantelle nodded. 'Let me just check the coast is clear,' she said. She took Sally into the hall and opened the front door. She looked left and right and then nodded. 'Good to go,' she said.

As Sally stepped out of the door, a white Prius arrived. She hugged Chantelle again, then rushed to get into the car. Ahmed twisted around and flashed her a dazzling smile. 'Sally?'

Sally nodded. She had used her own account to book the car. It wouldn't be a good idea to have a legend's journey ending close to MI5 headquarters. 'Did you get the address?'

Ahmed nodded. 'Millbank.'

'Excellent,' said Sally. She took a quick look over her shoulder. The road was clear.

'Having a good day?' asked Ahmed.

'So far, so good,' said Sally. She took out her phone as Ahmed put the car into gear and drove off. Hadley had called back twice after she had ended her call, and made another call ten minutes later. He had left a message each time. She listened to all three. They were short and sweet, telling her to call him back. She wasn't happy about calling Hadley while she was in the Uber, but she didn't see that she had any choice. She called his number and he answered almost immediately.

'Ian, I'm in a taxi, heading to the office now,' she said, letting him know that she couldn't have a secure conversation.

'Are you okay?'

'Yes,' she said. 'All good.' She looked at Ahmed's phone which was in a holder stuck to the windscreen. He was using the Waze satnav app and it was showing her arrival time as 39 minutes.

'I'll be there in about fifty minutes,' she said.

Ahmed twisted around. 'Not so long,' he said. 'Less than forty.'

That confirmed that he was listening to her. 'The driver says less than forty,' she said, letting Hadley know again that the conversation was not secure. 'Have you checked the house?'

'Yes, and as you said, it's a mess. Did you see who did it?'

'I saw one guy, Caucasian. Bald or shaved head. Black jacket.'

'Age?'

'Between thirty and fifty.'

'Anything else?'

'Not really. It was over in seconds, Ian.'

'But if we show you photographs, you'd be able to pick him out?'

'I think so.'

'Good girl,' said Hadley. There was a patronising tone to his voice that made Sally want to scream.

'They had a vehicle. A Mitsubishi Outlander. A black one.'

'An Outlander? What the hell is that?'

'It's a big 4x4. Like a Range Rover.'

'Registration number?' asked Hadley.

'Like this one,' said Ahmed. The driver was pointing through the windscreen. A black Outlander had just pulled in front of them.

'I didn't get the number,' said Sally. 'Look, Ian, we'll talk when I get there, okay.' There were two men sitting in the rear of the car ahead of her. She couldn't see if there was anyone in the front passenger seat. She frowned. It couldn't be the same car from the house, could it?'

The Outlander's brake lights came on. Ahmed muttered under his breath and braked. They were driving parallel to the common now. She looked to her left. It had only been a couple of hours since she had been jogging to work. She shuddered as she remembered what she had seen on the ground floor of the house.

Ahmed was looking in his rear-view mirror and frowning. Sally twisted around. There was another black Mitsubishi SUV behind them. She frowned.

'Sally, are you still there?' asked Hadley.

Sally's heart pounded as she recognised the driver of the car behind them. It was the man from the house.

'Ian, I'm going to have to call you back,' she said and ended the call. She tapped on the screen of her phone, put it in camera mode and took several pictures of the car. It accelerated towards the Prius and she continued to take photographs.

'What is he doing?' asked Ahmed.

The Outlander nudged against the rear of the Prius.

'He hit me!' shouted Ahmed, then he shouted something in another language. He was so busy looking in his rear-view mirror that he hadn't noticed that his front bumper was only feet away from the vehicle ahead of them.

'Ahmed!' she cried. 'Look out!'

His eyes flicked back to the front windscreen and he yelped and slammed on the brake when he saw how close he was to the car in front. Sally hadn't fastened her seat belt and her head slammed into the seat back.

'Sorry,' said Ahmed. 'Are you all right?'

'Just drive,' said Sally. 'Whatever you do, don't stop.'

The car ahead of them was still slowing. She took a quick look over her shoulder. The Prius was boxed in.

'What are they doing?' asked Ahmed, his eyes flicking between the rear-view mirror and the road ahead.

'Can you go around them?' asked Sally, but there was traffic coming their way so she knew the answer before he even shook his head.

'I can't,' he said.

'Okay, but don't stop, okay?'

Ahmed didn't reply.

Sally looked around. The Outlander nudged their rear bumper again. She changed her phone setting to video and pointed at the driver, then moved to film the passenger in the front seat. He saw what she was doing and put his hands over his face. The driver had no choice other than to keep his hands on the steering wheel and he glared at her with undisguised hatred. She finished filming and flashed him two fingers. She put the phone in her pocket and leaned closer to Ahmed. His face was bathed in sweat and he was breathing heavily.

She patted him on the shoulder. 'Don't worry, they're just messing about,' she said.

'They are fucking crazy!' he said.

'Look, Ahmed, I'm going to get out here,' she said.

He looked around. 'What? Why?'

'I've just changed my plans.' She opened her handbag, took out her wallet and gave him a ten pound note. 'Here's a tip for messing you around. I'll get out here and you end the job here. Okay?'

He took the money with his left hand and put it inside his jacket. 'You're sure?'

'I'm sure,' she said. The Prius lurched as the Outlander nudged the rear bumper again. 'Okay, just stop here.'

'He'll hit me.'

'He's already hitting you,' said Sally. 'Trust me, when you stop, he'll stop.' She patted him on the shoulder. 'It'll be okay.'

He nodded, hit the indicator and braked. The car behind them also braked but the one ahead continued on its way. As soon as the Prius had come to a stop, Sally pushed the door open. 'Thanks Ahmed,' she said. 'Five stars.'

She rushed out of the car, slammed the door shut, and hurried across the pavement. She didn't waste time looking at her pursuers, she was sure they would be coming after her. There was no way the cars could drive onto the common which meant they would have to follow on foot and with any luck they wouldn't be runners. Most people could run at full pelt for a few seconds or jog for a few minutes, but only a serious runner could keep going for longer than that. There was a line of trees separating the pavement from the common itself. They were starting to lose their leaves and several fell around her as she threaded her way through. She heard car doors slamming but she kept her head down and concentrated on the ground ahead of her, keeping her breathing as steady as possible. She took a quick look at her watch and made a mental note of the time.

CHAPTER 4

Ellie Cooper, the director's secretary, nodded at the door to the inner office. 'You're to go right in,' she said. She brushed a lock of blonde hair behind her ear and studied the screen of her phone, frowning and wrinkling her nose.

'Thanks, Ellie,' said Ian Hadley. He knocked on the director's door and pushed it open. There were already three people sitting in front of the director's desk. Hadley frowned. He'd hurried up from his office as soon as he got the message from Ellie so he wasn't late.

The director was sitting behind his desk. Hadley had never spoken to Giles Pritchard before, but he had seen him in the lift several times. He was in his early fifties, with slicked-back hair and metal-framed spectacles perched on his hawk-like nose. He had taken off his jacket and loosened his tie. 'Ian, good man, pull up a chair,' he said.

The three people already sitting there turned to look at him. He knew two of them. John Fretwell was in charge of B Section, which handled protective security for MI5 and vetted all staff. Next to him was Liz Bailey, who was responsible for building security at Thames House and MI5's operational properties around the country. The third chair was taken by a man in his late forties, maybe early fifties, square jawed and with close-cropped hair and a nose that appeared to have been broken several times. The man looked at Hadley, his face impassive, and Hadley knew instinctively that he was special forces, almost certainly with the SAS.

There was a spare chair by the window and Hadley carried it over. He placed it a couple of feet away from the stranger and sat down.

'So, just to bring you up to speed, the information given to you by Sally Page is in fact correct. The footie house in Wimbledon has been breached and we are looking at seven confirmed casualties. He looked down at a notepad on the desk in front of him. 'Jane Birkett, Anthony Watson, Drew Mountford . . .' He took a deep breath to compose himself. 'I'm sorry,' he said. 'Drew and I go back a long way.' He looked down at the notepad. 'Fiona Hyde, David Hansard, Mohammed Chowdhury and Afifa Farooqi. All dead. Clearly shot by professionals. The hard drives have been taken, as has the CCTV hard drive, and the thumb drives.'

'My God,' said Hadley.

'They were obviously well briefed and knew exactly what they were doing,' said Pritchard. 'We have absolutely no idea who they were or what they were after. I need to make it clear that at this stage we are keeping this under wraps as much as possible. If there is a terrorism element we don't want to be handing anyone any propaganda victories. The police have not been informed and we are handling this in-house, though we will be using police resources as and when necessary.'

'Forgive me, but it's going to be very hard to keep a lid on this, Giles,' said Fretwell. Fretwell was in his forties, and had been bald since his late teens. He had compensated by growing a beard that he kept neatly trimmed. 'The victims all have friends and family, and we had a team out to check on the house who obviously know what happened.'

'The team has already been spoken to,' said Pritchard. 'The director general's view is that we wait until we know who the perpetrators were before deciding how to handle any announcement. At the moment, the loop as to who knows what happened is small and will stay that way.' He turned to look at Hadley. 'Ian, what's the situation with Sally?'

The question caught Hadley by surprise. He was still trying to assimilate the information he'd been given: that seven of his staff were dead. He shook his head, trying to clear his thoughts. 'I'm sorry, yes. Err, I've spoken to her twice now and I'm afraid she's given me very little information. She said the occupants of the house were dead and that the killers were now trying to kill her. The first time she called she had just been shot at in the street and she had to cut it short because she saw their vehicle. A black Mitsubishi Outlander.' He saw the look of expectation on Pritchard's face and he shook his head. 'She didn't have the registration number. The second time she was in a taxi heading to Thames House. We were cut off, I think the car was attacked.'

'We need to know where the taxi picked her up,' said Pritchard. He looked over at Fretwell. 'Can you get on that, John?'

'Of course,' Fretwell said.

'And what's her situation now?' Pritchard asked Hadley.

'Her phone is off and we don't know where she is.'

Pritchard sat back in his seat. 'What can you tell us about her, Ian? She's been with the footies for almost two years, which is quite a bit longer than usual.'

Hadley kept a fixed smile on his face as he considered his options. The fact that the director knew how long Sally had been in the house meant that he had almost certainly looked at her file, which meant there was every chance that he had seen his assessments of her. Lying to your boss was never a good idea at the best of times, but when you worked for the Security Service an untruth could be a career killer. 'She performed well in her induction tests, but my feeling is that she has yet to live up to her potential,' he said, choosing his words carefully.

'I understand that, but most footies move on after six months. Most of them are very keen to work at Thames House, to be where the action is, as it were. They see being a footie as a chance to prove themselves.'

'And therein, I think, lies Sally's problem,' said Hadley. 'She doesn't seem to be much of a team player. Very much a loner and that's never a good thing, as you know.'

Pritchard didn't nod or smile, he just continued to look at Hadley, leaving a silence so that Hadley would fill it. A standard interrogator's trick. The counter was to sit in silence but Pritchard would spot that gambit immediately and conclude that he was being defensive so Hadley smiled and continued. 'Let me give you an example. Sally is a keen runner. She lives a few miles from the house and she runs to and from work, rain or shine. She showers in the house, and it's disruptive.'

'Did someone complain?'

'No, not officially. But as I said, it's disruptive.'

'We have people run to work at Thames House. And cycle. It's hardly a reason to block promotion.'

'Sally isn't being blocked,' said Hadley. 'I just feel that she isn't ready yet for a move.'

'Because she isn't a team player?'

'Exactly.'

Pritchard nodded but his face remained neutral. 'Do you have any idea why she wasn't killed in the house with her colleagues?'

'She didn't go into any details.'

'Did she say why she wasn't in the house at the time of the attack?'

Hadley shook his head. 'She was very rushed, both times.'

'What was she able to tell you about the attackers?' asked Pritchard.

'She couldn't say much because of the driver. But she gave me a very brief description of one of the men. A Caucasian man aged between thirty and fifty, bald or with a shaved head. Wearing a black jacket. That's all I got and then she said she had to go.'

Fretwell took notes on a small pad.

'Go?' said Pritchard. 'Go where?'

'End the call, I mean. She sounded stressed. I called back but her phone is off.'

'So all we can do is to wait for her to call again?'

Hadley nodded. 'I'm afraid so.'

Pritchard looked over at Fretwell. 'We need to ask the Met to increase their visible presence in the area and get any unused armed response vehicles out looking for black Mitsubishis.'

Fretwell nodded.

'But other than that I can't see there's anything we can do

except wait for Sally's call,' said Pritchard. He looked over at Liz Bailey. 'What's your take on this, Liz?'

Bailey was a former police officer, who had reached the rank of superintendent before transferring from Northumbria Police to MI5. She was a tough, no-nonsense Geordie with three grown-up children and a husband who produced wildlife documentaries. Her hair was greying but she refused to dye it, though her make-up was always flawless and her nails were perfectly manicured.

'It's obviously not a random home invasion,' said Bailey. 'They knew what they were after but more importantly they clearly knew the location of the property and that is a closely guarded secret. It's held by a shell company. All the bills are paid through a footie account, there's nothing to link it to MI5. All the footie properties are run on that basis.'

'So there's been a leak, either here or from the house itself.' Pritchard looked back at Hadley. 'How many footies are currently working out of the Wimbledon premises?'

'Sally, the seven who were . . .' Hadley couldn't bring himself to say 'killed'. He took a deep breath. 'I'm sorry. There were ten working out of the house today, two were on the road: Sonya McConaghy and Tom Peters. Three more are on holiday. One of them, Angela Lavin, is out of the country, actually on her honeymoon in Marbella. The other two – Louise Chadwick and Hamid Qadiri – are on short-term leave. Chadwick is back tomorrow, Qadiri is due back next week.'

'You've spoken to McConaghy and Peters?'

Hadley nodded. 'They'll finish their assigned tasks and then come here, to Thames House.'

'Let's pull them in immediately,' said Pritchard. He looked at Bailey. 'Keep them separated until they've been interviewed.' He looked back at Hadley. 'Get Chadwick and Qadiri in here, too. Again, separate rooms until Liz has arranged for them to be interviewed.'

'You don't really think they had anything to do with what's happened, do you?' asked Hadley.

Pritchard looked at him coldly over the top of his spectacles. 'I don't know, Ian, and I'm not rushing to make any judgement. We'll take it step by step.'

'Understood,' said Hadley.

Pritchard sat back in his chair. 'How many people would know the location of the house?' he asked.

'That's a difficult question to answer,' said Hadley.

'Try.'

'I don't mean I'm reticent about answering, it's just a difficult number to pin down,' said Hadley. 'Everyone in my department, obviously. So six, including myself. We would obviously know the locations of all the footie premises. Liz handles security for them, so her department would also know the locations. We have two in London, one in Edinburgh, one in Cardiff, one in Manchester and one in Bristol. But everyone who has ever worked in the house would also know its location. And that's the number that's difficult to pin down. We have anywhere between twenty and fifty people a year assigned to that house, depending on our recruitment figures. Those numbers have increased over the last few years, and the house has been in use for just over twenty years. So ballpark figure, anywhere between four hundred and a thousand. I can get you the exact figure, it won't take long.'

'Let's do that,' said Pritchard.

'Plus we have retired employees who finish their employment as a footie. Again, I can look at the files and put together a list.'

'Good,' said Pritchard. 'Somebody must have leaked the location of the house and we need to know who that somebody was. When Sally phones, does she call the office or your mobile?'

'Office.'

'You have someone monitoring your phone, I hope.'

'Of course.'

'Good. When she does call back, you need to get her location and tell John immediately. John, you need a collection team ready to go at short notice.'

'Not a problem,' said Fretwell. 'I was thinking two teams, and that we get one south of the river now. It might save time down the line.'

Pritchard nodded his approval. He looked at the man to Hadley's left. 'Allan, do you think we could have two of your people per car, so four in total? Suitably armed?'

The man nodded. 'I have four on standby as we speak,' he said, leaving Hadley in no doubt that he was with the SAS. In all probability he was a member of E Squadron, a composite group made up of special forces soldiers from the SAS, the SBS and the Special Reconnaissance Regiment who worked directly for MI6 and MI5. MI5 officers were not licensed to carry firearms, and E Squadron were used for the tasks that were too sensitive to be carried out by the police.

'Okay, now does anyone have any idea what's going on?' asked Pritchard. 'Why would anyone want to kill our footies? All they do is maintain legends, they're not involved in active investigations. The fact that the hard drives have been stolen suggests that they are after information – but what?'

'Do any of the legends use the Wimbledon house as an address?' asked Bailey.

Hadley nodded. 'Some, yes.'

'You're thinking revenge?' asked Pritchard.

Bailey nodded. 'If a target discovered that a legend using that address was moving against them, they might just turn up with guns thinking they'd find one man.' She smiled. 'Or woman. They burst in and discover seven people. They start shooting.'

'So they kill everyone without realising that it's an MI5 workplace?'

'The whole point is that it looks like a regular house,' said Bailey. 'But when they get inside they realise what's going on. That's why they've taken all the hard drives. They assume that it's an investigation centre.'

Pritchard nodded. 'Okay. That being the case we need to know every ongoing investigation that uses the Wimbledon house as an active address.' He looked at Hadley. 'Presumably Susan Murray would have a record of every legend she has given out, so she could compile a list of those legends that have the Wimbledon house on record?'

'Absolutely,' said Hadley. 'Neither she nor I would be aware of the nature of the investigations obviously, but we would have a list that you could work on.'

'Let's do that. ASAP,' said Pritchard. 'So in terms of investigations, we're looking at what? Drugs? Terrorism? Organised crime? And the perpetrators? Home-grown terrorists, local drug gangs, Russians, Eastern Europeans, the Balkans? The Chinese, maybe? The usual suspects. We need to narrow down that list, and we need to do it quickly.' He looked at his watch. 'Right, Ian can you go and talk to Susan Murray and get a list of active legends? And as soon as Sally calls in, I want to know.'

Hadley frowned. Was the meeting over, or did the director just want him out of the office? Pritchard nodded expectantly and glanced at the door. It was the latter, Hadley realised. He got to his feet and headed for the door. No one said anything but he knew that as soon as he left the office they would start talking again and that there was a good chance he would be the subject of at least part of that conversation.

CHAPTER 5

A red setter chased a ball off to Sally's right, barking happily. The owner was some distance away, looking at Sally. She knew that she looked strange, running across the common in a parka and regular shoes, but that was the least of her problems. She looked at her watch. She had been running for just under three minutes and at the pace she was going she knew she had covered almost half a mile. Ahead of her was the A3, the main road connecting London and Portsmouth. Once she crossed it she would be off the common and in the much larger Richmond Park.

The dog grabbed the ball and ran over to its mistress, tail wagging. The woman was still looking over at Sally. Sally took a quick look over her shoulder. There were a dozen or so people on the common behind her, but she spotted her pursuers immediately. There were three of them, big men with short hair, two of them wearing bomber jackets, the third in a long leather coat that flapped behind him as he ran. They were moving at a slow jog and even from a couple of hundred yards away she could see that they were struggling. They were empty handed but she was sure they had guns. They weren't trying to catch her, they were trying to kill her. The bald man must have stayed with his car and that was a worry because he might be driving to the A3, to cut her off.

The woman with the dog was now looking at her pursuers. If Sally looked strange then three men in jackets jogging across the grass was even more unusual. Would they kill her in front of witnesses? Maybe. And it wasn't a chance she could take.

Sally's right foot hit a bump in the grass and she pitched

forward. She managed to regain her balance and concentrated on the ground ahead of her.

There had been two Outlanders. There could have been six passengers in the two cars, maybe more if they had packed into the back seat. So there were three behind her; were there others off to the side? Or in the cars?

She heard a siren off to the left, getting louder, but then it faded off into the distance.

She took another look over her shoulder. She had pulled further away from the men. They looked gym fit, as if they spent hours lifting weights and doing squats, but gym fit and running fit were two different things. They were clearly already tired, there was no rhythm to their running and their heads were bobbing back and forth, mouths open as they gasped for breath.

She smiled despite the seriousness of her situation. In a locked room any one of them would probably be able to beat her to death with their bare hands, but out in the open, on the common, she was literally running them into the ground. In the distance she saw the traffic of the A3. She just hoped that the Outlanders weren't there waiting for her, because if they were then all bets were off.

CHAPTER 6

Hadley was sure that he had been asked to leave Pritchard's office because the director wanted to brief the others while he wasn't there. He just hoped that they weren't planning to blame him for what had happened at the Wimbledon house. And the questions about Sally's lack of promotion were completely out of order. Pritchard had no right to be second guessing him. Hadley was in charge of the footie houses, he decided who went where and when it was time for them to move on.

He looked back at the closed door to Pritchard's office. Part of him wanted to go back and continue the discussion, to argue his case that Sally Page simply hadn't been ready to move into Thames House, but he knew that the time wasn't right. He had to choose when to fight his battles and now definitely wasn't the right time. What was important right now was to find out who had attacked and killed his footies and to prove to everyone that what happened wasn't his fault.

He took the lift down to the second floor and walked along to the legends office. As with most of the doors in Thames House there was no sign, just a number. Hadley opened the door and Susan Murray looked up from her computer terminal. 'Ian, hello, this is a surprise,' she said. Murray had been with the Security Service for more than twenty years and prior to that had worked for the British Library for another twenty. She was close to seventy but there was no pressure on her to resign. She had a razor-sharp mind and an almost faultless memory. Her hair was a uniform dark brown and the wrinkles on her bird-like face suggested it was dyed, but Hadley had never seen grey roots and had come to assume that she had just been blessed with good genes. She wore a pair of reading glasses on a gold chain, but Hadley rarely saw her use them. 'Business or pleasure?'

Murray worked for Hadley, but her length of service and impeccable record meant that it often felt as if their roles were reversed. She kept a close eye on all the legends used by MI5 and dealt direct with the footies and shoppers when she had a specific request, though she always made sure to copy Hadley into any emails. It was Murray who generally handed out the legends as and when they were needed, and she had dealt with pretty much every officer working undercover at some point. Over the years a lot of those officers had moved up the ranks, which meant that Murray had a lot of friends in high places.

'I've a bit of an unusual request, Susan,' he said. 'I'm going to need a list of all legends out of the Wimbledon premises that have been allocated over the past six months, and who they were allocated to. Operational references too.'

'Easy peasy,' she said.

'Really?'

'It'll take me a couple of minutes,' she said. She peered down at her keyboard and tapped away on it with two fingers.

'I thought it would be quite complicated,' he said.

'No, it's all on the database. We label each legend with a code that tells us the premises it came from and the names of the footies and shoppers who had any input. So a simple search will give me all the cases.' She grinned up at him. 'And there we go.'

A laser printer started up and began spewing out pages. Murray looked at her screen. 'Twenty-two legends have been issued that were maintained in Wimbledon over the past six months,' she said. 'It's been quiet. There are another fifteen that were issued prior to six months ago so there has been no input from the staff.'

'Could I have them as well?'

'Of course,' she said. She tapped on her keyboard again. In total more than a dozen sheets were printed. She gathered them up and handed them to him. 'Has something happened?' she asked. 'Something I should know about?'

Murray knew all the footies and shoppers, present and former, and she would be hit hard when she found out what had happened to the Wimbledon staff. Hadley was under orders not to tell anyone what had happened but lying to Murray was not an option. She was a vital part of his team and without her support his life would be a lot more complicated.

'You can't tell me,' she said quietly, concern etched on her face.

She was as skilled at reading people as she was at handling legends, Hadley knew. 'Orders from the top,' he said. 'I'm sorry.'

'So it's bad?'

He held her look for several seconds and then slowly nodded. She looked pained and she reached for a small gold crucifix she wore around her neck.

'I think everyone will be told sooner rather than later,' he said. 'They're just trying to work out what to say.'

Tears swelled up in her eyes but there was a defiant thrust to her chin.

'I'm so sorry, Susan, if it was up to me . . .'

'It's all right, Ian, I understand.' She nodded at the printouts. 'I just hope they help.'

'I'm sure they will,' he said. 'And obviously, mum's the word until there's an official announcement.'

'Of course,' she said. She sat down and wiped away a tear with the back of her hand. 'I'm a silly old woman.'

'No you're not, Susan. Far from it.' He flashed her a sympathetic smile and slipped out of her office.

CHAPTER 7

Sally looked over her shoulder. She had pulled away from her pursuers and they were now almost three hundred yards away. They were moving at a slow jog and were getting slower by the second. She ran off the common and onto the pavement. As she feared, the traffic was heavy on the A3 but at least that meant the SUVs couldn't pull over and wait for her. She looked right and left and sighed with relief when she didn't see any black vehicles. The only Mitsubishi she saw was white with an elderly man at the wheel and a woman in a headscarf in the front passenger seat.

There were half a dozen cars almost nose to tail coming from her right, but after they had passed there was a gap of about thirty metres between the final vehicle and a white van. She jogged into the road, holding up an apologetic hand, but the white van driver was already pounding on his horn. To her left the traffic was equally heavy and she didn't see a suitable gap for about a quarter of a mile so she stood on the white line, said a silent prayer and cut behind a red Mini Cooper as it passed. The horn of the car behind the Mini blared like an animal in distress, but at least the driver was braking and the tyres squealed on the tarmac. The driver was a young woman and despite Sally's smile and wave she was clearly shouting obscenities at her.

Sally reached the pavement just as the woman stopped sounding her horn. She turned. The trees were blocking her view of the common, which meant her pursuers couldn't see her either. She ran into Richmond Park. At 2,500 acres it was the biggest of London's Royal Parks, criss-crossed by bridleways and cycle paths. As she ran, she gradually turned south, keeping to the more heavily wooded area. Thames House was to the north-east, which is where she had been heading in the Uber. They would probably assume she would continue to head in that direction. Providing she was out of sight by the time they entered the park she should be safe enough. For the time being, at least.

Her feet were hurting; her shoes were rubbing at the back and she knew she was heading for blisters. She was sweating, too, but it would be harder to run if she was carrying the parka as well as her bag. Her calves were burning but she wasn't tired and she knew she could run for at least another fifteen minutes at the pace she was at now. Over to her left a small herd of deer were watching her as she ran by.

Two runners were coming her way, two men in their twenties, wearing running vests, very short shorts and state-of-the-art training shoes. One of them said something and the other laughed, and they were both laughing as they ran by her. 'Pricks,' she muttered.

She was heading south-west now through a small copse, taking care where she put her feet because the ground was cluttered with roots and fallen twigs.

When she reached the edge of the clearing she stopped and looked back. There was no sign of them, and there was no way they could know which way she was headed. One of the houses she looked after was in Kingston upon Thames and she had the keys in one of the envelopes in her bag. She decided to go there. She took another look over her shoulder. Still no sign of her pursuers. Maybe they had given up at the road and were now back in their vehicles. That was good news and bad. They would be easier to spot but they would be able to move faster, though they would have to stick to the roads.

She raised her watch to her mouth. 'Call Ian Hadley, Office,' she said. The watch made the call as she started to jog again. Hadley's secretary answered and said that he wasn't in the office but that she would get him. Then she corrected herself and said that he had just returned. Within seconds he was on the line. 'Where are you?' he said.

'Richmond Park,' she said.

'What the hell are you doing there?'

'They rammed my taxi, Ian. I had to go on foot.'

'They're chasing you?'

'They did but I outran them.'

'Stay where you are and I'll send a car.'

'I can't stay in the park, Ian. I'm a sitting target here. Look, I have the keys to a house in Kingston upon Thames. I can be there in ten minutes, maybe fifteen.'

'What's the address?'

Sally told him.

'I'll send a car,' he said.

'Ian, I took a photograph of one of the SUVs.'

'One of them? You mean there were more?'

'Two. They hemmed in my Uber. I got a picture of the car's registration plate and the driver of the car behind us. The driver is the guy I saw at the house.'

'Can you send them to me now?'

'Give me your mobile number.' She stopped running and took out her phone. Hadley told her the number and she added it to her contacts list.

'Got it, Ian. I'll send it now.'

'Good girl.'

Sally fought back the urge to snap at him for his casual sexism. 'I'll call you again when I'm in the house, okay?'

'Okay.'

'Ian you never told me what you found at the house.'

He didn't reply.

'Ian?'

'It wasn't good, Sally.'

'What did you find?'

'They were all dead, Sally.'

'Everybody?'

'Everybody.'

The news hit Sally like a punch to the stomach. 'Oh my God,' she said.

'Sally, they were asking why you weren't there when it happened?'

'What?'

'You were outside, right?'

'I was getting coffees, Ian. I was on a coffee run. Who was asking?'

'The director was just wondering why you weren't in the house, that's all.'

'You mean he wanted to know why I'm not dead, is that it? What the fuck, Ian.'

'Calm down . . .' he began, but Sally cut him short.

'Don't tell me to calm down, Ian. You're not the one who saw their friends dead on the floor. You're not the one who was run off the road by the killers, and had to run for their life across Wimbledon fucking Common.'

'I know you're under a lot of pressure, Sally, I'm sorry if I offended you. But it was a question that Giles Pritchard asked and I didn't have an answer. Now I do. You were on a coffee run. End of story.'

'Okay, fine,' said Sally.

'You sound out of breath,' he said. 'Are you okay?'

'I'm running,' she said. 'I've been running for a while. Look, I'm going to end this call now. I'll send you the pictures I took.'

'Let me know when you arrive at the house.'

Sally ended the call. She had to stop to send the photographs and the short video but in less than a minute she was running again.

CHAPTER 8

Hadley flicked through the pictures that Page had sent him. The quality wasn't great because her hand seemed to have been shaking, but in one of the pictures the registration number was clearly visible. The driver was the man she had described earlier; Caucasian, bald, wearing a black jacket. He was wearing black gloves too. The man on the front passenger seat had his gloved hands up in front of his face but he was also Caucasian and had dark brown, slightly curly hair. In one of the pictures Hadley could see what looked like a diamond stud in his left ear.

He played the video. It was twenty seconds of shaky footage showing the black Mitsubishi Outlander banging into the rear of the car that Sally was in, but there wasn't anything to see that wasn't in the individual pictures.

He sat back in his chair and looked up at the ceiling. Strictly speaking he should pass the pictures and video on to Liz Bailey, but if he did that she would end up taking the credit. Then again, if he phoned Pritchard all that the director would do would be to tell him to pass it on to Bailey. He needed some way of sending the intel to Bailey while at the same time letting Pritchard know that it was he who was the conduit. He realised that email was the way to go, so he sent the pictures and video from the phone to his work address. They took several minutes to arrive, but when they did he attached them to an email to Bailey, copying Pritchard. He included a brief message: 'Sally just sent this. She is en route to a legend house in Kingston upon Thames. I'll call re details.'

He hit send and smiled to himself. No matter how Bailey dealt with it, Pritchard would at least know that he had been on the case. Credit where credit was due. He sat back and looked up at the ceiling.

His office phone rang and he grabbed for the receiver. He had assumed it was Sally but the voice that snapped 'Ian?' was older and more confident than the footie. It was Bailey.

'Liz, hi. Did you get my email?'

'This is the car that's in pursuit, right?'

'Yes. You can make out the registration number.'

'We're checking now, and we'll run facial recognition on the occupants. Where's she heading?'

Hadley gave her the address of the legend house.

'How did she sound?' asked Bailey.

'Tense. And out of breath. She was running, across Wimbledon Common.'

'They were still in pursuit?'

'She said they had been but she'd outrun them. But she sounded as if she was still under pressure.'

'Next time she calls, Ian, put her straight through to me.'

Bailey ended the call. Hadley smiled to himself. She was clearly unhappy that he had copied Pritchard into the email but that was her problem.

CHAPTER 9

Sally stopped jogging as she reached the road where the house was. People noticed runners and she didn't want to draw attention to herself. She pulled the hood of the parka off her head and looked around. The pavement was deserted. Both sides of the road were lined with cars but they all appeared to be empty and there was no sign of a black Outlander. She walked along to the house. It was a neat semi-detached with a garage. There was a burglar alarm box high up by the bedroom window. She carried on walking, wanting to make absolutely sure that she wasn't being followed. There was an Openreach van parked ahead of her and she slowed to give it a closer look. Both MI5 and the police used Openreach vans for surveillance purposes because there were so many of them and people were used to seeing them parked for long periods. Sally figured if the authorities used them there was every chance that the bad guys did too, but there was no one in the front seats and there were no signs of cameras.

She doubled back. There was a woman with a pushchair talking into a mobile coming towards her. The woman was so engrossed in her conversation that she didn't even glance at Sally as she went by. Sally took a final look around and headed down the driveway, taking her keys from her bag. Each key had a label, colour coded with red tags for front doors and black tags for back doors, along with a reference number rather than the address. She had memorised all the reference numbers and used the front door key to let herself in. She closed the door behind her and stood with her back to it, listening as she took slow deep breaths to calm herself down.

The house had been her responsibility for the last three months. Before that it was looked after by an arts graduate who had only spent five months in the house. His name was Ali Habib; he was tall and good-looking, and by virtue of his Egyptian-born parents and British public school education he was fluent in Arabic and English, which had got him fast-tracked to Thames House. The house had only been used twice since Sally had taken it over, and both times she had helped the dressers.

When the premises were used they had to be fitted out to match the personality of the legend that was supposed to be living there. The first time the legend was that of a GCHQ analyst who was planning to offer sensitive intelligence to a Russian Foreign Intelligence Service agent who operated out of Russia's embassy in Kensington Palace Gardens. They had initially corresponded through emails but when the Russian agent had requested a meeting, the MI5 officer had asked that he came to the Kingston upon Thames house late at night. The dresser, a gay man in his late fifties who had once worked for the National Theatre, brought in computers, books and toiletries, and stocked the kitchen cupboards and fridge with food that would be appropriate for a single man in his early forties. There had been framed family photographs of the man in university robes, and others with his family. All had been fabricated by the documents experts at Thames House.

The second time had been two weeks earlier when the house was kitted out to fit in with a legend of an MI5 officer posing as a former banker turned money-launderer. The officer was involved in the long-term penetration of a group of Belfast-born criminals with links to the New IRA. Two members of the gang were flying over to London for a meeting and the house needed to be set up just in case they decided to make a spot check on the banker's home address. Out went books on computing, vegetarianism and socialism, to be replaced by books on economics and finance and dozens of best-selling thrillers. The banker's fridge was stocked with champagne and foie gras, silk sheets put on his bed, and one of the bedrooms was converted into a home gym stocked with expensive German exercise machines.

The house was equipped with state-of-the-art cameras and microphones, though Sally was pretty sure they were only active when the house was being used. She headed to the kitchen and opened the fridge. It was empty; the dressers had moved everything out once the Belfast criminals were on the plane home. She found a jar of Nescafé and a bag of sugar so she filled the kettle at the sink. As she switched on the kettle, her watch buzzed to let her know she had a call. It was Louise Chadwick. Sally frowned as she stared at the screen. She let it ring for several seconds before answering, wondering what on earth she could say. When she took the call she tried to sound as cheerful as she could but Louise cut her short.

'What the fuck's going on, Sally?'

'What do you mean?' Louise was a year younger than Sally and had only joined MI5 three months earlier, just after Ali moved out. She was in no position to be swearing at Sally.

'I've been summoned to Thames House and no one will tell me what's going on. I've phoned Drew and Mo and Afifa and Fiona and no one's answering. I've left messages and they won't call me back. Am I being let go, Sally? Is that it? Are they sacking me?'

'It's not that,' said Sally quietly.

'Please don't lie to me,' said Louise. 'I thought we were friends.'

Sally smiled tightly. She had never considered Louise a friend. Louise worked on the ground floor of the Wimbledon house and in the twelve weeks she'd been there she'd done nothing more than nod and say good morning. She was ultra-competitive and only had time for those who could help her career. But she deserved to know the truth. 'Louise, the house was attacked this morning.'

'Attacked? What do you mean, attacked?'

'Men with guns went in and killed everybody who was there. Drew, Mo, Afifa, Fiona, David, Tony and Jane. They're all dead.'

There was silence on the line and for a moment Sally wondered if she had lost her connection. 'Louise?'

'Dead?'

'Yes. I'm so sorry.'

'Who? Why?'

'We don't know, Louise. It only happened this morning.'

'Someone just burst in and started shooting?'

'They're not sure. There weren't any witnesses that I know about.'

'I don't believe this,' said Louise.

'I'm having trouble processing it myself,' said Sally. 'But that's why they want you in.'

'Are you in Thames House?'

'I'm on my way.'

'You were working today, right?'

'I was out on a coffee run when it happened. Look, I have to go. I'm so sorry that I'm the one to break the bad news.'

'And what's going to happen? Will they shut down the house?'

'You're asking the wrong person, Louise. I'm as much in the dark as you at the moment. Sorry, I've got to go. Bye.' She ended the call and took a deep breath. The thought that it might have been better not to have taken the call sprang to mind. Clearly whoever had called Louise into Thames House hadn't told her what had happened and they presumably had a reason for that.

The kettle boiled and she made coffee in a bright yellow mug. She took her coffee upstairs and into the front bedroom. From the window she could look down on the street below. She took a sip and winced. She wasn't a fan of black coffee but she needed the caffeine. She looked at her watch. It was only a quarter past eleven. It had been just over two hours since she had walked into the house and found the carnage there but it felt like a lifetime ago. She took another sip of her coffee, then froze as she saw the black Mitsubishi turn into the road. 'No fucking way,' she muttered to herself as she stared at the vehicle in disbelief. So far as she knew, MI5 didn't use black Mitsubishis. And even if they did it was unlikely in the extreme that Hadley would send one to collect her after what she had told him.

She backed away from the window. A second black Outlander had appeared. The first one was pulling up outside the house. Her heart began to pound. How had they tracked her down? How the fuck did they know where she was?

She put the mug on the dressing table and ran downstairs. There was no way she could leave by the front door so she hurried down the hallway and into the kitchen. If they got into the house they'd know that she had been there, and there was nothing she could do about that. She pulled at the door handle and cursed when she realised it was bolted. There were two bolts, at the top and the bottom. She stood on tiptoe to pull back the top one, and then bent down to deal with the lower one. She grabbed at the handle and pulled. It was still locked. She needed a key. She took out her keyrings but there was only the one key to the front door. She looked around frantically. Where the fuck could it be?

She pulled open the kitchen drawer nearest to her and sighed with relief when she saw a steel key lying on a folded tea towel. She grabbed it, slammed the drawer shut and shoved the key into the lock. It turned and she pulled open the door. She heard car doors slam. She grabbed her bag and parka from the table. She wanted to run at full pelt away from the house but she knew it would be a mistake to leave the kitchen door open so she pulled it closed and locked it.

Hearing voices at the front of the house, she turned and ran across the lawn to a wooden shed with a grey felt roof. She hurriedly pulled on the parka and then squeezed between the shed and the hedge next to it, looking for a gap wide enough to get through. She heard more voices. At least two men had come to the back of the house. She pushed her bag through a gap in the hedge and then crawled through after it, stray twigs scratching across her face and catching in her hair. The garden she found herself in was a mirror image of the one behind her. She got to her feet and kept low as she ran over the grass, straightening up as she reached the house and taking a quick look behind her. There was no one following. She ran around the house and onto the street. She looked left and right but the roads and pavements were clear, so she headed back towards Richmond Park. She felt safer in the park; the SUVs couldn't get to her and she was fairly sure she could outrun any pursuers. She could go to ground in the park, call Hadley and arrange to be collected there.

CHAPTER 10

Ian Hadley's office phone rang and he grabbed at it. It was Liz Bailey. 'Ian, we have a problem. Our guys arrived at the Kingston upon Thames house but Sally wasn't there.'

'She said she was on the way, last time we spoke,' Hadley replied.

'We think she was there. Someone had made themselves a cup of coffee and we are assuming it was her. The kettle was still warm so something must have spooked her. Has she called you?'

'No.'

'As soon as she does, put her through to me. In the meantime, I'll try to call her myself. Let me have the number.' Hadley had to take out his mobile to get her number. He read it out to Bailey. She ended the call.

Hadley put down the receiver. Liz was obviously annoyed and he had the feeling that she was planning on blaming him for the whole debacle. He was going to have to watch his back.

CHAPTER 11

S ally jogged across Richmond Park. The ground was too uneven to risk running at full speed but even at her pace of about six miles an hour she was sure her pursuers wouldn't be able to catch her on foot. Every few minutes or so she looked over her shoulder but there was no one following her. The rest of the time she concentrated on the ground ahead of her, making sure that she avoided any pitfalls.

She eventually reached Wimbledon Common, then headed north to Putney Heath. She kept to the most wooded tracks as she headed towards the Green Man pub. Reaching the edge of the heath, she peered through the trees. The area in front of the pub was used by buses waiting to service the routes to and from central London. There were three double-deckers lined up, their engines running. One was a number 14, which ran over Putney Bridge to Fulham and eventually on to Russell Square. On the rare occasions she didn't run to or from work, the number 14 was her bus of choice. For now, she needed to cross the river and the bus was probably the best way of doing it.

She lifted her left hand and spoke to her Apple Watch. 'Call Ian Hadley,' she said. She looked at the watch and frowned, then pressed the side button to cancel the call. How had they found her at the Kingston house? They hadn't followed her, she was sure of that. And the locations of the premises linked to MI5's legends were classified. The only people she had spoken to were Louise and Ian Hadley. She hadn't told Louise where she was when she spoke to her, so Hadley was the only person who'd have known her location. Had he betrayed her? Was he behind

the attack on the house, and if he was did he have the backing
of his bosses?

She shook her head, annoyed at her overactive imagination.
Sally wasn't a great one for conspiracy theories; she was a hundred
per cent sure that Bin Laden had been behind the 9/11 attacks,
that Diana had died in a simple car accident, and that men had
walked on the moon. It made no sense at all for MI5 to be killing
off its own people. Her frown deepened as she walked. The black
SUVs had intercepted her Uber car. She'd assumed that had just
been bad luck, but it must have been more than that. She had
been wearing the wig and the parka; there was no way they could
have recognised her. If they had been outside the house when
the Uber arrived they could have followed her, but she had been
very careful to make sure that they weren't around. They had
come from nowhere when they'd been driving by the common.
How had they found the car? She looked at her Apple Watch
again. GPS. The watch and her phone could both be tracked. It
wasn't easy to do but the men in the black SUVs looked like
professionals and might well have access to the technology. If she
didn't ditch the watch and the phone then it wouldn't matter
where she went or what disguise she wore, they would always be
able to find her.

She took out her phone, scrolled through to settings, and chose
'Erase All Content And Settings' to remove all her data. Then
she took off her watch. She considered throwing the phone and
the watch away, but then she had a better idea. There were two
teenagers standing by the bus stop looking as if they were up to
no good and they both squinted at her as she walked up to them,
smiling brightly and slipping the watch into her pocket. One of
them had a hand-rolled cigarette and as she got closer she could
smell the earthy aroma of cannabis. He cupped his hand around
the joint and held it behind his back as she walked over. 'Hi guys,'
she said. She held out her phone. 'Did either of you guys lose
an iPhone X?'

The taller of the two lads narrowed his eyes and looked at her
suspiciously. 'What?'

She held up the phone. 'I found it earlier, when I was on the common. I was going to hand it in to the police.'

'Let me have a look,' said the shorter one. He was wearing a puffa jacket with the hood up.

Sally gave it to him. Then she reached into her pocket and took out the watch. 'There was this watch with it,' she said. 'It was on the grass, like somebody lost it.'

The taller one took the watch and examined it. He was wearing a New York Yankees jacket and a matching cap, with baggy jeans and gleaming white high top Nikes. 'Yeah, that's mine,' he said.

'Oh great,' said Sally. 'That was lucky, me finding you.'

'Yeah, we was over on the common before, I must have dropped it.' He already had a garish gold watch on his left wrist so he put the Apple watch on his right. He had to struggle to use his left hand to fasten the strap.

'What about the phone?' she asked.

'Yeah, I dropped that,' said the guy in the puffa jacket. 'We were doing some exercises and it must have fell out.'

'Exercises?'

'Yeah. Tai chi, that Chinese shit.' He slipped the phone into his pocket. 'Thanks, girl.'

Sally smiled. 'I'm glad I could help,' she said.

A number 37 bus pulled up at the stop and the door rattled open. The two guys hurried on. She gave them a small wave. 'You have a great day.'

As they walked down the bus she heard them laughing, then the door closed and the bus drove off. Sally looked around. There were plenty of cars speeding both ways along the A219 and many of them were SUVs, but there were no black Outlanders. The number 14 bus was still parked opposite but the driver was reading a copy of the *Sun* and chewing on a sandwich so he didn't appear to be in a hurry. There were three schoolgirls sitting in the bus shelter, gossiping away about boys and why they were so annoying, and an old lady stood by the side of the shelter, muttering to herself. The shelter was in full view of the road so she walked to the Green Man's beer garden and stood by the side of the pub. She could feel her heart pounding and she took several slow breaths to calm herself down as she considered her options. She actually didn't have that many, but her first priority had to be to get off the streets.

CHAPTER 12

Major Allan Gannon had just sat down in the Thames House canteen and picked up his bacon sandwich when his phone started to buzz in his pocket. He sighed and fished the phone out. It was Pritchard. He took the call. 'Where are you?' asked the director without any pleasantries.

'The canteen.'

'I need you in my office, now.'

'On my way,' said Gannon. He took a gulp of coffee and grabbed one half of his sandwich. He headed for the stairs and wolfed it down on the way to the director's office. Pritchard's secretary waved for him to go straight through. The director was behind his desk and without looking up from his screen, he motioned for the Major to sit. 'Be with you in a second, Allan, sorry,' he said. He tapped on his keyboard for a few seconds, then sat back. 'We've got a problem. The driver of the car following Page, he's one of yours.'

The Major's jaw dropped. 'You're sure of this?'

'Martin Hirst. He left the Regiment two years ago.'

Pritchard passed a sheet of paper across the desk. It was a printout of one of the photographs that Sally had taken on her phone. Gannon studied the face but he didn't recognise the man. Pritchard passed him a second sheet. This one contained Hirst's service record. Five years in the Paras and two years in 22 SAS. Gannon frowned. Two years was a short time to be in the Regiment; ten years or longer was the norm. The gruelling selection process meant that only the most committed made it through. SAS training was among the most expensive in the Army and there was no point in investing so heavily in a man if he was going to leave after just two years. Gannon scanned the sheet. There was a photograph on the left. A man in his late twenties with a roundish head and a receding hairline, a small nose and the cold, hard stare that suggested he had seen more than his fair share of action. His five years in the Paras had seen him do two tours of Afghanistan and one in Iraq. He had visited both arenas with the SAS, and had done three missions in Syria. According to the man's service record he had been discharged honourably, but Gannon knew that service records often didn't tell the full story.

'Have you crossed paths with him?' asked Pritchard.

Gannon shook his head. 'I'm afraid not. But I can ask around.'

'Two years is a very short time to be in the Regiment.'

'I was thinking the same.'

'Can you make some calls? Obviously we need to know who he's working for, and with.'

Gannon stood up. He held up the two sheets. 'Can I keep these?'

'Of course.'

Gannon nodded and headed for the door. He figured he might as well make his calls from the canteen; at least then he'd be able to finish his bacon sandwich.

CHAPTER 13

The bus reached the middle of Putney Bridge and crossed the divide between south and north London. Sally was sitting at the back of the top deck and kept looking over her shoulder, scared that at any time she would see a black Outlander. She had used the Oyster card of one of her legends to board the bus. It was difficult to track Oyster cards in real time but she didn't want to take the risk of using her own card.

There were a dozen or so people sitting in front of her, most of them engrossed in their mobile phones. Sally felt strange not having her phone and watch. The watch had been a gift from her previous boyfriend. He'd given it to her just two months before they had broken up and to his credit he hadn't asked for it back. But Tim was that sort of a guy. He'd been devastated when Sally had told him that she didn't want to continue their relationship and had tried to talk her out of her decision, but once he had understood that her mind was made up he had accepted it and hadn't bothered her since. His strength, physical and mental, was what had first attracted her to him. That and his skin the colour of mahogany and his soft brown eyes. She felt her stomach turn over and she pushed the thought of him out of her mind. She had to stay focused.

The bus drove off the north end of the bridge and headed up Fulham High Street. Sally looked over her shoulder. Still no sign of her pursuers. She needed to call Thames House and let them know where she was but for that she needed a phone. And she needed to decide who to call. Could she trust Ian Hadley? The fact that her pursuers hadn't followed her on the bus suggested that they were no longer tracking her, which meant she had been right about the phone and watch. It also meant that maybe Hadley wasn't involved – and her pursuers would now be following the two guys with the phone and watch.

The bus turned right at the roundabout and drove down Fulham Road. They passed the building site that had once been Fulham Police Station on the left. It was one of many that had been closed by the mayor as a cost-cutting exercise in 2017, shortly after Sally had moved into the area. The police station was demolished the following year and its place was being taken by a boys' school. The mayor had said at the time that closing so many police stations would have no effect on the crime figures because most people reported offences online. Even after the murder rate soared and knife crime reached record levels, he refused to admit that he had made a mistake, but as a local resident Sally knew that you were more likely to see a sheep on a bicycle than an on-foot police patrol. The only time that she had seen a cop in Fulham was when they drove by.

Not that it made any difference to her current predicament. She was an MI5 officer and it was made clear to her the day she joined the service that whenever an MI5 officer crossed paths with the police they were to deny who they worked for. If during the course of an operation they were picked up by the police, the officer was to say nothing and insist on a phone call. The only call they were to make was to an unlisted number. Once the person who answered the call was made aware of the situation, the officer was to remain silent until the matter was taken care of at a senior level.

There was no way that Sally could possibly tell the police what had happened. And even if she did, would they be able to protect her? Her pursuers had thought nothing of killing her friends and colleagues, all of them MI5 officers, so she couldn't imagine they would have any reservations about killing cops.

Sally got off the bus at Fulham Broadway. She needed somewhere to lie low while she considered her options. Home was only a few hundred yards away but she needed to be sure it was safe. She looked left and right several times, and once she was sure there were no black SUVs around she headed for the Cancer Research charity shop in the North End Road, a five-minute walk from the bus stop. She walked by the shop, checking reflections in the window to make sure that she wasn't being followed. She walked a dozen or so metres and then stopped at the roadside, looked right and left and jogged across to the other side of the street. She stopped and looked into the window of an estate agents, checking reflections again. No one followed her across, but if they were good they wouldn't. She started back in the direction she'd come from, looking across the road to see if anyone there did the same. It looked like she was in the clear but she walked for a hundred yards or so checking vehicles in the road, parked and moving. There were plenty of SUVs but no black Mitsubishi Outlanders.

She re-crossed the road and walked back to the shop, still checking reflections but secure in the knowledge that she wasn't being followed. She went inside, smiling at the middle-aged woman with short permed hair who was behind the cash register, then lowered the hood of her parka. She needed a complete change of image so she chose a pair of faded blue Wranglers, a dark blue pullover and a black North Face fleece. There were a dozen wool beanie hats on a shelf and she took three – a red one, a white one and a blue one. She went over to a rack of shoes. She baulked at the idea of wearing someone else's footwear but the flats she had on weren't ideal for running. There were several pairs that were her size but she narrowed the choice down to a pair of almost new brown Timberland boots for £35 and well-worn grey Nike Tanjun trainers. The Tanjuns weren't waterproof but the weather didn't look like rain and if she had to run again they would be lighter on her feet. She decided on the Nikes. She carried the trainers and clothes over to the counter and took out her credit card. She frowned as she stared at the card. If they were capable of tracking her phone, maybe they could follow her credit card transactions. She put the card back and took out a debit card belonging to one of her legends and used that. She was tempted to ask the woman if she could change in the back of the shop, but figured that would draw attention to her.

There was a pub, the Cock Tavern, a short walk away, so she headed there, keeping a close eye out for the black SUVs. The pub's blue and purple awnings were out and the soft lights inside made it appear welcoming. She walked between the potted trees either side of the main entrance, and pushed open the door. The buzz of conversations washed over her and for a second or two she wanted nothing more than to slide on a bar stool and down a glass of Prosecco. The feeling of safety was an illusion, she knew that. The difference between safety and carnage could simply be a man with a backpack of explosives, or a gun, or even just a machete.

The door closed behind her as she hurried along to the ladies, where she locked herself into a cubicle, took off her wig and changed into her jeans, sweater and fleece. She dumped her parka, trousers and shirt in the waste bin, then sat down on the toilet and swapped her shoes for the trainers. She was reluctant to throw away a perfectly good pair of shoes but she didn't have room for them in her bag so they followed the clothes into the bin.

She left the cubicle and tried the wig on again. She checked herself in the mirror and pulled on the blue beanie. It wasn't a good look and she decided to ditch the wig. The beanies would cover her hair, anyway. She tried on the white one and tucked her hair underneath it. It wasn't especially attractive but she figured it would probably fool anyone who was looking for her. She smiled at her reflection but she could see the fear in her eyes. She hoped it was a good enough disguise, because her life depended on it.

CHAPTER 14

The Special Forces Club was in a nondescript mansion block in Knightsbridge around the corner from Harrods. The Major wasn't a regular visitor, but he was a member and it was a useful venue for meetings that were best kept confidential. He walked up the steps and was reaching for the lion's head door-knocker when the door opened. He stepped to the side to allow two men to go past. They were in their early thirties and he knew immediately they weren't special forces, present or former. They didn't have the cold stares of men who had been in combat and they were both out of condition, carrying more weight than was good for them. They were wearing suits and ties and one of them was holding a briefcase. They were laughing and the Major could smell the drink on them. The club had been having financial problems and had widened its membership criteria to include the intelligence services and the police. Most of the members considered the drop in standards to be unacceptable, but there was no arguing with the accountants.

Gannon walked into the club as the two suits headed down the road, still laughing. Mark Renny was in the bar, a pint of lager in front of him. He stood up and shook Gannon's hand, his grip slightly firmer than it needed to be. Renny and the Major went back a long way. Renny had been a sergeant major, one of the best, and had left after twenty-five years' service. He was small and wiry, a good four inches shorter than Gannon, whippet-thin with his head shaved. There was a small scar on his neck, just below his right ear, courtesy of a sniper in Libya, and he was missing the tip of his left little finger. Considering the hotspots that Renny had been in during his career, he was remarkably unscathed. 'You're looking good, Renny,' said the Major. 'Civvy Street agrees with you.'

'I miss the adrenaline, but the money's good, boss,' said Renny. He waited for Gannon to sit before dropping down onto his own chair. He had left the Regiment two years earlier but there was no way he would call the Major anything but 'boss'. Even though ranks were rarely used within the SAS and he was no longer even serving, the Major knew that Renny would never be comfortable using first names.

A waiter walked over and Gannon ordered an orange juice. He grinned at the look of surprise on Renny's face. 'I'm working,' he said. 'And the people I'm working with don't appreciate drinking on duty.'

Renny raised his own glass. 'Well this is one of the perks of being self-employed.'

Renny had set up his own private security firm, mainly offering personal security to foreign VIPs visiting the United Kingdom. He had been involved in several operations looking after members of the various royal families in the Arab Emirates and had been very well regarded. Much of his work came from Dubai and Abu Dhabi. He was always busy and drew on several dozen former SAS troopers for manpower as and when needed.

The waiter returned with Gannon's juice and Renny sipped his lager until the man had returned to the bar. He put down his glass and leaned across the table. 'So, Marty Hirst,' said Renny. 'What's he been up to?'

'We're not sure,' said the Major. He didn't like lying to Renny but this was Secret Service business and being economical with the truth went with the territory. He had phoned Renny and confirmed that the former sergeant major knew Hirst before arranging their meeting, but Gannon hadn't explained why he was interested. 'When did you last see him?'

'About six months ago. He was looking for work but I didn't have anything for him.'

'I thought the private security business was booming?'

'It is.' Renny picked up his pint glass and drank. The Major

knew he was playing for time, getting his thoughts in order, so
he settled back in his chair and waited. 'You never met him,
right?' Renny asked eventually.

'He was only with the Regiment for two years and I was away
from Stirling Lines most of that time. We were probably both
there for the yearly regimental picture but I'm pretty sure I never
spoke to him. But you served with him, right?'

'In Afghanistan once. Syria twice.' He took another sip of his
pint. Again, Gannon waited. Renny put down his glass. 'He was
a difficult one. Breezed through Selection. Fit as the proverbial
butcher's dog. Took the Long Drag in his stride, navigational
skills second to none.'

The Major nodded. The Long Drag was the end of the endur-
ance phase of the SAS selection process, a forty-mile trek across
the Brecon Beacons with full kit and a fifty-five pound Bergen.
Only the fittest of men could complete it, and while Gannon was
in tip-top physical condition he was sure that at his age he would
struggle to finish.

'He aced the jungle phase too. He passed Selection first time
and passed with honours. We thought he was destined for great
things.' He took another sip of his lager.

'I'm sensing a "but" is coming,' said Gannon.

Renny shrugged. 'It was about three months after he'd passed
Selection that we realised we had a problem. He was out in
Afghanistan, tasked with taking out high-value targets. He was
in a couple of firefights where our boys came off worse and in
both cases they blamed Marty.'

'He froze?'

Renny shook his head. 'He made bad decisions. When he had
to make his own calls, he was as likely to make the wrong call as
the right one. He shot a civilian on one mission. Easy mistake to
make, his unit was under fire and he saw a face at a window that
he thought was a shooter and he took him out, but it was a teenager being nosy. There were no witnesses and the unit moved on.
He never put a foot wrong in training, he was damn near perfect
in the Killing House, but on the ground he just made mistakes.'

The Major nodded. He'd seen it before: men who were trained to perfection, who knew what they had to do and how to do it, but just couldn't function under combat conditions. The selection procedure was supposed to root out those who were unsuitable for the job, but occasionally a bad apple got through.

'The thing is, he was a bloody good soldier. A perfect Para. Tell him what to do and he'd go ahead and do it. But when he had to make his own decisions, his instincts had a tendency to let him down. To be honest, I think the fact he had a family was holding him back.'

'Wife? Kids?'

'Wife and a daughter. Married while he was in the Paras. If it was down to me I'd never have married guys in the Regiment – but it wasn't down to me.'

'So what happened?'

'We gave him extra training, a lot of extra training, but he was sent on a mission to Syria and fucked up again. His unit had been sent in to capture an ISIS commander for questioning. They went in and for some reason Martin shot him. No need for it; the man was armed but not a threat, and his bodyguards had been eliminated, but while the rest of the unit stopped shooting, Martin put two bullets in the officer's head. A perfect double tap. But the mission was a dead loss. Literally.'

'And that ended his career?'

Renny shook his head again. 'With hindsight, that was when he should have been let go. But he was given more training and went out on a job in Colombia, backing up a DEA operation against one of the cartels. I'm not sure of the details but the mission turned to shit and the DEA sent him back along with instructions that he never darkened their doorstep again.'

'So he was RTU'd?' That was what happened to the few SAS men who didn't make the grade – they were Returned To Unit.

Renny shook his head again. 'He was told he was being sent back to the Paras but he chose to leave the Army instead. You can understand why. Being RTU'd is a badge of shame.'

'But there's no mention of any of that in his service record.'

'No one wanted to fuck him over, boss,' said Renny. 'He was a good soldier. He followed orders, he gave it his all, he just wasn't Sass. The feeling was that the Regiment was as much to blame as he was. So when he said he didn't want to be RTU'd he was given an honourable discharge.' Renny took another sip of his drink as he studied Gannon over the top of his glass. 'How long have we known each other, boss?' he asked.

'Twelve years,' said Gannon.

'Closer to fifteen,' said Renny. 'And during all those years, have I ever let you down?'

'Not once.'

'So why not just tell me what the fuck is going on and let me help you, rather than playing this secret squirrel game where you're twisting yourself in knots trying not to let anything slip.'

The Major sighed. Renny was right. He was absolutely trustworthy and if nothing else would have signed the Official Secrets Act at some point in his career. 'Fair enough,' he said. 'But obviously anything said here stays here.'

'That goes without saying,' said Renny.

Gannon nodded. 'Okay, here's the story. We believe that Martin is part of a group who have killed seven MI5 officers and who are currently in pursuit of an eighth. They broke into an MI5 house in Wimbledon and killed everyone there and stole hard drives containing sensitive information. They disabled the CCTV and clearly knew what they were doing.'

Renny shook his head. 'Impossible,' he said. 'Martin is one of the good guys. He wanted to work in the private sector but he was talking about security, maybe contracting back in the Sandpit. He wouldn't start killing for money, he's not that sort. We both know people who've gone over to the dark side but that's not Martin.'

Gannon said nothing for several seconds, then reached inside his jacket and took out the picture that Pritchard had given him of the two men in the front of the black Outlander. He handed it across the table to Renny. Renny stared at the picture for a while and then slowly nodded. 'Fuck me,' he said.

CHAPTER 15

The house where Sally lived was in Musgrave Crescent, facing common land that was known as Eel Brook Common. Musgrave Crescent was higher than the surrounding land and some know-it-all in a local pub had told her that it was built on what was originally a Bronze Age mound. The mound could have been a military fortification or a burial site and Sally always hoped it was the former. The same know-it-all had told her that in the 1880s Fulham FC had played their home games there, and that during the Second World War an underground bunker was built to protect local residents from German bombers.

The common was bordered by several roads, including Effie Road to the north, New King's Road to the south-east and Musgrave Crescent to the north-east. Sally normally walked along Effie Road, past her favourite tapas restaurant, El Metro, and into the common. Musgrave Crescent was to the left. The road was about four or five feet higher than the common and access was barred by a wall topped by railings. She had to walk about a hundred yards to a ramp that led up to the road. It was an easy walk, but it was the obvious route so instead she headed south to Favart Road. She walked along the road then doubled back to check that she wasn't being followed before walking across the grass. There was a children's play area to her right and mothers were grouped together chatting as their kids ran and played. There was a group of dog walkers off to her left, deep in conversation as their charges romped around. Ahead of her a group of kids were kicking a football around.

She approached Musgrave Crescent at the midway point. Her flat was to the left but she went right, checking the cars that were parked there. She reached the end without seeing an Outlander, so she turned and retraced her steps, eventually arriving at the white-fronted terrace that she had lived in for the past eighteen months. It was built over three stories, including a basement with its own entrance. It had originally been a single home but over the years most of the houses in the road had been converted into flats. Sally lived on the first floor. Her bedroom overlooked the small back garden and had an original cast-iron fireplace, which the landlord had said wasn't to be used. She had two flatmates, and they all had individual contracts with the landlord, a fast-talking Indian man who owned more than two dozen properties in Fulham and Chelsea. Sally had only met him twice and each time he had turned up in a bright green Lamborghini. Business was obviously good.

Sally continued to walk parallel to the road, still checking cars. Her breath caught in her throat as she spotted the black Outlander. It was parked behind a white van so she hadn't seen it until she had moved down the road. There didn't appear to be anybody in the vehicle so she walked along the grass until she could see the registration plate. She couldn't remember the number of the car that had followed her in the Uber so she reached for her phone to check the pictures she had taken and then mentally kicked herself when she remembered that she'd given her iPhone away. It looked like the same model as the one that had been outside the Wimbledon house, but then there were probably hundreds of black Mitsubishi Outlanders in London.

She drew level with the car. There was no way of telling if it belonged to her pursuers or not, and staring at it wasn't going to help. And if it was them, where were they?

She walked along to the end of Musgrave Crescent. There was a black BMW SUV and a black Honda CR-V but no Outlanders. She walked back through the common and stopped at the Mitsubishi again. She couldn't see a resident's parking permit from where she was but that didn't mean there wasn't one on the windscreen. The only way to find out would be to go onto the pavement but that would mean walking up the ramp and exposing herself.

She stared at the house. She heard a voice shouting off to her right and she flinched, but it was one of the kids calling for the ball. As she looked back at the road, she recognised a figure walking along the pavement towards the house from the direction of the Tube station. It was Callum Jenkins, her flatmate. He had worked for an estate agency in Kensington before he had been let go the previous month. Now he was unemployed, which explained why he was returning to the flat in the middle of the day. He pretty much depended on handouts from his parents and had the smallest of the three bedrooms, paying a hundred pounds a month less than Sally. The third flat sharer was Laura, a girl who worked as a waitress at a local burger restaurant while she applied for jobs in journalism.

As usual, Callum was wearing Beats headphones connected to his phone. She wanted to attract his attention but he was too far away and even if she called out he wouldn't hear her over the sound of his music.

He walked up to the front door and let himself in. Sally's heart was racing. Even if her pursuers had found her road there was no way they would be able to get into her flat, was there? It was fitted with a Banham alarm and security locks. He'd be fine – at least that's what she said to herself.

She stared up at the first-floor windows. The sitting room overlooked the street and that was where they spent most of the time when they weren't in their bedrooms. It was comfortably furnished with two leather sofas and a big-screen TV. It even had a Bang & Olufsen music centre that Callum had brought with him.

She counted off the seconds as she pictured Callum climbing the stairs, then taking out his keys and opening the double locks. Once the door was open he'd walk into the hall and tap the four-digit passcode into the burglar alarm console. Then he'd probably go into the kitchen and switch on the kettle. Callum was a big tea drinker. Tetley teabags, milk and two sugars.

She jumped as something flashed in the front room window. Then flashed again. There was no sound but she knew immediately what had happened. Someone had just shot Callum with a suppressed weapon. The sound hadn't carried outside the room but the flashes told the whole story. She put her hand over her mouth and blinked away tears. She felt the strength drain from her legs and she grabbed at the railings for support. Behind her, a woman was calling for her dog. Sally stared at the window. A dark figure appeared, then just as quickly it moved away. They were waiting for her in her flat. But how? How did they know where she lived? She took long, slow breaths trying to calm herself down. She felt as if she was trapped in some weird dream, and part of her wondered if at some point she was going to wake up and she'd realise that she was safe and warm in her own bed. She gripped the railing so tightly that the knuckles of both her hands whitened. This was no dream.

She looked over her shoulder. There were no pursuers, just nice middle-aged, middle-class people walking their pampered pets, and teenagers kicking a ball around without a care in the world. High overhead, an airliner was heading towards Heathrow. Everything was going on as normal around her. She shook her head, trying to clear her thoughts.

She had ditched her phone and her watch so there was no way they could have tracked her to Fulham that way. She was pretty much certain that no one had followed her on the bus, or when she went to the charity shop for the change of clothes. They hadn't followed her across the common; they had already been waiting for her. That meant that they knew who she was and where she lived. And that could only mean that it was someone within MI5 who was after her. Was Ian Hadley behind this? Or was he only obeying orders? Had something happened, something so terrible that everyone involved had to disappear? Her grip tightened on the railings. That made no sense. Sally was a footie, she wasn't involved with any active investigations. No one at the house was. They bought stuff, they looked after flats and houses, they updated social media. They were the lowest of the low. There was nothing, absolutely nothing, that made them worth killing.

She let go of the railings, her mind racing. She needed somewhere to hide, somewhere she would be safe while she worked out what to do next. She was a sitting duck standing outside her home. She backed away, then turned and walked across the common. She took out all the keys she had in her bag. The three MI5 properties that she was supposed to visit that day were clearly no longer safe, not after her pursuers had turned up at the house in Kingston.

There were three sets of keys on her personal key ring. There were keys to her flat, which was clearly a no-go area. Then there were the keys to her parents' house in Croydon. If they knew her home address, there was every chance they also knew where her parents lived. Her heart began to race and she stopped in her tracks. What if they had already gone there? She felt as if a steel belt had been strapped around her chest and for a few seconds she fought to breathe. What if they were there now, waiting with guns like they were waiting at her flat? And if they were there, what had happened to her parents? Her heart was pounding and she stood rooted to the spot, gripped by a rising sense of panic that threatened to overwhelm her.

'Pull yourself together,' she hissed to herself. 'Get a fucking grip on yourself.' She took a deep breath, held it and then let it out slowly. There was no point in worrying about what might or might not have happened. She had to take what was happening one step at a time. And the first step was to find somewhere to rest up. A hotel maybe? She could check into a hotel while she worked out what to do next. Except if they could track her phone they might also have access to credit card records and almost all hotels would insist on seeing a debit or credit card. She could use a card that went with one of the legends she looked after, but she had no way of knowing any more if they were safe.

She looked back at her key ring. The third key was a Yale and she frowned at it for several seconds before she remembered what it was for. It was the key to Tim's flat. He had pretty much insisted that she had a key to his place, and during the last two months of their relationship had been pleading with her to move in with him. She had always kept her own place, and had never given him a key, even though he had dropped several heavy-handed hints that he wanted one. He lived in a one-bedroom flat in Maida Vale, above a corner shop close to the Tube station. His parents had helped him with a large deposit and he just about managed to pay the mortgage on his police sergeant's salary, but he was dependent on getting regular overtime. Sally had never told anyone at MI5 about the relationship, and she had met him after she had joined and been positively vetted.

She looked at the key, wondering if Tim had changed the lock after she had left. She smiled to herself. No, he wanted her back. He'd made that clear from the start. He didn't ask for the key back or ask her to return any of the gifts he'd given her. He wasn't the type. Tim was a genuinely nice guy, and the way things stood maybe the only person she could trust. But first she needed to get to Maida Vale.

The number 28 bus went from Fulham Town Hall to the end of Elgin Avenue, and took about half an hour, if the traffic was good. Or she could take the 414 which went down Edgware Road. She had made the trip more than a hundred times while she had been going out with Tim; she always preferred to spend the night in his flat rather than having him stay over at hers. She had always said it was because she didn't want her flatmates eavesdropping on them, but the real reason was that she was fiercely protective of her personal space and knew that if Tim did stay over it wouldn't be long before he started leaving clothes and toiletries in her room and she wasn't ready for that. Not yet and maybe not ever. But as things stood, Tim's flat was probably the only place where she would be safe.

CHAPTER 16

Martin Hirst's mobile rang and he fished it out of his jacket pocket, answering the call with a laconic 'Yeah?'

'I'm still in the girl's flat, there's a problem.' It was Billy Winchester. Like most of the members of Hirst's team he was a gung-ho former Delta Force soldier who had been working in the private sector for several years and who appeared to have absolutely zero reservations about killing for money. He was in his forties and had run to fat, and from the amount of fast food and beer that he guzzled down each day, Hirst was pretty sure he was heading for diabetes if he hadn't got there already. 'Some guy came in. He had a key so I'm guessing he's a flatmate.'

'Just tie him up and carry on waiting for the girl.'

'He caught me by surprise, Marty. I was in the bathroom with my trousers around my ankles. I had to shoot him.'

'Did anyone hear the shots?'

'I don't think so. I had the suppressor on.'

'So stay where you are. She could still be heading home.' Hirst ended the call. What the hell was the girl playing at?

CHAPTER 17

The Major waited until he had left the Special Forces Club before making two phone calls. The first was to a former MI5 high flyer who had left under a cloud, and he arranged to meet her within the hour. He hoped that she might have an idea who Martin Hirst was working for. The second call was to Debbie Gilmore, who worked in the SAS's admin office as well as being married to one of the Regiment's sergeant majors. 'Debbie, I need a favour,' he said. 'Can you see if the Regiment has an up-to-date address for one Martin Hirst? He left a couple of years ago.'

'No problem,' she said, and he heard the tapping of her fingers on her keyboard. 'Here we go. Looks as if he's still at his Hereford address.'

'What's his family situation?'

'Married, with a six-year-old daughter.'

'Excellent, thanks so much. Could you be an angel and send me the details in a text?'

Debbie said she would and she was as good as her word. Thirty seconds later his phone beeped and he had the address and the names of Hirst's wife and daughter. He went into a Costa and ordered a cappuccino, and sipped it at a seat by the window as he pondered who to call next. He decided on Darren Keighley, a sergeant with B Squadron, which was currently tasked with squadron training – basically bringing new recruits up to speed and making sure that the veterans didn't lose their edge. Gannon phoned the sergeant and explained that he needed him to pay a visit to the Hirst house. 'I'm pretty sure that he's not there, but his wife and kid should be,' he said, keeping his voice down so as not to be overheard. 'Can you pretend you're with Family Support, just checking that Hirst is adapting well to Civvy Street?'

'Sounds like you suspect he isn't, boss,' said Keighley.

'There's a suggestion that he's up to no good,' said the Major, reluctant to go into details even though he trusted Keighley with his life. 'See if you can find out where he's working, who he's been hanging out with, how he's been behaving, but softly, softly; make it appear to be a regular welfare visit.'

'When do you need this doing, boss?' asked Keighley.

'Soon as,' said the Major. He heard a flurry of gunshots and figured that Keighley was probably putting a team through their paces in the Killing House, the SAS's training facility for hostage rescue scenarios.

'Where's the house?'

Gannon gave him the address of the Hirst home, a fifteen-minute drive from the SAS's Credenhill barracks, and the names of Hirst's wife and daughter. 'I'll get back to you ASAP, boss,' Keighley promised.

CHAPTER 18

Sally kept checking reflections in shop windows but there was no one following her on foot. She had changed her white beanie for the red one and had put her bag into a large Marks & Spencer carrier bag that she had purchased from a shop off Fulham Road. She hoped the change in hat colour and different style of bag might be enough to momentarily confuse any followers, at least. She looked down the road ahead of her. No black SUVs.

In the distance was Fulham Town Hall. The bus stop was close to it but Sally kept some distance away, constantly checking the street for Mitsubishis. After eight minutes of anxiously waiting, the bus arrived. Sally waited until the door had opened and the first passengers had got on board before hurrying over and pressing an Oyster card against the reader. She used the card belonging to the legend of a junior civil servant who was supposed to live locally. Two more passengers followed her, both middle-aged women laden with shopping.

Sally kept her head down as she went up the stairs to the upper deck. A group of schoolboys were at the front, laughing and swearing. Sally headed to the rear. All the back seats were empty and she sat next to the window. She checked the street to her right. There was a line of cars but the only SUVs were being driven by women with children. The school run. It always amused Sally that the most strident supporters of global warming campaigns put their opinions on hold when it came to taking their precious children to and from school. Sally's parents couldn't afford to run a car and she had always walked to school, until the running bug had bit.

The bus moved off and Sally tried to force herself to relax. Nothing could happen to her while she was on the bus. She hoped.

CHAPTER 19

Major Gannon walked from Knightsbridge and into Hyde Park. He stopped to allow half a dozen teenage girls to trot by on glossy horses, all moving with the sort of grace that could only be achieved by hours of expensive lessons, then he headed across the grass to the Serpentine. It was a warm evening and he took off his jacket and draped it across his arm.

Charlotte Button was sitting at an outside table at the Lido Café, overlooking the forty-acre lake that bisected the park. She had a cappuccino in front of her and had stretched out her legs to enjoy what was left of the sun.

Gannon checked his surroundings automatically as he walked, though he knew that the sort of men and women Button had on her payroll were skilled at surveillance and would be hard to spot. There were people walking dogs, tourists heading to the Princess Diana Memorial Fountain, schoolchildren heading home and rollerbladers showing off their skills, but no obvious security. She spotted him and waved but he was pretty sure that she was faking it and that she had seen him the moment he had entered the park. He waved back, then pointed to the café building and mimed drinking, and she grinned and flashed him a thumbs up.

He walked into the café, bought himself a large black coffee and went out to join her. She was wearing a light blue cashmere sweater and a knee-length Burberry skirt and had hung a beige Burberry raincoat over the back of her chair. 'Thanks for coming at such short notice, Charlotte,' he said as he sat down.

'Always a pleasure to see my favourite military man,' she said. 'Are you still with the Increment?' Her chestnut hair was slightly shorter than the last time he'd met her, and she was wearing the same slim gold Cartier watch on her left wrist.

'They're calling it E Squadron these days, but it's a case of tomato potato,' he said. The Major had been running the group for several years. 'I'm still involved but I spend more time at Thames House these days advising on security. Shopping malls, stadiums, transport hubs, all the obvious targets.'

'The world is becoming a very unsafe place,' said Button.

The Major nodded. 'What happened in Sri Lanka showed that ISIS is still a threat, even though they're being defeated militarily. We've shut down half a dozen serious threats so far this year. It's like the IRA said about Thatcher: we have to be lucky all the time, they only need to be lucky once.' He sipped his coffee. 'Anyway, obviously this isn't a social call. Does the name Martin Hirst mean anything to you? Former SAS, left the Regiment a couple of years ago. He's been looking for work in the private sector.' He took the printout from his jacket pocket and gave it to her. 'Hirst is the driver.'

She nodded. 'He got in touch a year or so ago, looking for work. I had him in for an interview and he seemed perfect, but then I had some due diligence done and we decided he wouldn't be a good fit.' She gave him back the sheet of paper.

'Because?' said Gannon, taking the sheet, refolding it and slipping it back into his pocket.

Button tilted her head on one side. 'Now don't be coy with me, Allan,' she said. 'He's one of yours, you know better than me what his problems are, surely.'

Gannon smiled. 'I just wanted to know how much you knew,' he said.

'He's unreliable under pressure,' said Button. 'He was a grade A soldier, a first class Para by all accounts, but the Pool doesn't need soldiers. It needs men who make the right decisions. A lot of the time my people are working in pairs or alone so there's no place for someone who can't think for themselves.'

The Pool was the shadowy organisation now headed up by Button. Whereas E Squadron handled matters that were too

demanding for MI5 and MI6, the Pool operated in a whole
different league. It carried out tasks that the government couldn't
be associated with, up to and including assassinations. Whereas
the men, and women, of E Squadron had to follow the law of
the land, there were no such restrictions on the Pool. Any money
paid to them was paid offshore through holding companies,
ensuring that there was no paper trail linking it to the government. As part of the deal for taking care of the government's
dirty work, Button was allowed to sell her services within the
private sector, though she was prohibited from working with
other countries. It was a nasty business at best, and not one
which the Major would ever want to be involved with, but he
accepted that in the world of modern terrorism there were times
that governments needed to take action without getting their
hands dirty, and in that respect Button provided a necessary
service.

'He was only in the Regiment for two years,' said Gannon.
'He was offered the chance to return to his unit but turned that
down. We think he's now working in the private sector.'

'And not in a good way, I suppose,' she said. 'Otherwise you
wouldn't be so keen to track him down.'

'We suspect he's part of a team that have just killed seven MI5
officers in a footie house in Wimbledon.' Gannon knew that
Button had the highest security clearance, plus her sources were
so good that she would find out what had happened sooner rather
than later. The fact that her jaw dropped showed that she hadn't
been told already, and the swear word that slipped out was added
proof.

'Who the hell would do that?' she said.

'That's the sixty-four thousand dollar question,' said the Major.

'They were all footies that were killed?'

Gannon nodded.

Button frowned. 'That doesn't make any sense,' she said.
'Footies don't work active cases, they just maintain legends.'

'That's what your former bosses said. But what's done is done.'

Button nodded slowly. 'A former colleague was working with

the footies prior to retirement,' she said. 'Drew Mountford. Please tell me he wasn't caught up in this.'

The Major grimaced and Button picked up on the gesture immediately. 'Oh my God,' she said, her hand going up to cover her mouth.

'I'm sorry,' he said. 'Yes, he was in the house.'

'Why would anyone attack footies?' she said. 'They're either kids or about to leave the service.'

'They're not sure,' said the Major. 'They took the hard drives, that could have been the objective.'

'They killed everybody?'

'Everyone that was in the house. One girl was out and she came back and disturbed them. She managed to escape and they're trying to bring her in as we speak. I'm not sure how much she'll be able to tell them, to be honest.'

'Who is she?'

'Sally Page. She's been with the footies since she joined two years ago.'

'After my time,' said Button. 'So you think that this Hirst character is the killer and that he's now after Sally?'

'She took the picture. He was in a black Mitsubishi Outlander on her tail. The vehicle is registered to a shell company on the Isle of Man, before you ask.'

'So it's a professional operation, clearly. Russians, maybe?'

'We'd just be guessing at this stage,' said Gannon. 'The key is to find out who Hirst is working for, because he obviously isn't doing this for personal reasons. He's a hired hand.'

'Somebody hired him to kill seven MI5 officers?' She shook her head. 'Nothing I heard about the guy suggests he'd be the type to do that.'

'He wanted to join the Pool.'

'Allan, be serious. We're the good guys. We might operate outside of the law but we do it for the greater good, to keep our country safe and occasionally to punish those who would do us harm. We'd never do anything to hurt the forces of law and order, or innocent civilians. And we'd never hire anyone who would.'

'But the point I'm making is that the Pool does carry out "wet work", as the Americans like to call it. So Hirst was up for that, obviously.'

'That's what you trained him to do, isn't it? And then he finds out that after all that training, he can't put his skills to work for you. What else could he do? Look for work as a plumber or a florist? No, he'd look for a job that made use of his skills. But your guys usually have a strong moral centre. Queen and country. They don't become hitmen for hire.'

'Some do, unfortunately,' said the Major. 'But I hear what you're saying. Everything I've heard about the man says he's not the sort to go on a killing rampage. But there's no doubting that picture.'

'Pictures can be faked.'

Gannon shook his head. 'Sally took it on her phone and sent it straight to her boss. It's definitely him.'

'Something must have changed,' said Button. 'When we did due diligence on him, he came up smelling of roses on all counts. We would almost certainly have hired him if it wasn't for his reliability issue.'

'Could you do me a favour, Charlotte?'

'Of course.'

'Can you put out some feelers? I can't see that what happened is Hirst's idea so he must be working for someone. And that someone must have been recruiting. No one's going to talk to me, but you're in that line of work . . .'

Button smiled thinly. 'I'd be happy to help,' she said.

'I'd owe you one.'

Her smile widened. 'I took that for granted,' she said.

CHAPTER 20

Sally pressed the red button to stop the bus. She looked around nervously as it came to a halt and the side door opened. She was the only person to get off at the Elgin Avenue stop and she hesitated for a second before placing her foot onto the pavement. She looked left and right and then hurried away from the bus, clasping her Marks & Spencer bag to her chest. The engine of the bus roared as it pulled away from the kerb. Sally stood on the pavement and watched it go, then looked both ways up Great Western Road before crossing over and heading down Elgin Avenue. She walked against the traffic so that she could see who was driving towards her, and took frequent looks over her shoulder. Nothing.

She crossed over to Sutherland Avenue, past the laundrette where Tim took his shirts to be washed and ironed. Non-biological powder because he was allergic, and hangers rather than folded. Many was the time she had dropped off his laundry on the way to the bus stop.

She headed north up Elgin Avenue and began to relax a little. If they had been following her to Maida Vale, they would have intercepted her by now. Ahead of her she saw Maida Vale Tube Station, next to the Vietnamese noodle shop that Tim loved. His favourite meal was a bowl of pho noodle soup with grilled chicken and a Tiger beer.

She walked along the road, past the shops with their outdoor displays of fruit and vegetables, and turned the corner to the entrance to his flat. The door was on the ground floor and opened to a narrow hallway that ran up two floors to his flat. His was the only flat that used the hallway so he kept his bike and sports stuff there. But Sally didn't go inside just yet. Instead, she walked past the front door, heading towards Sutherland Avenue. There was an Everyman cinema there where she and Tim had often watched movies, curled up on a sofa with a bottle of wine and a pizza. She hadn't been back to Maida Vale since she had broken up with him and now all the memories came flooding back. She blocked them out, knowing that she had to concentrate on what was going on around her. She looked over her shoulder. No one had followed her down the road. She crossed over to the other pavement. There were no cars, either way. Her heart was pounding again and she took slow, deep breaths. If she had been wearing her Apple Watch she was sure her pulse would show as well above 120.

She stopped walking, took another look around, and then retraced her steps to the front door. There was a single doorbell to the right but she ignored it and put the key straight into the lock, saying a silent prayer that Tim hadn't changed it. She turned the key and it refused to move. Her heart pounded again. There was a knack to opening the lock, she remembered; it had caught her out on several occasions. You had to push the key all the way in, then pull it out a fraction, and then turn. She took a deep breath and tried again. This time the lock clicked and she pushed the door open. She took a last look over her shoulder and hurried inside, slamming the door behind her and pressing her back against it. She stood panting for breath, then took an extra deep breath to calm herself down.

Tim's bike was on its brackets on the wall but that didn't necessarily mean he was home – he used the Tube to get to work. His cricket bag was on the stairs, along with two tennis rackets and a squash racket. She went up the stairs, past the posters of his favourite movies: *The Godfather*, *Heat*, *Serpico*. 'The classics', he always called them. Sally preferred vampire movies and science fiction and he'd always let her choose the movie on the nights they had stayed in, though the quid pro quo was that he got to choose the pizza, which meant she had to put up with the pine-apple that she hated and that he loved.

The door to his flat was at the top of the stairs. There was a second lock there, but this one was operated by a keypad. Tim loved gadgets. He always upgraded to the newest iPhone on launch day, and he was one of the first in the UK to own an Apple Watch. When he'd bought Sally the same watch for her birthday, he'd delighted in showing her all the features. She looked now at the keypad. The number to open the lock was his month and year of birth; she tapped in the six digits and sighed with relief when the lock clicked and the door swung open. 'Tim?' she called. 'Tim, it's Sally. Are you there?'

There was no answer and she pushed the door wider, entering the main sitting room. There was a small kitchen to the left, a bathroom next to it and the bedroom was directly opposite the front door. 'Tim!' she called, but there was no doubt that the flat was empty. She sighed and closed the door behind her. All the strength faded from her legs and she sank to the floor. She drew her knees up against her chest and began to sob.

CHAPTER 21

The Major's phone buzzed in his pocket. He was sitting in the back of a black cab, heading back to Thames House. He looked at the screen of his phone. It was Darren Keighley. He took the call. 'Boss, the cupboard was bare, I'm afraid.'

'Any idea where they went?'

'I spoke to the neighbours both sides and Martin has been gone for about six months, but was around most weekends. The wife and kid were here but they went away a couple of days ago. They have two cars; his isn't there but hers is. According to one of the neighbours, Martin was here on Monday and seemed distraught. They heard shouting and banging inside the house.'

'What was he up to? Domestic violence, maybe?'

'Negative, boss. The wife and kid weren't there then. He was alone.'

Gannon frowned. This wasn't making any sense.

'After that he left and they haven't seen him or the family. I guess that's not what you wanted to hear, is it, boss?'

The Major smiled grimly. 'I'm just trying to find out what he's up to,' he said. 'Did you ever work with him?'

'Trained with him a few times,' said Keighley. 'Bloody good shot with a Glock and none too shabby at sniping. Always got a perfect score in the Killing House. He fucked up a couple of times is what I heard, on active ops. He quit rather than being RTU'd. That's pretty much all I know, boss. He wasn't really in the Regiment long enough to get to know.'

'All right, Darren, you can stand down. Thanks for your help.'

The Major ended the call and looked out of the window, trying to make sense of the limited information he had. An SAS trooper who couldn't make the grade sets out to find work in the private sector. Then he turns up at an MI5 footie house where seven officers are murdered. Then he starts chasing the only survivor from the house. Had he been hired to carry out the killings? There had been several cases of men leaving the Regiment to work in the drugs industry or using their military skills to rob banks, but killing MI5 officers was a whole different ballgame. And from what little Gannon had heard about Marty Hirst, he really didn't sound the type to go rogue.

CHAPTER 22

Sally wiped the tears from her face with the back of her hands. This was no time to be getting emotional. She stood up, took a deep breath, then went into Tim's tiny kitchen. It was barely six feet square but it had everything he needed, which was basically a sink, a small fridge and a microwave. There was a double hotplate but no oven — he usually either ate out or used Deliveroo. And the fact there wasn't room for a washing machine had never bothered him because he preferred to use the laundrette anyway.

She bent down and opened the fridge. As usual there was little in the way of fresh food, but there was a yoghurt that was only nudging its sell-by date so she took it out. She smiled when she saw the bottle of rosé wine lying on the bottom shelf. There had been a deal on at the local off-licence, buy six and get one free. That had been what, six months ago? She and Tim had drunk six of the bottles but he had obviously kept the last one. As a reminder of her? Was that creepy or romantic? She shook her head and took out a can of Dr Pepper. She sat on the sofa and turned on the television. It was tuned to Sky News and she watched it as she ate the yoghurt and sipped her soft drink. There was no mention on the TV of what had happened at the Wimbledon house, but that was to be expected. There was no way MI5 would go public. The opposite in fact; they would move heaven and earth to keep it quiet.

She lay back on the sofa and swung her feet onto the table. She needed to talk to someone at Thames House, but who? She was worried about Hadley, but if he was a traitor, who was he working for? And why kill everyone at the Wimbledon house? The fact that the computers had been ransacked suggested that there was something in the house that the men wanted. But if Hadley had wanted anything from the Wimbledon house he could have just turned up and taken it. He was a regular visitor – it was his domain.

She shook her head, trying to focus her thoughts. How were the attackers managing to find her everywhere she went? They could have been tracking her phone, but that wouldn't explain everything. She didn't have the phone when she went to her home in Fulham, and one of the black Outlanders was already there. So they also knew who she was and where she lived. Had that information come from someone within Thames House? Or the house in Wimbledon? Maybe the attackers hadn't killed everybody straight away; maybe they had kept someone alive and questioned them and that person had told them about her. Or maybe they had all been betrayed by someone who usually worked at the house but who hadn't been there today.

She took another drink of Dr Pepper and thought about who had been missing from the house. Three of the footies were on holiday. Angela Lavin was on her honeymoon in Marbella, and Hamid Qadiri and Louise Chadwick were on short-term leave. Louise had been redecorating a bedroom for her mother and was due back in the house tomorrow and Hamid had taken a week off to rehearse with his band. Could one of them have been involved? Louise knew where Sally lived but she didn't think Angela and Hamid did. And anyway what reason could they possibly have had for killing everybody? The only footie who had been involved with actual cases was Drew Mountford, but he was winding down in preparation for retirement. She felt as if she was going around in circles and getting no closer to solving the mystery. Her eyes were starting to get heavy and she blinked, trying to stay awake. She was dog-tired, partly from all the running she'd done but the stress was having an effect, too. She lay back, surrendering to the exhaustion.

CHAPTER 23

Liz Bailey pushed open the door to the director's office and Ellie Cooper smiled up at her. 'He says you're to go right in, Liz. Sounds like it's going to be an all-nighter.' Bailey nodded her thanks and went through to the inner office.

Giles Pritchard had taken his jacket off and rolled up his sleeves and was starting to look like a man under pressure. 'Please tell me you've got some good news for me, Liz,' he said, sitting back in his chair.

'I've got news, I'm just not sure if it's good or not.' She sat down opposite him.

'I'm all ears.'

'I ran a check on Sally's phone. It took a while because the phone company had a hefty backlog of police requests but I managed to elbow my way to the front of the queue.' She passed him a computer printout. 'That's her GPS location since 7 a.m. this morning up until twenty minutes ago,' she said.

'Good work,' said Pritchard. He took it from her and studied it.

'She starts off in her apartment in Fulham, then she runs to the house in Wimbledon. The phone confirms what she told Ian; she arrived at the house and shortly afterwards left. Again, as she told Ian, she seems to have gone to a coffee shop and then returned about ten minutes later.'

Pritchard nodded as he studied the map.

'That's when she goes on the run. Initially on foot. She spends about twenty minutes in a house close to our premises.'

Pritchard opened his mouth to speak but she beat him to the punch. 'We're sending someone out to find out who lives there.'

Pritchard smiled and nodded.

'She then moves by car, presumably an Uber. The car goes as far as Wimbledon Common which again confirms what she told Hadley. She then moves on foot through Wimbledon Common and on to Richmond Park, before running to the Kingston house. Then there's more foot traffic and now she's stopped.'

'So we know where she is?'

'We know where she was about twenty minutes ago,' said Bailey.

'Not home?'

'No, not Fulham. But we have the address.'

'Then we need to have her picked up, obviously.'

'That's what I need to check with you,' she said. 'We can send a team from here but it'll take time to get there. In view of what's happened it would speed things up if we get the police to send ARVs.'

Pritchard looked pained. 'I'd rather keep this in-house at the moment,' he said.

Bailey nodded. 'That's what I thought you'd say. So we use our people.'

'Can you handle it? Allan is on his way back to Thames House so you brief the team and get Sally picked up.' He smiled. 'Good work.'

'There's something else,' she said. 'Earlier on today the phone company acted upon a request for data on the same number.'

Pritchard raised his eyebrows. 'Authorised by whom?'

'It had an investigation number attached but the case had no connection with Sally Page.'

'So who was asking about her number?'

'The request didn't have a contact number. Just the case number.'

'And what time was the request put in?'

'Shortly after our people were killed.'

'So they knew that Sally was a witness and used MI5 resources to track her.' He swore under his breath, something Bailey had never seen him do before. 'You know what this means, Liz?'

She nodded. 'Unfortunately, yes.'

CHAPTER 24

Martin Hirst ejected the magazine from his Glock, checked the number of rounds and then slotted it back in. There was a suppressor screwed into the barrel. The three men with him in the car were all checking their weapons too. They were professionals and that's what professionals did. All of their guns were silenced. The target was in a residential area and one way or another at least one of the guns was going to be fired. There was no way that Sally Page was going to get out of this alive.

'Right, Josh deals with the lock. As soon as the door opens, I'll go in. Baz, you follow me. Josh, you're tail-end Charlie.' He turned to look at the driver. His name was Kristov and that was all Hirst knew. He'd been told that Kristov would be a member of his team and there was no questioning the orders of the men that Hirst worked for. Kristov barely spoke, though the few times he had it was clear he had decent enough English. He hadn't offered up any information on his background but Hirst was fairly sure he was former special forces, or *spetsnaz* as the Russians called them. There was no way of guessing which unit Kristov had served with, though it was clear from his cold, dead eyes that he had killed in the past. 'Kristov, you stay here with the engine running.'

'No problem,' said the Russian. There were seven men on Hirst's team and Baz and Josh were the only two that he trusted. He certainly didn't trust Kristov and was fairly sure that the Russian was reporting back to the men who had hired him. That was why he always kept Kristov close, more often than not driving his vehicles.

The rest of the team were all Americans and all former special forces, mainly Delta Force or Navy SEALs. They were a nasty bunch, and had clearly crossed over to the dark side some time ago. Hirst could understand the concept of killing for money, but not the fact that they took such pleasure from it. They were based in a large rented house in Ealing and when they weren't out on the road the Americans sat drinking beer and swapping stories, most of which seemed to involve people begging for their lives. When Hirst had been given the job, the Americans had come with it. They needed Hirst for his local experience but they were the muscle. Hirst wasn't sure that he could trust the Americans, and he was damn sure he couldn't trust the Russian, so he brought two men he knew onto the team: Barry 'Baz' McKenzie and Josh Taylor. He had known Baz for five years and Josh for double that, and trusted them both with his life. Both were proficient with weapons but only Josh had seen military service. Baz was from Glasgow where he'd been a bareknuckle fighter as a teenager, leaving him with a twisted nose and cauliflower ears. He'd abandoned the fight game at twenty-two after a barrage of punches to his chest had imploded a lung. He'd started working as an enforcer for a local bookie and it had been a short journey from breaking legs and arms to killing for money. Now, at twenty-four, he had a dozen kills to his credit, most of them related to drugs disputes north of the border. He had taken to dying his hair blond and growing it long enough to tie back in a short ponytail, and wore a diamond stud in his left ear.

Josh Taylor was a different matter. Like Hirst he was a former paratrooper and had seen action around the world. They had served together for almost two years before Hirst had gone off to join the SAS. Taylor was happy being a paratrooper and had been set for a twenty-year military career until it was cut short when he broke his hip during a NATO exercise in the summer of 2018. As part of Saber Strike, the Paras had joined eighteen thousand troops from nineteen NATO nations in operations across the Baltic states. Taylor's jump had gone wrong and while the Army gave him reasonable medical care they made it clear that he had no future as a soldier. Taylor managed to find work as a static security guard, mainly guarding building stores at night, and was pretty much living from hand to mouth. He had developed a drinking problem and after a year of soul-destroying solitary work had decided to use the skills that the Army had taught him. Hirst had heard on the Para grapevine that Josh had become a killer for hire and the man had jumped at the opportunity of working with Hirst, especially when he heard how much the job paid. Hirst had spent an evening drinking with Josh, gradually revealing what it is they would have to do, and he had been surprised at the lack of reluctance even when he disclosed the nature of the victims. The money was obviously a big attraction but the way the Army had treated Josh had clearly twisted his mind. Hirst understood – he wasn't doing it for the money either.

Marty wasn't happy at having to lead the breaching of the flat, but he didn't see that he had any choice. Sally had seen him outside the house in Wimbledon and truth be told he should have killed her there and then. He was armed at the time, she was in the house and he was outside, it should have been the easiest thing in the world to have put two rounds in her chest. He still wasn't sure why he hadn't. Or why she had been able to push him out of the way and run. MI5's self-defence training wasn't a patch on the SAS's, but she had obviously learned enough to catch him by surprise. Her punches had hurt, too. Luckily no one had seen her attack him and by the time Baz and Josh had joined him outside he had grabbed his sunglasses and told them that she had run off before he had reached the house. He wasn't sure if they believed him or not but either way they had to accept it because he was running the op and they were the hired help.

'Just so you know, she's probably got the thumb drive on her. It wasn't at the house and it's one of hers so that's a sound conclusion. If we get the thumb drive then we don't need her. End of. But if the thumb drive isn't there we need a hard interrogation to get the intel from her. So we go in hard and we take out anyone with her, but we don't shoot her until we know whether she has it or not. No itchy trigger fingers, okay?'

Baz and Josh nodded.

Hirst called Winchester on his mobile. 'Billy, we've got a location on the girl. You can clean up your mess and get out of there. It's all going to be over in a few minutes. This part of it anyway.'

'Where shall we meet?'

'Just park up and wait. I'll be in touch.' Hirst ended the call and put his phone away. He twisted around in his seat and nodded at Baz and Josh. 'Ready guys?'

The two men nodded.

'Right, here we go,' said Hirst. He opened the door and stepped onto the pavement. Josh and Baz followed him. They headed to the door.

CHAPTER 25

'A re you going to fucking share that, or what?' growled Wayne, gesturing impatiently at the joint in Marcel's hand.

'Chill, blud,' said Marcel. He took a hurried pull on the joint and then handed it over to Wayne.

Wayne continued to operate his controller with his left thumb as he took the joint with his right hand and took a long drag. Three enemy soldiers died in a hail of bullets as he handed the joint back to Marcel. Marcel was playing with the iPhone they had taken from the stupid bitch in the park. The Apple Watch was on Wayne's wrist. He had synced it to his own iPhone but he was starting to think that he had gotten the shitty end of the stick – the phone was worth two or three times the watch. And Wayne had been the first to spot the girl. He was the one who suggested they should roll her but then she had caught them by surprise by approaching them. Silly bitch. What sort of mug finds an iPhone and an Apple Watch and then fucking gives them away? He took a quick look over at Marcel, who was texting like a schoolgirl. Wayne already had an iPhone 8 but the one the girl had given them was an iPhone X Max with 512 GB of memory.

Marcel held up the phone. He grinned. 'Excuse me, have you lost a phone?' he said, mimicking the girl in a sing-song voice. 'What was that bitch thinking?' He took another pull on the joint. 'You know, we should have rolled the bitch. Should've taken her own phone and her money.'

'Then the cops would have been involved and all that shit,' said Wayne. 'This way, we got the phone and the watch and there's no comeback.'

There was a metallic click in the hallway and Wayne frowned. 'What the fuck was that?'

'The radiator,' said Marcel. 'It's always kicking off these days.'

There was a second click, slightly louder this time.

'Don't sound like the radiator,' said Wayne. He paused the game and looked over at the door. It led to a narrow hallway. The kitchen was to the right, the stairs and front door to the left. He was pretty sure the sound had come from the left.

'Chill, bruv, the cops will knock, they always do,' said Marcel.

There was a third click and then a scraping sound and Marcel frowned. 'The fuck?' he said, putting the phone down on the coffee table. He reached behind a cushion and pulled out a large machete, then got to his feet.

Wayne dropped the controller and bent down. There was a machete under his armchair and he grabbed it. As he got to his feet he heard a padding footfall in the hallway. It couldn't have been the cops; like Marcel had said they would have announced their presence and if the door wasn't opened they would have kicked it down. And if they had broken in they would have come charging down the hall waving their guns and screaming 'armed police' at the tops of their voices.

A floorboard squeaked. The only drugs in the house was their stash of weed and a few tablets of ecstasy they used to get girls in the mood. They had cash and in the attic there was a trunk full of valuables they had still to fence. There were several gangs in the area who were stupid enough to think that the house was worth turning over but if gangbangers were going to break in they would have probably come in through a window in the middle of the night, not through the front door in the early evening.

Marcel looked over at Wayne, his forehead creased into a frown. 'The fuck?' he repeated.

Wayne raised the machete and stepped towards the door. If they wanted a fight, they'd fucking well have one. Marcel did the same.

There was another wooden squeak followed by a muffled

whisper. Wayne's heart was pounding now. There was definitely someone in the hallway. Maybe two people. He gripped the handle of the machete and gritted his teeth as he took another step forward. He stopped short when a figure appeared in the doorway. The man was white and that surprised him because all the local gangbangers were black or Asian. The man was a few inches shorter than Wayne, built like a weightlifter with wide shoulders and a narrow waist. He was wearing a black bomber jacket and what looked like Versace jeans and Timberland boots. In his hand was a gun with the sort of silencer you only saw in movies. Wayne frowned. Was he a cop? There was no badge that he could see and the man wasn't identifying himself, just standing there and staring at them with blank eyes. A second man moved into view. Taller, thinner, with his blond hair tied back in the sort of tiny ponytail you only saw on sad middle-aged men who wanted to look young and hip. He also had a gun with a silencer. Wayne's frown deepened. The cops didn't use silencers.

He opened his mouth to speak but as he did Marcel rushed towards them, his machete held high. The bald man's face remained impassive as he pointed his gun at Marcel's face and pulled the trigger twice. The gun made a loud popping sound and the back of Marcel's skull exploded in a shower of blood, brain matter and bone fragments that sprayed across the sofa. Some of it splattered across Wayne's face and he flinched. The machete was above his head and he drew it back, ready to charge, but the bald man was already swinging the gun towards him. Wayne felt his stomach turn over as he realised what was about to happen and that there was nothing, absolutely nothing, he could do to stop it. He took a step forward and began to bring the machete down but the bald man had all the time in the world to point the gun at Wayne's chest and pull the trigger. The last thing he saw was the cold blankness of the man's eyes and then there was the sound of a balloon popping and everything went black.

CHAPTER 26

Sally was being chased but no matter how hard she ran she couldn't escape her pursuers. Her heart was pounding and her throat was red raw. She looked over her shoulder. Her pursuers were gaining on her and that didn't make any sense because she was a runner and she was younger and fitter than they were. She looked down at the grass. It seemed to be sucking at her feet, and lifting them was an effort. She was finding it hard to breath, as if there was a steel clamp around her chest. She didn't seem to be sucking in enough air, no matter how hard she tried. 'Sally! Sally!' They were shouting her name. She looked over her shoulder. There were three men chasing her, big men dressed in black carrying large guns with bulbous silencers. Where had they come from? They were in the middle of the park, there were no roads nearby, yet they had appeared from nowhere. They weren't tiring, either, they seemed fresh and full of fire. She turned away and concentrated on running but her feet were like lead. 'Sally!' she heard and then something grabbed her foot. She screamed and woke up.

Tim took a step back, shocked by her outburst. She was still confused and she rolled off the sofa and came up in a crouch, her hands in the air, fingers curled like talons.

Tim put his hands up to placate her. 'Hey, it's me,' he said. 'Calm down.'

She took a deep breath and straightened up. 'Sorry,' she said. 'I was having a nightmare.'

'I'd say so. You were tossing and turning and mumbling.'

'I've been having a rough day,' she said. She looked around the room. 'I didn't know where else to go.' She sat down and put her head in her hands.

'What the fuck's going on, Sally?' he said.

'I'm in trouble,' she said.

'I gathered that,' he said. 'I didn't think you broke in because you wanted to pick up where we left off.'

She looked up at him. 'Tim, I didn't have anywhere else to go.'

'Clearly. Look, you broke up with me, remember. You can't just waltz back in when you need somewhere to crash. That's what hotels are for. And how did you get in, anyway?'

'I still have a key,' she said. 'You never asked for it back.'

'And you thought that gave you the right to just let yourself in?'

'There are men out there trying to fucking kill me,' she said quietly.

It took a couple of seconds for what she had said to sink in, then his eyes widened. 'Say what now?'

'There are men, with guns, trying to kill me,' she said, saying each word slowly and clearly as if addressing a child.

'Who?'

'I don't know.'

'Why?'

'I don't know.'

'Have you been drinking?'

'No. Why would you ask that?'

His upper lip curled up in a look of disdain. 'Are you on something?'

She glared at him. 'Of course not.'

'Coke? Ice?'

She threw up her hands in frustration. 'Tim, what the fuck? I'm being hunted like an animal and you accuse me of being a drug addict.' She folded her arms and stared at the floor.

He sat down next to her and put his arm around her shoulders. 'What's happening? What's going on?'

She shook her head. 'You won't believe me.'

'Is it because of your job?'

She nodded. 'I think so.'

'So why aren't they helping you? Why are you here and not at work?'

'Because I can't trust anybody,' she said.

'Sally, I'm not following you,' he said. 'You need to tell me what happened, from the start.'

She sniffed and nodded. 'Okay,' she said. She looked at him and forced a smile. 'Look, despite what you said about me being a drunk and a drug addict, I could seriously do with a drink right now.'

He took his arm from around her shoulder and patted her on the leg. 'That's the spirit,' he said. 'There's still a bottle of that rosé you like in the fridge,' he said. 'You remember where the kitchen is?'

She ignored the sarcasm. He had every right to be annoyed, turning up the way she had and effectively breaking into his house. She pushed herself up off the sofa, went along the hallway to the kitchen and opened the fridge.

She took the bottle of wine out and opened the drawer to get a corkscrew, then took two glasses from the cupboard to the left of the cooker. She smiled at the thought that she was as familiar with Tim's place as she was with the flat she shared with Callum and Laura. Her heart lurched at the thought of what had happened to Callum.

She opened the bottle and took it and the glasses into the sitting room. Tim had already kicked off his shoes, loosened his tie and dropped down onto the single armchair. He leaned forward and opened a pizza box that he'd obviously brought with him. Sally groaned when she saw the pineapple. 'Who puts fruit on a pizza?' she asked, giving him one of the glasses and pouring wine into it.

'I do,' said Tim. 'It's my pizza and I'll eat it any way I want to. It's not as if I was expecting you.'

Sally sat down on the sofa. The pizza did smell good and she grabbed a slice. Tim watched her, clearly wondering if she was going to pick off the pineapple. It was one of the things that had driven him crazy when they were a couple. She grinned, left the pineapple where it was, and took a large bite.

Tim took a gulp of wine and grabbed a slice of pizza. 'You're looking good, Sally,' he said, taking a bite of his slice.

'I look like shit,' she said.

'I've not seen you dressed like that before.'

'I went to a charity shop,' she said.

He stopped eating, his pizza suspended in the air on the way to his mouth. 'You what?'

'I needed to change my appearance,' she said.

'Which brings me back to my original question – what the fuck is going on?'

She looked at him for several seconds, unsure what she should say. Under her employment contract, she was forbidden to discuss Secret Service matters with anyone outside MI5. And the Official Secrets Act, which she had signed on the day she had joined MI5, meant she could go to prison for revealing any of the service's secrets. She sighed, gulped down her wine, then told Tim everything that had happened, from the moment she had discovered the bodies in the Wimbledon house, to running across the common, giving away her phone and watch and getting the bus over the river. His jaw dropped when she explained how she had seen the Outlander near her flat, and the flashes when Callum had gone inside. Tim had met Callum several times when he had visited her in Fulham.

'You're saying that these guys killed Callum?'

Sally swallowed. Her mouth had gone suddenly dry. 'There were two flashes. I think they shot him, Tim. I think he walked into the flat and they fucking shot him.'

'You don't know that for sure.'

'No, I'm sure.'

'Have you tried calling Callum?'

'I don't have his number. I mean, I had it, but only on my phone.'

'You seriously think he's dead?'

She nodded. 'They killed seven people in Wimbledon,' she said. 'I doubt that one more would worry them.'

'There's been nothing about this on the TV,' he said.

'They'll have kept it quiet,' said Sally. 'D-notice, the works.'

And these guys in the black SUVs, they're still after you?'

'So far as I know, yes.'

'It's . . .'

'Unbelievable?' she finished for him.

He nodded. 'Yeah.'

'I keep having to pinch myself. But it happened, Tim.'

'I believe you.'

He looked at her earnestly and she held his look for several seconds. 'Thank you,' she said eventually.

'For what?'

'For believing me. For being on my team. I turn up out of the blue with a story that even I'm having trouble believing and you just accept it. I don't deserve you, Tim. I never deserved you.'

'I wouldn't say that. And one thing I can say about you, Sally, you are never boring.' He paused. 'The question now is what are we going to do?'

'We?'

'I'm in this with you now, Sally. I'll do whatever I can to help you.' He ran a hand through his hair. 'And you think they were tracking you through your phone? Or the watch?'

'I was heading back to the office in an Uber, and they forced us off the road,' she said. 'How else could they have known what car I was in?'

'Maybe they saw you getting into the car?'

'I didn't see them outside the house, and I was wearing a wig.'

'What?'

'This woman gave me a wig. And a parka. So even if they had seen me getting into the car, they wouldn't have known it was me. But they found me while we were on the road.'

'But you got away?'

'Like I said, I ran, across the common. They came after me but they weren't runners.'

Tim smiled. 'Nobody runs like you,' he said. 'Mo Farah, maybe.'

'Then I went to one of the houses I look after. I called my

boss and he said he'd send help but the bad guys turned up. So that means either my boss told them where I was, or they were tracking my phone.'

'Except that sort of tracking ability is the province of GCHQ and MI5, right?'

'These days, who knows?' said Sally. 'The Russians can probably do it. The Chinese maybe.'

'Your boss – you said he might have told them where you were?'

'I said it was a possibility. But I don't see why he'd do that. He's a cantankerous bugger but I don't think he'd be involved in the murder of his staff.' She shrugged. 'It's way more likely that they managed to track my phone.'

'So in theory, having dumped the phone and the watch, you're okay now?'

'Except that they knew where I lived. They didn't follow me there, they were waiting for me. So no, I'm not okay now. I'm very far from okay.'

'What do you want to do, Sally?' he asked. 'Just tell me and I'll help you.'

She sat forward and put her head in her hands and stared at the floor. 'I wish I knew,' she said.

CHAPTER 27

There were two men in the front seat, both in their thirties with beards and suntans that suggested they had been somewhere hot and sunny for several weeks at least, presumably somewhere quite dangerous. They were polite and deferential to Simon Wilsher, the MI5 officer sitting in the back of the SUV, but there was no doubt that they were alpha males. The vehicle was similar to the ones driven by the Met's Armed Response Units but the paintwork was black with no markings. The car had arrived at Thames House to collect Wilsher and the two men had introduced themselves as Dave and Rob. Wilsher wasn't sure if their names were genuine or not; so far as he knew special forces were as reluctant to use real names as MI5. He'd shaken their hands and given them the name Roger.

'Roger that,' Rob had said, as he shook his hand with a grip that seemed to suggest he was exerting just a fraction of its available power. Rob had black hair and dark brown eyes with a hardness that belied his easy smile.

Dave was driving. He had brown hair and his beard was much shorter than Rob's, more of an extended stubble. Both men wore G-Shock watches, as did most of the special forces men that Wilsher had come across. They had spent most of the day parked up close to the Thames, near to Waterloo Bridge. There hadn't been much chit-chat. Wilsher had tried to start a conversation several times, but was unable to get them to talk about anything other than football, the weather and any reasonably attractive women who walked by.

The call from Liz Bailey came as Wilsher was starting to think he was involved in nothing more than a training exercise. His briefing had simply been that he was to ride shotgun with two SAS heavies and wait for instructions.

Bailey gave him an address, and told him that he was to pick up an MI5 officer by the name of Sally Page. 'Sally might well be in danger so let the SAS guys take care of any problems,' said Bailey. 'I'll send you a photograph now.'

She ended the call, and by the time he had given the destination to the guys in the front, the photograph arrived. Wilsher didn't recognise the name or the picture. He handed the phone to Rob. 'Sally Page,' he said. 'We're to collect her and take her to Thames House.'

'Roger, Roger,' said Rob. He showed the picture to Dave, who acknowledged it with a curt nod, then he handed the phone back to Wilsher.

They sped across Waterloo Bridge and continued to head south. Rob had tapped the address into his phone and was giving Dave instructions.

Wilsher settled back in his seat and tried to relax.

CHAPTER 28

Josh hurried down the hallway into the sitting room. There had been four shots, two groups of two – followed by the dull thuds of bodies falling to the floor.

Hirst was standing in the doorway, his gun lowered. Baz was behind him, looking over his shoulder.

'What the fuck happened?' asked Josh.

Baz turned to look at him. 'She's not here,' he said.

'How can she not be here?' asked Josh. He peered over Hirst's shoulder. There were two bodies on the floor.

'Fuck, fuck, fuck,' said Hirst as he stared down at the two men.

'Marty, didn't you say easy on the trigger finger?' asked Josh behind him.

'They were armed,' said Hirst, nodding at the machete lying on the floor next to the dead black man who had rushed him.

'No question of that, but you did say no shooting unless it was absolutely necessary.'

'She's not here, and they were coming at us, so they're collateral damage so yeah, it was fucking necessary.' He stepped over the body. There was an iPhone on the coffee table and he picked it up. 'Is this her phone?' he asked.

'Fuck me, mate, how would I know?' asked Baz. 'They all look the same.'

The second man that Hirst had shot was lying face down by the sofa. Hirst had put two shots in the centre of the man's chest. He'd also been brandishing a machete. Hirst couldn't see it. He flipped the man over and that revealed the weapon. There was an Apple Watch on the man's left wrist. He pointed his gun at it and looked over at Baz. 'She's a smart one,' he said. 'She dumped the watch and the phone and we've been tracking them for the last couple of hours.'

Josh joined him and stood looking down at the body. 'Now what?' he said.

Hirst scowled. That was a good question and one that just then he didn't have an answer to.

CHAPTER 29

Tim put a mug of Ovaltine down in front of Sally. She laughed when she saw what he had brought her. It had always been her comfort drink of choice. 'You're like an elephant, you never forget a thing, do you?'

He sat down next to her. 'To be fair, elephants don't really have much to remember.'

She picked up the mug and felt tears prick her eyes. 'I'm sorry,' she said.

'For what?'

'For everything. For breaking into your flat. For dumping all my problems on you.'

'For breaking my fucking heart?'

She nodded. 'I'm sorry.'

'I was joking,' he said, sitting down next to her.

'No you weren't. Not really. And I am sorry.'

Tim shrugged. 'I'm over it now.'

'Really?'

'I think so. It used to be that you were the first thing I thought about when I woke up and the last thing before I went to sleep. Now some days I don't even think about you.'

'Are you seeing anyone?' She sipped her Ovaltine.

He laughed, and there was a harshness to the sound that made her feel sad and guilty in equal amounts. 'I haven't been looking, and in the job I either meet cops, villains or victims and everyone is usually stressed. But I'm not looking. You?'

'I don't want a relationship, not at the moment.'

He laughed again. 'Yeah, you made that pretty clear.'

'I'm really sorry, Tim. It was my fault.'

'It's not you, it's me, is that what you're saying? Seriously?'

She sipped her Ovaltine. 'It was always me, Tim. You were the perfect boyfriend. Still are. But I didn't want what you wanted.'

'And what was that exactly?'

She saw the defensive look in his eyes and she tried to smile, to make him feel better. 'You wanted a family. You never had one when you were growing up, and you want one now. You want a wife and kids and a house with a garden.'

'Isn't that what everyone wants?'

She shook her head. 'No. Not everyone.'

'I never said we had to have kids. I'd have been happy just getting married. Hell, I was happy enough just living with you.'

'I wasn't living with you, Tim.'

'As good as.'

'We both had our own places.'

He threw up his hands and leant back. 'Drink your Ovaltine,' he said.

She drew her legs up underneath her. 'You still have Ovaltine. You hate Ovaltine.'

He shrugged. 'No point in throwing away a perfectly good powdered beverage,' he said.

'I'm glad you didn't.' She took another mouthful of Ovaltine. 'What am I going to do, Tim?'

He smiled thinly. 'If it was up to me, we'd go to the station and you'd give a full report. You'd tell them what happened at the house in Wimbledon and the fact that they've been chasing you across London. And you'd tell them what you saw at your flat.'

'You know I can't go to the police.'

He grinned. 'Sally, you sort of have done already.'

'I'm here because you're Tim, not because you're Detective Sergeant Tim Reid.'

'Good to know.'

'You know what I mean. And you know that I can't go to the cops. It'd be the end of my career.'

'Sally, if these guys catch up with you, it won't just be your career that comes to an end.'

Sally raised her mug. 'Thanks for that,' she said.

'I'm just telling you the way it is,' he said. 'They killed seven MI5 officers already. They might well have killed your flatmate. You have to do something and it seems to me that going to the police is the best option.'

She shook her head. 'It's not an option. They drum it into you from day one. If something goes wrong in an operation, you never, ever, go running to the cops. You report in and you tell your superior what happened and then they will decide how best to deal with it.'

'So do that then. Call the office.'

Sally sighed. 'And talk to who? The last time I spoke to my boss the killers turned up and I only just managed to get away.'

Tim frowned. 'So you do think your boss is behind this?'

'I don't know. That's the problem, I don't know who I can trust any more.'

'Except me?'

She laughed despite the seriousness of her situation. 'Yes, except you. But seriously, I can't just call the Thames House switchboard and ask to be put through to the director general.'

'Why not?'

'Because that's not how it works. Could you call Scotland Yard and ask to speak to the commissioner?'

Tim wrinkled his nose. 'Maybe not.'

'They'd take your name and phone number and get someone to call you back. But it wouldn't be the commissioner.'

'True enough,' said Tim.

'So if I did call Thames House, there'd be no guarantee that they wouldn't tell Hadley that I'd called.'

'You could specifically tell them not to do that.' Sally raised her eyebrows archly. 'Right, okay, I can see how that wouldn't work. But what about someone lower than the director general? Someone you know you can trust.'

'Liz Bailey, maybe,' said Sally. 'She runs building security. But how do I know I can trust her? How can I trust anybody after what's happened?'

'Why don't I just take you to Thames House? Surely nothing can happen to you once you're in the building.'

Sally shrugged. 'What if it's MI5 that wants me dead?' she said.

Tim's jaw dropped. 'Oh come on, now. Why would you say that?'

'I don't know,' she said quietly.

'No come on. Why would you even think that?'

She shrugged again. 'Who knows what sort of black ops they get involved in?' she said.

'But killing their own people? Why would they do that?'

'To cover something up, maybe.'

'I'm sure there are better ways of doing that than killing a house full of people. Why use that level of violence if they want to keep a lid on something?'

'Okay, but there has to be at least one person at Thames House helping these guys, and I've no way of knowing who I can trust. What's to say that I turn up at Thames House and the next minute they put me in a car and take me to God knows where?'

'I'll come with you.'

She shook her head. 'They won't let you inside, Tim. MI5 is a whole different world.' She sipped her Ovaltine.

'So let's go to the cops but at a very senior level. They can protect you.'

'Tim, you're not listening to me. Going to the police in any capacity isn't an option.'

'Only if you intend to carry on working for them,' he said. 'And after what's happened, is that seriously an option?'

'I haven't done anything wrong,' she said. 'What's this got to do with my career?'

'Are you serious?'

'Yes, of course I'm serious. I'm the victim here, I'm caught up in something that's not of my making, and once it's over I'll be back in my job.' She saw the look of disbelief flash across his face. 'Bad things happen to you all the time, that doesn't put you off being a cop, does it?'

'I catch villains, I don't expect them to be nice people.'

'No, but you were always moaning about the stupid PC rules you had to follow, and that more often than not the system favours the criminals rather than the victims.'

He smiled. 'That's true. But if someone within the Met wanted me dead, I'd probably review my career choice.'

'No you wouldn't. You love being a cop. You'd never leave, no matter how much shit they threw at you. If something like this happened, you'd fight it, you wouldn't run.' She forced a smile. 'I'm sorry, I'm not fighting with you, Tim. I'm just trying to work out what's going on.'

'I want to help.'

'I know you do. And I appreciate it.' She held up the mug of Ovaltine. 'And I especially appreciate this.'

'The guys who attacked you – you got a good look at them?'

'One of them. He was bald, white, maybe five ten. Looked a bit like a bouncer. I saw him waiting by his car outside the house in Wimbledon. Then he came to the back door while I was inside. I had to hit him to get away.'

'You hit him?'

'I was just reacting,' she said. 'It wasn't a fight. I just pushed him and ran. Then I saw him again when I was in an Uber. They were trying to run me off the road. I took his picture on my phone.'

'And he saw you take his picture, obviously?'

'Sure.'

Tim frowned. 'So chasing you doesn't make much sense.'

'Why not?'

'Well he must know you work for MI5, right? So wouldn't he assume that you'd send the picture to the office? That'd be the obvious thing for you to do, right?'

'I guess so.'

'But despite that, they were still chasing you.'

Sally frowned. 'What are you getting at?'

'You're assuming that they were trying to kill you because you could identify them. But if they saw you take their picture then that's no longer an issue. At that point the obvious thing for them to do would be to cut and run. Instead they chased you around London and presumably had someone at your flat. Maybe it's not about taking care of a witness. Maybe it's something else.'

'Like what?'

'You said they took the hard drives from the computers and other stuff.'

Sally nodded. 'I only saw the ground floor but it looked as if they had looted the thumb drive safe as well.'

'The what now?'

Sally hesitated, knowing that she had already told him enough to breach the Official Secrets Act but telling him about office procedures was most definitely against the law. But that ship had pretty much sailed and she had reached the point where she might as well tell him everything.

'We look after houses and apartments that belong to the different legends that our officers use, and we maintain various safe houses. All the data on each property is kept on encrypted thumb drives which are stored in various safes. They're supposed to be locked away when they're not being used.'

'And the killers took the thumb drives with them?'

Sally nodded. 'Oh my God,' she said.

'What?'

She grabbed for her bag and began rooting through it. She pulled out the three envelopes that she had taken from the house and lined them up on the table. 'I was going to be using these today,' she said. She picked up one of them. 'This has the details of the house in Kingston that I went to this morning.' She opened the envelope and showed him the thumb drive and the keys.

He took the thumb drive from her. 'What's on it exactly?'

'Details of the premises, the location, a floor plan, photographs, an inventory of everything inside, details of bills paid, who it's been used by and when.'

'Is it encrypted?'

'No, but it's password protected. But I don't think that would stop anyone who knew what they were doing. Each time I visit a property I update the thumb drive with what I did and what, if anything, needs to be done.'

'But there's nothing on the drives that wouldn't be on MI5's main computer?'

She shook her head. 'No, that's the whole point of using them. The idea is to keep all the information confidential. Sure, there are people at Thames House who know about the various properties but the information isn't for general consumption. Almost everything about the legends used by MI5 officers is kept on a strictly need-to-know basis.'

She frowned as she stared at the other two envelopes. 'What if what they wanted wasn't at the house? What if they were after one of the thumb drives that I had with me?' Sally sat back and ran her hands through her hair. 'Maybe they're not trying to kill me because of what I saw. Maybe they want what I've got.'

Tim nodded. 'You might be right.' He gestured at the envelopes. 'So what are they, these two?' he asked.

Sally pointed at the one on the left. 'That's an apartment in Notting Hill. It's used by an officer who has a legend as a free-lance journalist, mainly for the *Guardian* and the *Observer*. He's close to a female attaché at the Russian Embassy and they use it for meetings.'

'What do you do for him?'

'I maintain the flat, make sure the bills are paid and the meters are read, collect the mail, organise newspaper and magazine subscriptions. I also run his Oyster card and loyalty cards and buy books and stuff on his Amazon account. And I place articles for him that run under his byline and run the bank account that the payments go into. Plus his tax and stuff. And I handle his social media accounts. Facebook, Twitter, Instagram.'

'That's a hell of a lot of detail.'

'It has to be these days,' said Sally. 'Everyone leaves a footprint, and anyone without one looks dodgy. But the officers don't have the time to do what's necessary, so the footies and shoppers do it for them.'

'That's a real job? They pay you to do that?'

'Sure. For some people it's a career. That's all they do, all they want to do. But generally it's a stepping stone. They put new recruits in until they find them a suitable posting. Or they put old timers there on the run to retirement, instead of sending them on gardening leave.'

'You say stepping stone but you've been with MI5 for two years now.'

Sally nodded. 'I'm pretty sure my boss is blocking me. He made a pass at me in the pub and I wasn't interested.'

'While you were living with me?'

'I wasn't living with you, Tim.'

'Going out with me, then. The bastard made a pass at you while you were going out with me?'

She nodded again.

'Why the hell didn't you tell me?'

'I'm a big girl, Tim. I can take care of myself.'

'I didn't mean that. It's just that when a guy hits on you, you should have told me.'

'That's in the boyfriend manual, is it?'

'You know what I mean.'

'Tim, I never expected you to tell me every time a girl gave you her telephone number. I trusted you.'

'It's not about trust, it's about . . .'

He struggled to find the words to express himself, and Sally couldn't help but laugh at his discomfort. 'About wanting to be the alpha male, I get it. I was your girl so any guy who wants to approach me has to go through you.'

'That's not what I meant,' he said.

She leaned over and patted him on the leg. 'I'm only teasing you, Tim. I used to love the way you'd get jealous if another guy so much as looked at me. But this was different. For a start, we both work for MI5 so there was no way I could tell you even if I wanted to.'

'Official Secrets Act? Come on.'

'I'm serious. I'm not supposed to even tell non-family that I work for Five. I'm supposed to say I work for the Home Office and leave it at that. I told you far more about my work than I ever should have.'

'Which was fuck all, frankly. I'm only now learning about the footies and shippers.'

'Shoppers.'

'Whatever.' He sighed and pointed at the second envelope. 'And this one?'

Sally picked it up. 'It's a safe house in Hampstead. It's an easy job, there's no legend attached to it, I just have to make sure the meters are read and the bills are paid, and that the place is clean.'

'So you're a bloody cleaner?'

'No, I'm not a cleaner. I just check that the cleaners do their job.'

'So you supervise cleaners? Remind me again what your degree is in?'

Her eyes narrowed but he grinned and she realised he was only teasing her. 'Bastard,' she said. She opened the envelope and looked inside. There was a set of keys and a black thumb drive.

'So it's possible they're after one of these thumb drives. Or the keys?' said Tim.

'I suppose so,' said Sally, staring down at the envelopes. 'But let's think that through. Say the Russians got wind that the flat in Notting Hill is being used by an MI5 officer. They'd already know where the flat was, wouldn't they? All right, the thumb drive would have evidence that the flat was an MI5 property, but so what? It's not as if they'd be trying to build a court case.' She looked back at the Hampstead envelope. 'But the safe house, that's a different matter. No one outside the service would know about the house. And even within the service, only a few people would know where it was.'

'Including you.'

'Exactly. And I'm only privy to it because I have to take care of it.'

'Your boss would know where it was, right? Hadley?'

Sally nodded. 'Yes, of course. And anyone who ever used the

safe house would know where it was, obviously. But a civilian wouldn't. The only way they could get the details would be to get the thumb drive. Or the footie.' Sally's eyes widened as she remembered what had happened that morning. 'The house is being used,' she said. 'I had an email saying I wasn't to go there today.'

'There you are then. Maybe we should go and take a look for ourselves.'

'Are you serious?'

'What's the alternative? You can't hide forever, Sally, much as I enjoy having you back here.'

'I'm not back, Tim.'

He grinned. 'Well you sort of are, actually.'

CHAPTER 30

'That's the place, up ahead,' said Rob, pointing at a line of terraced houses. Dave nodded and pulled the BMW over to the side of the road and stopped.

Wilsher reached for the door handle. 'Mate, you'd be better off staying put,' said Rob, twisting around in his seat.

'Sally's one of us, I should be there,' said Wilsher.

'Suit yourself,' said Rob. 'But remember, we were told we could be going into a hot situation.'

Rob and Dave got out of the SUV and Wilsher joined them. He was feeling a lot less confident than when he had been sitting in the back seat.

The two men started walking towards the house. Wilsher suddenly realised they weren't armed and he frowned. Surely the whole point of having the SAS on the case was that they had the guns? MI5 officers were never armed, despite what they showed in films and on TV. When they needed firepower they relied on the police's specialist firearms officers or the SAS. He'd expected Rob and Dave to have high-powered carbines at the very least but the two men were strolling along the pavement as if they didn't have a care in the world.

That all changed when the three men emerged from the door of the house they were walking towards. They were all carrying the sort of weapons Wilsher expected the SAS men to have, large carbines with bulky suppressors on the end of the barrel.

The men had their guns across their chests and they were looking left and right as they stepped out of the doorway. Rob and Dave moved immediately, pulling handguns from out of their jackets.

Rob stepped into the road, Dave moved to the left. They were separating, Wilsher realised, putting distance between themselves. It also put him clear in the line of fire. His heart began to pound. As an MI5 officer he'd done some self-defence training, but no one had ever told him what to do if someone pointed a gun in his direction.

Rob and Dave were still moving. Rob was getting behind a Toyota Prius, his gun in both hands. Dave was moving close to the building to his right, his gun arm at right angles with the barrel pointing upwards.

All Wilsher could think of doing was to drop down into a crouch to make himself a smaller target but even as he did that he realised he was still completely exposed on the pavement.

Time seemed to slow to a crawl, even though he could feel his heart pounding so quickly that the beats were practically running together.

The first man out of the house was bald and his face was totally impassive as he raised his gun.

The man behind him had a baseball cap pulled low over his eyes. He was pointing his gun towards Rob but hadn't yet pulled the trigger.

The third man was taller with blond hair. His gun had been pointing at the pavement but was already swinging up. Wilsher's bowels turned liquid as he realised that the gun was pointing directly at him. He threw himself towards the road, hoping to use a car as cover. As he jumped bullets raked the pavement behind him, chipping the flagstones. He misjudged his jump and hit the wing of a grey Nissan, knocking the breath out of him. He fell back, his arms flailing for balance.

Rob and Dave both fired. They both shot at the man who had fired his gun and the two rounds both smacked into his chest. He staggered back but stayed on his feet and both the SAS men fired again. This time their target slumped to the ground.

Wilsher clambered around the Nissan. There was a second burst of automatic fire and Dave fell backwards. The bald man had fired, and as Wilsher stared in horror the man fired again and Dave's head split apart, blood and brains splattering over the pavement.

Rob swung his gun towards the bald man but the shooter in the baseball cap already had his weapon aimed at Rob and a burst of automatic fire tore into him. Rob's gun fired three times as he collapsed onto the pavement but the rounds went wild.

Then there was just silence and the acrid stench of cordite, so strong that Wilsher could taste it. His breath was coming in short ragged gasps as he peered over the car.

The bald man was standing on the pavement, looking around. People were looking out of their windows. How many shots had there been? A dozen? Two dozen? Someone would have called the police, surely. But how long before they turned up? Five minutes? Ten?

The guy with the baseball cap walked over to Rob, muttered something, then pointed his gun at the man's chest and pulled the trigger. Wilsher gasped and the man's head swivelled so that he was looking at him. The man said something to the bald guy and then started walking purposefully towards Wilsher.

Wilsher stood up and raised his trembling arms in the air. 'I'm unarmed,' he said.

'More fool you,' said the man, raising the gun. There were two loud pops and the rounds smashed into Wilsher's chest. There was surprisingly little pain, he realised, as his legs collapsed underneath him and everything faded to darkness.

CHAPTER 31

As soon as Pritchard's secretary ushered him into the office the Major could see from the look on the director's face that something was wrong. Gannon didn't sit down; he wanted to hear the bad news standing up. Pritchard's secretary closed the door. 'Allan, I'm so sorry about this but two of your men have been killed south of the river. Rob Tyler and Dave Chapman.'

'Taylor,' said Gannon. 'Rob Taylor.'

'My apologies, I'm sorry,' said Pritchard. 'I must have misheard. Rob Taylor, yes. And we lost one of ours. An MI5 officer. We had tracked Sally Page's mobile phone to a house in Wandsworth so we tasked your guys with bringing her in. So far as we understand, Sally's pursuers got there first.'

'Sally's dead?' asked Gannon.

Pritchard shook his head. 'They killed two low-lives who appeared to have her phone and her watch. We don't know if they stole them from her or if she ditched them, but either way it was their death sentence. As the killers were leaving the house, your men arrived. They were outgunned and . . .' He left the sentence unfinished. 'I'm sorry,' he said.

The Major sighed and sat down. 'They had UCIWs, they shouldn't have been outgunned.' He saw the frown on the director's face. 'Ultra-compact individual weapons,' he said. 'Less than two feet long with the stock collapsed and capable of firing six hundred rounds a minute.'

'They weren't carrying them,' said Pritchard. 'They had hand-guns.'

'Who briefed them?'

'That would have been Liz Bailey.'

The Major nodded but didn't say anything. Someone had fucked up. Taylor and Chapman were highly trained and had been in hotspots around the world. If they had gone in expecting to meet no resistance then they had been badly briefed, but at the end of the day they were in charge of their own destinies. They had been carrying the UCIWs in their vehicle, they must have made the decision not to carry them.

'What about Sally?' asked the Major.

'No news,' said Pritchard.

'Assuming she ditched her phone, she must have known that they were using it to track her. Or at least assumed as much.'

Pritchard looked pained. 'She might well be right,' he said. 'The only evidence we had to lead us to the house in Wandsworth was that the phone was there. The fact that Sally's pursuers were also there suggests they had the same intel.'

The Major frowned. 'How would they do that?'

Pritchard looked even more uncomfortable. 'There are commercial services available but it's starting to look as if they have had help from within Thames House, at least initially.'

The Major tried to conceal his surprise but couldn't stop his eyes widening. 'Which means what?'

'I'm not sure yet,' said Pritchard. 'All we know is that a request was put in for GPS details on her phone early this morning. That request wasn't at my behest, and Liz Bailey wasn't involved.'

'What about the Wandsworth premises?'

'We got the information from the phone company. Ours was the only check made. But having got her number, it's possible that her pursuers are now using other methods.'

The Major rubbed his chin thoughtfully. 'Is there any possibility that whatever is happening is being sanctioned within MI5?'

'The left hand not letting the right know what's going on? That's not how we work, Allan. Plus, I can't see the left hand wanting to kill seven of our own people.'

'So you've got a traitor in Thames House? Someone who is helping the killers?'

'As I said, I'm not sure yet. But it does look that way, yes.'

The Major sighed and folded his arms. 'Do we have any idea why any of this is happening? Why would they target a team of low-level officers who weren't even working on active cases?'

'We're still thinking that they didn't go into the Wimbledon house expecting to kill everyone. That they wanted something in particular and were surprised to see so many people there.'

The Major frowned. 'But that wouldn't explain why they are continuing to hunt Sally Page.'

'She was a witness. They don't want to be identified so they want to kill her.'

The Major wasn't convinced, but he didn't see any point in arguing. 'I suppose so. And the two people they killed at the Wandsworth place?'

Pritchard shrugged. 'They went in looking for Sally and found two guys with machetes. They probably had no choice other than to shoot. They come out of the house and see your people and our officer. And they start shooting again.'

'So we have seven deaths in the house and another five in Wandsworth. For what? What the hell were they after?'

Pritchard threw up his hands. 'I wish I knew,' he said. 'If I did, we might have a better idea of who is behind this. What about this Hirst character?'

'Not making much progress on that front. But nothing in his past suggests he'd be the type to start killing MI5 officers. He didn't make the grade with the SAS so he was sent packing. But he was applying for other jobs in the private sector.'

'Money problems?'

'He didn't ask the Regiment for help. There's a fund for helping our guys who have fallen on hard times, but he seemed to be okay. No drink or drugs problems that I know, he has a mortgage on a house in Hereford.'

'Married?'

The Major nodded. 'With a young daughter. We haven't been able to speak to the wife, she's not at home.'

'What jobs was he applying for?'

'Security, mainly. He approached the Pool.'

'Did he now? That suggests he doesn't have an aversion to killing people.'

'True. But the Pool is on the side of the angels and everyone knows that. It's a world of difference between working for them and running around London shooting MI5 officers and former colleagues.'

'I suppose it could be some sort of breakdown.'

The Major shook his head. 'He seems to be operating efficiently, he's not acting as if he's out of control. Maybe you could use your resources to see if you can track down the wife. She might have a better idea of what he's up to.'

'Give me the details and I'll get someone on it.'

'All I have is her name, unfortunately. And their address in Hereford.'

'That's enough to be getting on with,' said Pritchard.

Gannon gave him Mrs Hirst's address.

'If you do get a lead on her, let me know,' said the Major.

'Of course.'

Gannon looked at his watch. It was almost nine o'clock. 'I'm going to head to the Special Forces Club in Knightsbridge. I've got a room there and I'll grab a bite to eat. If anything changes, call me and I'll be right back in.' He stood up. 'And we're honestly still none the wiser what this is all about?'

Pritchard shook his head. 'It's a bloody mystery,' he said. 'And I hate mysteries.'

CHAPTER 32

The driver dropped Tim and Sally on Hampstead High Street, close to the King William IV pub and about a hundred yards from the safe house. They waited for the Prius to drive away before walking to the side road where the house was. 'I'm not sure this is a good idea,' said Sally.

'I don't agree,' said Tim. 'If the house is being used, then that suggests that the bad guys are trying to find it. And if the bad guys don't know where the house is, that almost certainly means you can trust that bastard Hadley.'

'Why do you say that?'

'He's a bastard because he hit on you.'

'No, I mean why do you say I can trust him?'

'Because if he was involved with the bad guys then he could simply tell them where the house is. So if this is all about finding the safe house, you call him and get him to bring you in. Which one is it?'

'Further along. One of the detached houses.'

'Let's cross over the road then. Best not to make it too obvious.'

Sally looked around. She had a dull ache in the pit of her stomach. At any time she expected to see a black SUV turn into the road. Tim put his arm around her. It took her by surprise and she flinched. He laughed and gave her a squeeze. 'If anyone sees us, we're just a regular couple out for a stroll,' he said.

She smiled, knowing that he was right. She slipped her arm around his waist and was surprised at how natural it felt. They crossed the road. Tim seemed relaxed enough but Sally was tense, scanning the pavement ahead of her and looking over her shoulder.

'Relax,' he whispered.

'I'm trying,' she said.

'I thought they trained you in this sort of thing.'

'I'm relaxed,' she said, but she knew that wasn't the truth. It was all right for Tim, he hadn't seen the bodies in the house in Wimbledon. He hadn't seen the blood spreading across Tony's chest, Afifa slumped over her keyboard, or Jane lying in a pool of her own blood. She shuddered.

'Are you cold?' he asked.

'I'm okay,' she said.

The house was about fifty yards ahead of them. It was Victorian and detached, with a small garden at the front and a garage to the right. Sally knew that behind the house was a large garden with several rockeries and a white gazebo. A gardening firm went in once a month to cut the grass and weed the rockeries and do any watering that was necessary. Safe houses could have a number of possible uses, but generally they were to keep people out of public view, usually because their lives were in danger. The footies were never told what the safe houses were used for, just that they were occupied and to be left alone until instructed otherwise.

There was a wrought iron gate blocking the driveway and through it they could see three cars. Two were white SUVs, the other was a dark saloon.

Tim stopped but Sally urged him on with her hand. 'Keep walking,' he said. 'Check the windows, make sure no one is looking out.'

'There are lights on inside,' he said.

'I see them.'

She took another look over her shoulder. The pavement behind them was clear. She took another look at the gates. She didn't see anyone standing guard but she knew that the exterior of the house was fully covered by CCTV. There was a light on in one of the upstairs windows. It was one of the bedrooms. The blinds were down in the front room.

They walked by the house and kept on going until they reached the junction with Fitzjohn's Avenue. They stopped. 'What do you think?' asked Tim. 'Do you recognise the vehicles?'

Sally shook her head.

'Do MI5 use white SUVs?'

'Not usually.'

'And those SUVs weren't the ones after you?'

'The ones chasing me were black Mitsubishi Outlanders. The ones outside the house were white Ford Explorers. Chalk and cheese.'

'What about the other car?'

'Volkswagen Jetta. Could be a pool car.'

'I'd like to check out the SUVs. See who they belong to. Are you okay to walk back?'

'I don't see why not. There didn't seem to be anyone looking out.' They crossed over the road and walked back towards the house. As they reached the wrought iron gates, Tim took out his phone and snapped pictures of the registration plates with his left hand as he kept his right arm draped over her shoulder.

They carried on walking past three more houses then stopped. Tim tapped on his phone and put it to his ear. He identified himself, gave his warrant card number, and then asked for two vehicle checks. He spelled out the numbers of the two Fords. He waited, thanked whoever was doing the PNC check for him, and put the phone away. 'That's interesting,' he said.

'What?'

'The SUVs are owned by the US Embassy.'

'They what?'

Something hard pressed against the back of Sally's neck and she stiffened. Tim reacted more aggressively and a gun was whacked across the back of his head. 'Move and you're dead,' hissed the man behind Sally.

'I'm a police officer,' said Tim, raising his hands slowly. 'My warrant card is in my jacket pocket.'

'I don't care if you're fucking Batman,' said the man who had hit Tim. 'You keep your hands where I can see them or I'll put a bullet in your head.'

CHAPTER 33

'Pull over here, Kristov,' said Hirst, gesturing at the side of the road. Kristov did as he was told. 'You guys stay put,' he said. The second Outlander drove by and Hirst pointed for them to park up. He walked away from the SUV before calling Javier. It wasn't the sort of call that he wanted the others to hear.

'Tell me you have it,' said Javier.

'I'm sorry. She wasn't there.'

'How could she not be there?'

'There was some sort of fuck up,' said Hirst. 'The girl's phone was there. And the watch. But there were two guys in the house and they came at us with machetes so we had to deal with them.'

'No great loss,' said Javier.

'It gets worse,' said Hirst. 'As we were leaving the house, three guys approached us. Two of them were armed. Plainclothes but they had guns. We had to shoot to protect ourselves.'

'Your team is okay?'

'We lost one man. McKenzie.'

'The men who shot at you, were they cops?'

'I don't think so,' said Hirst. 'In the UK the cops always identify themselves when they pull out their weapons, even the ones working undercover. These guys just pulled out their guns.'

'And what happened?'

'They were outmanned and outgunned. They didn't stand a chance.'

'They were probably MI5,' said Javier. 'They are also looking for the girl.'

'So what do you want to do now?' asked Hirst.

'We wait,' said Javier. 'Unless you have any idea where she might go.'

'She'll be lying low somewhere,' said Hirst. 'She's clearly not going to go back to Thames House.'

'As soon as I get a location for you, I will tell you. In the meantime, I suggest you move closer to Thames House. If they send someone out to check on Flores, I will be told. I want you and your men close by.'

'I want to talk to my wife and my daughter.'

'Listen to me and listen to me carefully. If you do not take care of this matter you will never see your wife or daughter again. You have my word on that.'

Javier ended the call. Hirst gritted his teeth. He wanted to throw back his head and scream his frustration at the night sky, but such an outward display of emotion wasn't an option, not when he needed to keep the respect of his team. He took a long, slow, deep breath. He wanted nothing more than to be able to put two rounds in the head of the man he knew only as Javier, but in his heart he knew that it would never happen. Javier was too cunning and too well protected. All he could do was to perform the tasks he was given and hopefully he and his family would at some point be together again. He put the phone away.

CHAPTER 34

Sally looked across at Tim. 'Sorry,' she said. They were in the dining room of the Hampstead safe house. She figured the men had put them there because there were no windows in the room, just sliding doors that led to the kitchen. Whoever had done the interior design work on the house had compensated for the lack of a window by installing a large mirror on one wall. She could see her own reflection and winced at the fear in her eyes.

'Nothing to apologise for,' he said. 'I should have seen them coming.'

The men who had seized them on the street had brought them in through the wrought iron gate and around to the back of the house. One of them, the one who had hit Tim, was huge, close to seven feet tall. The other was Hispanic and shorter than Sally but he made up for his lack of height with bulk; he had wide shoulders and weightlifter forearms that stretched the material of his jacket. There were two more men there with guns in underarm holsters and they had stared sullenly at Sally and Tim as they were taken inside. The kitchen lights were on but there was no one there. Their captors had taken them into the dining room, sat them down on wooden chairs, and used zip ties to bind their wrists behind them and their ankles to the legs of the chairs. 'We're not going to gag you because no one will hear you if you do shout,' the bigger of the two men had said. 'But trust me, any sound out of you and I'll slap you into the middle of next week.'

'I'm a police officer . . .' Tim began but the man had silenced him with a pointed finger.

'Shut the fuck up,' scowled the man. He patted Tim down,

found his wallet and warrant card and put them in his own pocket. He went through Sally's pockets and took her purse.

The two men had left, pulling the sliding doors shut behind them.

'They're Americans, right?' she asked.

'Sounds like it,' said Tim. 'Why would Yanks be in an MI5 safe house? You're sure they're not the ones who were chasing you?'

'I don't recognise them, but then I only saw two of them, and one of them I didn't get a good look at. Maybe.'

'Well if it is them, they obviously found their way here.'

'You don't think that Americans would have killed those people in the Wimbledon house, do you?'

'Who knows?'

'The Americans are our allies.'

'In my experience Americans only care about their own interests,' said Tim. 'But yes, killing the footies and chasing you around London does seem a bit excessive.'

Sally smiled despite the seriousness of their situation. 'Excessive?'

'You know what I mean. If it was the Russians, they wouldn't care, but the Americans . . .'

'It doesn't make any sense,' said Sally. 'But then nothing that has happened does. Anyway, I'm sorry I dragged you into this. Whatever this is.'

'You didn't drag me, Sally.'

'I know. But you didn't have to be the white knight.'

'How could I not be? You're my . . .' He laughed. 'I was going to say girlfriend.'

'I'm sorry about that, too.'

'You never really explained why you left, not properly.'

'I didn't really leave. I wasn't living with you.'

'Would you rather I asked why you dumped me?'

'I didn't . . .' She didn't finish the sentence because she knew that at the end of the day that was exactly what she had done.

'I just wanted to concentrate on my career,' she said.

'Shopping? And playing around on Facebook?'

'That's how you start at MI5.'

'So you wanted to be James Bond, is that it? You dropped me because you wanted to be 007?'

'Well, first of all, James Bond works for MI6, not MI5. And second of all, he's a fictional character.'

Tim shook his head. 'Do they teach you to evade questions? Is that part of your training?'

'I wanted to concentrate on my career. I'm twenty-four years old, I don't want to settle down and be a wife and mother.'

'I don't remember proposing to you.'

'We were heading that way.'

'Says who?'

Sally sighed. 'I don't want to argue.'

'Clearly,' said Tim. 'That's why when you dumped me you just gave me the silent treatment. You hate confrontation.'

'I just don't see the point in arguing.'

'There's a difference between arguing and discussing. It might have been nice if you had at least talked to me. Explained a bit more. Maybe even apologised.'

Sally frowned. 'Apologised? For what?'

'For breaking my bloody heart, Sally.' He looked away and bit down on his lower lip.

'Tim . . .'

'I'm sorry,' he said.

'Stop apologising. You've got nothing to apologise for. It's all down to me.'

He opened his mouth to say something but they were interrupted by the sound of the doors sliding back. The man who opened them was balding with a goatee beard and a pair of glasses hanging on a chain around his neck. He was wearing a dark blue pinstripe suit and a light blue tie. As the doors slid back, Sally could see the two Americans standing in the kitchen. The man stepped inside, leaving the doors open. He walked over to Sally and stood looking down at her. Sally stared back defiantly, refusing to show fear.

'You are Sally Page, right?'

He was English, Sally realised. 'You took my purse and my driving licence is in there, so you know who I am.'

'Don't get clever with me, Ms Page,' the man said. 'You're in a great deal of trouble and if you are anything less than honest with me you are going to make it worse for yourself.'

'I'm a police officer, and you're the one in trouble, mate,' said Tim. 'Assault, kidnapping a police officer and God knows what else.'

The man turned to look at Tim, his face impassive. 'The very fact that you came here with Ms Page puts you in breach of the Official Secrets Act and makes you liable for a prison term of up to fourteen years, so you need to just shut the fuck up. Okay?' He turned again to look at Sally. 'Your manager at Thames House would be Ian Hadley, is that correct?'

Sally nodded.

The man took out his mobile phone and walked out of the room. He left the doors open but Sally couldn't hear what he was saying. The two Americans stared at her with undisguised hostility and she looked away.

The man returned with his phone. He held it to her face. 'Say who you are,' he ordered.

Sally swallowed. 'This is Sally Page,' she said.

'Sally? What the fuck are you playing at?'

It was Ian Hadley. 'Ian?'

'Why didn't you call? Why didn't you come to Thames House? We've got people combing the city for you.'

'I wasn't sure what to do,' she said.

The man took the phone away from her. 'Can you confirm that she's Sally Page?' he asked. He grunted, then ended the call. He put the phone into his pocket and nodded at the two men in the kitchen. 'She's with us.'

The bigger of the two men pulled a knife from a wooden block and walked through the doorway into the room. He held the knife and moved towards Sally. She began to tremble and shake her head. 'Don't worry, honey,' he said. 'I'm not going to hurt you.' He knelt down and used the knife to cut away the ties around her ankles. 'Bend forward,' he said. She did as she was told and he cut the ties from her wrists.

'Thank you,' she said, massaging her wrists.

The man went over to Tim and cut his bonds.

Tim stood up.

'You need to stay here,' said the man with the goatee. 'This isn't over yet.'

'Who are you?' asked Tim.

'I'm the man who is telling you that you have to stay put. And these two gentlemen are the men who will stop you if you don't follow my instructions. Are we clear?'

'Yes,' said Tim.

'Excellent. Now sit down.'

Tim did as he was told.

'Can you at least tell us what's going on?' asked Sally.

'Your boss is on the way in, he'll explain the situation to you,' said the man. He and the Americans went through the sliding doors and closed them, leaving Sally and Tim alone.

Tim hurried over to Sally and put his arms around her. 'Are you okay?' he asked.

'I thought he was going to kill us.'

'Thankfully not,' said Tim. 'So Mr Goatee is with MI5?'

'I guess so, but I don't know him.' She rested her head against his shoulder. 'I'm exhausted.'

'After what you've been through, I'm not surprised. But it looks like it'll all be over soon.'

'God, I hope so.'

CHAPTER 35

Ellie Cooper looked up as Liz Bailey walked in carrying a clipboard. 'He says you're to go straight in, Liz,' she said. 'Can I get you a coffee or a water or anything?'

'Actually a coffee would be marvellous,' said Bailey.

'Milk and no sugar?'

'You have such a good memory.' Bailey walked into Pritchard's inner office. The director smiled up at her. 'Please tell me you have some good news for me, Liz,' he said. He was looking tired, with dark patches under his eyes.

'I've got the GPS tracking on Hirst's wife, and there's definitely something strange going on,' said Bailey.

Pritchard waved for her to sit down. 'I'm all ears.'

Bailey looked at her clipboard. 'Okay, so three days ago, everything is normal. Amanda Hirst is at home, then goes shopping, then takes her daughter to a local playground. Mother daughter stuff. Then at five o'clock in the evening, she moves. Heads east, towards London.'

'But her car is at home,' said Pritchard.

'She was taken,' said Bailey. 'At seven o'clock in the evening she makes a call, to her husband. One call, lasting thirty seconds. From then on the phone is off the grid. Not just switched off, because we can still track phones that are turned off, but dead. Battery out, SIM card destroyed, whatever. But the phone hasn't been seen since. The last time it was used she was about forty miles from her home in Hereford, in a service station outside Oxford.'

'So she was taken and whoever took her had her call her husband?'

Bailey nodded. 'That's how I read it, yes. And they were prob- ably taking her to London.'

'So we've no way of tracking her?' Pritchard sighed. 'That's a pity.'

'All is not lost, as they say. It occurred to me that GCHQ could run a check of all mobile phones at the Hirst house at the time of her abduction, and again at the location where she made the call to her husband. Any matches would almost certainly be phones belonging to her abductors.'

'Sounds like a plan.'

'It'll take time, and it's late so there's a manpower problem, but I'm on it,' she said.

They were interrupted by Pritchard's secretary, carrying a cup of coffee for Bailey and a bottle of Evian water for the director. 'Thank you, Ellie. You should really go on home now,' said Pritchard.

'I'm here for the duration,' she said. 'I wouldn't dream of leaving you now, not with all this going on.'

'You're an angel, thank you.' He took the bottle of water from her and flashed her a grateful smile.

They were interrupted by Ian Hadley bursting in. 'Sally Page has turned up,' said Hadley, his cheeks flushed red.

'Here?' asked Pritchard.

Hadley shook his head. 'The safe house in Hampstead.'

Pritchard put down the phone. 'She's okay?'

'It seems so, yes. I'm going to head out there now to talk to her.'

'We need her back here, Ian. Now.'

'Absolutely. But she's gotten herself into quite a complicated situation.'

Pritchard frowned. 'How so?'

'The house is being used by the DEA at the moment.'

'The drugs case we broke? The Mexican?'

'Exactly,' said Hadley. 'The Mexican. Sally was outside the house and the DEA pulled her in. They're reluctant to release her at the moment.'

'Are you telling me the DEA are holding one of our officers?' snapped Pritchard.

'I'm sorry, am I missing something here?' asked Bailey. 'We have DEA agents in an MI5 safe house?'

'It's in connection with a drugs investigation we were running,' said Pritchard. 'The DEA became involved and they needed a short-term safe house. Their presence was on a need-to-know basis.'

'I would have assumed that as the person responsible for the physical security at all our safe houses, I would have been deemed need-to-know.'

'I am sorry, Liz, but the Americans were insistent.'

'So the Americans now set operational policy for MI5?'

Pritchard held up a hand. 'Liz, I hear you. But this was – is – a very special case. Only Ian and I were privy to what was going on.' He looked over at Hadley. 'You should go, now,' said Pritchard. 'And explain to the DEA that we want Sally back here to be debriefed.'

'There's a car waiting for me downstairs,' said Hadley.

'And call me as soon as you've spoken to her,' said Pritchard.

Hadley nodded and left the room. Bailey was glaring at Pritchard. She was clearly unhappy at being left out of the loop and there was nothing that he could say that would soothe her feelings.

CHAPTER 36

Amanda Hirst stared up at the ceiling, her mind in turmoil. How long had she been in the room, bound and gagged? Three days? Four? She had lost all sense of time. She was lying on a double bed, next to her daughter. At least Sophie was asleep. Amanda hadn't slept more than a few hours since they had taken her. She'd been in the kitchen, making tea for Sophie, when the men had appeared. They had pressed something against her neck and there had been a crackling sound and she had passed out. When she had woken up she was in the boot of a car with her daughter. At one point they had stopped and a man had opened the boot, thrust a phone at her and told her to speak to her husband. She hadn't said more than a few words to Marty before they'd taken the phone away from her.

The last thing Marty had said to her was that everything would be okay and that he'd make sure they released her. And that he loved her and Sophie.

But what did they want from him? He wasn't rich, far from it, and since he'd left the Regiment they had been pretty much living from hand to mouth. He'd had such big plans, he was going to make serious money working in the private security sector, but none of that had come to anything and over the months their savings had dwindled and their credit card debt had risen. She had spoken to their bank manager and raised the possibility of increasing their mortgage but he had been adamant that with Marty's slump in earnings there was no way the bank could agree to increasing their loan. If the kidnappers were expecting Marty to pay a ransom they were going to be disappointed. He barely had enough money to pay for their daughter's shoes.

Sophie began to mumble and Amanda rolled over to check that her breathing was okay. She'd begged her captors not to gag her daughter but they wouldn't listen to her pleas. The only time the gags were taken off was when they were given food and water. They had to eat and drink while a man in a ski mask sat in front of them holding a gun. That happened twice a day and the food was always pre-packed sandwiches and a bottle of water. And twice a day they were allowed to use the bathroom. It was an en suite with a cramped shower and again they were watched all the time by a masked man with a gun. Amanda had asked for a toothbrush and toothpaste but her request had been met with a shake of the head.

The gag in her mouth was a strip of cloth, and they used duct tape to bind her wrists. Each time they released her to eat they cut off the tape with a knife, and then retied her with fresh tape. They kept the roll on the dressing table. The last time they had taken off her gag she had tried to explain that her husband had no money and that they were wasting their time but she had been slapped, hard, and told that every time she spoke without being spoken to she would be slapped again. Sophie had started to cry and the man had raised his hand to hit her but Amanda had begged him to stop and told Sophie that she mustn't cry. The man had pointed a warning finger at her and told her that she needed to do as she was told. He was an American, she realised. And white. That would be something she could tell the police if they ever released her. She still hoped that they would let her go eventually. She had read somewhere that kidnappers always covered their faces if they intended to release their hostages. If they kept their faces covered they couldn't be recognised. If they let their hostages see their faces it was because they were planning to kill them. That was the one hope that Amanda clung to as she lay staring up at the ceiling. So long as they didn't reveal their faces, she had hope.

CHAPTER 37

Sally and Tim looked around as the sliding doors slid apart. It was the man with the goatee. He stood to the side and Ian Hadley walked in. Sally gasped with relief when she saw her boss. 'Ian, thank God,' she said.

She stood up and took a step towards him but he waved her away dismissively. 'You've no idea the trouble you've caused,' he snapped. 'What the hell did you think you were doing, coming here?'

'That was my fault, I'm afraid,' said Tim, getting to his feet.

Hadley turned his icy stare on him. 'And who the fuck are you?' he asked.

'Detective Sergeant Tim Reid,' said Tim, holding out his hand.

Hadley sneered at the proffered hand. 'The fact that Ms Page brought you here puts you both in breach of the Official Secrets Act,' he said.

'Yeah, your colleague already told us that.'

'Well, I hope he also said that you could well end up being sent down for fourteen years.'

Tim raised an eyebrow. 'In view of what's happened today, I think that's highly unlikely,' he said.

'You had no right to come here, and by doing so you may have jeopardised an ongoing operation and put lives at risk.'

'Sally's life is already at risk,' snapped Tim. 'She's been chased all over London by men who killed seven of your people. I would have thought you'd have been more concerned about that than who may or may not have breached the Official Secrets Act.'

Hadley turned back to Sally. 'You went to the police? What the hell were you thinking?'

'Tim's a friend.'

'And that makes it better, does it? Are you insane?'

'Ian, I called for your help and the killers turned up. You were supposed to have me collected from the house in Kingston, remember? Then I tried to get to my flat in Fulham and they were waiting for me there.'

Hadley frowned. 'You're sure about that?'

'There was one of their cars in the street. At least I think it was one of theirs. Then my flatmate went inside and I think they shot him.'

'You think? Did they or didn't they?'

'I don't know, Ian. I saw flashes.'

'Didn't you check?'

'I could hardly have knocked on the door.'

'You didn't phone your flatmate?'

'I haven't got my phone.'

Hadley smiled thinly. 'You didn't by any chance give your phone to a couple of petty criminals, did you?'

Sally nodded. 'I figured they were using my phone and watch to track me.'

'Your watch?'

'It was an Apple Watch. I gave the watch and my phone to a couple of guys in Putney.'

'Yeah, well those guys are now dead,' said Hadley.

'What?'

'They're dead. Someone broke into their home and shot them.'

'Oh my God.'

'So it looks as if you were right. They were tracking your phone.'

Sally put her hand up to her mouth. She had assumed that the men in the Outlanders would follow the phone but once they realised they were on a wild goose chase she figured they would just give up.

'It looks as if you were responsible for the death of two civilians,' said Hadley. 'On top of everything else.'

'That's not fair,' said Tim. 'All she did was dump her phone.'

'I never thought they'd be killed,' said Sally. 'I just wanted them to stop following me. I thought that they'd realise I'd given them the slip and just . . .' She threw up her hands. 'Why would they kill them?'

'Because they burst into the house and were met with two guys waving machetes.'

'So not really civilians, then,' said Tim.

Hadley turned to glare at him. 'What?'

'You said they were civilians, but in my experience regular civilians tend not to attack people with machetes.'

'You are on very thin ice, Detective Sergeant Reid.'

'You're the one making allegations about Sally. You're the one who claimed she is responsible for the deaths of two civilians.' He smiled but his eyes stayed hard. 'Look, we're on the same side here. Why don't you just tell us what's going on?'

Hadley looked as if he was going to argue, but then the fight seemed to go out of him. 'Sit down, both of you,' he said.

He pulled a chair away from the table and sat down, carefully adjusting the creases of his trousers. Sally looked over at Tim and he nodded. They both sat down. 'Obviously anything I say here is not to be repeated,' said Hadley. He flashed Tim a warning look. 'And that includes your superiors at the Met.' Tim nodded, showing that he understood. 'Two nights ago, an MI5 investigation into a major London drugs gang was concluded, with the arrest of half a dozen gang members. We had an undercover officer who had been on the case for close to a year, and we had all the evidence we needed. But unbeknown to our man, two of the leaders of the gang were meeting a senior member of a Mexican drugs cartel that controls a big chunk of the cocaine and cannabis trade in Texas and New Mexico. The cartel is run by a guy by the name of Carlos Martinez, a nasty piece of work, even by Mexican standards. He has been responsible for the torture and death of three DEA agents and dozens of DEA informers. He tortures and kills his opposition and more often than not kills their families too. He's particularly fond of having his men rape and kill the wives, girlfriends and children of his victims before killing them.'

Sally winced and Hadley smiled at her discomfort. 'It's a whole different world over there,' he said. 'We think we have a problem with drugs gangs in the UK but it's nothing compared to what's happening in the US and Mexico. But that could well change. Martinez is looking to expand into Europe. He sent his number three to London, an enforcer by the name of Diego Flores. Flores is one of the cartel's most ruthless killers, the DEA think he has murdered hundreds of people over the years, but mainly in Mexico where the cartel is pretty much untouchable. Flores was in a meeting with two members of the gang in a club they use in Mayfair. We had the place bugged so we have a full record of the conversation, a conversation in which he went into great detail about the cartel's operations in Mexico, in the United States, and his plans for Europe. All of it caught on tape and camera. Flores was arrested along with the UK gang, but once we realised who he was we brought him here and contacted the DEA. The DEA were obviously very interested in what we have, and it was decided at a very senior level that we would hand him over to them, along with the tape.'

'So he won't face charges in the UK?' asked Tim.

'We would have enough evidence to charge him with conspiracy to import Class A drugs, but the information we have on tape is far more useful to the DEA. We are holding Flores here and if all goes to plan, tomorrow he'll be flown to the United States.'

'So that's what all this is about?' said Sally. 'The cartel found out and they're looking to rescue Flores before they ship him out.'

'That's what it looks like,' said Hadley. 'But don't worry. No one knows he's being held here.'

'You know,' said Sally.

'Yes, but I'm on a very short list and that list is entirely need-to-know,' said Hadley.

CHAPTER 38

M arty Hirst stared at the house. There was no way of knowing how many men were inside, but they were almost certain to be armed. There were three vehicles parked in the driveway beyond the wrought iron gates – two white Ford Explorers and a Volkswagen Jetta. There was a fourth vehicle parked outside the gate, a blue Vauxhall Corsa that Hirst had followed from Thames House. The call from Javier had come just in time. The man was driving to the house in Hampstead where Flores was being held and on no account was Hirst to lose him. The fact that they knew that Hampstead was the destination made the pursuit easier, and the two Outlanders took it in turns to be the lead car.

They had seen the Corsa pull up outside the large detached house and watched as the driver went inside, then both vehicles had driven a few hundred yards away and parked in a darkened mews.

'We're going to have to move quickly,' Hirst said. 'It could be they're planning to move Flores. Kristov, you'll be going in, I'll stay with the car. Let's go talk to the other guys.'

He and Kristov climbed out while Josh got out of the back. They walked over to the other Outlander. The driver, Aaron Miller, was already out. 'What's happening?'

'We need to go in, now,' said Hirst. 'You drive this vehicle, I'll drive the other.'

The four men in Miller's vehicle, including Billy Winchester, got out. All of them were big Americans, wearing bomber jackets and jeans. They listened intently as Hirst continued. 'We kit up here and drive back to the house. The guys go in and Aaron and I wait outside, engines running. Kristov and Josh can go in through the rear, the rest of you through the front. Shock and awe, shoot anything that moves, make sure Flores is dead, and move out. Shouldn't take more than a minute. Two at the most.'

He looked at them all one by one, checking that they were paying attention. 'Any questions so far?'

He was faced with a wall of shaking heads.

'Right, you need to go in to the front and back simultaneously, obviously,' he said. 'Regard anyone inside as hostile, though Flores is the prime target. And we need photographs of Flores so that Javier knows that he's dead. Do not forget that. A video would be better. Javier has promised a fifty-thousand dollar bonus for the man that kills Flores.'

The men nodded enthusiastically.

'On the way in, I want trackers putting on all their vehicles, just in case.' He reached into his pocket and took out four metal discs. They were magnetic and had adhesive pads so could be affixed to almost anything.

'Just in case we fail?' said one of the men. It was Hank Schmidt. He was one of the youngest members of the team, but he still had five years with the Navy SEALs on his CV.

'I'm just covering all the bases,' said Hirst. He handed the trackers to Schmidt. 'As you're so interested, you might as well take care of them.'

'No problem,' said Schmidt.

There were Kevlar helmets, vests and ski masks in the rear of Miller's Outlander and the men took them out and put them on. Kristov and Josh jogged back to the other Outlander to get their carbines while the rest of the men grabbed their weapons and climbed back into the SUV. Miller nodded at Hirst and got into the driving seat of his vehicle.

Hirst walked back to his Outlander where Kristov and Josh were checking their guns. 'Okay?' he asked.

All three men nodded.

'Okay, in you go,' said Hirst.

They all climbed back into the SUV. Hirst reversed out of the mews and started driving back towards the house. He drove slowly, waiting until he saw Miller follow him out of the mews, then he accelerated.

'Rock and roll,' said Kristov.

'Hell, yeah,' said Hirst.

He drove to the house and pulled up a short distance away. Miller found a parking space on the other side of the road.

'Go to it, guys,' said Hirst.

Kristov and Josh climbed out and quietly closed the doors. The three men in the second Outlander jogged over and together they headed to the gates. Hirst took a deep breath. One minute, two at the most, and it would all be over. And he would be reunited with his wife and daughter.

CHAPTER 39

'Two sugars, and easy on the milk,' said Hadley. He was sitting at the kitchen table while Sally made the tea. Tim was also sitting at the table, clearly uncomfortable at the way Hadley was treating her like a maid, but Sally didn't object. She was actually grateful to have something to do. The kettle boiled and switched itself off. She poured water into three mugs and dropped in Tetley tea bags. She knew without asking that Tim liked his tea milky and without sugar. Sally always preferred hers black.

'How were they able to track my phone?' asked Sally.

'It's doable these days, and not just by the authorities,' said Hadley.

'But how did they have my number? And how did they know where I lived?' She turned around to look at him. 'It all happened so quickly. They were in the house, I ran and managed to find someone to hide me for half an hour or so while I called an Uber. I'm sure they didn't see me getting into the car and I'd changed my appearance, but somehow they managed to intercept me by the common. How could they do that?'

'As you said, they must have been able to track your phone. It's easy enough these days now that they all have GPS.'

'But that doesn't explain how they knew my number in the first place, does it?'

Hadley shrugged but didn't say anything.

'And they knew where I lived. That means they know who I am.'

'I suppose so,' said Hadley. He shifted uncomfortably on his chair.

'There's no suppose so about it,' said Sally. 'It seems to me that there are two possibilities. Either they knew who I was before they went into the house, or they found out after they saw me. And either way, they must have had help from someone at Thames House.'

'Are you pointing the finger at me?' asked Hadley.

Sally shook her head. 'I'll admit, earlier on today I wondered if you were involved, but now it looks as if they were after details of this safe house and as you obviously knew about the house you could have just told them, right?'

'You thought I was a traitor? A mole?'

'Ian, someone must have given them my name, address and phone number.'

'It could have been a friend.' He nodded at Tim. 'Or a boyfriend.'

'What the fuck?' said Tim. 'What the fuck are you saying?'

'She's making allegations about the service, I'm simply pointing out that the information could have come from elsewhere.' He held up a hand. 'Having said that, there was a GPS request put in to your service provider regarding your number earlier this morning.'

Sally's jaw dropped. 'Are you serious?'

'We haven't been able to ascertain who placed the request, and at present we have no way of knowing why the information was sought.'

'Ian, will you listen to yourself? It's as clear as the nose on your face what went down. They went looking for the details of this safe house, and when they realised I had the thumb drive they got someone at Thames House to get my location.'

Hadley opened his mouth to reply but before he could say anything the kitchen window exploded and his face erupted into a red pulp. He slumped across the table, blood splattering across the floor.

Sally turned to look at the window. There was a man standing outside wearing a black ski mask. He was holding a carbine, a big black weapon with a large silencer on the end of the barrel. She stared at him in horror. Tim was already on his feet, backing away from the table.

There were more loud bangs from the front of the house. Then more shots, louder this time.

The man at the window was moving now, bringing his gun to bear on Tim. Sally began to scream. She grabbed the kettle, took two steps across the kitchen and hurled it at the masked figure. He saw it coming and started to raise the gun to block it but he was too slow and it hit him in the face. He screamed as the boiling water splashed over his head and chest.

Sally ran towards the door. Tim opened his mouth to shout at her but she was already committed. The man in the mask was screaming in pain now. He dropped his gun and reached for his mask.

Sally suddenly realised that the back door was almost certainly locked. She switched her attention to the window, where the man in the mask was still howling in agony.

'Sally, no!' shouted Tim but it was just background noise, adrenaline had taken over and she was in full fight or flight mode.

The shot had smashed most of the glass from the window. She vaulted onto the worktop and jumped out. The man was clawing at his ski mask, trying to get it off his face. She twisted in mid-air and smashed her shoulder into his chest and he staggered back, his arms flailing, his screams turning into curses.

Sally bent down quickly and grabbed the gun. There was a second man in the garden, she realised, bigger than the first and also carrying a weapon. The man she'd scalded was in front of her so the other attacker couldn't get a clear shot. She had no idea what sort of gun she was holding, but the man had fired it so the safety must have been in the off position.

She slipped her finger over the trigger. Her heart was pounding but her mind was sharply focused. The second attacker was moving to the side. He was also wearing a ski mask. Sally held the gun steady with her left hand. The man she'd scalded managed to get his mask off but before he could react she kicked him in the stomach, putting all her weight behind the blow. He staggered back, his wet mask in his right hand, his left flailing out for balance. She pulled the trigger and was surprised at how little recoil there was. The bullet smacked into the middle of his chest and he gasped.

The man behind him was still trying to get a clear shot. Sally kept moving, bending low to make herself a small target. The man she'd shot was still on his feet and there was no blood on his chest. He was wearing a bulky black vest over his jacket and she realised it must be bulletproof. He took a step towards her and she shot him again, this time in the throat. Blood spurted over his body but he remained upright. She darted to the right and got a clear view of the second man's face. She aimed and fired but the shot went wide. She fired again and this time she managed to hit him, but only in the shoulder. He too was wearing a bulletproof vest and she wasn't sure if the shot had wounded him or not. 'Bitch!' the man shouted. He swung his gun around but she ducked to the left and when he fired a short burst most of the rounds hit his colleague who was slumping to his knees.

Sally was down in a crouch now and she aimed upwards and fired three times. The first two missed but the third caught him in the centre of his face and he fell backwards. Sally straightened up. 'Sally!' She turned to see Tim staring at her, wide-eyed. 'What the fuck?'

She bent down and picked up the gun of the second man she'd shot, then jogged over to the kitchen window. She passed the carbine to him. 'I'm not trained in firearms,' he said.

'Neither am I,' she said. 'You just point and pull the trigger.'

He stared at the gun in his hand. 'Are you serious?'

'It's for self-defence, Tim.' They heard more shots from the front of the house. Sally headed to the driveway. Tim called her name but she had already blotted him out.

As she turned around the corner, she saw a black Outlander in the road. There were two more bangs from inside the house. She hurried along the driveway. There was a man sitting in the driving seat of the Outlander. The street lights were reflecting off the windscreen so she couldn't see his face or if he was looking in her direction. She raised her carbine. She had no idea how many shots she had fired or how many rounds were in the magazine.

She put the stock against her shoulder and took aim at the passenger side window. She pulled the trigger and a round thudded into the car door. The engine of the SUV roared and she fired again. This time the passenger window shattered into a thousand cubes. The Outlander pulled away from the curb, accelerated and sped off down the road.

Sally moved to the front of the house. There was a second Outlander parked on the other side the road. Sally raised the carbine again and shot at the rear tyre. The bullet ricocheted off the pavement and she fired again. This time the rear window of the SUV disintegrated and it also sped off down the street, the tyres squealing on the tarmac.

She heard more gunshots from inside and ran to the front door. It was ajar and she pushed it open with her foot as she kept the gun up against her shoulder. There were more bangs that sounded like suppressed fire, and cracks from unsilenced handguns.

As she pushed the door open, she saw a man in black at the foot of the stairs. He had his back to her and he was aiming his silenced carbine at the upper floor. He was wearing a helmet and a bulletproof vest, and under other circumstances she would have assumed he was a specialist firearms officer with the Met. The man fired twice and his bullets smacked into the wall at the top of the stairs. Another man was in the hallway, heading towards the kitchen.

A figure emerged from the sitting room. It was one of the DEA agents, the Hispanic one. He was holding a handgun and he fired twice. Both shots hit the man at the bottom of the stairs in the face and he slammed against the wall and then slid down it.

The man in the hallway turned and was swinging his gun towards the DEA agent. Sally fired twice and both shots hit the man in the chest. He took a step backwards but then started moving forward again. She fired again and hit him in the face and he slumped to the floor.

The agent stepped into the hallway and aimed his gun at Sally. 'It's me!' she shouted, holding her gun in the air. 'Don't shoot!'

He looked at her coldly and nodded.

Tim appeared in the kitchen doorway and the agent swung his gun around. 'No!' shouted Sally. 'He's with me.'

'I can see that,' growled the American. 'I'm not stupid. Where did you get the guns from?'

'Two guys attacked us through the kitchen.'

'And you overpowered them? What the fuck?'

'I had a kettle.'

'A what?'

'I threw a kettle of water over one of them and grabbed his gun.' She shrugged. 'Looking back it wasn't the smartest thing to have done.'

'It worked,' said Tim.

The agent waved for them to be quiet, then shouted up the stairs. 'Eric, we're all clear down here!'

A large man with a crew cut and a square jaw moved cautiously across the upper landing. 'Sitrep?' he shouted.

'Two dead in the hallway,' came the reply. The agent looked at Sally. 'The guys you took the guns from?'

'Dead. Both of them. In the back garden.'

Eric came slowly down the stairs. He was holding a large semi-automatic. 'We've got two bad guys dead upstairs so that's six in total.'

'There were two vehicles outside. Black Mitsubishi Outlanders,' said Sally. 'I fired at them and they drove off.'

He frowned at her. 'Who are you?'

'Sally Page.'

'She's the girl who didn't get killed in Wimbledon,' said the other American. 'Where's Harris?'

'Dead. He took a bullet when they burst in.'

'Who's Harris?' asked Sally.

'One of your bosses,' said Eric. 'Toby Harris. He was running the operation that captured Flores.'

'Is Flores the cartel guy?'

Eric smiled thinly. 'Yes, the cartel guy. Harris was our MI5 linkman.'

'All academic now that he's dead,' said the other agent. 'What about the other MI5 guy that turned up? Hadley?'

'He's dead,' said Sally. 'They shot him in the kitchen. They came through the back garden.'

'And you killed them?'

Eric peered through the front door, and then closed it. 'This is one hell of a clusterfuck.'

Eric noticed Tim for the first time. 'Who the fuck are you?'

'Detective Sergeant Tim Reid,' he said. He nodded at Sally. 'I'm with her.'

Eric nodded. 'Right, to bring you up to speed, Detective Sergeant Tim Reid, I'm Eric Mitchell and this is Luis Mendoza, and we're with the DEA. Upstairs I've got one more guy, Sam Butler, who's guarding our prisoner. Two of my men are dead up there. And Harris.' He looked over at Mendoza. 'Jim and Larry bought it.'

'Shit,' said Mendoza.

Eric grimaced. 'They caught us by surprise up there. It was a fucking massacre.' He frowned. 'Where's Rick?'

'I'm sorry, Eric. He got hit when they burst in. He managed to get back into the room but bled out.'

'Fuck,' said Eric. 'So we're down to three of us, plus Sally and Tim makes five.'

'How did Harris die?' asked Sally.

'He was in the room with Flores. First guy in started spraying bullets and took out Harris and my two guys. He was about to shoot Flores when I got him. And the guy who was with him. I got them both. But it was touch and go.'

'I thought they wanted to rescue Flores?' said Tim.

Eric shook his head. 'They came here to kill him,' he said.

'But Flores is all right?' asked Sally.

'My men stepped in front of him,' said Eric. He looked at his watch, a bulky black G-Shock. 'The plane won't be here for another six or seven hours.' He looked over at Mendoza. 'Got any thoughts?'

'If two of them got away, they could well come back.'

'That's what I was thinking. And we're going to have to ask ourselves how they fucking found us.'

'Yeah,' said his colleague. 'It can't be a coincidence that they turned up on Hadley's heels.'

'He knew where the safe house was and probably knew that you guys were using it,' said Sally. 'He could have just told them, they wouldn't have had to kill everyone in Wimbledon or chase me across London.'

Eric cocked his head on one side. 'So what are you saying? They followed him?'

'That seems more logical,' said Sally.

'She's right,' said Mendoza.

'But I think that the killers have an inside man at Thames House,' said Sally.

'Thames House?' queried Eric.

'That's where MI5 is based,' said Sally. 'Someone did a check on my phone this morning. And it's possible that the same person tipped off the killers that Ian was heading out to see me. He wouldn't have been expecting a tail, obviously.'

Eric grimaced. 'Like I said, it's a clusterfuck.' He looked over at Mendoza. 'We're going to have to saddle up and ride out, because they're not going to give up.'

'Agreed,' said Mendoza. 'But where?'

Eric gestured at Sally with his chin. 'Do you have any bright ideas?'

'There's Tim's flat in Maida Vale. Five don't know about him.'

'How far away?'

'Fifteen, twenty minutes. You'd have to park on the street, though.'

'Any other possibilities?'

'What about checking into a hotel?'

'I'd be worried about involving civilians if they attack again,' said Eric. 'Plus it might arouse suspicions if a group of men check in together with no luggage. Especially with one of them in handcuffs.'

'We also don't know who's involved,' said Mendoza. 'If the cartel has a mole inside MI5 then they might well have access to credit card information and hotel records. We need to take care of this ourselves.'

'Agreed,' said Eric. He looked at Sally. 'Any other thoughts?'

'I have the keys to a flat in Notting Hill.'

'Is it safe?' asked Eric. He looked at his watch again, clearly worried about the time.

'It's not a safe house, it's a flat used by undercover officers.'

'Would Hadley have known about it?'

Sally nodded.

'How many other people at MI5 would know about it?' asked Eric.

'Difficult to say. But not many.'

Eric nodded at Mendoza. 'What do you think?'

'We need to get the hell out of Dodge, that's what I think.'

'I hear you.' He looked back at Sally. 'Okay, Notting Hill it is. You'll have to come with us. From now on you're our MI5 liaison.'

Sally opened her mouth to protest but he cut her off with a wave of his hand. 'We don't have time to argue.'

'I'm coming with you,' said Tim.

Eric smiled thinly. 'From the way you're holding that gun, I'm not sure you'll be much use to us, buddy.'

Tim grinned. 'You just point and pull the trigger, right?'

Eric grinned back. 'Just make sure you don't point it at me,' he said. 'Okay. You're on board.' He turned to Mendoza. 'What do you think? One vehicle? Two?'

'There's six of us, we're going to need two. We'll take one of the SUVs and Sally can lead the way in the car that Harris was using. I'll get the keys.' He nodded at Eric. 'Let's get ready to move out.'

Eric went to the bottom of the stairs. 'Coming up!' he shouted. He jogged upstairs.

Tim walked over to Sally, letting the barrel of his gun swing towards the floor. 'Are you okay?' he asked.

'I've been better.'

'How did you learn to do that? You were on fire.'

'It was instinctive,' she said. 'They'd killed Ian and I knew we'd be next.'

'You were amazing. Me, I just froze. It's like my feet were rooted to the floor.'

'It happens,' said Mendoza. 'You have to be trained to overcome the freezing reflex. It's crazy that British cops aren't armed.'

'We have armed cops,' said Tim. 'But they're specially trained and they specifically volunteer for it. Most British cops wouldn't want to carry a gun.' He gestured at the Glock that Mendoza was holding. 'Speaking of which, how do DEA agents get authorisation to carry guns in London?'

'Bearing in mind this gun saved your life, you might not want to be looking that particular gift horse in the mouth.'

Sally figured it would be a good time to change the subject. 'You're flying Flores out, right? From which airport?'

'RAF Northolt,' said Mendoza. 'If all goes to plan.'

Sally frowned. 'What's that, a military base?'

'It's a Royal Air Force airport in South Ruislip,' said Tim. 'It's about eight miles from Heathrow. It handles a lot of private civilian flights as well as RAF traffic. A lot of the Russian oligarchs land there in their private jets.' He looked at Mendoza. 'Why not go straight there?'

'The airport is having technical problems and there is a chance the flight will be diverted,' said Mendoza. 'We're waiting until we know for sure that it'll be landing.'

'And what's the plan once you get him to the States?'

Mendoza grinned. 'After what's happened tonight I don't think there'll be any problem getting Flores to give evidence against the cartel. But even if he refuses, your people have more than enough evidence to put him away forever.'

Eric reappeared at the top of the stairs, his gun in his hand. 'Luis, check we're good to go outside. Sally, you can drive Harris's car. We'll follow. I'll drive and Sam will ride shotgun so Tim you sit in the back with Luis and Flores.'

'I don't have the authority to get involved with a DEA operation,' said Tim. He held up the carbine. 'And I most definitely
don't have the authorisation to be carrying this.'

Eric came down the stairs. 'Tim, the President himself has
declared Carlos Martinez and his cartel a priority target. He'll
smooth out any problems, trust me. But I take your point about
the gun. It's maybe more than you need.' He took the carbine
from him and gave him the Glock. 'The principle's the same,'
he said. 'Point and shoot.'

'Tim, come with me and check out the street,' said Mendoza.

Tim looked at Sally. 'Are you okay with this?'

'We've come this far,' she said. 'We might as well follow it
through.'

'To the bitter end?'

She laughed. 'Always the pessimist.' She patted him on the
shoulder. 'It'll be fine.'

Tim grinned but she could see the concern in his eyes. He
followed Mendoza out of the front door.

Two more men appeared at the top of the stairs. One was
black wearing a leather jacket and pale blue jeans, the other was
Hispanic with his wrists zip-tied in front of him. 'The good-
looking guy is Sam Butler, he's with me,' said Eric. 'The other
guy is the one they were after.'

'What the fuck is going on?' shouted Flores. He was in his
forties, dark-skinned with glossy black hair and piercing brown
eyes. He was wearing a white jacket over a tight blue T-shirt and
there was a large gold medallion hanging from a thick gold chain
around his neck.

'We're keeping you alive, that's what's going on,' snapped Eric.
He pointed a finger at the man. 'And if you don't keep a civil
tongue in your head I'll put the bag back on.'

'How did they find us?' asked Flores, lowering his voice. 'You
said this was a safe house.' He nodded at the body at the foot
of the stairs. 'How is this fucking safe?'

'The house was compromised but you're alive, so just be
grateful for that,' said Eric. 'Three of my men weren't so lucky.'

Flores nodded. 'The men with me, they died bravely,' he said.

'Their job was to protect you,' said Eric. 'And that's what they did.'

'I'm sorry for your loss, I know they were your friends.'

'They were, yes.'

'Were they married?'

Eric frowned. 'Why would you ask that?'

'They weren't wearing wedding rings, but I got the impression they had family back in the States.'

'Jim Henderson is married with two young kids.' He grimaced and corrected himself. 'Was married. The older guy, Larry, is – was – divorced. His kids are at college. He was due to retire next year. They were both good men.'

'I'm sorry,' said Flores. 'When this is over, I would like to help their families.'

'What?' said Eric.

'They saved my life, the least I can do is to help those they left behind.'

Eric's eyes widened in disbelief. He opened his mouth to respond but was interrupted by the return of Mendoza and Tim. 'We're good to go,' said Mendoza.

Eric handed Sally the keys to Harris's car. 'Stay below the speed limit, obviously,' he said. 'Keep it nice and calm. Watch out for traffic lights, we don't want to get caught with a red light while you carry on your sweet way. What's the parking situation near the flat?'

'This time of night it's fine.'

'Great. Let's go.'

Mendoza and Tim went back out. Sally followed them. Eric and Butler took Flores through the door.

Butler went over to the gates and pulled them open, while Eric put Flores into the back of one of the Ford Explorers.

'What do I do with this?' Sally asked Eric, holding up her carbine.

'Keep it close by,' said Eric.

Sally nodded and got into the front of the VW. She closed the door and put the weapon in the passenger footwell. She started the engine.

Eric got into the driving seat of the Explorer. Tim and Mendoza were in the back, either side of Flores.

Sally edged out of the driveway and onto the road. The Explorer followed. Once the two cars were out of the driveway, Butler closed the gates then jogged over to get into the front passenger seat next to Eric. Sally realised she was gripping the steering wheel so tightly that her knuckles had whitened. She took a deep breath and clenched and unclenched her hands. 'Come on, relax, we're only going for a drive,' she said. She checked in her mirror that Eric was ready to go, then eased her foot down on the accelerator.

CHAPTER 40

Marty Hirst called Javier with a heavy heart. He didn't know how Javier was going to react, but he was sure he wouldn't take the news well. Javier was a dangerous man with a killer's ice-cold eyes, but so far he had never raised his voice to Hirst. Men like Javier didn't need to rant and rave. They told people what they had to do and if they didn't do it then they died and they usually died horribly. Hirst's mouth had gone dry and he was having trouble swallowing. He had parked about half a mile away from the Hampstead house once he was sure that he wasn't being followed. He called all of the six men who had gone into the house, and Aaron, but in every case the call had gone straight through to voicemail.

'Yeah?' growled Javier as soon as he took the call.

'There's been a problem,' said Hirst.

'What happened?'

'I sent a team into the house and they fucked up. I don't know how or why but I'm pretty sure they're all dead.'

'You don't know for sure?'

'I called Aaron but his phone is off, I'm guessing he's lying low. He was outside the house in the other car. The rest left their mobiles with Aaron and they're all still switched off. If any of them had got out they would have contacted me. So I'm assuming that I need a new team.'

'Where were you while this was going on?'

'I was waiting in one of the cars outside and I came under fire.'

'From who?'

Hirst took a deep breath. 'The girl who got away from the Wimbledon house.'

'The runner?'

'Yeah. The runner.'

'What the fuck was she doing there?'

'I don't know,' said Hirst. 'She came around the back of the house and from the look of it she'd taken the gun off one of my men. She fired at me so I had to drive off. Aaron drove off, too.'

'You were scared of a fucking girl?'

'Didn't you hear what I said?' Hirst snapped. 'She was fucking shooting at me with an automatic weapon.'

Javier didn't say anything. The silence went on for a few seconds and it was Hirst who spoke first. 'I'm sorry,' he said. 'It all turned to shit. I'm a bit stressed out.'

'You need to calm down,' said Javier. 'And you need to put this right.'

'I will, I will. But I need more manpower. And vehicles. I've got a smashed window and bullet holes in my car and I'm going to have to dump it.'

'I'll send you more people. What about Flores?'

Hirst looked at the iPad mini on the passenger seat. It showed a street map of London and two small green dots showed the progress of the Explorer and the Volkswagen as they headed west. 'We put trackers on their vehicles before we went in, so I can find them,' he said.

'At least you did something right,' said Javier. 'I'll arrange the manpower and vehicles and I'll call you back.'

The line went dead. Hirst felt sick to the stomach even though he hadn't eaten all day. He was disgusted at himself for what he was doing, but he was out of options. He had to do everything Javier asked of him. If he didn't . . . He shuddered at the thought of what would happen.

CHAPTER 41

The traffic lights ahead of her were green but Sally had a feeling they were about to turn so she eased off on the accelerator and checked her rear-view mirror. The Explorer was five car lengths behind her. The lights changed and she smiled. She'd made the right call, though the smile tightened as she realised that they were more vulnerable when they weren't moving.

She kept both hands on the wheel as she scanned left and right, looking for potential threats. She took another quick view in her rear mirror. Eric and Sam were also looking around. The seconds ticked off. Several cars were held at the lights facing her, but there were no SUVs and all had just a driver, no passengers. Sally was pretty sure that the bad guys would be in large vehicles and that there would be several passengers, all male. There were no vehicles fitting that profile nearby but that didn't make her any more relaxed.

The lights turned green and she pulled away. As she crossed the junction, her eyes flicked to the rear-view. The Explorer was following.

She jumped as a siren kicked into life behind her. She checked the side mirror. A police car was overtaking the Explorer, blue lights flashing. She tensed, wondering if it was them the police car was after, but it sped on down the street. She sighed with relief, but she could still feel the tension in her neck and arms. 'Come on, relax. This is a walk in the park,' she muttered to herself. She smiled at the image. She'd certainly be a lot more relaxed on foot and outdoors. She was a better runner than most men and in better condition, and on foot she was in control. The car was stronger and faster, but she felt confined by it. She was limited to where the car could go and if it was blocked in she would be trapped. She remembered how quickly the Outlander had fled after she had fired at it. Cars were made of thin metal and glass and were no match for a bullet from a high-powered rifle.

She got to thirty miles per hour and eased off the accelerator, checking that Eric was still with her. He was. She looked down at the gun in the footwell next to her. She had never fired a gun before today. Never even held one. But when she had picked it up off the grass in the back garden of the house in Hampstead, it had felt like the most natural thing in the world to aim it and fire. She was also surprised at her lack of reaction to killing three men. She was a vegetarian, she abhorred cruelty to animals in any form, but she had taken the lives of three men without a second thought. How was that possible? She was under pressure and the adrenaline reflex had kicked in, there was no doubt about that, but did that mean that her natural instincts were those of a killer? Maybe she was still in shock and had yet to come to terms with what she'd done. But she didn't feel as if she was in shock. She felt tense, and she was definitely apprehensive about what lay ahead of her, but she wasn't wracked by guilt or paralysed by fear, and that surprised her.

She tensed as she saw a black SUV in a side road wanting to turn ahead of her. She slowed and the vehicle took that as a signal that he could pull out in front. She gripped the steering wheel and took a quick look in the rear-view mirror. Eric didn't seem to have spotted the SUV. Her eyes flicked back to the windscreen and she breathed a sigh of relief when she realised it was a Range Rover and that the driver was a middle-aged lady. 'Relax,' she said to herself. 'You need to stop jumping at shadows.'

CHAPTER 42

Liz Bailey burst into Pritchard's office with Ellie Cooper in her wake. 'Have you heard?' asked Bailey, her voice shaking. 'The house in Hampstead has been attacked. Ian Hadley is dead. So is Toby Harris.'

'What? No, when did this happen?'

'The cops have just turned up. Neighbours reported hearing shots.'

Pritchard stood up and walked around his desk. 'What about Sally? And the DEA?'

'We don't know. There are eight bodies in the house in addition to Ian and Toby, six of them seem to have been the attackers. They were wearing bulletproof vests, Kevlar helmets and carrying heavy-duty carbines.'

'So what the hell happened?'

'It looks as if they stormed the house but somehow bit off more than they could chew. There were two DEA agents dead upstairs, which is presumably where they were keeping Flores.'

Ellie looked as if she was about to faint and held onto a chair for support. 'Oh my God,' she gasped.

Bailey put her arms around the secretary and helped her sit down. 'When the police got there they thought it had been a Met firearms team that had been killed, but there were no police markings and no police vehicles. Whoever they were, they had state-of-the-art equipment.'

'Presumably working for the cartel,' said Pritchard. He began to pace up and down. 'What a bloody nightmare. Okay, we need to make sure the press don't get hold of this. Liaise with the commissioner's office and get a D-notice in place. I'll talk to the

DEA in London.' He looked at his watch and grimaced. 'Though I doubt they'll be answering their phones this time of night. I'll put in a call to their Washington office, too. Do we have any idea where they might have gone?'

Bailey shook her head. 'I can get a team monitoring CCTV footage in the area but it'll take forever and I'll have to bring people in.'

Pritchard stopped pacing and rubbed the back of his neck. 'This is just getting worse and worse, isn't it? What about IDs of the men killed in the house?'

'No IDs, and no phones. Dead ends, literally.'

Ellie was sobbing into her hands. Pritchard went over and put his hand on her shoulder. 'Ellie, you really should go home.'

She shook her head vehemently. 'No, I'm okay,' she said. 'You need me here, there's a lot to be done.'

'You're exhausted.'

She took a deep breath and shook her head again. 'No,' she said. 'I'm okay. It's just Ian . . .'

'I know.'

'He was only just here. And now he's . . .'

'I know,' said Pritchard again. 'Look, seriously, I can get someone else to answer the phones, Ellie.'

'No, please, I want to stay,' she said. 'Plus it's after eleven, there are no spare staff around. I'll go and splash some water on my face and I'll be good to go, I promise.' She stood up, composed herself enough to flash him a smile, and then hurried out of the office.

'She's taking it hard,' said Bailey.

'We all are, Liz. It's just that some of us have learned to hide our emotions.' He sighed. 'We have to get these people, Liz. We have to put a stop to this.'

CHAPTER 43

Sally indicated right, slowed, and turned. She checked in her rear-view mirror to confirm that Eric was following her and then started looking for a place to park. She found a space and reversed into it. Eric waited behind her then drove by and found a spot to park the Explorer further down the street. Sally switched off the VW's engine. She looked down at the carbine. There was no way she could carry it on the pavement. There were three-storey white stucco terraces either side, most of which had been converted into flats and bedsits, and there were hundreds of windows overlooking the street. She shrugged off her fleece and wrapped it around the gun. She wrinkled her nose. It still looked like a weapon, just one that had been covered with a jacket.

She got out of the VW and locked it, then fished the envelope for the flat out of her bag. She took the keys from the envelope and walked along the pavement to the Explorer, where Eric was already opening the rear door for Tim. Tim had tucked the Glock into his belt and he fastened his jacket as he got out.

'We need something to cover the cuffs,' said Eric.

Mendoza took off his jacket and dropped it over the cuffs binding Flores's wrists.

Sally kept her gun pressed against her side, hoping it wasn't too conspicuous. She scanned the houses nearby and while many had lights on inside no one appeared to be paying them any attention.

'Where do we go?' asked Eric, as Tim helped Flores out of the Explorer. Sally nodded at the building behind them. 'First floor.'

'So there's access from the garden behind?'

Sally shook her head. 'English first floor. You call it second floor, right?'

'Because it is. The bottom floor is obviously the first floor so the one above it is the second.'

Sally laughed. 'Yeah, well we call it the first. And no, there's no access from the back. The only way in is through the front door and up the stairs.'

Eric nodded. 'Let's go.' Butler locked up the car as Sally took Eric to the front door. Tim and Mendoza followed, either side of Flores, who was looking around anxiously.

'This is not good,' muttered Flores. 'You should have your guns out.'

'This is England, not Mexico,' said Eric. 'You can't wave guns around here.'

'The men who attacked us didn't seem to have a problem,' said Flores.

'Shut the fuck up, Flores,' snarled Eric. 'We're doing this to save your fucking life.'

'No,' said Flores. 'You're doing this because you want to take down the cartel, and you need me to help you do that.'

'Either way, Martinez's men are out to fill you full of lead so you need to stop bitching.'

An engine revved behind them and they all turned to look. It was a Deliveroo driver on a motorbike. He went by and parked further down the road.

Sally unlocked the main door and pushed it open. There was a time-delay light switch to the right and she pressed it. The hallway was flooded with light. There was a line of mailboxes and two doors leading left and right to the ground-floor flats.

Sally led the way up the stairs and Eric followed her. She unlocked the door to the flat and pushed it open. Eric pulled his Glock from an underarm holster and went in first. Sally switched the light on for him. The burglar alarm began to buzz. Eric went along the hallway, checking the rooms, as Sally tapped in the four-digit number to silence the alarm.

Mendoza and Tim brought Flores into the flat and Butler brought up the rear. He closed the door and flicked a bolt across.

Eric came out of the main bedroom. 'All clear,' he said. He pointed at the living room. 'Sam, pull the blinds shut, will you?'

Butler nodded and headed into the room.

'Is there anything to eat?' asked Flores.

'Not really,' said Sally. 'The flat isn't being used at the moment. There might be something in the freezer.'

'What about coffee?'

'Coffee I can do. But it'll have to be black.'

'You're not his maid, Sally,' said Eric.

'I'm happy to make coffee,' she said. She unwrapped the carbine. 'What do I do with this?'

'Keep it close by,' said Eric. 'On second thoughts, let me have a look.' He took it from her and examined it. 'It's an HK. Heckler & Koch. But I've not seen this model before.'

Butler switched on the sitting room lights and came back into the hall. Eric handed him the gun. 'Sam's the gun nut,' he said. 'What do you think, Sam?'

Butler hefted the weapon in his right hand and nodded his approval. 'Nice piece of kit,' he said. 'HK416, based very much on our own Colt M4 carbine but it's a lot more reliable. Delta and the Navy SEALs use them. This is the shorter version with a ten-inch barrel. More than seven hundred rounds a minute, effective up to four hundred yards, pretty much. I've never seen them with suppressors, so that's a first.' He gave it back to Eric.

'So the question has to be asked, where did they get guns like this?' asked Eric. He turned to look at Tim. 'Have you heard about weapons like this being available in London?'

'It's not my field,' said Tim. 'We normally come across hand-guns or the occasional Ingram or Uzi. That's more like something a soldier would use.'

Eric then turned to look at Mendoza. 'Luis, take Flores to the bedroom at the back of the apartment. Draw the curtains.'

Flores raised his arms. 'Can you take the cuffs off, they're cutting into me.'

Mendoza took his jacket and examined the man's wrists. 'They look okay to me.'

'I'm in fucking pain,' said Flores.

'We'll take them off when we're on the plane,' said Eric. 'Get him out of my sight, Luis.'

Mendoza grabbed Flores by the arm and frog-marched him to the bedroom at the back of the property.

'Let's talk,' said Eric, taking them into the sitting room. There were two sofas at right angles to each other, with a wooden chest used as a coffee table between them. Eric dropped down on one of the sofas, still holding the gun, and Butler took the other sofa. There was an armchair by a big-screen television and Tim sat there, while Sally dropped down onto a dark leather pouffe. Eric held up the gun. 'This is special forces kit, no question,' he said. 'Plus they had Kevlar helmets and jackets. We weren't attacked by gangsters, they were professionals. If I hadn't been in the other bedroom when the first two came upstairs, they'd have got me as well. And if Sally hadn't taken care of the two at the back of the house – well we probably wouldn't be sitting here now.'

'And presumably they were working for the cartel?' said Sally.

'No question of it,' said Eric. 'Have you heard of Carlos Martinez?'

'Only what Ian Hadley told us,' said Sally. 'A nasty piece of work who tortures and kills his competitors.'

'He's the worst of the worst. And he's not going to give up until Flores is dead. He'll keep sending killers until he succeeds or until we have Flores in custody in the States. Even then, and even if we bury Martinez in a supermax somewhere, Flores is going to be looking over his shoulder for the rest of his life.'

'He'll definitely testify against his boss?'

'He doesn't have any choice,' said Eric. 'Did your boss tell you how they caught him?'

'He was caught on tape, right?' said Sally.

Eric laughed. 'You couldn't make it up, what happened. Your people were about to move against a London drugs gang that they'd been investigating for months. As part of that operation they had bugged several of the places that the gang used, including a couple of restaurants and a nightclub. On the night they were about to bust the gang, they met with Flores. They had dinner in one of the restaurants that MI5 had bugged but the conversation was pretty guarded, as you'd expect. Then they moved onto the nightclub. Several bottles of Cristal and many lines of cocaine later, their tongues loosened and they started swapping war stories. The London boys were keen to impress Flores so they opened up about the cannabis they were bringing in from North Africa and the heroin they were buying from Afghanistan. Flores then starts to get all competitive and tells them about the cocaine and cannabis his guys are moving across the Mexican border, and how the cartel pays off border guards to let their shipments through. Then he started telling them how they deal with their competition, especially the Colombians. That's when it got really interesting. He detailed three murders that he had personally carried out. He was actually charged with one of those murders but got off. Flores said it was because they had bribed the judge and threatened members of the jury.'

'It defies belief that he would open up like that,' said Tim.

'It was partly the booze and the drugs talking,' said Eric. 'But Flores was trying to show them how powerful the cartel was, and how the cartel could help them expand in the UK and Europe. That's when he started to big up Carlos Martinez. He told them far more than he should have done about the guy. About killings Martinez had carried out himself, his connections with Mexican politicians, about the judges in Mexico and the States that he pays bribes to. And every word was captured on tape. Martinez must have gone apoplectic when he heard what Flores had said. If nothing else, he'd have ordered his death because of his stupidity alone.'

'When was this?' asked Sally.

'Three nights ago.'

'Haven't you wondered how Martinez found out so quickly?'

Eric frowned. 'We assumed that one of his people realised what happened and called it in.'

'Doesn't it seem more likely that someone within MI5 is on his payroll?'

Eric rubbed his chin. 'That's a definite possibility.'

'Probably the same person who ordered a check on my phone this morning. And I'm guessing that's who had Hadley followed.'

'But if it's someone within MI5, wouldn't they have known about the safe house?'

Sally shook her head. 'Not necessarily. The details of the safe houses are not widely known. It's need-to-know, mostly.'

'Do you have any thoughts on who the inside man might be?'

'Initially I thought it was Ian Hadley, but he definitely knew about the Hampstead house and almost certainly would have been told that it was in use. If he had told the cartel what he knew there would be no point to the attack on the Wimbledon house.'

'No one else comes to mind?'

She shook her head. 'Sorry.'

'But you're probably right. The inside man heard about Flores being arrested and told Martinez. Martinez sent in his own men.'

'Would he have that sort of manpower in England?'

'The cartel has people all over the world. But he could have flown a team over from the States. He's got a load of former special forces people on his payroll. But he might well already have a crew in place here in anticipation of problems down the line.'

Sally nodded thoughtfully. 'Same with getting people on the payroll at MI5 and with the cops, maybe. It would make sense to have them in place before making any serious moves here, right?'

'Exactly.'

'So he could well have someone working for him at a very senior level within MI5?'

'That's a definite possibility. One of the things Flores told the London guys was that the cartel had one of the top DEA agents in Dallas on the payroll. There's always someone who will either accept the money or bow to the pressure. "Silver or lead" was the choice that Escobar gave people. You take his money or you get a bullet. The Mexicans follow a similar philosophy. Is it possible it could be someone at Hadley's level, or above? Someone who was near the top but who wouldn't know the location of the safe house in Hampstead?'

'It's possible,' said Sally. 'But presumably allowing you to use the house must have been cleared at a very senior level. The more I think about it, the more it looks like their MI5 source – if they have one – is quite junior. Someone who knew the location of the footie house in Wimbledon, and someone able to get my phone tracked, but not at a high enough level to know where Flores was being held or what you planned to do with him.' She ran her hands through her hair. 'I just wish I knew who it was.'

'You and me both,' said Eric. He looked around the room. 'I'm hungry,' he said. 'Is anyone else hungry?'

'You know what I could eat?' said Butler.

Eric grinned. 'Pizza.'

'Damn right.' He looked over at Sally. 'Can we get pizzas delivered?'

'Sure. There's one close by, I can go and pick up a couple.'

'I'd prefer we all stay inside,' said Eric. 'But a delivery works for me. I want extra pineapple on mine.'

Tim laughed and Eric frowned at him. 'What?'

'What is this with guys wanting fruit on their pizzas?' said Sally.

'Tomatoes are fruits and everyone has tomato on their pizza,' said Eric.

'That's different. Tomatoes aren't really fruits.'

'Tomatoes are totally fruits,' said Eric. 'Anything with the seed on the inside is a fruit.'

'But pineapples are so sweet, why would you want something sweet on a pizza?'

'Because it tastes good,' said Eric and Tim at exactly the same time, and they both laughed.

Eric's mobile phone buzzed and he checked it. He put the phone away as Sally walked back into the room. 'The jet has just left Dallas,' he said. 'Flight time of about ten hours so ETA at RAF Northolt is 9 a.m.'

'The plan is to stay here until when?' asked Sally.

'How long do you think to get there?'

'Early morning, half an hour, forty-five minutes maybe. Most of the traffic will be coming the other way.'

'So we can leave at about eight,' said Eric. 'Give us a chance to get a few hours' sleep.'

'Why not leave now and wait overnight at the airport?' asked Tim.

'My bosses vetoed that,' said Eric. 'They don't want us drawing attention to Flores. We stay away until the plane is refuelled and ready to go. Then we go straight onto the airport and away. This isn't exactly a rendition flight but the US came into so much shit for its Guantanamo flights that they've been treading on eggshells ever since.' He looked over at Sally. 'So pizza, yeah?'

'With extra pineapple?' She mimed using her fingers to make herself sick as she headed for the kitchen.

CHAPTER 44

Hirst squinted at the iPad. Both vehicles had stopped in Notting Hill. They hadn't moved for almost twenty minutes so it looked as if they had gone to ground. Hirst had parked in a quiet side street in Bayswater. He didn't want to drive around in a vehicle with broken glass over the seats and bullet holes in the doors. He took out his mobile phone and called Javier. Javier answered on the third ring. 'Okay, I have a replacement team ready for you. They are not as professional as the one you had before, but there are more of them. The leader is called Dean.'

'Are they former soldiers?'

'You're not in a position to query the backgrounds of the men you will be working with. At this short notice you will take what you get.'

'I understand,' said Hirst. 'I just wanted to know who I'll be dealing with, that's all.'

'They are men who are being paid to do whatever is necessary,' said Javier. 'They have been told to carry out your instructions without question. I will text you the address where you are to meet them.'

'What about Aaron?'

'Aaron is with me now,' said Javier. 'He'll be staying with me until this is over.'

'Okay, all good,' said Hirst. 'Do they have new vehicles? My current car sticks out like a sore thumb.'

'They will have three vehicles between them. Where are you?'

'Bayswater.'

'And Flores?'

'They've stopped in Notting Hill, I assume they're in a safe house there.'

'I am told that the plane that will collect him is en route with an estimated time of arrival of 9 a.m. According to my source the jet will land at RAF Northolt.'

'Okay, I know where that is.'

'If anything changes, I will let you know. Just to be clear, Flores must not get onto that plane,' said Javier.

'He won't,' said Hirst.

'Good,' said Javier. 'Because you know what will happen if you fail.'

The line went dead and Hirst glared at the phone. 'Fuck you, fuck you, fuck you,' he shouted. He knew swearing at an inanimate object wouldn't change anything, but it made him feel a bit better for a few seconds at least.

CHAPTER 45

Flores raised his hands and nodded at Mendoza. 'Luis, these cuffs are really hurting now. They're cutting off the circulation to my hands.'

'They look fine to me.'

Flores was sitting on the double bed. Mendoza had switched on the lights and drawn the blinds and was now sitting on a rattan chair by the window.

'I'm on your side, right? You could at least cut me some slack.'

'You're never going to be on my side, Flores. Let's not go kidding ourselves. You're helping us because Martinez wants you dead and without us he'll get what he wants.'

'You need me to put Martinez away. That puts me on your team.'

Mendoza laughed. 'Diego, my friend, I heard some of the tapes they have of you in the club. There's enough evidence to put you away forever. For murder, for conspiracy, for drugs. What the fuck were you thinking?'

'I had been drinking. And we had been testing the product.'

'You gave them the names of Texas judges you're paying off. You told them about men you had personally killed. If it was you we were after then you'd never see daylight again. But it's Martinez we want and if that means doing a deal with you, then so be it. But you're not on my team. You never can be. You killed colleagues of mine. So I'll help to keep you alive, but that's as far as it goes.'

Flores nodded and smiled. When he spoke again he switched to Spanish. 'So how much does a DEA agent earn these days?'

Mendoza flashed him a tight smile. 'I'm sure you know exactly what I earn.'

'Starting salaries are about fifty thousand dollars, right? What are you, Luis? Are you a level GS-13? Just over ninety thousand dollars, right?'

Mendoza shrugged. 'Sounds like you know our salary structure.'

'I do, I do. They don't pay you guys enough, Luis. Not for the risks you take.'

'Yeah, well tell that to my bosses.'

'I will do, my friend. I will do.'

'You're not my friend, Flores.'

'I could be your friend, Luis. I could be a good friend to you.' He stared at Mendoza for several seconds, then leaned forward and lowered his voice, still speaking Spanish. 'If you were my friend, I could put five million dollars in your bank. Today.'

'How would you do that?'

'With one phone call, my friend. I make one phone call and five million dollars will be paid into any account you want.'

'And my bank manager wouldn't ask any questions?'

'We could open an account for you offshore. The Cayman Islands. Switzerland. Luxembourg. Anywhere you want.'

'And what would I have to do for five million dollars?'

'Let me go. Just let me go.'

Mendoza gestured at the door. 'I doubt that my colleagues would be happy with that.'

'I could be their friend, too. Five million for each of them. And for the English girl and her boyfriend.'

'You think he's her boyfriend?'

'Didn't you see the way they look at each other?'

Mendoza shook his head.

'Well I did, and they have fucked, I'm sure of that. So what do you think? Can we all be friends?'

Mendoza shook his head again. 'Eric wouldn't even think about it. Neither would Sam. And to be honest, neither would I.'

'You couldn't use five million dollars? Think how happy your wife would be.'

Mendoza's eyes narrowed. 'My wife?'

'I assume that was who you were talking to last night, on the phone. It could have been a girlfriend I suppose, but you did ask about the kids. I suppose she could be a single mother but it seems more likely that she is your wife. Think what she could do with five million dollars, Luis. College fees for kids are so expensive these days, aren't they?'

Mendoza stared at Flores without speaking.

Flores smiled amiably. 'Oh come on, my friend, you were speaking in Spanish, how could I not overhear. And what does it matter? I have a wife, too.' He chuckled. 'Actually I have three. And many children. It is good for a man to have children, don't you think? So that when you finally go to meet your maker, you leave something behind.'

'And?' said Mendoza quietly.

'And?' repeated Flores, still smiling.

'You've offered me the carrot, and I told you to stick your carrot where the sun don't shine. So now you're going to offer me the stick.'

'The stick?'

'The stick. You're going to tell me that if I don't help you, if I don't let you get away, then you'll kill my family. You'll kill everyone who loves me. And then you'll kill me.'

'You have a very vivid imagination, Agent Mendoza.'

Mendoza stood up, pulled his gun from its holster and pointed it at Flores's face. His finger tightened on the trigger but Flores showed not a trace of fear. 'Tell me what you're going to do,' hissed Mendoza. 'Say the fucking words.'

Flores smiled as if he didn't have a care in the world. 'I don't have to, my friend,' he said. 'You've already done it for me.'

Mendoza stepped forward and whipped the barrel of his pistol across the side of Flores's head. Flores grunted but didn't cry out, and when Mendoza stepped back, Flores was still smiling.

CHAPTER 46

The address that Javier sent to Hirst was close to Wormwood Scrubs prison in Hammersmith, just north of the A40 and around the corner from the Old Oak Primary School. He was tense throughout the drive, constantly checking his mirrors for any sign of a police presence. There was a chance that they wouldn't realise that the window had been shot out, but there would be no mistaking the bullet holes in the side door. When he arrived, there were three vehicles waiting for him: two SUVs, one white and one green, and a Mercedes with tinted windows. There were houses only on one side of the road and the other wasn't well covered by street lights, so it was as good a place as any for the meet.

He parked at the rear of the convoy and climbed out. He couldn't see who was in the Mercedes, but as he reached it the rear door opened. 'Get in,' said a voice.

Hirst bent down to look inside. There was one man in the back, and two in the front. They were all in their thirties, well muscled with short haircuts and hard eyes, but he placed them more as bouncers than soldiers.

The man in the back had a thick moustache and jet-black hair and had the look of a young Freddie Mercury, with slab-like teeth that his lips seemed to have trouble sliding across. 'You're Marty?' he asked. He was wearing a brown leather bomber jacket and as he offered a handshake, Hirst saw the butt of a gun in a holster under his left shoulder.

'Yeah,' said Hirst. He shook the hand. The man had a tight, firm grip.

'I'm Dean.' He had a north of England accent. Manchester, maybe. 'Dean Barrett.'

'Good to meet you.'

Barrett introduced the two men in the front of the Mercedes. 'This is Simon, we call him Simple, but he isn't really. Andy's driving. Andy Pandy we call him.'

Andy shook hands with Hirst.

'How much have you been told?' Hirst asked Barrett.

'That you're in charge and when you say jump we ask how high.'

'And you're okay with that?'

Barrett shrugged. 'Javier said you're former SAS and that you know your stuff.'

'Did he now?' Hirst wasn't happy at Javier broadcasting his CV but knew there was nothing he could do about it. Javier called all the shots. Literally and figuratively.

'We're up for whatever you need,' said Barrett.

'You're being well paid?'

'It's not always about the money with Javier. It's about staying in his good books. He's not a man you say no to, am I right?'

Hirst nodded. 'I hear you. So how many men do you have and what skill sets do they have?'

'There's nine of us in total. Most of the others work for a security company I run and they're all dead solid and as hard as nails. Simon and Andy have been with me for going on ten years. I'd trust them with my life.'

'Any former military?'

'Two of the guys are former Irish special forces.'

'Ranger Wing?' asked Hirst.

Barrett nodded. 'That's it. They're good in a scrap so long as they don't put their balaclavas on the wrong way round.' He started to laugh but stopped when he saw the look of disgust on Hirst's face. 'Sorry, just trying to lighten the moment,' he said.

'Yeah, well I need to be brought up to speed, not entertained,' said Hirst. 'Who else has military experience?'

'Two of the guys in the front car were squaddies. Both did tours in Iraq but they were there after all the shit had happened.

One of the guys in the second SUV is a former Para. Jimmy. Jimmy the Para they call him. He's a weapons expert. He took a group of us over to Croatia boar-hunting and he obviously knows his stuff. We did some small arms fire while we there and he's shit hot.'

'And what ordnance do you have?'

'Ordnance?'

'Weapons. What are you carrying?'

Barrett opened his jacket and Hirst had a better look at the gun in the holster. A Glock. 'We've all got handguns. We've a few shotguns, and an Uzi. The Ranger Wing guys have got some bigger guns. I don't know what they are. Hecklers maybe. And Jimmy the Para has a Kalashnikov.'

'A Kalashnikov? Are you serious?'

'It's a souvenir, Jimmy said. God knows how he got it back. But he's got the ammo and everything.'

'What about comms?'

'Comms?' repeated Barrett.

'Communications,' said Hirst.

Barrett pulled a face. 'We've been using our phones. WhatsApp, mainly. WhatsApp is encrypted so it's safe, right? For calls and messages.'

'Okay,' said Hirst. 'And what about protection? Kevlar vests and that?'

'A few of the guys have the anti-stab vests they use on the doors, but that's about it.' He saw the look of concern on Hirst's face. 'Is that a problem?'

'I'd prefer us all to be kitted out in Kevlar, but it's not the end of the world.' He rubbed his nose with the back of his hand as he considered his options. His last crew had been mainly highly trained former American special forces personnel, and they had failed miserably. He couldn't see how this rag-tag group of misfits would fare any better, but beggars couldn't be choosers and he would just have to make the best of what he had been given. 'Okay, here's what's going to happen,' he said. 'Jimmy the Para and the two former Rangers are with me. We're the A team. You run the B team. I'll brief you and you brief them.'

Barrett nodded. 'No problem.'

'The DEA jet is due to land about 9 a.m. this morning,' said Hirst. 'Whatever happens, the target must not get onto that plane.'

'We'll do whatever has to be done,' said Barrett.

CHAPTER 47

The door buzzed and Eric's gun was in his hand immediately. 'It'll be the pizzas,' said Sally. Eric went over to the window and checked outside. There was a pizza delivery bike parked by the kerb. He nodded and motioned for her to get the door. Butler also had his gun out and he tip-toed across the floor with her. She went to the intercom unit and picked up the handset. 'Pizza delivery,' said a man's voice.

'I'll be right down,' she said. She replaced the handset.

'Okay, you go down and get the pizzas, but stay inside the building,' said Eric. 'Stay in the shadows, don't show your face. Sam and I will stay here but at the first sign of any trouble we'll be down.'

'It's just the pizza guy,' said Sally, opening the door.

'I hear you,' said Eric. 'But better safe than sorry.'

Sally went downstairs and opened the front door. A young Asian man in a parka and a red crash helmet was standing on the pavement with a stack of pizza boxes and a carrier bag of soft drinks. Sally looked over his shoulder. A middle-aged woman was walking by with a Labrador on a lead, and on the other side of the street a young couple were walking hand in hand.

Sally gave the guy £40 and told him to keep the change. She closed the door and went upstairs. Eric and Butler put their guns away. 'Excellent,' said Eric, taking one of the boxes. He nodded at Butler. 'Take a pizza through to Luis.'

Butler took one of the boxes and two cans of Coke and headed to the back bedroom.

Eric sat down on the sofa and opened his box. He grinned down at the pizza, grabbed a slice and took a bite. Sally put the rest of the boxes and the soft drinks onto the coffee table. She hadn't realised how hungry she was. She grabbed a slice and wolfed it down. Tim grinned at her. 'What?' she said.

His grin widened. 'Nothing,' he said.

'I'm hungry.'

'Clearly.'

Tim went into the kitchen and returned with plates and pieces of kitchen roll. Eric had already eaten his first slice and had started on the second. Butler returned and dropped down on the sofa next to Eric before helping himself to a slice.

'How's Flores?' asked Eric.

'He's developed a bruise on the side of his head,' said Butler. 'He says he bumped into a wall.'

'Is he okay?'

'He is now,' said Butler.

'Luis hit him?'

Butler held up his hands. 'The man says he bumped into a wall, who am I to argue with that? Anyway, he seems happy enough. Luis cut his ties so that he can eat.'

'He can stay like that so long as he behaves himself,' said Eric. He popped the tab on a can of Coke and drank thirstily.

'So Flores is Mexican, right?' asked Sally.

'As Mexican as tacos, tequila and mariachi.'

'But I thought it was the Colombians who ran the drug trade?'

Eric nodded. 'It used to be, but since the death of Pablo Escobar, the Colombians have lost their fire. The Mexicans were the junior partners but in recent years the DEA has named them as the number one criminal drug threat to the United States. Colombia still produces most of the world's cocaine but it's the Mexican cartels who are doing the lion's share of the trafficking. And the Mexicans have been buying coca plantations and importing their own engineers and agronomists to boost productivity. At the same time they've been forming links with criminal groups across South America.'

'And the Colombians have just let them do it?'

'Like I said, the Colombians have lost their fire. Partly because of what happened to Escobar and his people. And partly because of the political pressure the president has been putting on the Colombian government. And the Mexicans have raised murder and torture to a whole new level. They don't just kill the bad guys, they kill their families and everyone who loves them. The Colombians didn't shy away from killing cops or soldiers, but the Mexicans have been carrying out massacres wholesale. The official death toll in the drug wars in Mexico last year was thirty thousand, with another thirty thousand missing. They've taken that level of violence into Colombia and I can tell you that if they get a foothold in your country the first thing they'll do is export their violence here.' Eric took a big bite of his slice, smearing tomato sauce across his upper lip. 'That's why catching Flores is such a big deal,' he continued. 'It stops his cartel dead in their tracks here, but we can chop the whole head off the snake with what Flores has already told us. Assuming he does cooperate, the cartel will be finished, pretty much.'

'Has he said he will cooperate?' asked Tim.

'Not yet. But he's seen how much the cartel wants him dead so he knows he doesn't have any choice. If he refuses to help us then he'll be tried and convicted and there isn't a prison in the States where the cartel can't get to him. Plus he has a wife and kids. And a mistress and more kids. Brothers, sisters, aunts, uncles. His father passed away but his mother is alive. They became at risk the moment Flores was arrested, and he knows that. What happened at the house in Hampstead has shown him that he has only one way out. And that's to cooperate with us.'

'And if he does?' asked Sally. 'What then?'

'We'll put him and his family in witness protection. New names, new lives; he'll have to spend the rest of his life looking over his shoulder but it's better than the alternative. And the more of the cartel he helps us put away, the safer he'll be.'

Tim took a sip of Coke. 'And what about the guys who attacked us in Hampstead? They didn't look Mexican.'

'Martinez buys in expertise when he needs it,' said Eric. 'In Mexico he's been hiring former Mexican special forces by the boat-load. Cops, too, if they want to switch sides, but he prefers cops to stay on the job so he can get inside information. In the States he pays a small fortune in bribes to DEA agents, cops, judges, customs agents; anyone he finds useful he pays off. He's been hiring former Navy SEALs and Delta Force guys; he pays top dollar and there are plenty of men around who aren't fussy about who they kill.'

'You think they were Americans?' asked Tim. 'The guys who attacked the house in Hampstead?'

'The gun your girlfriend grabbed suggests so,' said Eric.

'I'm not his girlfriend,' said Sally quickly.

Eric held his pizza over his plate. 'I just assumed . . .' He shrugged. 'Sorry. No offence.'

'We used to go out,' said Tim, but stopped speaking when Sally flashed him a warning look.

'Any relationship Tim and I might have had isn't really the issue,' said Sally. 'What matters is that we get through this without any more casualties.'

'We're on the same page there,' said Eric.

'So why don't we get Tim to contact his bosses at the Met and get some ARVs over here?'

'ARVs?' repeated Eric.

'Armed response vehicles,' said Tim. 'With specialist firearms officers.'

'We need to keep this low profile,' said Eric. 'The fewer people who know where we are and what our plans are, the better.'

'But if they do find us, and they come with reinforcements, we'll be outgunned,' said Sally. 'What do we have, three handguns and two of the HKs we took from them?'

'They don't know where we are,' said Eric. 'But the more people we tell, the more likely it becomes that they will know. So let's just leave things as they are, shall we?' He took another large bite of his pizza and chewed happily.

CHAPTER 48

Hirst studied the iPad on his lap. 'Turn right ahead,' he said. He was in the front passenger seat of a white BMW SUV that was being driven by Jimmy the Para. Jimmy was in his forties and had done fifteen years with the Paras, including spells in Afghanistan and Iraq. He was a chain smoker and stank of stale tobacco, and his teeth were a yellowish brown. He was a little over six feet tall and broad shouldered, probably too big to have ever made it to the SAS but the perfect build for a Para. He was taciturn, which suited Hirst, and as Barrett had said, he had a Kalashnikov and several magazines. Hirst had checked the weapon and it had clearly been well cared for. Jimmy was also well presented, wearing a black leather jacket over a blue sweater, dark jeans and brown boots.

Sitting in the back of the vehicle were the two former Ranger Wing soldiers. Sean O'Rourke was from Dublin, Pat Walsh was from the opposite side of the country, Galway. O'Rourke was in his late thirties, Walsh was about five years younger. In Hirst's experience Irish special forces weren't that special – hardly surprising when the Ranger Wing could only draw on a military population of fewer than nine thousand men – but O'Rourke and Walsh seemed to know their stuff. They both had Glocks in underarm holsters and Hirst had transferred three HK416 carbines from his Outlander to the BMW. The former Rangers had a nylon bag containing HK MP5s and 9mm ammunition, but Hirst figured they were underpowered for the job they had to do so he planned to give them to the junior members of the crew. All three of the men claimed familiarity with the 416, though Jimmy had made it clear he wanted to stick with his Kalashnikov.

They had listened as Hirst outlined what he planned to do, and they hadn't expressed any reservations about what was expected of them.

Jimmy made the turn and Hirst scanned the sides of the road. He saw the Ford Explorer first, and then the Volkswagen. He pointed the vehicles out. 'They'll be in one of the houses close by, but there's no way of knowing which,' he said. 'Find somewhere to park that gives us a decent view of the cars.'

Jimmy found a parking space and reversed into it.

'Now what?' asked O'Rourke.

'All we can do is wait,' said Hirst.

'That's all well and good, but four grown men sitting in a car for hours is going to look suspicious, isn't it?'

Hirst nodded. 'Any thoughts how we could be less conspicuous?'

O'Rourke grimaced. 'This time of night, we don't have many options, do we?'

'Not really,' said Hirst. 'Maybe we walk around. But that might attract attention, too. And we can hardly walk around with the guns.'

'I'm thinking home invasion,' said O'Rourke. He gestured at the line of houses to his left. 'We pick a ground-floor flat with a view of the vehicles and we move in. They'll be one or two-bedroom places, so I reckon we'll be unlucky to get more than two occupants. We tie them up and settle down for the night.'

Hirst nodded. 'That should work. What do you think, guys?' In the SAS it was traditional to talk through an operation at the planning stage and give every member of the team a chance to throw in ideas and suggestions, and express any reservations up front. It was referred to as Chinese parliament and was a way of building team spirit.

'Sounds good,' said Walsh.

'I don't want witnesses blabbing to Five-O,' said Jimmy.

'We just make sure our faces are covered,' said Hirst. 'We can tie, gag and blindfold them. It's no biggie.' The three men nodded in agreement. 'Right, let's get it done,' Hirst said.

CHAPTER 49

There was one slice of pizza left and Eric looked at Sally and Tim. 'Either of you guys want that?'

'I'm good,' said Sally. She turned her wrist to look at her watch and shook her head when she realised yet again that she wasn't wearing one.

Tim had seen what she did and he grinned. 'I'll buy you another one,' he said.

'Another what?' asked Eric. He bit into his pizza.

'It's a private joke,' said Tim.

'Eric, what happens to Tim and me after you put Flores on the plane?' asked Sally.

'We take Flores back to the States and you get on with your life.'

'You mean we go back to work as if nothing has happened?'

Eric wiped his mouth with the back of his hand. 'I'm assuming your bosses will want an extensive debriefing but other than that, sure. You've had one hell of a day but that's because the cartel are after Flores. Once Flores leaves the UK, the heat will be off.'

'Will it, though?' asked Tim, leaning forward and resting his elbows on his knees. 'They know who Sally is, and they know where she lives. She killed three of their people. How do you know they're just going to let that be?'

'The guys that attacked us were paid professionals. It wasn't personal. I'm pretty sure the cartel will realise that.'

'Eric, I'm not convinced that we can rely on "pretty sure" where Sally's life is concerned. We've all seen those documentaries that say how vicious the cartels can be. What if this Martinez decides he wants revenge?'

'It's unlikely,' said Eric. 'He's going to be more concerned about the damage that Flores is going to do. Once Flores opens up, Martinez will be behind bars for the rest of his life.'

'Assuming you can get him.'

'Oh, we'll get him, you can be sure of that,' said Eric. 'The Mexicans hate Martinez as much as we do.' He took a swig of Coke. 'Martinez is going to have too much on his plate to worry about you, trust me.'

CHAPTER 50

The door intercom buzzed and Peter McKee looked over at his wife. 'You're not expecting anyone are you, Maggie?'

His wife looked at her watch. 'It's after midnight. Barbara said she might pop around but she didn't confirm and she wouldn't come at this late hour, obviously.'

They were watching *Breaking Bad* on Netflix. It was the second time for them both but the first time they had binge-watched and they had forgotten most of it. Peter picked up the remote and pressed pause, then stood up and went to the hallway. The intercom buzzed again. 'I'm coming, I'm coming,' he said.

'If it's one of those students on the top floor, don't let them in,' called Maggie. 'They don't have enough keys, they need to talk to the landlord. They're ringing half a dozen times a day.'

'I will,' said Peter, but he knew in his heart he wouldn't. It was easier just to press the button to let them in rather than explain why he was refusing to help. Plus the mail was held in the communal hallway in unlocked pigeonholes and the last thing he needed was a bunch of angry students making his life a misery. He picked up the receiver. 'Yes?'

'Courier delivery,' said a man. 'Sorry about the late hour, the traffic's been a bitch.'

'It's almost half past twelve,' said Peter.

'Yes I realise that and I apologise but if I don't make all my deliveries tonight they cut my pay.'

'Are you expecting a delivery?' he called to his wife.

'A couple of books from Amazon,' said Maggie. 'Sainsbury's are delivering tomorrow. Let me know if you want to add something.'

'We could do with some more of that Prosecco if they still have it on special offer,' said Peter. 'But this is a delivery now.'

'Well it could be Amazon, but they really shouldn't be delivering this late.'

Peter pressed the button to open the front door.

'Make sure you tell him not to deliver this late in future. We could have been asleep,' called Maggie.

'I will do,' said Peter.

There was a double knock on the door and he opened it. There was a large man standing with his back to him, but as he opened the door the man moved, grabbing Peter by the throat and pushing him back into the room. He tried to shout but he couldn't even breathe. Two more men appeared, both wearing ski masks. They hurried into the hall and pushed their way into the sitting room. He heard his wife gasp and then he was pushed to the floor, face down. 'Please, take whatever you want, just don't hurt us,' he managed to gasp before something was shoved into his mouth. His hands were taped roughly behind his back and more tape was used around his mouth, then a strip of tape was plastered across his eyes. 'Listen to me and listen to me good,' said a voice next to his left ear. 'You stay quiet and give us no trouble, and we'll be gone in a few hours,' said the man, with what sounded like an Irish accent. 'But you fuck us around and you and your lovely wife will be heading to the emergency room.'

Peter tried to speak but the gag made it impossible to do anything but grunt.

He was lifted up and carried along the hallway to the bedroom, then he was thrown onto the bed. A minute or so later something was tossed next to him. It was his wife and he assumed she was bound and gagged the same as he was. He inched across the bed to her, then rolled over so that his back was towards her. He reached out with his hands and managed to find her arms. He ran his fingers down her arms until he found her hands. She gave him a gentle squeeze and relief washed over him. She was alive. And if the man was telling the truth, in a few hours it would all be over, whatever it was.

CHAPTER 51

Hirst was sitting in an armchair. He figured it was where the woman of the house usually sat because there was a bag of knitting at the side and a magazine rack full of copies of *Hello!*. His phone rang. It was Javier. He didn't want to have a conversation in front of O'Rourke, Walsh and Jimmy the Para, so he walked into the hallway. The occupants of the flat had been bound and gagged and put in the back bedroom, with pillow cases over their heads. The rest of Hirst's team had followed them into the flat and were now in the kitchen.

'Yes,' said Hirst, taking the call.

'Where are you?'

'Notting Hill. We've taken over an apartment that gives us a clear view of their vehicles.'

'What do you intend to do?'

'We might be able to get Flores as they're loading him into the vehicle,' said Hirst. 'If not, we can follow them to the airport and get them on the way.'

'Flores must not get on that plane, you understand that?'

'You've made that clear several times, Javier.'

'And I trust I have made it clear what will happen if you fail.'

'I'm doing my best.'

'Then I hope your best is good enough.'

'I want to speak to my wife and daughter.'

'That's not possible at the moment.'

'Why not?'

'I am not with them. When I am, I will arrange a call.'

'Are they okay?'

'Yes, they're okay and they'll stay that way so long as you do as you are told.'

Javier ended the call, leaving Hirst grinding his teeth in frustration.

He walked down the hallway to the kitchen where the six men there were helping themselves to the fridge-freezer and were in the process of frying eggs and bacon and making toast. When they had first gone into the flat they had grabbed bottles of wine from the fridge but Hirst had vetoed alcohol to much swearing and grumbling. He'd told them to take off their shoes and boots and to cut down the noise to a minimum.

'All right lads?' he asked and was answered with a few grunts and nods. He grabbed a couple of bacon rashers and slapped them between two slices of bread. He didn't have much of an appetite but he knew that his body needed fuel. He made himself a cup of Gold Blend coffee and took it and his sandwich back to the sitting room.

'Problem?' asked Jimmy the Para.

'Nah, all good,' said Hirst, sitting down. He picked up his iPad and he ate his sandwich as he watched the two blinking dots.

CHAPTER 52

Giles Pritchard's mobile rang and he looked at the screen. It was Liz Bailey. He took the call. 'Giles, I thought you'd want to know straight away that GCHQ have managed to get a match on three phones that were at the Hirst house in Hereford and at the location where Mrs Hirst called her husband.'

'Excellent,' said Pritchard. 'Well done.'

'It gets better,' said Bailey. 'The same two phones are now in a house in Ealing. If we're lucky, that's where Mrs Hirst and her daughter are being held.'

'Some luck would be nice,' said Pritchard. 'I'll talk to the Major; at this stage I'd rather not involve the police. Let me have the address.'

As he scribbled down the address, his office door opened. It was his secretary. 'Is everything okay?' she asked. 'Do you need me for anything?'

'All good,' said Pritchard. 'You really should go home, for a few hours at least. You've been at your desk for almost eighteen hours.' He looked at his watch. 'It's two o'clock.'

'I'm fine,' she said. 'Really. And you've been here longer than me. Is everything okay?' she asked again.

Pritchard nodded. 'We're getting there,' he said. 'Slowly but surely.'

'Is there anything I can do?'

'Just make sure that any calls are put straight through,' he said.

'What about a coffee? And a sandwich?'

'That would be a life-saver,' said Pritchard. As she closed the door, he called Major Gannon on his mobile. The Major answered almost immediately which suggested he wasn't asleep, though most of the special forces people that Pritchard had come across appeared to be able to sleep with one eye open. 'I hope I didn't wake you, Allan,' said Pritchard.

'I'm in my room but not sleeping,' said Gannon. 'What's up?'

'We believe we have the location of Mrs Hirst and her daughter. It looks as if they were kidnapped.'

'Do we know by who?'

'All we have are their phone numbers and GCHQ has them in a single location. A house in Ealing. We're assuming that's where they are holding Mrs Hirst and her daughter.'

'Excellent,' said Gannon.

'I'm going to inform the police but I think things will move faster if we use them as back up and you mount a rescue operation. The police have a lot of procedures to follow so they tend to move slowly and for us, time is of the essence. Do you think you could put together a team?'

'No problem at all,' said the Major. 'We've got men on standby at Wellington Barracks. I'll head over there now and get things started.'

'I'll text you the address,' said Pritchard. 'There's something I need to make you aware of. This evening one of our safe houses was attacked in Hampstead. It was being used to hold a potential informant in a drugs case. The DEA are planning to fly him back to the States. The men who attacked the house seem to be the same ones who hit the house in Wimbledon. Six of them were killed.'

'What? Who killed them?'

'We're not sure. The DEA agents have fled the scene with the informant and haven't been in touch yet.'

'They were armed? The DEA agents?'

'I assume so. I'm playing catch up at the moment. It's all a bit of a mess. We got a call that Sally Page had turned up at the house and we sent Ian Hadley around to collect her. The next thing we hear is that Ian and our colleague Toby Harris and three DEA agents are dead, along with six of the men who attacked the house. The DEA agents have fled with the informant, and we assume have taken Sally with them.'

'So this is obviously connected to what happened in Wimbledon.'

'I would say so,' said Pritchard. 'It looks as if the attack in Wimbledon was an attempt to get the location of the Hampstead safe house so that they could rescue the informant.'

'And what do the DEA have to say for themselves?'

'At the moment, not much. We've put in calls to their New York and Washington offices but they're shut and no one has called us back. But if Marty Hirst is behind these killings, we need to talk to his wife, and soon.'

'I'm on it,' said Gannon.

CHAPTER 53

Sally yawned and covered her mouth. 'Sorry,' she said. 'I'm exhausted.'

'You've had one hell of a day,' said Tim. He looked over at Eric who was dozing on the sofa with his feet on the coffee table. 'You should get some sleep if you plan to go with them to the airport this morning.' Butler was asleep in an armchair, his head back with a dribble of saliva running down his chin.

'Do you think we've got a choice?' she asked, keeping her voice low so as not to wake the DEA agents. 'I think they're not going to let us out of their sight until Flores is on the plane.'

'Are you saying we're prisoners?'

'You know, I'm not sure. The only way to know is to insist that we leave.'

Eric opened one eye. 'If either of you make a move for that door, I'll put a bullet in your leg.' He laughed at the looks of astonishment that flashed across their faces and swung his feet off the coffee table. 'I'm joking, guys,' he said.

'I knew that,' said Tim.

'I wasn't sure,' said Sally.

'The thing is, we are short handed and there's no way we can bring in extra manpower before the plane lands so you'd really be doing us a solid by helping out. Plus the way the bad guys have been chasing Sally here all over London, she's probably better off staying with us.'

'I'd like to see this through to the end,' said Sally.

'And I'm not letting you out of my sight,' said Tim.

Eric rooted through one of the pizza boxes and pulled out a

cold slice. 'Why don't you two catch some shut-eye. There's a bedroom spare.'

'What time are we heading to the airport?'

Eric looked at his watch. 'Half eight, I guess. Just over four and a half hours from now.'

Sally looked at Tim. 'Sleep sounds like a good idea,' she said. 'You okay to share the room?'

'Sure, why not?' asked Sally.

Tim shrugged. 'You know . . .'

She shook her head. 'We're not teenagers, Tim.'

Tim held up his hands in surrender. Sally laughed and pushed herself up off the sofa before heading down the hallway. As Tim followed her, Eric leered, winked, and threw him a mock salute. 'We're just friends,' Tim protested, but that just made the American laugh out loud.

CHAPTER 54

Major Gannon looked at his watch. There were four men in the room with him and there were two more on the way. He grunted impatiently. He was in a ground-floor room at Wellington Barracks, just three hundred yards from Buckingham Palace. The barracks were the base of the five regiments of the Queen's Household Division – the Irish, Scots, Welsh, Grenadier and Coldstream Guards – who were tasked with protecting the royal palaces. The SAS used the barracks on an ad hoc basis, and there had been two members of the Regiment there when he arrived. He had called another two troopers who were due to be on duty at the Westfield shopping mall in White City that morning.

Four would probably be enough to take the house, but he needed drivers and had been allowed to requisition two members of the Coldstream Guards. The guardsmen could barely contain their enthusiasm at being involved in an SAS operation and were sitting together at the back of the room, dressed in casual jackets and jeans. The SAS troopers already there were Kevin 'Burt' Reynolds and Ricky 'Mustard' Coleman. Gannon knew Reynolds of old – he had been with the Regiment for close to ten years – but it was the first time Gannon had met Coleman, who had only been with the SAS for two months. Coleman was preparing for his first Syrian posting with the Regiment and was growing a beard and spending hours a day on a tanning bed so that he would blend in with the locals as soon as he arrived.

Gannon heard footsteps in the corridor outside, then Mike Travis and Chris Wheeler appeared. Travis was big for an SAS trooper, almost six feet six tall, though he was spindly thin with arms that always appeared slightly too long for his jackets. He had acquired the nickname Thrombo on SAS Selection, after one of the directing staff had called him a slow-moving clot. Wheeler had been given the kinder nickname of Three. Both men were SAS veterans, in their late thirties with ice-cold eyes but easy smiles, always ready with a joke but more than capable of carrying out any task they were given. 'Sorry about the short notice,' said Gannon. 'It's all kick-bollocks-scramble.'

'Not a problem, boss,' said Wheeler.

Wheeler and Travis had been tasked with providing undercover protection at the Westfield shopping centre after MI5 had picked up chatter that a group of home-grown jihadists were planning an attack there. They spent the day wandering around the mall with Glocks in underarm holsters and were both keen to get involved with real work.

'Right, let's get to it,' he said. 'Gather round.'

The two guardsmen came over and Gannon introduced them. 'This is Roger and Luke, they'll be driving. We have a Range Rover and a Volvo. Thrombo and Three will be with me in the Range Rover. Luke will be driving us. Burt and Mustard will be with Roger in the Volvo. We'll be driving to the target house in Ealing. Luke and Roger will stay with the vehicles while we do the necessary. When we come out, Thrombo and I will take the hostages to the Range Rover; Three, Burt and Mustard go to the Volvo. We then return to Wellington Barracks. Any questions so far?'

The two guardsmen were clearly perplexed at the use of nick-names, but they both shook their heads.

Gannon spread a map out on a table. He had marked the house that Pritchard had identified, and marked a route from where they were. The six men leant over to get a better look as Gannon ran his finger along the roads leading to the target. He also had printouts taken from Google Earth and Google Maps, showing a satellite view of the house and its surroundings, and a photograph of the front of the building.

The house was in the middle of a terrace, with a small yard

behind that led to an alley. 'We have two small shaped charges and we'll go in front and back simultaneously. We have flashbangs but we'll only use them if we have to.'

'Night vision?' asked Travis.

'There should be enough light getting in from the street,' said Gannon. 'Now so far as hostiles go, we haven't the time to mount any sort of surveillance operation so we don't know how many are in there. We're told that there were probably three men involved in the abduction but there could be more or fewer in there now. The hostages are Amanda Hirst and her daughter, Sophie. Sophie is six years old. So any male on the premises is to be regarded as hostile.' He had a head-and-shoulders photograph of Mrs Hirst, taken from her passport application, and he tapped it with his finger.

The four men nodded.

'As soon as we have the hostages, we're out of there. No hanging about.'

'What about the police?' asked Coleman.

'They're holding back several streets away,' said Gannon. 'As soon as we move out, they will move in and secure the location. So, any more questions? Speak now or forever hold your peace.'

'Are we looking to be taking prisoners, boss?' asked Wheeler.

'It'd be nice if we had at least one prisoner to interrogate, but our prime mission is to get the hostages.' He checked that they were all happy, then he nodded. 'Right, let's get this done.'

CHAPTER 55

The man was wearing a ski mask but Sally could see the grin on his face as he levelled the gun at her face. She looked around frantically for something she could use to defend herself but the room was bare. There was no furniture to hide behind, nothing she could grab to throw at her attacker. She opened her mouth to cry out but she couldn't breathe; it felt as if there was a steel band around her chest. The gun was pointing directly at her face now and the man's finger was tightening on the trigger. She finally had enough air in her lungs and she started to scream.

'Sally!' She woke to see Tim looking down at her. He was shaking her gently.

'I'm okay, I'm okay,' she said, gasping for breath.

'You were trembling and moaning.'

'It was a nightmare, that's all.' She took a deep breath and let it out slowly. 'I'm okay.'

They were in the small second bedroom in the Notting Hill flat. There was a double bed and they had both collapsed onto it fully clothed and been asleep within seconds. She blinked her eyes and tried to focus, then raised her left arm and cursed when she realised yet again that she wasn't wearing a watch. 'What time is it?'

'Just after five,' said Tim. He had taken off his jacket and trousers and hung them on the back of an armchair.

'You couldn't get me a glass of water, could you?'

Tim grinned. 'Remind me again of what your last slave died of?'

She laughed. 'I'm sorry.'

'You've been saying that a lot today.' He ruffled her hair. 'I'm only joking.' He got up and padded over to the door. Sally couldn't help but smile at the sight of him in his shirt, underpants and socks.

He returned after a couple of minutes with a glass of water. He sat down on the bed and gave it to her. 'The DEA guys are playing poker,' he said.

'Do you think we're safe here?' she asked, sitting up.

'I think if we weren't we'd know already. It's not as if they've been hanging about, is it?'

Sally sipped her water. 'I don't know why they just don't call in the police,' she said. 'They could flood the place with armed cops and take him to the airport in an armed convoy.'

'After what happened in Hampstead? They presumably think they can't trust anyone. I mean, it was supposed to be a safe house, right? Three of their men died. I doubt they'll be trusting anyone for a while.'

She took another sip of water and nodded. 'I suppose so.'

'I guess this is the life you wanted, right? When you joined MI5?'

'Hardly,' she said. 'This isn't what MI5 officers do. They handle intelligence, they mount surveillance, they don't go around shooting bad guys and causing mayhem.'

'Well, you seem to be a natural.'

She grinned. 'I'll take that as a compliment.'

'Seriously, what you did in the kitchen, when that guy was shooting at us – you were epic.'

'I wasn't even thinking.'

'Your instincts were perfect. I froze. I seriously froze. My mind just went blank. But you?' He shook his head. 'You were awesome. You grabbed the kettle, threw it at the guy and jumped through the window. Then you shot him and the other guy. And I still hadn't moved.'

'I was lucky, right? It could so easily have ended badly.'

'No, you did exactly the right thing. If you'd frozen the way I did then we'd both be dead. If you'd tried to run, he'd have shot you in the back.'

She put her glass on the bedside table.

'Are you okay?' he asked.

'I guess so.'

'What was the nightmare about?'

She flashed him a thin smile. 'A guy was about to shoot me. You don't have to be Freud to work out what that's about.'

'After this is all over, you won't have any problem with promotion,' he said. 'They'll probably give you a medal.'

'You don't get medals in MI5,' she said. She looked into his eyes. She'd almost forgotten how brown they were. Almost black. It was so easy to get lost in them.

'You know you saved my life, right? There's a Chinese proverb that says if you save someone's life you're then responsible for them forever more.'

'I can live with that.'

'You're sure?'

She kept looking into his eyes as she nodded. 'I'm sure.' She reached up and stroked his cheek. 'You can kiss me if you want.'

His eyes narrowed a fraction. 'I'm not after a pity fuck,' he said, and she couldn't tell if he was joking or not.

She continued to look into his eyes and stroke his cheek. 'First of all, I didn't say anything about a fuck. And second of all, there's no pity involved. I miss you. I haven't been with anyone else since we split up.'

'Me neither,' he said. 'How sad am I?'

'I'm sorry.'

'Again with the sorry.'

'Just kiss me.'

'Yes, ma'am.' He leaned forward and kissed her, slowly and softly at first. She moaned and kissed him back, slipping her hand behind his neck. She'd forgotten how good he tasted. She brought her other hand up and caressed the back of his head. He was the one who broke away first and she could see there were tears in his eyes.

'You broke my fucking heart,' he whispered.

'I know.' She kissed him again, on the lips, then pulled back. 'A fuck isn't out of the question.'

He laughed.

'And it wouldn't be a pity fuck.'

'What sort of fuck would it be?'

She laughed and kissed him again, then rolled him over so that he was lying on his back and she was on top of him, gripping him with her knees. She pulled off her pullover and tossed it onto the chair. She dropped down and kissed him again and could feel him growing hard underneath her. 'I fucking love you,' he said.

'I know,' she said.

This time he rolled her over so that he was on top and he took off his shirt as she pulled off her Wranglers. She raised her eyebrows at his chest and six-pack. 'When did that happen?' she asked, gesturing at his abs.

'I've been in the gym a lot,' he said. 'It's not as if I've had much else to do.'

'Looking good,' she said. She threw her jeans on the chair then pulled him down and kissed him again hard as he ground himself against her.

CHAPTER 56

The black Range Rover pulled up at the side of the road. Luke was driving, the Major was in the front passenger seat and Travis and Wheeler were in the back. Gannon took an Airwave radio from his pocket and spoke to the police commander who was parked up a hundred yards away with an armed response vehicle and a Mercedes Sprinter van belonging to the Territorial Support Group, the Met's heavy mob. Two ambulances were also on standby. The Major told the commander that his people were in place and that they intended to move in within the next fifteen minutes.

The Volvo parked a short distance away. Reynolds and Coleman got out and walked over to the Range Rover. The Major, Travis and Wheeler joined them on the pavement and the Major opened the car door. There were five black nylon holdalls in a line. The men took one each. The Major closed the door and checked his watch. 'We go in in exactly fourteen minutes,' he said. He looked at Coleman. 'You listen for our charge, you go in immediately.'

'Got it, boss,' said Coleman. He and Reynolds walked away, towards the alley that led to the rear of the terrace.

Gannon nodded at Travis and Wheeler, and the three men headed for the house. There were lights on in the downstairs room, which was good news and bad news. It meant that the house was occupied but it also meant that at least one of the men inside was close to the front door and they would have to keep any noise to an absolute minimum. There was a tiny garden that had been paved over and was now used as a storage area for rubbish bins. The Major kept checking his watch as if that would make the time pass more quickly. It didn't. The minutes crawled by.

Eventually there were two minutes to go. He nodded at Travis, who knelt down and unzipped his holdall. He took out a wooden frame, about twelve inches square, onto which had been taped C4 explosive. The shaped charge was designed to blow out a lock, as opposed to the large version that the SAS often used, which would take out a complete door. There were adhesive strips on one side of the frame and Travis peeled off the protective cover and pressed it around the lock. The detonator was kept separately and he inserted it into one side of the charge, then ran the wires out so that he could get six feet away. He took his Glock from his holster with his right hand and held the detonator in his left, then nodded at the Major to show that he was ready.

The Major and Wheeler opened their holdalls and took out their guns, CQB carbines manufactured by Colt Canada. The guns had ten-inch barrels and telescoping stocks which made them perfect for close protection work and room clearing, and they had replaced the MP5 submachine guns that the SAS used to use. The carbines had cylindrical suppressors on the ends of their barrels. They wouldn't make the weapons silent but they would cut down on a lot of the noise. Both men had flashbang grenades and they shoved one into each pocket of their jackets.

Gannon took a final look at his watch and then nodded at Travis. Travis flashed the Major a tight smile, turned his head away from the door and pressed the trigger. There was a loud bang and a small cloud of white smoke and when they looked back the door was hanging on its hinges. Almost immediately he heard a muffled bang from the rear of the house.

The Major kicked the door, hard, and it fell back with the sound of splintering wood. He took three quick steps into the hall and turned to the left. He had the CQB up to his shoulder and his finger on the trigger. He saw movement, then a man appeared, holding a handgun. The Major fired twice, a double tap to the chest. As the man fell to the ground, Gannon stepped into the room to give Wheeler a clear view of the hallway. He kept his gun to his shoulder as he swept the room with his eyes. 'Clear!' he shouted.

He heard two shots from the kitchen and turned back to the door.

Wheeler was moving down the hallway.

The Major headed out of the sitting room. There was a body on the floor by the kitchen door. Reynolds was in the middle of the kitchen, his carbine up to his shoulder. 'Clear!' shouted Reynolds. Wheeler had paused and was swinging his carbine around.

There were stairs to the right. Two bodies accounted for and at least one more still in the house. Wheeler took a step towards the stairs but the Major stopped him with a hiss. Gannon would never ask anyone to do something he wouldn't do himself and this was very much his operation. He put his foot on the first step and started up, keeping close to the wall to minimise any noise. The stairs were carpeted and in good shape so he made no noise as he ascended.

Wheeler had moved along the hallway so that he could cover the upper landing. Reynolds followed the Major upstairs, keeping plenty of distance between them.

If there was anyone upstairs they would have been certain to have heard the shaped charges going off and the gunshots. There hadn't been any shots from the upper floor so the Major hoped that Mrs Hirst and her child were okay.

He saw movement at the top of the stairs and his finger tightened on his trigger but he couldn't get a clear shot. Wheeler clearly didn't have a problem acquiring a target and fired twice. The two shots were followed almost immediately by a loud groan and a man pitched forward, a handgun clattering to the floor. Three down. The phone records had spotted three phones but the Major didn't let his guard down. He continued to move up the stairs, with Reynolds close behind. He reached the top. There was a man face down on the landing, a Glock on the carpet by his head. Blood was pooling around his chest. The Major kept low as he ducked around the corner. There was an open door behind the body. He ducked back and looked right. Two more doors in that direction. One was open and seemed to be the bathroom. The other was closed. A second bedroom, maybe.

He motioned for Reynolds to move to the right, then began moving himself, stepping carefully over the body and crouching low to make himself as small a target as possible.

The bedroom door was ajar but all he could see was a dressing table. There was a large mirror but the only thing reflected in it was the blue curtains. Gannon was breathing evenly and steadily, his eyes focused on the end of the barrel and the view beyond. He moved towards the door, took his left hand off the gun and pushed the door gently. It swung open. He took two quick steps forward and turned to his right. There was a figure there. Two figures. In less than a second he had processed the visuals and held his fire. There was a man with a square jaw and a crew cut, holding a gun to the neck of a bound and gagged woman. A child was lying on the bed, also bound and gagged. The woman was struggling but the man had his left arm around her neck. Her fear-filled eyes stared at the Major in horror. He knew he was an intimidating sight with the carbine at his shoulder but the man didn't seem fazed.

'You need to get the fuck out of the room or the woman dies,' said the man, his voice flat and emotionless, almost mechanical. His gun was a Glock 19, the 9mm compact handgun that was favoured by undercover cops and concealed carriers around the world. Not that the model or calibre mattered – that close to the target any gun would fire a fatal shot. The man's finger was already on the trigger. There was no safety on the Glock and a trigger pull of about five pounds. It wouldn't take much for the gun to go off.

'I'm staying right where I am,' said Gannon.

'Then the woman dies.'

'And immediately after that, you die. So the exercise seems a bit pointless, doesn't it?' He was aiming in the centre of the man's face. The man was over six feet tall and Mrs Hirst was a little over five feet two, so there was no way she was ever going to provide complete cover. If this were an exercise in the Killing House back in Hereford, Gannon would have already put two shots in the target's face. But this wasn't the Killing House and it wasn't an exercise.

'What's your name?' asked the Major.

'Zach.'

'American?'

Zach nodded. 'You need to back away now or the woman dies.'

'That's not going to happen, Zach. You former special forces?'

Zach's eyes tightened, then he nodded.

'SEAL? Delta?'

'Delta.'

'Okay, then you know there's no way we just let you walk out of here, not after everything that's happened. We want to keep collateral damage to a minimum, obviously, but there are four men behind me and there's only one way out. Killing Amanda there doesn't make your situation any better. In fact it makes it worse because the moment you pull that trigger I will put two rounds in your head. You have my word on that.'

Zach swallowed. 'So I'm fucked. No matter how this pans out, I'm fucked.'

'No, you're not fucked, Zach. You're in a fucked-up situation but if you handle it right you can get out of it. You haven't killed anyone yet, Zach. The situation is salvageable.'

'Please, let me go,' sobbed Mrs Hirst through the gag. It muffled what she was saying but the Major could pick up the gist. 'I haven't done anything,' she said.

The Major kept his gun trained on Zach's face. He had a clear shot and was reasonably sure that if he pulled the trigger he could take the American out before the American could kill his hostage. But there was no rush, and the longer that Zach talked, the less likely he was to shoot her. 'Amanda, it's okay,' said the Major. 'Zach here doesn't want to hurt anybody. He knows you're a mum and he's got a mum too and he wouldn't want anyone hurting her. He's a professional, he knows that men don't go around killing women and children, isn't that right, Zach?'

Zach didn't answer. Wheeler moved behind the Major and Zach stiffened. His finger tightened on the trigger.

'Give me room here, Chris,' said the Major, without taking his eyes off Zach. 'Everything is okay.'

'Roger that, boss,' said Wheeler, and he backed down the hallway.

'I am so fucked,' said Zach.

'You keep saying that, but it's not true. Just drop your gun and let Mrs Hirst go and we can all walk out of here.'

Zach shook his head. 'You don't understand,' he said. 'The people I work for, they'll kill me in a heartbeat. Me and everyone I love. They're animals.'

'Why would they kill you, Zach?'

'Because I've failed. If I'm still alive at the end of this, they'll come for me and my family.' He gritted his teeth. The Major could see the American's eyes start to mist over.

'Zach, you need to listen to me and listen good,' said Gannon. 'You can walk out of here with us and no one needs to know that you didn't die with everyone else. There are three bodies outside and we can just as easily say that there are four. Your name will be released as one of the casualties.'

'Then what?'

'Then you cooperate, you tell the powers that be what they want to know, and they put you in witness protection.'

'The people I work for, they can find anyone. They can find anyone and they can kill anyone. If I help you, everyone I love will die.'

'It's your best shot, Zach. It's the best way of un-fucking your fucked-up situation. And I know you're looking for a way out because if you weren't you'd already have pulled the trigger. You're a decent guy, Zach, I can tell that. You don't get into Delta by being an arsehole. And we both know Delta don't kill women and children.'

Zach swallowed and his Adam's apple bobbed up and down as if it had a life of its own. He was having trouble swallowing, the Major could see. His mouth had gone dry. But his finger was still tight on the trigger. Gannon had an even clearer shot now that Mrs Hirst had turned her head away from her captor. One squeeze of the trigger and it would be all over.

'Amanda here hasn't done anything to hurt you, Zach. Killing her would be plain wrong. And look at her daughter. Do you want the last memory she has of her mum to be you blowing her head off?'

'I am FUBAR. Fucked up beyond all repair.'

'But killing a mum in front of her kid doesn't make it any less fucked up, Zach. We can get you out of this. We can take you in. Everyone will think you died here.'

'You've done this before?'

The Major nodded. 'Several times,' he said. 'If ever you hear about the SAS being involved in a shootout and that all the bad guys were killed, you can pretty much bet your bottom dollar that at least one of the bad guys was taken to a place of safety. My orders are to take back at least one source, and you're the only one left. Put down your gun and we're out of here.'

Zach tried to swallow again.

'Just put the gun down, Zach.'

'How can I trust you? What's to stop you putting a bullet in my head as soon as I let her go?'

'Zach, I've had a clear shot for the last thirty seconds,' said the Major. 'I could drop you now before you had a chance to pull your trigger. But I don't want you hurt. I want you to walk out of here and help us bring down the bastards who hired you.'

Zach stared at Gannon for several seconds, then slid his finger off the trigger and held the gun up in the air. He released his grip on Mrs Hirst who staggered over to the bed and sat down.

Gannon kept his carbine trained on the American's face. 'Put the gun on the floor, Zach, nice and slowly,' he said.

Zach stared at him but the gun stayed where it was. The Major could see the American's brain racing as it tried to process what was happening. Zach was considering all his options. If he died in that room, it would be over. Over for him, sure, but his family wouldn't be in danger. If he lived, if he cooperated, he would spend the rest of his life in witness protection and his family would be forever in danger. That was what Zach was considering as he held the gun aloft – a quick death now or an uncertain future. Gannon said nothing, but kept his finger on the trigger and the sights aimed at Zach's head. There was nothing else he could say. It was now up to Zach. It was his call.

Zach swallowed again, then slowly nodded. He let the gun swivel in his hand so that he was holding it by the grip with his finger and thumb. The Major relaxed a little but stayed alert. 'We're good,' said Zach, as he bent at the knees and slowly placed the gun on the floor, then he straightened up and put his hands behind his head.

'In you come, Chris,' said the Major, stepping to the side but keeping his weapon aimed at the American.

Wheeler entered the room. He let his carbine hang on its sling as he used a plastic tie to bind Zach's wrists. Only when the American's wrists were bound behind his back did the Major relax. 'It's going to be fine, Zach,' he said. 'We'll take you back to our barracks and we'll take it from there.'

Zach nodded and forced a smile, but he didn't say anything as Wheeler took him out.

The Major let his weapon swing from its sling as he took a Swiss Army knife from his pocket. He flicked the main blade open and used it to cut the duct tape from around Mrs Hirst's wrists. As she untied the gag around her mouth, Gannon cut the tape from her daughter's wrists and ankles. Mrs Hirst threw herself at her daughter and hugged her, then undid her gag. 'You're okay now, Mrs Hirst,' said Gannon. 'Everything is fine.'

Mrs Hirst blinked away her tears. 'No, it's not fine,' she said. 'Where's Marty?'

'We're not sure, we're looking for him now. When was the last time you saw him?'

'A week ago. I spoke to him on the phone when they took us. They're forcing him to do something, but I don't know what it is.'

'Don't worry about it. We're looking for him as we speak.'

'I want to go home,' said Mrs Hirst, holding her daughter to her chest.

'Soon,' said Gannon. 'We're going to take you to our barracks and you can have a shower and we'll see if we can get you some fresh clothes. And we need to talk to you. But as soon as that's done, we'll have you back in Hereford.'

He took out his mobile phone. 'I need you to record a message for him, okay? So that I can show him that you're all right.'

She nodded again and forced a smile.

He pressed the button to record video and nodded for her to speak. 'Marty, honey, we're okay,' she said. She kissed her daughter on the head. 'Sophie's fine, too, though we're a bit shaken up. I'm so sorry what we put you through, honey. I know this has been a nightmare for you but everything is okay now, we're safe and they're going to take us back to Hereford soon. I miss you so much.'

'Me too, Daddy,' said Sophie. 'Come and see us, please. I was scared but everything is okay now.'

The Major ended the recording and thanked them.

Mrs Hirst nodded tearfully. 'And what about Marty?'

'Like I said, we're looking for him. As soon as we've found him we'll have you back together again.' He smiled reassuringly, but he knew that the chances of the Hirst family living happily ever after were slim to none.

CHAPTER 57

Amanda Hirst and her daughter climbed into the back of the Range Rover. They were in shock but unharmed. Travis closed the door, flashed the Major a thumbs up and went around to the other side of the vehicle. The Major looked up and down the street. There were lights on in many of the windows but no one seemed to be taking any notice of what had happened. The shaped charges had been muffled and the shots fired inside the house had been suppressed and most people were probably asleep in bed.

Reynolds and Coleman escorted Zach over to the Volvo. Wheeler was already waiting with the boot open. Zach began to protest but Reynolds cut him short with a slap across the back of his head. They helped the American into the boot and slammed it shut.

As the three men climbed into the Volvo, the Major took out his Airwave radio, called up the police commander, and explained that they were moving out, that the hostages were safe and that there were three dead bodies in the house. 'Sounds like a good night's work,' said the commander.

The Major climbed into the front passenger seat of the Range Rover and nodded at Luke. 'Back to the barracks,' he said. 'Soon as you can but let's not go breaking any speed limits.'

As Luke pulled away from the kerb, the Major's mobile phone rang. It was Giles Pritchard. 'I was just about to call you, we have Mrs Hirst and her daughter, safe and well,' said the Major. 'The cops are moving in to secure the location. We have one of the kidnappers in custody, three were KIA. We're taking the kidnapper and the hostages to Wellington Barracks.'

'I think we'd prefer the kidnapper here at Thames House,' said Pritchard.

'Understood, but I'd rather keep everyone together at this stage, plus I'd prefer to get our ordnance off the streets as soon as possible.'

'Okay, that makes sense. I'll send a team to the barracks and they can collect him from there.'

'That will work,' said the Major. He ended the call. He was being less than honest with Pritchard. They could quite easily have delivered Zach to Thames House but Gannon wanted a quiet word with him first. The Major still didn't know what Marty Hirst was up to, and the American might have the answer.

CHAPTER 58

The second bedroom didn't have a bathroom so Tim padded out into the hallway, naked. As he reached the bathroom door, the door to the main bedroom opened. It was Eric. The American grinned when he saw Tim. 'Going well, is it?' he said. He closed the door behind him.

Tim shook his head in disgust.

Eric held up his hands. 'Hey, sorry, didn't mean to offend you. It's just I'm not surprised, you can see from the way she looks at you that she's got the hots for you.'

'Sally and I go back a long way,' said Tim.

'She's cute. And as hard as nails. I imagine she'd be tough to handle.'

'A fucking nightmare,' agreed Tim. 'But she's worth it.' He turned to face Eric, totally unfazed by the fact that he was naked. He spent enough time in men's changing rooms not to be embarrassed by his body. Truth be told, after months of hard training in the gym he was pretty darn proud of his physique. 'How do you think this is going to play out?' he asked.

'With Flores? We're on the home stretch. I don't see any problems.'

'You think we're safe here?'

'Don't you? They had no problems attacking the house in Hampstead. I'm sure they'd do the same if they knew we were here.'

'I don't know about that,' said Tim. 'The Hampstead house was detached and not overlooked. Easy enough to mount an attack. This is Notting Hill, it's busier and we're in a flat that can't be accessed from the rear. The only way in is through the main door, up the stairs and through the front door. It's as close to impregnable as you can get and as soon as any shots were fired people would be calling the police.'

'I'm fairly sure we weren't followed, and if we were, they would have attacked us when we got out of the vehicles.' Eric shrugged. 'I think we're okay.'

'Sally was right when she said we should call in armed cops,' said Tim. 'We could form a convoy with ARVs front and back and even if they did know where we were they wouldn't dare come near us.'

'How do you think they found us, at the supposed safe house?' asked Eric.

Tim shrugged. 'I don't know.'

'There had to have been a leak. Presumably within MI5. That's how Martinez works. He bribes or coerces people within law enforcement to work for him. Police, the judiciary, the intelligence services. His cartel is worth billions, so money is no object. And if money doesn't work, the threat of violence usually will. It takes someone very brave – or very foolhardy – to stand up to them.'

'You're saying the cartel will have British cops on their payroll?'

'Almost certainly, yes. So you can see why I'd be reluctant to ask them for help.'

'What about people you can trust? Get in more DEA agents?'

'You're looking at our full strength out of the Embassy,' said Eric. 'Three of my men died in the attack, the three of us is all that's left. There'll be more men on the plane but that isn't much use to us.' He shrugged. 'We'll be okay, Tim.'

'I hope so.' Tim went into the bathroom and closed the door. He stared at his reflection. Most Americans he had met were imbued with a confidence that everything would work out for the best, that the prize belonged to the strong and that good old American ingenuity would overcome all obstacles. He just hoped that in this case that confidence wasn't misplaced. He stepped into the shower, turned it on full blast, and closed his eyes as he let the water play over his body.

CHAPTER 59

'What's happening?' asked Amanda Hirst. She had her hands cupped around a mug of hot sweet tea. 'Where's Marty? Is he all right?'

They were sitting in the officer's mess in Wellington Barracks. Amanda was remarkably composed considering what she had been through. Her daughter was sitting on a sofa playing with an iPad that the Major had found for her. 'We're looking for him,' said Gannon. 'Amanda, can you talk me through what happened to you?'

She took a sip of tea. 'I was at home, with Sophie. They must have gotten into the house somehow. It was in the afternoon and Sophie had just got back from school. They knocked me out with something. A stun gun maybe.' She rubbed her neck. 'My neck still hurts. They put me in the boot of a car with Sophie.' She looked over at her daughter, who was engrossed in the iPad. 'Who does that to a kid? What sort of animals are they?'

'That's what we're trying to find out,' said Gannon. 'Okay, so at some point they let you talk to Marty, right?'

Her eyes narrowed. 'How do you know that?' she asked.

'They took you for a reason,' said Gannon. 'I'm assuming it was to put pressure on your husband.'

She nodded. 'They took the bag off my head and gave me a phone and it was Marty. He asked me if I was okay and I told him what had happened and then they took the phone off me and one of the men spoke to him. Something about if Marty did as he was told we would be all right.' She looked at the Major and her lower lip trembled. 'What do they want Marty to do?'

'Something he wouldn't normally consider doing,' said the Major.

'Is he in trouble?'

Gannon didn't want to lie to her, but he didn't want to upset her, either. Her husband was in a whole lot of trouble. He forced a smile. 'We're going to do what we can to help him, Amanda,' he said.

'I want to go home,' she said.

The Major nodded. 'I'll arrange for someone to drive you back to Hereford, and they'll stay with you until this is over.'

She frowned over her mug of tea. 'What do you mean? Over?'

Gannon was finding it harder to smile but he made the effort. 'When we get him back to you,' he said. 'And that should be a lot easier now you're safe.'

He stood up. 'I've asked them to bring you some sandwiches and biscuits. I'll come back and see you once we've got transport fixed up.'

She reached up and grabbed his hand. 'Don't let anything happen to Marty, please. He's a good man. If he's done something wrong, it's because he was trying to save us, that's all. He was being a good husband and a good father.'

'I know,' said Gannon.

She tightened her grip on his hands. 'Promise you'll bring him back to us.'

Gannon looked down at her. The pleading in her eyes made his stomach turn over. 'I promise,' he said.

He left the room and walked down the corridor to where they were holding the American. They had untied Zach's hands, given him a mug of coffee and put him in a windowless storage room. Wheeler and Travis stood guard outside the door and they nodded as the Major walked up. 'How's he been?' asked Gannon.

'As good as gold,' said Wheeler.

The Major opened the door. Zach was sitting in the far corner of the room. He scrambled to his feet, leaving his coffee on the floor. 'Am I out of here?' he asked.

'MI5 want to debrief you first, then they'll work out what happens to you,' said Gannon.

'No one knows I'm here, right?'

'The police think that everyone in the house was killed in an SAS operation. That's the story that will be given to the media.'

'Thank you,' said Zach. 'I'm sorry about what happened.'

'Holding a gun to the head of an innocent woman and threatening to kill her in front of her daughter? Yeah, you should be sorry.'

'It wasn't personal. It was a job.'

'So tell me, how does someone from Delta, the best of the best, end up threatening to kill a civilian, in front of her child? How does that happen, Zach?'

The American looked down at the floor, his cheeks flaring red. 'You wouldn't understand,' he mumbled.

'Look me in the eye like a man, son, and tell me.'

Zach looked up. He straightened his spine and pulled his shoulders back. 'I made some bad choices,' he said, his voice stronger now.

'I'd say so,' said the Major.

'I left Delta two years ago. I'd been promised a job with a civilian contractor but that fell through. Seems the company had been playing fast and loose with its taxes. I was looking for work for a few months then I got approached by another former Delta guy. It was security work, he said. Guarding shipments from Mexico.'

'Drugs?'

'I didn't ask and they didn't tell, but sure, yes, of course. We worked in Mexico, riding shotgun on trucks heading to the border. And we worked in the States, guarding trucks as they drove through Texas and beyond. It was good money. Easy work. We had a few attempted hijacks but we were well equipped and well trained and we never lost a shipment.'

'It's a hell of a jump from protecting trucks to taking a civilian hostage.'

Zach nodded. 'They pull you in. Bit by bit. We started as

defensive security but before long they wanted us to be more proactive. We were tasked with attacking the opposition.' He shrugged. 'It was difficult to say no.'

'Did you try?'

Zach looked pained. 'The people we were working for don't take no for an answer. And to be honest, we were taking out trash. You've heard about the Mexican cartels, right? They kill and torture each other and their families, they murder cops, they assassinate judges.'

'What about you? Did you kill cops?'

'No!' said Zach, quickly. 'Absolutely not.'

'But what if you had been asked to? Would "no" have been an answer then?'

His eyes flashed dire. 'I'm not a cop killer.'

The Major shrugged. 'So tell me about Marty Hirst.'

'Tell you what?'

'You kidnapped his wife and daughter and threatened to kill them.'

'We wouldn't have actually killed them.'

'You looked pretty serious in the bedroom a couple of hours ago.'

'I was just looking for a way out.'

Gannon nodded, not convinced. 'Who was giving you instructions?'

'A guy called Javier.'

'Mexican?'

Zach nodded. 'One of Martinez's right hand men.'

'Martinez?'

'Carlos Martinez. He runs the cartel. He lives in a near-fortress outside Mexico City. He has guys like Javier do his dirty work for him. We flew over in a private jet.'

'Who's we?'

'About a dozen guys.'

'All former Delta?'

'A mixture. But yeah, special forces.'

'You say about a dozen. How many exactly?'

Zach frowned as he considered the question. Then he nodded. 'Thirteen. Someone made a joke about it being unlucky.'

'And your brief was what?'

'To do whatever Javier told us.'

The Major's eyes hardened. He didn't know if the American was being deliberately evasive but there wasn't time to mess around. 'Specifically?'

'Javier met us at the airport. We were split into two groups. Javier spoke to the groups separately. That was always his thing, to not let the left hand know what the right hand was doing.' He bent down and picked up his coffee mug. It was displacement behaviour, Gannon figured, a clear sign that the American was uneasy with the line of questioning. 'Me and three others were tasked with picking up Mrs Hirst.'

'So you don't know what the other group was doing?'

Zach shook his head.

The Major studied him for several seconds, wondering if Zach really didn't know that his colleagues had gone into the house in Wimbledon and brutally murdered seven innocent men and women. And that Marty Hirst had led them. And if Zach had been tasked with the Wimbledon murders, would he have refused, knowing what refusal would entail? 'So Javier told you what? To go and get Mrs Hirst and her daughter and take them to the house in Ealing?'

Zach nodded. 'Exactly.'

'And at some point you had Mrs Hirst speak to her husband?'

Zach nodded again. 'Javier gave us the number. We were to have her speak to him and tell him what happened, then I took the phone from her and told him that if he didn't do what Javier was asking, he'd never see his wife or daughter again.' He grimaced. 'I wouldn't have killed them, I swear. It was a threat.'

'A threat that Marty took very seriously.'

'He was one of yours, right? SAS?'

'Did Javier tell you that?'

'He said that Hirst was a Brit and that they needed a Brit to lead the team. To make things easier. We were all Americans, he needed someone on the ground and didn't have time to bring in someone new.'

'Marty had worked for them before?'

'No. But they knew him.'

'How exactly? How did Javier have Marty's name?'

'They'd crossed paths in Colombia, a few years ago.'

The Major's eyes narrowed. 'In what way, exactly?'

'I'm not sure. He didn't say. He just gave me the address and told me to take the wife and daughter and have the wife speak to the husband on the phone.'

'So the plan was to force Marty to work for Javier?'

'I got the impression that Marty had already done some work for him in London. But he was getting cold feet.'

'Because of what Javier was asking him to do?'

Zach nodded. 'That's what they're like, the Mexicans. They make you do what they want, one way or another.'

'How did you contact Javier? While you were in Ealing.'

'I didn't. He rang me. Usually landlines.'

'You don't have a mobile number for him?'

Zach shook his head. 'He wanted to keep minimal contact.'

'You didn't call him to confirm that you had Mrs Hirst? And that she had spoken to her husband?'

'He called me. Once to confirm that we had her, and again to confirm that she had contacted her husband.'

'Landlines both times?'

Zach nodded. He leaned forward. 'So what's going to happen now?'

'To you? MI5 will need a chat. Then I assume they'll pass you onto the DEA. I'm guessing the intel you have will be useful, and that being the case they'll debrief you and arrange for witness protection for you and your family.'

Zach transferred his coffee mug to his left hand and offered his right. 'Thank you,' he said.

The Major shook his hand, but he felt nothing but contempt for the man. He wasn't generally a fan of American special forces. All US special forces personnel – more than seventy thousand of them – came under the US Special Operations Command, and they included Navy SEALs, Delta Force, Army Rangers and Green Berets. The Major doubted that one in a hundred would have been up to the SAS's demanding standards, but leaving that aside, he had a problem sympathising with any former special forces soldier who sold his skills to criminal gangs. Mercenaries were one thing – a professional soldier carrying out his duties against armed forces had at least a degree of respectability – but killing for drug dealers was just plain wrong. And taking women and children hostage and threatening to kill them was what thugs and villains did, not highly trained soldiers. When Gannon had burst into the bedroom in Ealing, he had no doubt at all that Zach was ready and willing to pull the trigger and end Mrs Hirst's life.

'Thank you,' Zach said again.

The Major pulled his hand away and resisted the urge to wipe it on his trousers. 'No problem,' he said. 'MI5 should be on the way – let the guys outside know if you need to use the bathroom.'

The Major left the room. Two middle-aged men in dark suits were waiting in the corridor. 'Speak of the devil,' he said.

'I'm sorry?' said the older of the two, his grey hair swept back as if he hoped that would disguise his bald patch.

'You're from Pritchard?'

The man nodded. 'We're here to collect . . . err, actually we don't have a name.'

'Zach. I don't have a family name. Do you have armed support?'

'Good God no, do you think we need it?'

The Major's eyes widened. 'What did Pritchard say?'

'We were just told to collect the person you removed from the house in Ealing.'

'Okay, just so you know, the man in there is prepared to provide intelligence about a major Mexican drugs cartel, the same cartel that killed seven of your people this morning. If the cartel even has an inkling that you have him, they will bring the wrath of hell down on you. So yes, I would think that armed support would be a good idea.'

The two men looked at each other in astonishment. It was clear that they had been badly briefed, to say the least.

'Look,' he said, gesturing at Travis and Wheeler. 'These two guys are cleared for weapons carry in London, they can ride with you.'

'Thank you,' said the grey-haired officer. 'Much appreciated.'

CHAPTER 60

Javier's phone buzzed, heralding the arrival of a WhatsApp message. He read it and cursed under his breath. He was in the kitchen of a house in Camberwell where he had based himself until the matter of Diego Flores had been resolved. There were two men with him, both Americans and both former special forces. After the debacle in Hampstead, Aaron Miller had dumped his Outlander and had caught a black cab to join Javier. The second man was Pedro Gonzalez, who had worked for the cartel for more than five years. Javier was using him as personal security. Wherever Javier went, Gonzalez stayed close by. Gonzalez's parents were from Mexico but he was a US citizen and had served five years with the Navy SEALs. Miller was former Delta Force. The two men hadn't met before but had bonded instantly. They were sitting at the kitchen table, drinking coffee, and they looked at him expectantly.

'We've got a problem,' said Javier. 'They found the hostages and have released them. Zach is at an Army barracks and will shortly be moved to the headquarters of MI5.'

'MI5?' said Gonzalez.

'They're like your CIA,' said Javier. 'We have to stop him talking to them. He knows about the two of you, so you know what has to be done.'

The two men nodded. 'When?' asked Miller.

'Now,' said Javier.

CHAPTER 61

The Major watched the grey Vauxhall Vectra drive away from Wellington Barracks. The two MI5 officers were in the front and Zach was in the back, sandwiched between Travis and Wheeler. They had zip-cuffed his wrists despite his protests, though they had agreed that his hands could be bound in front of him. The American was ashen-faced, clearly worried about what lay ahead of him. But the Major had zero sympathy for him. He had made his bed and now he was going to have to lie in it, bloody sheets and all.

He took out his phone and called Mark Renny, immediately apologising for the time of his call. 'So, I just need to pick your brains again,' he said to the former sergeant major. 'Specifically about his time in Colombia.'

'Not sure I can help you there, boss,' said Renny. 'That was after I'd left.'

'Can you think of anyone who might be able to fill me in?'

'Let me check and I'll call you back,' said Renny. 'Presumably you want to talk to someone who was out there with him?'

'That's exactly what I want, Mark,' said Gannon. 'Soon as you can, will you? I'm on a ticking clock here.'

'I'll make some calls, boss.'

The Major ended the call and put the phone away. He needed caffeine so headed for the officers' mess and ordered a coffee and a club sandwich. He ran through his conversation with Zach as he chewed on his sandwich. Zach had said thirteen men had flown in from the States. Presumably Javier had reported back that Flores had been caught in the MI5 sting and Martinez had sent out reinforcements. Four of the team had been tasked with kidnapping Hirst's family, and three of them were now dead.

The rest of the team had presumably gone to the Wimbledon house with Hirst. And the same team had then attacked the safe house in Hampstead. He sipped his coffee. Six had died at Hampstead. Another had died along with the MI5 officer and two SAS troopers on the abortive attempt to collect Sally Page. So ten out of thirteen were dead. Zach was in custody. That meant there were still two out there. Plus Marty Hirst. Presumably the cartel was still determined to get to the informant, which meant they would need more manpower. There wouldn't be time to fly in reinforcements from the States so they would have to use locals.

His phone rang and he picked it up. It was Renny. 'Boss, do you know Colin Peckham? He's with B Squadron.'

'Del Boy? Sure.' Colin Peckham had *Only Fools and Horses* to thank for his nickname, Peckham being the area of London associated with its main character.

'That's him. Anyway, Del Boy was with Hirst in Colombia. I thought it best you talk to him direct so I've told him to expect your call. Is that okay?'

'That's perfect, Mark. Thanks.'

'I'll text you his number.'

The Major thanked him and ended the call. A few seconds later his phone buzzed with a message containing Peckham's number. Del Boy was a fifteen-year veteran of the SAS, a forward air control specialist. He had extensive training in calling in aircraft to attack ground targets, a skill he had used to good effect in Iraq, Afghanistan and Syria. He was a good, solid operator and the Major had used him on several occasions for operations carried out by the Increment. FAC specialists had to perform well under pressure as any mistake could result in civilian casualties.

He called the number but it went through to voicemail. He left a short message, just saying who was calling and that it was urgent. The man was clearly screening his calls because within thirty seconds he rang back. 'Sorry about that, boss, but my ex-wife has set lawyers on me.'

'Sorry to hear that,' said Gannon. 'Alimony?'

'She's trying to get blood out of a stone, but what can you do? My first wife gets the lion's share of my paycheque because we've got two kids. Anyway, my problems are my problems, what do you need?'

'Guy called Marty Hirst. You were in Colombia with him.'

'Ah. Has he got himself into trouble again?'

'Again?'

'He was a bloody Jonah. Bad luck follows him around.'

'Bad luck or bad judgement?'

Peckham laughed. 'Well, Marty would always say he was unlucky, but yeah, he made more than his fair share of bad calls.'

'What happened?'

'We were assigned to the Colombian Army who were identifying and destroying cocaine labs in the jungle. The Colombian Army isn't great in the jungle.' He chuckled softy. 'Actually they're fuck all use at pretty much everything. Plus the Army leaks like a sieve. As soon as the troops know which area they're searching, the cartel is tipped off. So they would send us in and we'd do the location and targeting and call in an airstrike or send in choppers so they could get there before the cartel knew what was happening. We were in two-man teams. We'd go in and once we found a lab we'd lie up in an observation post and then call it in. We were on a three-month attachment and generally it worked well.'

'And what happened with Hirst?'

'We've only really got his word for it and I'm not sure if we got the full story. We were about ten miles apart and in radio contact. Me and a guy called Rusty had found a large processing factory and had set up an OP. All good. We stopped using the radio because we were dug in, pissing in plastic bags and the like. Hirst was with Ronnie Goldman, Goldilocks.'

'I remember Ronnie,' said the Major. 'He killed himself, right?' The Regiment had more than its fair share of suicides.

Posttraumatic stress disorder was a common problem, and many men had trouble adapting to Civvy Street after an adrenaline-fuelled career with the SAS.

'A few months after he got back from Colombia, yeah,' said Peckham. 'In a nutshell, anyway, Marty and Ronnie got caught. Not by the Colombian cartel but by a Mexican group. The Mexicans were making inroads into the cocaine business in Colombia and they were always getting into scraps with the Colombians. They were vicious bastards. If they felt that the Colombians were in what they regarded as their territories they'd move in and skin everyone alive and hang their bodies from the trees.

'So they caught Marty and Ronnie, and normally they'd just have been killed and buried in the jungle but for some reason they were kept alive and tortured, mentally and physically. Fake executions, water torture, the works. Rusty and I didn't know they had a problem because we weren't using the radio. So, we call in our location and they send in choppers to destroy the factory and arrest as many of the workers as they could. It was a good bust, they got two Russian chemists and several tons of coke. Job well done. Then we realise that Marty and Ronnie had gone missing. The Colombians went looking and found them eventually in a Mexican camp. They went in with guns blazing. A lot of them got killed but they found our guys. They were flown back to Hereford a few days later. They were in a pretty bad state, mentally more than physically. I'm sure that's why Ronnie topped himself.'

'But Marty was okay?'

'I wasn't that close to him, truth be told. But he left the Regiment sometime afterwards, right? The rumour was that he'd been told he was being RTU'd but had decided to quit instead. Can't say I blame him.'

'Did you talk to Ronnie about what had happened in the jungle?'

'Ronnie was a taciturn fucker at the best of times, boss, if you'll excuse my French. But he wouldn't say a word about what had happened out there. Just that they had been picked up by a patrol and beasted something rotten.'

'How did he kill himself?'

'Ah, it wasn't put down as a suicide. He was out drinking and he was driving back to Stirling Lines when he hit a lamppost. He wasn't wearing his seatbelt and they reckon he died instantly.'

'So it was an accident?'

'He had a wife, and two kids, so the investigators bent over backwards to say that it was an accident brought on by drink, but he'd left a note in the barracks about his will and what he wanted doing with his personal stuff. His mate found the note but he didn't tell the cops and the coroner was never told about it.'

'I get it,' said the Major. He thanked the trooper and ended the call. He took a gulp of coffee and bolted down the rest of his sandwich, deep in thought.

CHAPTER 62

'So you guys are SAS?' asked Zach. He looked at Travis on his right, but Travis ignored him. He turned to his left but Wheeler was staring straight ahead. 'What's with the silent treatment?' he asked.

'We've had a busy day,' said Wheeler.

'You and me both,' said Zach.

Wheeler turned to look at him. 'What?'

'I just mean, we've all been through a hell of a lot.'

'You were holding a woman hostage,' sneered Wheeler.

'I was under a lot of pressure,' said Zach.

Wheeler placed his hand on Zach's leg, just above the knee, and squeezed. 'I'll give you pressure, you prick,' hissed Wheeler.

'What the fuck!' said Zach.

'Do you know the names Rob Taylor and Dave Chapman?'

Zach shook his head. 'No.'

'Because Rob and Dave were shot dead in the street earlier today. By your fucking mates.' He tightened his grip on Zach's knee. Zach squirmed but couldn't escape the pressure. 'They were just heading over to pick up an MI5 officer your guys had been chasing, and they died in the fucking street. So don't tell me you've been through hell. You have no idea what that word means.' He squeezed harder and Zach yelped.

The MI5 officer in the passenger seat twisted around. 'Is that right?' he asked.

'Yeah, that's fucking right,' he said. 'And his pals killed seven of yours.'

'Ten,' said the MI5 officer. 'One of ours was shot in the street with your guys. Simon Wilsher. He'd only been with Five for a few years, still wet behind the ears. He wasn't even armed. And they killed two of our senior people – Ian Hadley and Toby Harris – in Hampstead.'

Zach looked away. Wheeler squeezed even harder and the American yelped.

Wheeler took his hand away. 'You know what we should do?' he said. 'We should drive to somewhere nice and quiet and put a bullet in his fucking head.'

'Your boss said you had to deliver me to MI5,' said Zach.

'Yeah? Do you always obey orders?'

A motorcycle gunned its engine behind them. The driver checked his side mirror. 'Come on, plenty of room,' he muttered.

'I'm a soldier,' said Zach.

'Nah mate. You were a soldier. Now you're a fucking mercenary.'

'That's what professional soldiers do, they get paid to fight.'

'Yeah, but you clearly don't give a fuck who's paying you,' said Wheeler. 'That's the difference.'

The motorbike dropped back and the driver looked in his rear-view mirror. 'Are you going to overtake or what?' he muttered.

Wheeler turned around. It was a big bike, with two people on it, both wearing full face helmets.

'What's going on?' asked Zach.

'Shut the fuck up,' snapped Wheeler, reaching inside his jacket for his Glock.

The motorbike engine revved and it came up on the passenger side. Travis had also picked up on what was happening and was reaching for his gun.

'Accelerate!' Wheeler shouted.

'What?' said the driver, twisting around in his seat.

'Fucking accelerate!'

The bike was on the left of the car now. The pillion passenger had a gun in his right hand. It was an Ingram MAC-10, Wheeler realised, with a suppressor. The machine pistol was notoriously difficult to control on full automatic, but at close range accuracy wasn't an issue. The pillion passenger twisted around so that he could get his left hand on the suppressor to steady his aim. Wheeler got his gun out of its holster but he knew he was out of time. The car accelerated but it was too late: the window exploded and bullets raked through the vehicle, ripping through the three men in the back as the bike roared off down the road.

CHAPTER 63

Sally rolled over half asleep and stiffened when she realised she wasn't alone. It took her a few seconds before she remembered where she was and who was in the bed next to her. Tim was on his side, with his back to her. That was his way, always had been. 'I'm a huggee, not a hugger,' he'd always said whenever she'd remarked on it. He didn't know why but he could never get to sleep if he was holding her. But he dropped off within seconds if she was holding him. To be honest, Sally always preferred to sleep alone. That was her way.

She slipped an arm around him, then slid her leg over his hip. He was warm, and soft, but there was no mistaking the strength he had. She kissed him softly between the shoulder blades, then licked his flesh. She always loved the salty taste of his skin. He moved in his sleep, but then went still again. His breathing was slow and even and she started to match his rhythm. She felt calm and safe lying next to him, despite everything that had happened that day. She had always felt that way with him. It wasn't just his physical presence and strength, there was a quiet confidence about him that reminded her of her father. Some policemen she had met had a game face they put on when they were working; they faked hardness and aggression and confidence but underneath they were usually fraught with uncertainty. With Tim, authority came naturally.

She kissed him on the back again. If she had wanted to settle down and get married, Tim would have been the perfect choice. But she had met him at a time when she was totally focused on her career, and settling down wasn't an option. It wasn't then and it wasn't now.

'What are you thinking about?' he asked quietly.

'How do you know I'm not asleep?' she asked.

'The way you're breathing. Are you worried about what's going to happen?'

'With Flores? Not really.'

'What then?'

She considered the question for a while, then gave him a gentle squeeze with her arm and her leg. 'You know I love you, right?' He didn't answer and Sally wondered if he'd heard her or not. She squeezed him again. 'You know I love you, right?'

He chuckled softly. 'I heard you the first time,' he said. 'I just wanted you to say it again.'

'Bastard,' she said, and he turned around, rolled on top of her, and kissed her.

CHAPTER 64

The Major's mobile rang. It was Giles Pritchard. 'I've bad news, Allan,' said the director. 'The car bringing your prisoner to Thames House has been attacked. The prisoner has been killed, as has one of your men, Mike Travis. The other member of your team, Chris Wheeler, has been taken to A&E, but the prognosis isn't good.'

'How the hell could that have happened?' asked Gannon.

'Apparently the killer was on a motorbike.'

'I mean how could they have known that we had him? And how could they have known we were taking him to Thames House?'

'We don't know.'

'Well, we bloody well should know,' snapped Gannon. 'How is it that they know everything we're doing? You've got a problem over there, Pritchard. A big fucking problem and you need to get it sorted.'

'I hear you.'

The Major took a deep breath to calm himself down. He rarely snapped but then most days he didn't have to deal with three dead troopers and a fourth in hospital. Something had clearly gone very wrong. 'I need to see you, face to face.'

'I'm in the office.'

'No, I need to see you outside. We can meet on Lambeth Bridge. Mid-way. That way I can see if you're being followed.'

'I'm perfectly capable of carrying out my own counter-surveillance procedures,' said Pritchard frostily.

'That ship has well and truly sailed,' said Gannon. 'Now

we're going to do it my way. I'll text you when I'm there. And don't tell anyone where you're going or who you're going to see.'

Pritchard began to protest but the Major ended the call. He was done with talking.

CHAPTER 65

Jimmy the Para lit a cigarette and blew smoke towards the television. He was sitting on the single sofa with Sean O'Rourke and Pat Walsh. O'Rourke had found a packet of Jaffa Cakes in the kitchen and Walsh had liberated two packs of Walkers crisps and was working his way through them. Dean Barrett was standing at the window, watching the two target vehicles and taking the occasional sip from a can of Coke.

'How long do I have to stay here?' asked Barrett. He wiped his moustache with the back of his hand.

'Do half an hour and then I'll get you relieved. We need eyes on the vehicles at all times. They could move at any time.'

'Got you,' said Barrett. 'It's just as boring as fuck, that's all.'

'You should try lying in the jungle for three days, pissing and shitting into plastic bags.'

'You did that?'

'Many times,' said Hirst. 'It's part of the job. Lying up in an OP and watching the enemy.'

'OP?' said Barrett.

'Observation post,' said Hirst. 'A hole under a bush or beside a rock. Trust me, standing at a window for half an hour is no big thing.'

They heard the roar of a helicopter overhead and Hirst tensed. Barrett peered upwards through the gap in the curtains.

'They're not here for us, are they?' asked Walsh.

'They wouldn't bother with a chopper, they'd set up armed cops outside and send in a negotiator,' said Hirst.

The roaring toned down as the helicopter flew away. 'Could

be the cops on a pursuit or an air ambulance,' said Hirst. He lifted his mug of coffee to his mouth but stopped and frowned. His frown deepened as his mind raced, then his face broke into a smile. 'Fuck me, I've just had an idea,' he said.

CHAPTER 66

The Major turned up the collar of his overcoat against the wind that was blowing down the Thames. He saw Giles Pritchard on Millbank, heading towards the north side of the bridge. Gannon was standing at the midpoint, facing the traffic.

He watched as Pritchard walked along the bridge. There were no signs that he was being followed. Pritchard had his hands in the pockets of his coat when he reached the Major, and he didn't offer to shake, he just acknowledged him with a curt nod. 'I don't appreciate being dragged outside like this,' said Pritchard.

Gannon shrugged. 'Your appreciation is pretty far down my list of priorities at the moment,' he said. 'Chris Wheeler died on the operating table ten minutes ago.'

Pritchard sighed. 'I'm sorry.'

'Yes, well sorry doesn't really cut it. There are four names now that have to be added to the base of the clocktower in Stirling Lines. That's where we honour our dead. And there are four sets of relatives who are going to have be told that their loved ones have died. And for what?'

'There's no way we could have known that they were going to attack the car,' said Pritchard.

'But they did. And we need to ask ourselves how they knew. I phoned you and told you that we had the Yank and we were taking him to Wellington Barracks. Other than you, no one else knew that he was alive. You sent your two guys to pick him up, so who else knew?'

Pritchard shrugged. 'John Fretwell and Liz Bailey. They needed to know that he was on the way in.'

'That's all?'

'Allan, you phoned me, I notified John and Liz. I don't know if they mentioned it to anyone else.'

'Liz Bailey would have known about the Hampstead safe house, right?'

'Sure.'

'And John?'

'Probably.'

'Did either of them know that the DEA were holding Flores in Hampstead?'

Pritchard shook his head. 'That was strictly need-to-know. Ian Hadley knew, of course.'

'And when Hadley went to the house, it was attacked.'

'You're suggesting he was involved? I don't think so.'

'No, but he could have been followed, if they knew he was on the way to the house.'

Pritchard shrugged but didn't say anything.

'We have to find out who their inside man is, or this is going to get worse.'

'Do you have any thoughts?' asked Pritchard.

'Actually, I do,' said the Major.

CHAPTER 67

Hirst spread the map out on the coffee table. Dean Barrett was at the window, peering through the curtains. Jimmy the Para, Sean O'Rourke and Pat Walsh gathered around Hirst. Jimmy had a lit cigarette and as he looked down at the map, he scattered ash over it. 'Sorry,' he said, brushing away the ash with his hand.

'For fuck's sake, Jimmy, get a grip,' said Hirst.

'Sorry,' said Jimmy, taking a step back.

'Right,' said Hirst, tapping Notting Hill on the map. 'This is where we are.' He moved his finger north-west, and tapped the location of RAF Northolt. 'This is where they'll be headed. The most obvious route is along the A40, but just because that's the obvious route doesn't mean that's the way they'll go.'

The three men nodded.

'As soon as we see them get into the cars, we'll move out. If everything goes to plan we'll take them down in the street. But these guys are professionals so it might not be straight-forward. In which case we'll follow them and look for an opportunity to hit them en route. If that's the way it plays out, you three will be our ace in the hole.' He tapped the map again, further south. 'You come from here, and intercept them as they head north-west. It might well be on the A40 but you'll need to be flexible.'

Walsh nodded. 'And what, we force them off the road?'

'Just do whatever needs to be done. Jimmy's Kalashnikov will do a lot of damage and you and Pat have your Hecklers. The cars they're using don't look armoured so you shouldn't have any issues.'

The three men nodded as they stared down at the map.
'Any questions?' asked Hirst.
'Looks good to me,' said O'Rourke.
Walsh nodded. 'Easy peasy.'

CHAPTER 68

Liz Bailey and John Fretwell arrived at Pritchard's office together. 'What's the story?' asked Fretwell.

Bailey shrugged. 'I don't know, I was just told it was important.'

Pritchard's secretary smiled up at them. 'He says you're to go straight in.'

'Thanks, Ellie,' said Bailey. She opened the door. Pritchard was at his desk, his eyes flicking between his two screens.

'Ellie, Major Gannon should be calling shortly, put him straight through.'

'Will do,' she said.

Pritchard waved for Bailey and Fretwell to sit down as he continued to stare at his screens.

'Is everything okay, Giles?' asked Bailey.

'Allan thinks he might have a lead on where the guy who hired the Americans is. A Mexican they call Javier. He was in London when Flores was caught.'

'How come?'

'I don't know and I don't really care,' said Pritchard. 'I just want to get this over with.' He sat back in his chair and sighed. 'This has been a nightmare of a day. A bloody nightmare.'

'What about Rod and George?'

'Shaken up but not badly hurt. The killer was shooting at the three men in the back. Any injuries Rod and George have were caused by the car crashing.'

'They don't care about collateral damage, do they?' said Fretwell.

'I assume that's rhetorical, John.'

'You know what I mean, Giles. Shooting up a car in the middle of London, with a what, a bloody machine gun?'

'An Ingram MAC-10 they think. The killer just pointed it and kept his finger on the trigger until the magazine was empty. They didn't stand a chance.'

'Who does that?' muttered Fretwell.

'The Mexicans don't care,' said Bailey. 'They've torn through the Colombian cartels and they think nothing about assassinating politicians, judges, police, soldiers. Even the Colombians have been shocked by the violence.'

'It's always the way,' said Pritchard. 'The underdogs have less to lose. Once they become top dog they tend to quieten down. At the moment the Mexicans are doing whatever they have to do to take over. All the signs are that it's going to get worse before it gets better. Which is why it's so important that the DEA get their man back to the States.'

One of the phones on his desk rang and he answered it. 'Just wait one moment, Allan, I'll put you on speakerphone.' He pressed a button and replaced the receiver. 'Okay, Allan, go ahead. Liz Bailey and John Fretwell are here.'

'This is just to let you know that we know where Javier is. We have a team going over there now.'

'Allan, it's John,' said Fretwell. 'How did you come by this information?'

'John, the way things are at Thames House just now, I'm not prepared to say. But we expect to have Javier in custody within the hour.'

'What about Hirst?'

'No, he's still off the grid. But once we have Javier, we should be able to find Hirst and his team.'

'That's great news, Allan. Really great news. Let us know what happens.'

'I'll get back to you,' said the Major and he ended the call.

'Well that's a turn up for the books,' said Pritchard.

'I have to say, I'm not happy about him withholding information from us like that,' said Fretwell.

'So long as we get this Javier under wraps, I don't think it matters,' said Pritchard.

'Even so, he was as good as saying that he didn't trust us.'

Pritchard shrugged. 'He might have a point there.'

'What are you implying?'

Pritchard shrugged again. 'Nothing. I'm just saying that as things stand, the fewer people who are in the loop, the better.'

Bailey stood up. 'I'll be staying in Thames House until this is resolved.'

'That goes without saying,' said Pritchard.

Bailey headed out of the office. She went along the corridor to the toilets and slipped inside. There were four stalls. The doors to three were open but the fourth, the one closest to the wall, was closed. Bailey bent down. She could see the feet of the woman inside. Sensible black shoes.

Bailey straightened up, took a breath, and then kicked the door by the lock. She managed to get most of her weight behind the kick and the lock splintered and the door crashed open.

Ellie sat with her mouth open in surprise, both hands on her smartphone. The lid was down on the seat and she hadn't lifted up her dress. She looked at Bailey, then at the phone in her hands, and back to Bailey.

Bailey held out her hand. 'Give me the phone, Ellie,' she said quietly.

CHAPTER 69

Fretwell and Pritchard shook their heads as Bailey walked in with Ellie. Bailey held up the phone. 'She was about to send a text. Allan was right, she was the rotten apple.'

Ellie collapsed onto a chair, buried her face in her hands and began to sob.

Major Gannon walked into the office and glared scornfully at the crying woman.

'Your little ruse worked perfectly, Allan,' said Pritchard. 'Now that we have Javier's phone number, we'll get a location for him within the hour. Once we know where he is I intend to send in a CTSFO team.' Counter terrorist specialist firearms officers had been brought into play in the lead up to the 2012 London Olympics. They were better trained than the average firearms officers, including stints with the SAS at their base in Hereford. There were fifteen constables and one sergeant in each CTSFO team and when it came to hostage rescue and terrorist takedowns they were pretty much the equal of the SAS.

'Sounds like a plan,' said Gannon.

'If you want to be there when it happens, that would be okay with me,' said Pritchard. He held out his hand for the phone and Bailey gave it to him.

The Major nodded, then gestured at Ellie. 'What about her?'

'She'll be questioned, obviously.'

'And then what?'

'That will depend on the police and the CPS,' said Pritchard.

'I hope they throw away the key,' said Gannon.

Ellie looked up. 'I'm so sorry,' she said. 'But they said they'd kill my parents if I didn't help.'

The Major threw her a withering look. 'Four of my men died today. Along with ten of your colleagues. So don't be expecting anyone to shed tears over what happens to you.'

Pritchard held up a hand to silence him. 'Ellie, what happened? Who said they'd kill your parents?'

She swallowed and coughed, then patted her chest. Pritchard picked up a bottle of Evian water off his desk and gave it to her. She unscrewed the top and drank greedily. 'I met a guy, a few months ago. In a bar, after work. He said he was from Argentina. He was . . .' She shrugged. 'He swept me off my feet. Presents, dinners. He said he worked for an oil company and he had an expense account so we ate at some amazing restaurants. Michelin stars. Gordon Ramsay and Heston Blumenthal and everything.'

'What was his name?'

'Santino. Santino Rossi.'

Pritchard held up the phone. 'His number is in here?'

Ellie nodded. 'Under Santa.' She forced a smile. 'My secret Santa, I used to call him.'

'Why? Why secret?'

'Because I never met his friends and he didn't seem interested in meeting mine. I used to think he might be married but he swore he wasn't. And he met my parents. And my sister.'

'And when did he start asking about your work?'

'From the first time we met. He knew I worked in Thames House and he guessed I was with MI5. I didn't admit it at the time but it seemed stupid to keep denying it.'

'Did you give his name to the vetting department?'

She shook her head. 'No. I'm sorry.'

'So you meet a stranger who knows you work for MI5 who asks you about your work and you don't think that might be a problem.'

'I wasn't sure how the relationship would go.'

'Were you sleeping with him?' said Pritchard.

She nodded.

'Well that answers your question,' said Pritchard.

'I didn't tell him anything, not until . . .' She grimaced and looked away.

'Until when?'

'Two days ago. I was in his flat and a friend of his turned up. Javier. He said he was from Argentina, too. We drank some wine and then he took out some photographs of my mother and father and my sister, and pictures of where they lived. Javier said that they needed my help and that if I didn't help them then something bad would happen to my parents. And my sister.' Tears welled up in her eyes. 'I'm sorry.'

'This isn't about being sorry,' snapped the Major. 'Just tell us what happened.'

Pritchard flashed the Major a warning look. Bailey took a pack of tissues from her pocket and gave one to the secretary, who used it to dab her eyes.

'I said I couldn't possibly help them, and anyway I was only a secretary, I don't have access to secrets, and then Javier slapped me. Hard.' She rubbed her cheek as she recalled the pain. 'He had a gun and he pointed it at me. He said he wasn't going to shoot me, but that if I didn't help he would shoot my mother and my father and my sister, but not before his friends had raped my mother and castrated my father.' She dabbed at her eyes again. 'I've never been so afraid. He meant it, Mr Pritchard. There wasn't a shadow of a doubt that he meant it.'

'And what did Javier want you to do?'

'He said that a friend of his had been captured by MI5 and that he was in a safe house. He wanted to know where the safe house was. I didn't know, obviously. And I said so.' She blew her nose and Bailey handed her another tissue. 'They asked me about the safe houses and how they worked and who took care of them.' She stopped talking and stared at the floor.

'So you told them about the footies? And about the Wimbledon house?'

Ellie nodded and then began to sob.

'Seven people died,' said the Major.

'They didn't say they were going to kill anyone,' she said. 'I told them that the information about the safe houses was in the footie house. I assumed they'd break in at night and steal the files. I didn't think for one minute . . .' She began to sob again.

'And you were sending Javier a text now, telling him that we knew where he was.'

She nodded. 'But I didn't send it. I was still writing it when . . .' She looked at Bailey and left the sentence hanging.

'And it was you who put in the request to track Sally Page's phone?'

Ellis nodded tearfully. 'Javier called me yesterday morning. He said he had a man outside my parents' house and that if I didn't do what he wanted they'd be tortured and killed and he'd send me a video of it.' She looked at him pleadingly. 'He meant it, I know he did.'

Pritchard gave the phone to Fretwell. 'Get GCHQ on this as a matter of urgency. Any problems, let me know immediately. We need a location for Javier's phone, and for Santino.' He looked at the Major. 'As soon as I get Javier's address I'll call you.'

The Major nodded, threw a last scornful look at Ellie, and left the room.

Pritchard pulled up a chair and sat down next to his secretary. She turned her head away and continued to sob. 'Ellie, when Ian Hadley told me that he was going out to the safe house in Hampstead, you told Javier, didn't you?'

She nodded. 'I am so so sorry,' she said. 'I'll do whatever I can to make this right. I'll give evidence against them. I'll tell you everything that happened. But I was under duress, you understand that, right? I didn't have a choice.'

Pritchard shifted uncomfortably. 'Actually you did have a choice, Ellie. You could have come to me straight away and explained what had happened. We could have protected you and your family.'

She shook her head vehemently. 'They said there was nothing you could do to stop them.'

'You should have come to me, Ellie. A lot of people have died today because of what you did.'

Ellie began to sob uncontrollably. He stood up and patted her on the shoulder. He flashed Bailey a tight smile. 'We'll keep her here until this is over,' he said. 'Then we can pass her on to the police and the CPS can decide what to do from then on.'

'I'll cooperate,' said Ellie, looking up at them hopefully. 'That has to count for something, doesn't it?'

'I'm sure it will,' said Pritchard, though in his heart he knew that she was facing some very serious prison time. She could argue duress all she wanted to, but at the end of the day her decisions had cost the lives of ten MI5 officers and four SAS troopers.

CHAPTER 70

There were six weapons on the kitchen table – an Uzi, three MP5 carbines, and two shotguns. Hirst picked them up one at a time and professionally checked them as the six members of Barrett's B team watched him.

'I bags the Uzi,' said the one they called Andy Pandy.

'The Uzi is bloody inaccurate beyond twenty feet or so,' said Hirst dismissively. 'But you can use it to spray the car.'

'Spray and pray,' laughed Andy.

'You'll be driving me in the Merc. But you can put the Uzi under the seat, just in case we get stopped.'

Hirst picked up one of the MP5s. 'These are quality kit, but not great against vehicles. But once we've stopped the convoy they'll do the job.'

'What about the shotguns?' asked Barrett, picking up another of the MP5s. It was clear from the way he handled the weapon that he was familiar with it.

'We'll have one in the SUV, one in the Mercedes,' said Hirst. 'We can use them to shoot out the tyres. That's assuming we have to take them out on the move. Hopefully we'll get them in the street, but if not we'll need something to take down the vehicles.'

He put down the MP5 and picked up one of the shotguns. It was a pump-action Mossberg; the barrel had been cut down to a few inches while the stock had been cut and shaped to a pistol grip. It held five shells and packed enough of a punch to destroy the tyre of an SUV. 'We'll have this in the Merc,' he said. 'Who's used it before?'

One of the men raised a hand. 'It's mine,' he said. He was in

his early twenties with his long reddish hair pulled back in a
ponytail, his cheeks peppered with old acne scars.

'Perfect, you'll be in the Merc with me, then. What's your
name?'

'They call me Alf.'

Despite the long hair, Alf had the look and bearing of a military man. 'You been in the Army?'

Alf nodded. 'Three years. Fucking hated it.'

Hirst grinned. Alf was a common enough nickname in the
armed forces – it stood for Annoying Little Fucker.

The second shotgun was also a sawn-off but this was
double-barrelled and only held two cartridges, each fired by a
separate trigger. Its only serious use would be to put the fright-
eners on a bank cashier or post office worker. He handed it to
the one they called Simple Simon. 'You take this in the SUV,' he
said. 'You can ride shotgun, pun intended. But you'll need to be
right up against the target car to do any damage.' He gestured
at the MP5s. 'You can decide among yourselves who has these,
best that the guys who have had some military experience use
them. You've all got shorts?'

'Shorts?' queried Simple Simon.

'Handguns. We call handguns "shorts", and carbines and rifles
"longs".'

All the men in the kitchen produced their handguns. There
were four Glocks, a pristine SIG Sauer and an ancient Colt
45.

'Right, I want you to all strip down and clean your guns.'

Some of the men looked hesitant.

'Now!' he said.

The men started breaking their guns down. Hirst folded his
arms and stood in the hall doorway, watching them. You could
tell a lot about a man from the way he handled his gun. And
first impressions weren't good. Most of the team lacked confidence, and Simple Simon seemed to have no idea what he was
supposed to do. He was watching Andy Pandy and copying his
every movement.

Dean Barrett seemed to know what he was doing; he stripped and cleaned his Glock with smooth, economic movements. Hirst decided that Barrett would be in the Merc with him. The other three would be in the second SUV, but he doubted that they would be much use in a firefight.

CHAPTER 71

Major Gannon knocked on the side door of the mobile command centre. The door opened and a CTSFO looked out. He was dressed in a wolf-grey bulletproof vest, shirt and pants and had a Glock 19 in a grey nylon holster. Gannon smiled at him and nodded. 'Major Gannon. Inspector Bird is expecting me.'

The constable turned and spoke to someone inside and then opened the door. Inspector Craig Bird was in his early thirties, wearing the same wolf-grey gear as the constable but without the sidearm. There was an Airwave radio clipped to the left shoulder of his protective vest. He shook hands with Gannon. 'Good to see you again, Major.'

Bird had met Gannon twice at Stirling Lines as part of his training and the Major had a lot of respect for the man. While Bird's overall fitness probably fell a little short of the SAS's demanding standards, his weapons skills were second to none. He was running this operation, though, and wouldn't be going into the building. 'How's it going, Craig?'

Bird gestured at a screen showing a live feed of an overhead view of the house, presumably from a drone. There were four greenish figures in two of the downstairs rooms. 'We have an infrared feed and the quality's good so we know we have only four targets. The quality isn't good enough to see if they're armed, however.' The house was in Camberwell, south London, close to Kennington Park.

'I think it's safe to assume they are,' said the Major. 'We've tracked the phones of two of our targets, Javier Silva and Santino Rossi. They're Mexicans, so far as we know. There's a good chance that the other two are Americans, probably former special forces, and as I said, almost certainly armed. They're part of a group that attacked an MI5 safe house earlier today and they were wearing body armour and carrying Hecklers.'

Bird raised his eyebrows. 'That's not good news.'

'Well, they were prepared for an assault,' said Gannon. He nodded at the screen. 'These guys think they're safe, so I doubt that they're fully geared up, though there will almost certainly be weapons in the house.'

'I was hoping to continue surveillance for a while.'

'Not really an option, I'm afraid. The clock is very much ticking and we need to get in there sooner rather than later. The one called Javier is in touch with a group of mercenaries that we need to shut down. We need his phone and we need it yesterday.'

'So this isn't about taking prisoners?'

'I doubt if we capture Javier or Santino that they'll talk. Down the line, maybe, if they cut a deal with the DEA, but not right now.'

'DEA? How is the DEA involved?'

'These men are trying to kill a cartel member who is cooperating with the DEA. The DEA is getting ready to fly him out of the country and these guys are determined to stop that from happening.'

'And where are the DEA at the moment?'

The Major smiled thinly. 'They've gone off the grid. There was a – how shall I put it – trust issue. So at the moment we have no way of contacting them.'

Bird rubbed his chin as he stared at the screen. The four figures didn't appear to be moving. 'They've drawn the curtains so snipers aren't an option,' he said. He pointed at two figures at the front of the house. 'This is the sitting room. They've been static for a while.' The other two figures were at the rear of the house. 'These two have been moving around. The hotplates have been on and what was probably a kettle or a coffee maker came on, so I'm guessing they're cooking.'

'What's access to the rear like?'

There was a map of the area stuck on a corkboard and Bird pointed at it. 'Access is via a path at the side of the house. There's a gate there which could well be locked. The only other way would be to go through the garden of the house backing onto it. Through or over the hedge.'

'It would be quicker through the back. They'd hear you coming if you have to smash the side gate.'

'We could go over it,' said Bird. 'It's about seven feet tall. A ladder would do it. And with the curtains drawn they wouldn't see us.'

'And what about the doors to get access?'

'I was thinking just regular Enforcers.'

The Major nodded. The Enforcer was the standard battering ram used by UK police forces, also known as the 'big red key'. It was made of steel and weighed just sixteen kilos but when swung by an expert could exert a pressure of three tonnes which was more than enough to take down most locked doors, even ones that had been reinforced. 'And you're ready to go in now?'

'If time is an issue, yes, we're good to go.'

The Major nodded again. 'Let's do it.'

CHAPTER 72

Sally flinched as something touched her shoulder and she opened her eyes to see Tim standing by the bed, smiling down at her. 'Wakey, wakey,' he said. He was holding a blue mug. 'I made you coffee.' He had showered and dressed and looked remarkably fresh considering everything they had gone through in the past twelve hours.

She sat up and took the coffee from him. 'Thanks,' she said. 'What time is it?'

'Seven. The Yanks are up and getting ready to move out.'

'Did they say when?'

'Eight, eight thirty.'

'Are you okay?'

He sat down on the bed. 'In what way?'

She sipped her coffee as she wondered how best to answer his question. She settled on a shrug and a smile.

'About what happened?' He nodded at the bed. 'Yeah, I'm very okay. But a bit confused.'

'I'm sorry.'

He reached over and stroked her hair. 'Can we make today a day when you don't feel you need to apologise?'

'I'll try.' She sipped her coffee again and he took away his hand. 'Confused about what?' she asked him.

'About what we are. Are we boyfriend-girlfriend? Friends with benefits? Ships that pass in the night?'

'Do we need a label?'

He chuckled. 'I guess not. It just makes it easier for me to understand where we are.'

'Did I really break your heart?'

He nodded earnestly. 'Fuck, yeah.'

'You never said anything. You just let me go.'

He shrugged. 'Would it have made any difference if I had said anything? You seemed pretty definite about what you wanted. Or what you didn't want.'

'It wasn't that I didn't want you. I just . . .'

'Wanted something else?' he finished for her.

'That's what I thought.'

'And now?'

'Now I'm not sure.' She took another sip of her coffee. He'd made it exactly the way she liked it. Milky with two sugars.

'And that's why I'm confused, Sally. My feelings never changed. You came into my life and I fell in love with you and then you left me.'

'I'm back now,' she said quietly.

'Are you, though?' he said with a frown. 'Are you?'

She nodded. 'Yes. But can we not give it a label?'

He grinned. 'Deal.'

She slipped her hand around his neck and drew him closer, then kissed him on the lips, hard.

CHAPTER 73

'Here we go,' said Inspector Bird, nodding at the monitor showing the view from the drone overhead. Sixteen greenish figures moved towards the house. The Major knew that one of the figures was the sergeant leading the operation, but there was no way of telling who was who.

The group split into two. Eight men moved towards the front door, eight went down the side of the house. The infrared showed the men but didn't show their equipment: their SIG MCX carbines, the two Enforcers, or the ladders they would use to scale the side gate.

The group at the front stopped and went into a huddle. The two men who would be first in would be holding bulletproof shields. Those behind would have their carbines aimed and ready to fire. The armed police's approach to operations was very different to that of the SAS. When the SAS went in, they almost always shot to kill, moving quickly and efficiently to double tap the targets. Usually a four-man team was enough. They mostly didn't bother with shields or defensive measures, though they would often throw in flashbangs, to disorientate the opposition. The aim was to neutralise the threat as quickly as possible.

The police approach was to try to control the situation without firing a shot. The great British public was very much against the concept of the police shooting to kill, no matter what sins the perpetrators had carried out. Any police officer who fired his weapon was immediately taken off active duty, and any killing was treated, initially at least, as a murder investigation. When the police went in armed, they hoped to control the situation by shock and awe, by so outgunning the opposition that they had no choice other than to surrender.

The eight figures at the side of the house grouped together, and then one by one they went over the gate. Gannon and Bird couldn't see the ladders they were using, but there was no doubting that was how they were climbing over. Once they had scaled the gate, they moved around the house in single file and gathered at the kitchen door.

The Airwave radio clipped to Bird's vest clicked twice. After a few seconds there were two more clicks. The teams were on radio silence, but they could communicate by clicking the transmit button. Two clicks meant the teams were in position and ready to go. Bird looked across at Gannon as if seeking reassurance that it was time to move in. The Major flashed him a tight smile and nodded. Bird clicked the transmit button twice.

Almost immediately, the figures at the front door and back door went into action, breaching both doors with the Enforcers and piling inside. The Major watched the greenish figures, knowing that the first two would be holding their shields as a defence against hostile fire, while the men behind would be sweeping the rooms with their carbines and shouting 'armed police' at the tops of their voices. That was another way the police behaved differently in armed situations – they had to announce who they were and give the opposition a chance to surrender. The SAS never announced themselves – they just went in, guns blazing.

There was a flurry of activity in the front room and the kitchen. The two green targets in the front room were now getting down onto the floor. Things were more hectic in the kitchen: the two target figures were moving and then both fell backwards. As the Major watched, the two figures twitched and went still.

'It's over,' said Bird. 'Come on.'

They left the mobile command centre and walked quickly to the house. The unit's sergeant came out of the front door, his SIG carbine at his side, as Inspector Bird and the Major walked up.

'All clear, sir,' said the sergeant. He was wearing a Kevlar helmet and goggles in addition to his vest and protective knee and elbow pads. 'The two men in the front room surrendered without a struggle, the two in the kitchen went for their guns despite our warnings. Both dead.'

'Good job,' said Bird. 'I'll see you back at the mobile command centre for a debrief and then we'll head on back to base. There's a forensics team on the way and obviously Professional Standards will start an investigation into the deaths.'

'Fucking leeches,' muttered the sergeant.

No one liked the anti-corruption cops, least of all armed police officers who had been involved in clearly justifiable shootings. No matter the circumstances, once someone had been shot by an armed officer, Professional Standards moved in and removed the police involved from duty, cautioned them and treated them as suspects rather than heroes. And a final decision as to whether action would be taken against the shooters could take months.

'I concur with your sentiment but perhaps better not to express those thoughts out loud,' said Bird.

The sergeant nodded. 'Yes, sir.'

'Who were the shooters?' Bird asked.

'Neil Thomas and Bob McDonald. It was totally justified, sir. No question. They knew we were cops. As soon as the door was open Terry and Gazza went in with the shields. Everyone was shouting "armed police", you'll see that on the bodycam footage, but they had no intention of coming quietly. They were cooking or something and their guns were on the table. Heckler and Koch 416s.'

The Major nodded. 'The Navy SEALs like to use them.'

'They ignored our shouts to get down on the floor. Terry and Gazza rushed them with the shields and we moved in, still shouting but ready to fire if we had to. They grabbed their guns and moved backwards, trying to aim. One of them pulled the trigger too early and shot Gazza in the foot. At that point we had no option other than to shoot. If he'd raised his gun we'd all have been hit.'

Bird patted the sergeant on the shoulder. 'You all did good, don't worry. Professional Standards will just be going through the motions.'

'I hope so, sir,' said the sergeant.

'Have you ID'd them?'

The sergeant nodded. 'They were both carrying American passports.'

'I need to talk to Javier,' said the Major.

'Let's do it inside,' said Bird.

The two men went into the house. There were two Hispanic men sitting on a sofa. Their wrists had been zip-cuffed and they were watched over by two armed officers. 'Which one of you is Javier Silva?' asked Gannon.

The older of the two men nodded. 'I am.' He was in his forties, his jet-black hair slicked back. He was wearing a suit that looked made to measure and a dark blue silk shirt. There was a heavy gold chain around his neck. 'I want to speak to my lawyer.'

'You have a lawyer?' asked Gannon.

'Of course I have a lawyer. And I demand to speak to him.'

'I need your phone,' said the Major.

'For that you will need a warrant,' said Javier. 'And you will need to talk to my lawyer.'

The Major leant over him and went through his pockets. 'You have no right to search me,' said Javier.

'Actually under the Police and Criminal Evidence Act we do,' said Bird.

The Major looked at the phone, a new-model Samsung. 'I need the pin number to open it.'

Javier shook his head.

The Major glared at him. 'Stop fucking around and give me the code,' he snapped.

Javier looked up at him and smiled. 'Or what? You'll hit me? You'll beat me up? You'll use a cattle prod on me?' He laughed. 'This is England, my friend. Not Mexico. Here I have all the rights in the world. So no, I will not tell you the number. You will have to get a warrant. Now stop throwing your weight around and allow me to call my lawyer.'

The Major held out the phone. 'You can call him on this.'

Javier chuckled. 'You really think I am that stupid? I demand that someone calls my lawyer.'

'You can do that at the station,' said Bird. He looked at the Major. 'It's not one of those phones with thumb print recognition or facial recognition, is it? Because we could knock him out and get into the phone that way.'

'You need a password,' hissed Javier.

'Pity,' said the Major. He grinned at Bird. 'But I like the way you think.'

The Major patted the other prisoner down and took out his phone. Javier spoke quickly in Spanish and the other man grunted. 'I want to speak to my lawyer,' he said.

Gannon tried the phone but it too needed a passcode.

'What are we charged with?' asked Javier. 'What offences do you think we have committed?'

'There are two men in the kitchen with high-powered weapons who tried to kill my men,' said Bird. 'That would be a start.'

'My security staff,' said Javier. 'London is a dangerous city and a man such as myself needs protection. But if they decided to protect themselves against aggressive policemen waving guns and shouting at the top of their voices, then that is their problem, not mine.'

'We both know what you've been doing,' said the Major.

Javier shrugged. 'I want to talk to my lawyer. We both do. We won't be making any comments until our lawyers are present.'

The Major's eyes hardened. 'How do you think Carlos Martinez will react when he finds you are cooperating with the authorities?'

'I'm not cooperating,' said Javier.

'Really? It seems to me that you are. And I know a couple of journalists who I am sure would be happy to write stories saying that a leading member of a Mexican cartel is being very helpful following his arrest on conspiracy to murder charges.'

'Conspiracy to murder who exactly?'

'Ten members of the Security Service and four of my colleagues.'

Javier shrugged.

'I notice you don't have to ask who Carlos Martinez is.'

Javier shrugged again.

'We both know how eager he is to see Diego Flores killed. I'd imagine he'd be putting the same amount of effort into having you terminated. And I don't think anyone in the UK is going to be that interested in stopping him.'

'You don't scare me,' said Javier quietly.

'Maybe not. But I'm damn sure that the thought of what Martinez is going to do to you will keep you awake at night.' He held up the phones. 'Let's see what we have on these, shall we?'

'You can't touch our phones without a warrant,' said Javier, but the Major was already walking out of the room. Bird followed him.

Once he was outside the house, the Major called Giles Pritchard. The director answered almost immediately. 'All done, Giles,' said Gannon. 'We have Javier Silva and Santino Rossi in custody. There were two Americans with them, both were killed. Almost certainly former special forces, guns for hire.'

'No great loss,' said Pritchard. 'Any casualties on our side?'

'One of the firearms officers took a bullet in the foot but it's not life threatening.'

'Excellent.'

'I have Javier's phone. And Santino's. Unfortunately they're not prepared to give me the passcodes and are demanding to see lawyers.'

'If you have someone bring the phone into Thames House our technical guys can take a look,' said Pritchard.

'I could bring it in myself,' said Gannon.

'I think you'd be better off staying put with the police there so that you can be ready to move as soon as we have Hirst's location.'

'No problem,' said the Major, and he ended the call. He waved at Inspector Bird. 'I'll need someone to run the two phones over to Thames House,' said Gannon. 'They have people there who can get into locked phones.'

'The quickest way would probably be by motorbike,' said the inspector. He used his radio to summon a police biker. While they waited for the bike to arrive, the Major took two Post-it notes from a white-overalled forensics specialist and wrote down the names of the owners of the phones. The police motorcyclist collected the phones and sped off west towards Thames House.

CHAPTER 74

Hirst joined Barrett at the window. He pulled the curtain back to give him just enough of a gap to peer out. He saw Jimmy the Para, Walsh and O'Rourke walk out of the front door of the block and head towards the SUV. They walked past the white Explorer that the Americans were using to transport Flores. They were carrying holdalls containing their Hecklers and Jimmy's Kalashnikov.

'This guy we're supposed to hit,' said Barrett. 'Why's he so important?'

'Didn't Javier tell you?'

'He tells me what he needs doing, that's all. He never explains himself.'

'Let's just say the guy is one of the few people who can damage the cartel.'

'So he's a snitch?'

Hirst nodded. 'Yeah.'

'I fucking hate snitches,' said Barrett.

Hirst didn't say anything. He knew that Flores was only prepared to give evidence against the cartel because he knew that the cartel wanted him dead. He was caught between a rock and a hard place and helping the DEA was pretty much his only option. Hirst was also acting under duress, and he too had run out of options. All he could do was to do whatever Javier asked of him and hope that his wife and daughter would eventually be released.

The three men got into the SUV and a few minutes later they drove off. Hirst looked at his watch. It was just after seven fifteen. Javier had said the plane was expected to land at RAF Northolt at nine. The Americans would have to bring Flores out in the next hour or so. 'Keep your eyes peeled,' he said to Barrett, and patted him on the shoulder.

He went down the hallway to the bedroom and opened the door. The man and woman lay on their backs, bound and gagged with pillowcases over their heads. They had been untied once during the night and allowed to drink water and use the bathroom, but the rest of the time they had been securely tied. 'Mr and Mrs McKee, just to let you know that we will be leaving shortly,' he said. 'Once we've gone I'll call the police and they'll send someone around. I'll leave the door on the latch so they don't have to break in.' There was no reaction from either of them. 'Mr McKee, just move your legs so that I know you can hear me.'

Mr McKee shifted his legs.

'Thank you,' he said. 'You won't have to wait much longer.'

He closed the door on them and went along to the kitchen. The five men there were finishing off fried egg sandwiches and drinking coffee. 'Right, we need to get ready to move out at short notice,' Hirst said. 'Alf, do the washing up will you, let's try to leave this place as we found it. The Americans could be moving out at any time so I want you all in the front room, dressed and ready to go.' The men were still shoeless, following his instructions to keep noise down to a minimum. 'Shoes and boots on, obviously, but move quietly. Hopefully we'll take care of this in the street. As soon as it's done, Dean, Alf, Andy Pandy and I will head off in the Merc. The rest of you in the SUV. Assuming Flores is dead, the mission will be over and we can disperse. If we're not able to deal with Flores outside, we follow them to the airfield. Whatever happens, Flores is not to reach the airfield. Any questions?'

'Seriously, I have to do the washing up?' said Alf.

'Damn right,' said Hirst. 'And make sure you wipe down all surfaces and anything that you might have touched. We don't want to be leaving any prints or DNA behind.'

CHAPTER 75

The two mobile phones that Major Gannon had taken from the house in Camberwell arrived at MI5's headquarters and were taken up to Giles Pritchard's office. As soon as the Major had ended his call, Pritchard had phoned Amar Singh, one of MI5's technical experts and a wizard with mobiles. Despite the early hour, Singh had promised to get to Thames House within thirty minutes and was as good as his word. As always he was immaculately dressed in a Hugo Boss suit, a Ted Baker shirt and carrying a Louis Vuitton briefcase when he walked into Thames House.

Pritchard was waiting in the technical lab. He thanked Singh for coming in so early and explained the provenance of the two phones. Singh took off his jacket and hung it from a wooden hanger on the back of the door.

Pritchard pointed at the phone that belonged to Javier Silva. 'A senior Mexican cartel boss has, we think, been using this to stay in touch with a team of hired killers who have been running amok in London,' he said. 'We need the number he's been communicating with so that we can get GCHQ to track it.' He pointed at the phone that had been taken from Santino Rossi. 'This one we think has been used to communicate with a member of staff here at Thames House so we need to see any texts that are of interest.'

Singh took Silva's phone and connected it to one of his computers. He tapped on the keyboard for a minute or so, then sat back as lines of code flashed across the screen.

'How long does it usually take?' asked Pritchard.

'It varies, it depends on how much software is in the phone.

If it's a standard Android, just a few minutes. A bit longer for an iPhone.' He leaned forward and looked at the screen, frowning, then tapped on a couple of keys. 'Naughty, naughty.'

'What's wrong?'

'There's a sub-program here specifically designed to stop anyone doing what I'm trying to do,' he said. 'If it senses that someone is trying to access the passcode while the phone is attached to a computer, then it deletes everything on the phone.'

'I thought nothing was ever deleted, it was just moved to another part of the memory?'

'True. But this program will fragment everything and make it very time consuming to put it back together.'

'So we're screwed?' said Pritchard.

Singh flashed his trademark confident grin. 'The program is clever, but I'm cleverer,' he said. 'I can get the passcode through Wi-Fi and bypass the sub-program. It won't take me long to set it up.'

Singh's office phone rang and he answered it. He listened and then held it out to Pritchard. 'It's the switchboard. Call from the States.'

Pritchard took the receiver from him. The caller was the director of the Dallas office of the DEA. Pritchard looked at his watch. It was just before eight which meant it was 2 a.m. in Texas, which accounted for the man's annoyed tone. His name was Cory Bryant and he listened in silence as Pritchard explained what had happened. When he had finished, Bryant spoke quickly and quietly, almost as if he was reading from a script. 'There is a DEA flight en route to the UK as we speak, scheduled to land at RAF Northolt at nine o'clock your time. The last we heard from Eric Mitchell was that he had Flores in custody and that he would be at the airport.'

'That might well still be his intention. When was the last time you had contact with Agent Mitchell?'

There was a long pause and Pritchard knew that he had asked the right question.

'I spoke with Agent Mitchell about eight hours ago,' said

Bryant, and again Pritchard felt that the man was reading from a script.

'So that would be after he and his men were attacked in Hampstead?'

'I assume so, yes.'

'You assume so?' snapped Pritchard.

'I misspoke,' said Bryant. 'Yes, Agent Mitchell did explain what had happened, and that three of his agents had perished. He felt it best that they went off grid until the plane arrived and I agreed.'

'Did Agent Mitchell tell you that he had one of my people with him? Sally Page.'

'He did, yes.'

'And yet no one at the DEA thought to pass this information on to MI5?'

There was another long pause. 'Agent Mitchell felt that your organisation was probably the source of a leak that led to the attack in Hampstead,' Bryant said eventually. 'His judgement call was that the DEA should minimise contact with MI5 until Flores was out of the country.'

'He doesn't trust us?'

'In a nutshell, that's his view, yes.'

'Do you know where he is?'

'Specifically, no. He said he was in London, lying low in a safe location, and that he intended to stay there with Flores until the plane arrived.'

'How many agents does he have with him?'

'Two,' said Bryant. 'Luis Mendoza and Sam Butler.'

'And they are armed?'

'Yes.'

'And at what point were you going to tell us what had happened?'

'Once the plane had taken off. I understand that this is not what you want to hear, Mr Pritchard, but you have to understand the position we are in. Our people were in what was supposed to be a safe house, but it turned out to be anything but and three of our people died. There must have been a leak somewhere within your organisation, so it makes sense to cut our ties with you until the objective has been achieved.'

Pritchard didn't like what the American was saying, but considering they had just caught his secretary in the process of texting sensitive information to a member of the cartel, he couldn't really fault the man's logic. 'I understand,' said Pritchard.

'Shall we speak again once the plane has taken off?'

'I think that's a very good idea,' said Pritchard. He ended the call and immediately phoned Major Gannon. 'The Americans have sent a plane to pick up Flores at RAF Northolt,' he said. 'It might be an idea if you put together a team and head out that way.'

'I will do,' said the Major. 'Any joy on Hirst's location?'

'We're working on it,' said Pritchard. 'As soon as I know, you'll know. But if Hirst is still pursuing Flores there's a good chance he'll be heading out to the airfield.'

CHAPTER 76

Jimmy the Para lit a cigarette and took a long drag on it. It was the third he'd lit since they had parked their SUV at the London Heliport. They had been there since a quarter to eight, which was forty-five minutes after the heliport officially opened, but the office they were waiting for had a sign in its glass door saying that they were open from 8 a.m. until 9 p.m.

'At least open the window,' growled Sean O'Rourke in the back seat.

Pat Walsh pressed the button to open the front passenger window. 'It's a fucking disgusting habit,' he said.

'It relaxes me,' said Jimmy.

'Well it's fucking winding me up,' said O'Rourke. He opened his window and the wind blowing off the Thames ruffled his hair.

The heliport was on the south bank of the Thames, between Wandsworth Bridge and Battersea Railway Bridge. The site was small and the helicopters using it landed on a jetty that protruded into the river. The office they were waiting for offered chartered flights and sightseeing tours. Parked near to the office were two Eurocopter AS350 Squirrel helicopters. The heliport was surrounded by high-rise buildings and cranes but the jetty meant that landings were relatively simple.

'Here we go,' said Jimmy, nodding at a white Honda Civic with the name of the helicopter firm on the side as it turned into the parking area. A middle-aged blonde woman in a beige rain-coat with a large bag on one shoulder climbed out and walked to the office, a mobile phone pressed against her ear. She continued to talk on the phone as she unlocked the door and went inside.

'Right, so Pat and I will go in and do the talking,' said O'Rourke. 'You keep an eye on things out here.'

Jimmy blew a plume of smoke. 'Sounds good.'

'Send Marty a sitrep text,' said O'Rourke, as he opened the door. He and Walsh climbed out and walked over to the office.

The blonde woman had taken off her coat and was slotting a pod into a coffee machine. She flashed them a beaming smile as they walked up to the counter. 'Good morning, gentlemen, how can I help you?'

'We'd like to book a sightseeing trip,' said O'Rourke.

'That's what we do,' said the woman, flipping open a ledger. 'What day were you thinking of?'

'Today,' said O'Rourke. 'In fact, the sooner the better.'

'Oh my gosh, we're booked up all this week,' said the woman. 'Our first flight leaves in an hour and then we're booked right through until this evening.' She ran her finger down the ledger. 'The earliest I could book you in would be next Tuesday. In the afternoon.'

'That's too late for us,' said O'Rourke. 'To be honest, it's more of a business matter. We're in the property business and want to look at some sights from the air.'

'Ah, then a sightseeing trip really isn't what you want,' said the woman. 'Our trips stay over the river. We have a twenty-minute or a thirty-minute version and you get to see all the sights. It sounds as if you need a charter. Whereabouts are you interested in looking?'

'North-west London.'

'Ah, well you have to be careful there because you have Heathrow Airport so there is a lot of restricted airspace. What I'd suggest is that you sit down with one of our pilots and see if there's a flight plan that he could file.'

'It's possible, then?'

'It should be, yes.' She grinned. 'But I'm not a pilot.' The door opened and a young man in a dark blazer and light blue trousers came in carrying a large flight bag. 'But Daniel here is.'

The young man grinned. 'Daniel Chadwick at your service,' he said. 'Are you my nine o'clock tour? You're a bit early.' He was in his mid-twenties with ginger hair and freckles over his nose and cheeks. He'd cut himself shaving and there were two small pieces of tissue stuck to cuts on his chin.

'These gentlemen would like to talk to you about a charter,' said the woman.

Walsh pulled his gun from its holster and pointed it at the woman. 'We'd like to do more than talk,' he said.

The pilot opened his mouth to protest but O'Rourke pulled out his gun and pointed it at the man's stomach. 'Trust me, Daniel, there is nothing you can say that will change the outcome of what's about to happen. Put the bag on the floor, kneel down, and put your hands behind your head.'

The pilot obeyed. 'There's no need for anyone to get hurt,' he said.

O'Rourke grinned. 'That's exactly what I was going to say,' he said. O'Rourke walked over to the glass door and waved to attract Jimmy the Para's attention, then he flicked the 'OPEN' sign around so that it read 'CLOSED' and pulled a bolt across.

There was another door behind the counter leading to an internal room. O'Rourke gestured with his gun. 'Right, leave your bag where it is, Daniel. Stand up with your hands behind your head and walk to the room over there.'

'You too,' Walsh said to the woman. 'What's your name?'

'Tracey.'

'Well, Tracey, providing you do exactly as we say you'll be fine. We're not here to hurt you. We just need to borrow a helicopter.'

'You can't . . .' began the pilot, but he was silenced by a wave of O'Rourke's gun. He stood up and O'Rourke took him behind the counter. Walsh opened the door. It led to a windowless storeroom with shelving containing boxes of spare parts, uniforms, and aviation equipment and books.

'Right, both of you down on your knees, hands behind your head,' said Walsh. His captives obeyed. He covered them with his gun as O'Rourke went back into the office and opened the door for Jimmy the Para.

'Okay?' asked Jimmy. He was carrying his holdall.

'All good,' said O'Rourke. He relocked the door and followed Jimmy through to the storeroom, picking up the pilot's flight case on the way.

'Can I say something?' said the pilot, looking up at them fearfully.

'Sure, go ahead,' said Walsh. 'Just keep it short, we've got work to do.'

'You can't just borrow a helicopter,' said the pilot. 'There are rules and regulations that have to be followed. You have to be in contact with air traffic control, there are places you aren't allowed to fly, you have to file flight plans and you can't deviate from those flight plans. If you do, they'll scramble jets. After 9-11, no one takes chances any more.'

'Jets fly at five hundred miles an hour, helicopters hover,' said Walsh. 'What are they going to do, keep flying by?'

'They'll shoot you out of the sky,' said Chadwick.

'I seriously doubt that an RAF jet is going to shoot down an unarmed sightseeing helicopter over London,' said Walsh. 'But you'd better hope that they don't because you'll be at the controls.'

'This is madness,' said Chadwick.

'No, it's well planned,' said Walsh. 'We'll keep low, very low. By the time air traffic control realises there's a problem, we'll be finished.'

'Where do you want to go?'

'We'll tell you when we're on board,' said Walsh. 'Are you married, Daniel?'

The pilot nodded.

'Kids?'

'A boy. Two years old.'

'Well, you do exactly as we say and you'll be able to tell them all about your little adventure when you get home tonight. Okay?'

The pilot nodded.

Jimmy the Para took a roll of grey duct tape from his holdall and used it to bind Tracey's wrists and ankles, then slapped a piece across her mouth. He stood up and nodded at O'Rourke and Walsh. 'Right, we're good to go,' he said.

CHAPTER 77

'Done!' said Singh, punching the air in triumph. Pritchard walked over and put a hand on his shoulder. 'I'll do you a printout of all calls and texts,' added Singh.

'You're a star, Amar,' said Pritchard.

'I suppose now would be a good time to ask for a pay rise,' said Singh, his fingers tapping on the keyboard.

'It's never a good time, as you well know,' said Pritchard.

Singh peered at the screen. 'Interesting,' he said. 'Your man Javier got very busy at just after ten forty-five this evening. He received a call and then made another dozen or so calls over the following fifteen minutes.'

Pritchard looked over at Liz Bailey. 'That was just after the Hampstead house was attacked,' he said. 'The inward call was probably Hirst calling to tell Javier what had gone wrong and that six of his men were dead. Which suggests that the calls afterwards were Javier putting together a new team. Can you get a list of the numbers to GCHQ and tell them we need them GPS tracked as a matter of urgency. And we need them to arrange a real-time tracking feed – ideally of all the phones, but at the very least of Hirst's.'

'No problem,' said Bailey.

'I'm printing out the numbers now,' said Singh. A printer on a table behind them burst into life.

CHAPTER 78

O'Rourke closed the door and locked it using the key he had taken from Tracey's bag, then followed Walsh and Jimmy as they escorted the pilot towards one of the two Squirrel helicopters. They were carrying holdalls and kept their right hands close to their Glocks in underarm holsters. As they reached the helicopter, Chadwick stopped and put down his flight bag.

'What are you doing?' snapped Walsh.

'I have to do the pre-flight checks,' said Chadwick.

'Checking for what?'

'That the helicopter is flightworthy, that we have fuel, that the controls work.'

'You flew it yesterday, right?'

'Sure.'

'And when was it refuelled?'

'Last night, after the final flight.'

'So we're good to go,' said Walsh.

'We have to do the pre-flight checks. It's the law.'

Walsh put his hand on the butt of his gun. 'The only law you need to worry about is the one in my holster,' he said. 'Just get in the bloody helicopter and take off. Do anything else and I'll put a bullet in your leg.'

'If you do that then I won't be able to fly you anywhere.'

'In which case I'll cut to the chase and shoot you in the head and your wife and son can have dinner on their own tonight.'

'You don't have to keep threatening me,' said the pilot.

'Then just do as you're told,' said Walsh. 'And don't think about trying anything clever. We've all flown in choppers before so we know the drill. You stay off the radio, you don't squawk any ident, you fly exactly where I tell you to fly. Now get in the fucking chopper and get us in the air.'

Chadwick climbed into the pilot's seat and Walsh got into the front passenger seat. Jimmy the Para and O'Rourke climbed into the main passenger compartment with the holdalls. There were four seats in a row. They fastened their harnesses. There were headsets hanging on hooks and they all fitted them. 'Can you all hear me?' asked Chadwick, and they replied that they could.

'What's our heading?' asked Chadwick.

Walsh frowned. 'Heading?' he repeated.

'Which direction do we go?'

'North-west.'

'It would be easier if you gave me a destination.'

'Just fly where I tell you to fly,' said Walsh. He took out his Glock and laid it on his thigh for emphasis.

Chadwick nodded, and began flicking on a series of switches. He started the helicopter's high-powered single engine and the rotor blades began to spin overhead. The helicopter vibrated violently and even with the headphones on, the noise was uncomfortable. Chadwick looked across at Walsh as if he hoped he would change his mind but Walsh merely glared at him. Chadwick increased power to the blades, the engine roared and the helicopter lifted off and moved forward, over the river.

'Stay as low as you can,' said Walsh.

Chadwick nodded. 'You're the boss.'

The helicopter flew about twenty feet over the Thames, heading north-west, the rotor wash flattening the waves below them.

CHAPTER 79

Eric checked the action of his Glock and slid it into his holster. Sally and Tim were sitting at the kitchen table drinking coffee. Their carbines were on the table. Eric had broken the weapons down and checked and reassembled them and was satisfied that they were in good working order. He pulled up a chair and sat down with them. 'Guys, if you want you can pull out now. We're going to be driving to the airport so you can call it a day.'

'You're letting us go?' asked Tim.

'You're making it sound as if we've been keeping you hostage,' said Eric. He laughed and ran a hand through his hair. 'Yeah, I suppose that's what we did. But you understand why, right? We needed to stay hidden and we could hardly do that if you and Sally were back in circulation.'

Tim raised his coffee mug in salute. 'No hard feelings,' he said.

'You're not getting rid of me that easily,' said Sally. 'I'm seeing this through to the end.'

Eric grinned. 'I kinda thought you'd say that,' he said.

'And where she goes, I go,' said Tim. Sally looked over at him, smiled, and patted his hand.

'Okay, great. Thanks. So how does this sound? Sam, Luis and I will take Flores out to the SUV. You and Tim can cover us from the window of the apartment. You'll have a good view of the street and if we have a problem you should be able to take care of it with the Hecklers. Once we're in the SUV and on our way, you guys can get into the VW and follow us. Stay a hundred

yards behind us and protect our rear. We should get to RAF
Northolt within half an hour.'

'Sounds like a plan,' said Sally. Tim nodded in agreement.

'Great,' said Eric. 'Give me your phone numbers and I'll give
you mine.' They exchanged numbers, then Eric stood up and
headed for the sitting room. Sally and Tim picked up their carbines
and followed him.

Mendoza and Flores were together on the sofa in the sitting
room. Butler was standing by the window, peering through the
blinds at the street below. 'Sam, get the windows open so that
Sally and Tim can give us covering fire if necessary.'

Butler nodded and raised the three blinds covering the windows.
They were sash windows with brass screwable locks on the top.
He undid the locks on the two side windows and opened them
so that there was a gap of about a foot at the bottom.

Eric waved for Tim and Sally to take up position. They knelt
in front of the window and sighted through the gaps. They both
had a clear view of the Ford Explorer.

'Right, it's time to go,' said Eric.

Mendoza stood up and helped Flores to his feet. Flores held
up his bound hands. 'Can't you at least take these off?' he said.
'You took them off when I was eating my pizza and I didn't try
anything.'

'You're still our prisoner,' said Eric.

'But I'm cooperating. And you're responsible for my safety.'

'We're just walking you to the car,' said Eric. 'Nothing's going
to happen.'

Flores gestured at Sally and Tim with his hands. 'So why are
they there then?'

'Insurance,' said Eric. He nodded at Butler. 'Okay, Sam?'

Butler nodded and patted the gun in its shoulder holster.
'Locked and loaded.'

'Right, we walk down the stairs and out into the street. We
don't rush, we walk casually but we keep our eyes open. We
walk to the car, I get in the driver's seat, Sam you ride shotgun,
Luis you're in the back with Mr Flores. Sally and Tim will be

covering us. Sally, Tim, first sign of a threat you fire at least a warning shot. If you see attackers with guns, you shoot to kill. Got it?'

'Got it,' said Sally.

'Got it,' echoed Tim.

Eric smiled thinly. 'Right, let's do this,' he said.

CHAPTER 80

'I see them,' said Simple Simon. He was standing at the window peering through a gap in the curtains. Hirst hurried over to join him. He had his Heckler on a sling and was holding the iPad mini that showed the location of the Ford Explorer and the VW Jetta. Down below, four men were walking along the pavement. The two in front were looking around, checking their surroundings. They were followed by Flores and another man who was also looking around nervously. Flores had his hands in front of him, either handcuffed or zip-tied.

'Right, we're on, let's go!' said Hirst. He shoved the iPad into his jacket pocket and held his carbine with both hands as he hurried into the hallway. His team followed him. Hirst grabbed the front door handle and looked over his shoulder. Barrett, Andy Pandy and Alf were close by. Andy Pandy had the Uzi and Alf was cradling the sawn-off shotgun. Hirst didn't think that either weapon would be much good in a firefight but Barrett was holding an MP5 and Hirst had his own Heckler.

Hirst pulled upon the door but as he did he heard the clatter of footsteps coming down the stairs and the sound of laughter. Not one person, not two, but three or more. He cursed under his breath and half closed the door. Andy Pandy bumped into him and Hirst hissed at him to keep back. The clattering got louder. A teenager in tight jeans and Doc Marten boots came into view, followed by a girl with long blonde frizzy hair. Behind them was another guy, this one carrying a bike. They were laughing about something the girl had said and were teasing her. Hirst cursed again and closed the door.

'Simon, get eyes on the vehicles,' he whispered. Simple Simon headed for the front room.

'What is it?' whispered Barrett.

'Students,' said Hirst. The front door banged open and there were more footsteps on the stairs above.

'They're getting into their cars!' shouted Simon.

'Tell him to keep his fucking voice down,' Hirst hissed at Alf. Alf went into the sitting room.

'Right, we're going to have to use the cars,' said Hirst. 'I've got trackers on both vehicles so we won't lose them. Hide your weapons, and as soon as we get on the pavement, split up, okay? Let's try not to look like a gang.'

Hirst had a nylon backpack. He telescoped the Heckler's stock, and put it in the bag and shouldered it. Alf returned with a crestfallen Simon who studiously avoided eye contact with Hirst. Hirst pulled the door open and hurried across the hallway.

CHAPTER 81

Sally and Tim watched as the three DEA agents loaded Flores into the Ford Explorer. They scanned the street either side. There were pedestrians – three men in suits with briefcases, a couple of young mothers pushing buggies, and a postman – but nothing that looked remotely like a threat.

The car drove off and they stood up. Tim closed the windows. Sally took off her fleece and wrapped it around her carbine. Tim did the same with his jacket. It wasn't the best camouflage but they didn't have far to walk to their car. They hurried out of the flat, down the stairs and through the front door. They looked both ways and headed for the VW, resisting the urge to run.

CHAPTER 82

'That's the girl,' hissed Hirst. 'Fuck me, that's the girl.' He was walking down the pavement with Barrett beside him. Simple Simon and Andy Pandy were a few steps behind. Barrett had put his MP5 in a Marks & Spencer reusable carrier bag that he'd taken from the kitchen. He reached inside but Hirst stopped him with a shake of the head. 'Not here,' he said. 'Flores has already gone and if we start shooting now, someone will call the cops. Let them go. We can deal with them on the way.'

The girl and her male companion climbed into the VW Jetta without looking around, clearly in a hurry to get away. They had made a half-hearted attempt to hide their weapons with clothing, but it was clear they were armed.

Hirst reached the Mercedes. Andy Pandy pressed the fob to open the doors. Hirst stood by the front passenger seat watching the VW as it drove away. He pulled the iPad from his pocket. Two flashing green dots marked the progress of both vehicles.

Barrett and Alf got into the back of the Mercedes. Hirst took a final look around, got in and fastened his seat belt.

Andy Pandy shoved the Uzi under his seat and started the engine. Hirst kept the iPad on his lap as Andy Pandy followed the VW.

Hirst took his mobile phone out and sent a text message to O'Rourke. 'TARGET MOBILE, HEADING FOR A40'.

A few seconds later he got a text back. 'ROGER THAT. AIRBORNE'.

CHAPTER 83

The Major's phone rang and he answered it. It was Pritchard.
'Allan, where are you?' asked the director.

'In a layby about half a mile from RAF Northolt,' said Gannon.

'GCHQ have managed to get a fix on Hirst's phone, and they've patched a live feed through to Thames House and we're looking at it now. He was in Notting Hill and is now en route to the A40, clearly in a vehicle. The assumption is that he is following the DEA.'

'What about the rest of his team?'

'GCHQ are still looking at the numbers that Javier called. But Hirst's is the only one we are tracking at the moment. I can't see any way of getting this feed to you in the short term so I'll have to stay in touch via the phone. The good news is that we obviously know where he's going.'

'Do we know what vehicle he's in?'

'I'm afraid not. But the DEA will almost certainly be in a white Ford Explorer which shouldn't be too hard to spot. I suggest you start driving east along the A40 with a view to intercepting Hirst.'

'Agreed,' said the Major. He ended the call. Luke the guardsman was behind the wheel of the Range Rover while Kevin Reynolds and Ricky Coleman were in the back seat. Like soldiers the world over, Reynolds and Coleman had grabbed some sleep, resting their heads against the windows and snoring softly. They woke up as Luke put the car in gear and pulled into the traffic, heading east into London.

'What's the story, boss?' asked Coleman, immediately awake and alert.

'Hirst is on the way, we're going to try to intercept him.'

'About bloody time,' said Reynolds. He had his CQB carbine on his lap and he began checking its action. Coleman and the Major also had CQB carbines. Hirst wouldn't give up without a fight so they needed the heavy firepower.

CHAPTER 84

'Can you see them?' Sally asked Tim. They had just turned onto the A40. Wormwood Scrubs prison was off to their right, behind Hammersmith Hospital.

'I'm not sure,' said Tim, squinting through the windscreen. 'There's a white SUV ahead but I'm not sure if it's a Ford.'

'They won't be speeding, they'll be blending in,' said Sally. 'If we go just above the speed limit we should catch up with them soon enough.'

Her Heckler was on the back seat, covered with her North Face fleece. Tim had his weapon down between his legs, the barrel pointing at the floor. He smiled across at her. 'I can't believe how calm you are,' he said.

She grinned. 'I'm the proverbial swan,' she said. 'I'm only calm on the surface.'

'My heart is pounding,' said Tim. 'It's like I'm running a marathon.'

'You were never a runner,' she laughed. 'The number of times I offered to run with you and you always said no.'

'I did once, remember,' he said. 'You ran me into the ground.'

'I did not.'

He nodded. 'You're bloody competitive when it comes to running. Actually, you're competitive at most things.'

'You say that as if it's a bad thing.' She pulled to the right to overtake a removal van, stamped on the accelerator and then remembered she hadn't indicated as she sailed past it. The white SUV was a few cars ahead of them. It was a Honda CR-V.

'No criticism intended,' he said. 'But if the offer is still open, yeah, I'll run with you.'

'We'll see,' said Sally, putting her foot down again.

CHAPTER 85

Hirst stared down at his iPad. The second flashing green dot was gaining on the first. He twisted around in his seat. Dean Barrett was sitting behind him, his MP5 in his lap. 'Where's Simple Simon and his guys?' asked Hirst.

Barrett turned and looked through the rear window. The green SUV being driven by Simon was three cars behind them. 'I see him,' said Barrett.

'We need to take out the VW before we go much further,' he said. 'They've got guns and we can't attack Flores with them in the picture.'

'Got you,' said Barrett, taking out his phone.

Hirst looked back at the iPad. The lead vehicle was still about twenty minutes away from the airfield. Plenty of time. But first they had to get rid of the girl and her companion.

Barrett relayed the instructions to Simon, and a few seconds later the green SUV roared by them.

CHAPTER 86

'I think I see them up ahead,' said Sally. Tim peered through the windscreen and nodded. The white Ford Explorer was about eight cars ahead, in the inside lane. 'I should get a bit closer,' she said, pressing down on the accelerator. She took a look in the rear-view mirror. A green SUV was coming up behind her and her eyes narrowed when she saw that the man in the front passenger seat was holding what looked like a sawn-off shotgun. 'Tim,' she said, 'I think we might have a problem.'

The SUV got to about thirty feet behind her before it slowed to match her speed.

Tim started to turn but Sally hissed at him not to. 'Check your wing mirror,' she said.

Tim dropped down in his seat slightly to give himself a better view. 'Shit,' he said. 'That's a fucking shotgun. Do you recognise them?'

'No,' she said. 'Look, they're going to have to overtake to attack us, and they'll be on our right.' She pressed the button to lower the window by the right passenger seat. 'They won't be able to shoot us until they're almost level, so you'll be able to get a shot in first.'

'Are you sure?'

'Sure about what?'

'Sure about shooting at them? We could be prosecuted.'

'Tim, if we don't, we'll be dead.'

The wind was blowing through the open window and they had to raise their voices to be heard.

'Okay, okay,' he said, sitting up again. 'But if I have to shoot through the window behind you, the barrel is going to be bloody close to your head. It could seriously damage your ears. Plus I'll only have a very small angle to fire through.'

Sally's eyes flicked back to the rear-view mirror. The green SUV was closer now. At least one of the windows was open.

'How about this – get them to overtake on my side,' said Tim. 'I'll get a clear shot and the guy with the shotgun will have to fire through their car to get to me.'

'And how do I do that?' She accelerated a little but couldn't go too fast as there was a truck ahead of her.

'Move over to the right lane. Then brake hard and they'll have no choice other than to come up on our left.'

Sally nodded. 'Okay,' she said.

Tim pressed the button to open the passenger-side window. He raised the gun so that it was in his lap, then leaned forward and pulled the lever to push his seat back a few inches.

Sally checked the rear-view mirror again. The SUV was closer now. Then she looked at her wing mirror. There was a line of three cars moving up the outside lane behind her, led by a black BMW.

'Ready?' asked Sally.

Tim swallowed. 'As I'll ever be.'

Sally took a final look in her rear-view mirror. The SUV driver was looking to his right, checking out the cars that were overtaking. She realised he was getting ready to make his move. She turned the wheel to the right, moving to the edge of her lane and then crossed into the outside lane. The driver of the BMW pounded on his horn and as he did Sally stamped on the brake. She felt her seat belt tighten across her chest and the tyres squealed. She concentrated on keeping the car going straight but she managed to flick her eyes to the rear-view mirror and saw the green SUV coming up on their left.

Tim had his carbine up and he slipped his finger over the trigger.

The SUV's windows were open and there were two handguns pointing out.

Sally took a quick look to the left. The driver of the SUV was snarling like an angry dog. The front passenger had the shotgun up but he was on the wrong side to take a shot.

Tim swung the carbine out of the window. For a moment Sally thought he was going to shoot the driver but then he dropped his aim and fired three shots at the front tyre. The tyre exploded and the front of the SUV dropped. There was a shower of sparks from the wheel hub scraping along the tarmac and then the vehicle flipped and rolled.

Sally moved back into the left-hand lane. The BMW accelerated past her.

The SUV continued to roll down the road behind her with a scream of tortured metal and breaking glass. Tim pulled his carbine back in and pressed the button to raise his window. Sally closed the rest of the windows. She checked in her rear-view mirror. The SUV had finally come to a halt, upside down. The traffic behind it was slowing but cars were still driving past the wreckage.

'Nice,' said Sally.

'I can't believe I just did that,' said Tim, resting back in his seat.

'I'm glad you did,' said Sally.

'I guess all those years playing Grand Theft Auto finally paid off.' He laughed but she could hear the tension in his voice. She was just as edgy. They had put one car out of commission but it was far from over.

CHAPTER 87

'Did you see that?' asked Alf. 'Did you fucking see that?' The Mercedes was in the outside lane. Traffic had slowed to a crawl as drivers slowed to survey the damaged SUV. It was about a hundred yards ahead of them. The inside lane wasn't moving at all and traffic was merging to get by.

Hirst knew that it would be only a matter of minutes before the police turned up and blocked off the road.

'They fucking shot the wheel off,' said Alf.

Hirst ignored him and studied the iPad on his lap. The two blinking lights were close together and moving quickly. He ran his finger along the route, then took out his phone and sent a text message to O'Rourke. 'INTERCEPT NOW. COMING UP TO TESCO SUPERSTORE AND PITSHANGER PARK'.

A few seconds later he received a reply. 'ROGER THAT'.

The Mercedes continued to crawl along the road. They could see the SUV now. It was upside down and all the windows were smashed. There was steam billowing out of the bonnet and black smoke was pouring from the exhaust. The occupants were hanging from their seat belts. They all appeared to be unconscious.

One driver had got out of his car with a small fire extinguisher and was spraying foam around the bonnet. 'Whatever happens, keep moving,' said Hirst. 'We don't stop for anything.'

CHAPTER 88

Walsh could see the park ahead of the helicopter, then the A40 running east to west, and beyond the park the large 'TESCO SUPERSTORE' sign. 'Head that way, towards Tesco,' he said over the intercom as he gestured with his Glock. The helicopter was over Ealing, about fifty feet above the rooftops.

The pilot obeyed and the helicopter banked to the left and then straightened up again. The park was directly ahead of them, a large open space with meadows and woods and with the River Brent meandering through it. There was a golf course to the north and a car park with several dozen vehicles lined up close to a large brick building, presumably the club house.

'You need to go lower,' said Walsh.

'You're crazy!' shouted the pilot, but Walsh prodded his leg with the barrel of the Glock and the pilot guided the helicopter down until it was just twenty feet or so above the houses below. They flashed beneath them in a blur.

Walsh frowned as he saw the tailback stretching towards London. There had been some sort of accident and the westbound traffic was crawling past it. The eastbound lanes were moving just fine but the traffic was slowing as drivers craned their necks to see what had happened. The accident was about a mile east of the Tesco Superstore so their target wouldn't be affected.

In the passenger compartment, Jimmy the Para and O'Rourke were checking their weapons; Jimmy with his Kalashnikov and O'Rourke with a Heckler & Koch 416. Satisfied that their guns were primed and ready to fire, they opened the side windows. The wind rushed through the cabin, grabbing at their hair and whipping it around. Below them flashed the green of the golf course, dotted with sand-filled bunkers.

CHAPTER 89

'Do you think we should get any closer?' Sally asked Tim. The white Ford Explorer was four cars ahead of them in the middle lane, sticking to the speed limit.

'I don't see there's any point,' he said. 'We need to protect their rear and if we're right behind them we won't get any warning of an attack. I think we're better off here.'

She nodded. He was right. She looked in the rear-view mirror. The green SUV was too far away to see now, and the traffic behind her was moving normally. She doubted that her pursuers had been using only one vehicle so there was a real threat of another attack.

'He's flying low,' said Tim, looking through the side window.

Sally turned to see what he was looking at. A helicopter was flying over the park to their left, maybe just thirty or forty feet above the ground.

'I thought they weren't supposed to fly that low,' said Tim.

Sally frowned as she saw something sticking out of the helicopter's side window. As she watched, the helicopter reached the edge of the park then went into a hover, close to the entrance to a golf course. Sally's heart raced as she realised what was happening. She accelerated and began to pound on her horn, trying to attract the attention of the occupants of the Explorer. She pulled out into the outside lane forcing a Jaguar to brake sharply. The Jaguar's horn blared and Sally continued to sound hers. The helicopter was now moving parallel to the road, about twenty feet above it – and the barrels of two guns were pointing out of the side window. It was coming up behind the Ford Explorer.

CHAPTER 90

Mendoza twisted around in his seat. Two cars were banging on their horns behind them. Flores also turned to look. 'What's going on?' he asked.

'It's an English thing,' said Mendoza. 'They're as polite as fuck one on one but put them behind the wheel of a car and they turn into monsters.'

Eric twisted around. 'Can you see who it is?' His phone rang. It was Sally Page. 'Yes Sally?'

Before she could say anything, bullets ripped through the side of the car and the windows exploded.

Butler cursed and fought to keep control of the car but both tyres on the passenger side had been ripped apart and the vehicle lurched to the left.

'What the fuck's happening?' screamed Flores.

Mendoza grabbed him and pulled him away from the smashed window. Eric tried to pull out his Glock but the SUV was already starting to skid. They jerked to the right as Butler twisted the wheel around, compensating too much and slamming into a car in the outside lane with the crunch of buckling metal. More shots thudded into the front of the car and then the bonnet sprang open, blocking their view.

Butler was still fighting to bring the SUV under control. It twisted to the left again and then the steering wheel kicked in his hands and the vehicle began to roll. Flores was screaming in Spanish. As the SUV turned over, Eric caught a glimpse of a helicopter suspended in a cloudless sky, gun barrels protruding from an open window.

CHAPTER 91

Sally stared in horror as the Ford Explorer overturned and rolled along the inside lane in a shower of sparks. The helicopter sped on, then went into a tight turn to the left, clearly getting ready to make another pass. She stamped on the brakes and pulled over. 'Come on!' she shouted. She twisted around and grabbed her Heckler & Koch from under her fleece, then pulled open the door and stepped out. Tim followed her. They both stood next to the VW and leaned on the roof as they sighted on the helicopter. It was about a hundred yards away, still in a tight turn. Sally fired three times in quick succession, aiming at the middle of the main rotor, but couldn't tell if her shots were hitting their target.

Tim began firing, slowly and methodically, but again there was no way of telling if his rounds were hitting the helicopter. It was over the golf club building now, still banking. Sally could clearly see the barrels of two guns sticking out of the window. She fired two shots at the side of the helicopter, aiming for the barrels, then two more shots in quick succession. Her eyes were stinging from the cordite and she could feel the heat from the hot metal on her cheek. She continued to fire, moving her aim along the body of the helicopter, and then as she reached the tail the small rotor there exploded. Pieces of metal flew off the tail and the helicopter began to spin.

Tim was still aiming at the main body of the helicopter and he grunted with satisfaction as one of the windows exploded. The helicopter was spinning haphazardly now and the engine was screaming. It was heading away from the road, towards the golf club car park, and black smoke began to belch from the engine.

They stopped firing and straightened up, watching with open mouths as the helicopter spun over the golf course and then crashed into the car park. Almost immediately there was a loud explosion and a flash of yellow light followed by a plume of grey smoke that funnelled into the sky.

Traffic was coming to a halt all around. Then there was the crack of automatic fire from behind them and bullets thwacked into their car. Tim grunted and slumped against the VW. Blood blossomed on his shoulder and he grunted again as he turned around. 'Sally, I'm hit,' he said, then he slowly slumped to the ground.

CHAPTER 92

The Range Rover was on the other side of the road in the outside lane approaching the Tesco Superstore and the Major had a clear view of the helicopter's attack on the white SUV. His jaw had dropped when he saw the rear tail rotor fall apart and the machine spin and crash into the car park of the golf course on the far side of the A40. 'Pull over!' he shouted at Luke. 'Pull over now!'

The guardsman turned the steering wheel hard and cut across to the side of the road before jamming on the brakes. 'Come on, guys,' shouted the Major, opening the passenger door. 'We've got work to do.'

Reynolds and Coleman bailed out of the car. The traffic was slowing as drivers tried to get a better look at the burning helicopter.

They heard shots from the other side of the road. Three men had climbed out of a Mercedes and were firing at a man and a woman standing by a VW Jetta. As the Major watched, the man collapsed against the car. He'd been hit. The woman raised a carbine to her shoulder and began to fire at the men by the Mercedes. One of them was Hirst, Gannon realised, and he was firing a Heckler & Koch. The woman was Sally Page and she clearly wasn't fazed at all at being in a firefight. He pointed his carbine at Hirst and fired two quick shots, even though he knew at that range he had little chance of hitting his target. He just wanted to get the man's attention, and he succeeded. Hirst turned away from Page and peered over at the Major.

Gannon waved at Reynolds and Coleman and pointed at the men by the Mercedes. 'Come on!' he shouted, as they ran into the road.

CHAPTER 93

Sally aimed at the bald man who was holding a gun similar to the one she had. He was standing by the passenger door of a Mercedes. It was the man she'd seen outside the house in Wimbledon, she was sure of that. There was another man behind him and as she squeezed the trigger she realised a third man was getting out of the other side of the car. Her bullet smacked into the vehicle's radiator. Her second shot smashed the offside headlight. The bald man took aim and fired. She was already ducking and the round whined over her head. She straightened up and was about to fire when she saw he was aiming at her again. She threw herself to the side as more rounds whizzed by her. She knelt down and put the carbine to her shoulder and fired two quick shots but they went high.

There was a barrage of shots to her left and the bald man ducked. The man who was standing at the rear of the Mercedes screamed in pain and dropped his weapon before slumping to the tarmac. The bald man rested his carbine on the roof of the Mercedes and began firing across the road and the man with him fired what looked like a shotgun. There was a loud explosion and the windows of a car in front of them shattered.

Sally turned to see what they were shooting at.

There were three men on the far side of the eastbound lanes. Traffic was moving, albeit slowly, and the three men were weaving their way through the cars, firing guns similar to the one she was holding.

Sally knelt down and looked at Tim. He had put his gun down and was holding his hand over the shoulder wound. He'd been shot from the rear so he was pressing the exit wound; there would still be a hole in his back. She pulled open the passenger door and grabbed her fleece. She moved him forward, pressed it against his shoulder and had him lean back against the car to keep pressure on it.

'Don't worry, help will be here soon,' she said. She got to her feet.

'Where are you going?' he asked.

'I've got to help Eric,' she said.

For a moment she thought he was going to ask her to stay with him but then he forced a smile. 'Go,' he said. 'I'll be okay.'

She kissed him on the cheek. 'I know,' she said. She stood up, holding the carbine to her chest. The bald man and the man with the shotgun were crouching behind the Mercedes. The three men over the road were still shooting at them.

Sally kept her head down as she ran towards the Explorer. It was on its roof and clouds of steam were coming from the bonnet. The rear passenger door had opened and Flores was trying to crawl out, hindered by the fact that his wrists were still zip-tied. Sally reached the vehicle and helped him out onto the road. 'Are you okay?' she asked. He nodded. She looked inside the car. Mendoza was hanging from his seat belt, his face covered with blood, but he was breathing and his eyes were half open.

Both front airbags had inflated, pressing Eric and Butler back in their seats. Butler seemed to be unconscious and Eric was bleeding from his head. Sally couldn't tell if it was a gunshot wound or a result of the car crashing.

Eric forced a smile. 'A fucking chopper,' he said. 'That came out of left field.'

'It's not a threat any more,' said Sally.

'What happened?'

'We shot it down, Tim and I.' She flinched at the sound of more gunshots behind her.

'What's happening?' asked Eric.

'The guys who are after us are shooting at us. But someone is shooting at them. Undercover armed cops maybe. I don't know. But they're keeping the bad guys busy.'

Eric tried to undo his seatbelt but winced with pain and cursed. 'I think my arm is broken,' he said.

'I'll help you.'

There were more shots from behind her. 'No, there's no time,' he said. 'Get Flores away from here. Keep him safe until the cops arrive.'

'I will,' she said.

She stood up, but bent at the waist to keep her head down. She looked to her left. The entrance to the golf course was close by and she could see the cloud of smoke from the burning helicopter still rising into the sky. She grabbed Flores by the scruff of the neck and pulled him to his feet. 'Stay close to me,' she said. 'We've got to get away from here.'

CHAPTER 94

The Major reached the barrier between the east- and west-bound lanes and he paused to fire two more shots at the Mercedes, then ejected the empty clip and slapped in a fully loaded one. The traffic in the westbound lane had come to a halt and he used a Jaguar as cover. One of the men who had been in the Mercedes was down on the ground. Hirst and the other man were standing behind the car. Hirst had a Heckler and obviously knew how to use it, but his companion had a pump-action shotgun which even in the hands of an expert wasn't effective at more than twenty feet or so. The man had fired twice and done nothing more than pepper vehicles with lead shot and broken a couple of windows.

Reynolds was to Gannon's left and Coleman was to his right. They were both moving away from him along the central reservation to widen their angles of attack.

Off to the right, Sally had taken a Hispanic man from the upturned Ford Explorer and was running with him to the entrance to Ealing Golf Club, which bordered the north side of the park. The man was presumably the DEA's informant.

Hirst was staring after Sally and Flores and the Major fired two quick shots at him. One went high, the other thudded into the Mercedes. Hirst looked in his direction and shouldered his carbine. The Major ducked for cover behind the rear wheels of a large container truck before Hirst started shooting.

CHAPTER 95

Sally and Flores ran down the lane that led to the golf club. Flores was in shock and was having trouble running so she slung her carbine over her shoulder and put an arm around him to help. 'Where are we going?' he gasped.

'Away from the shooting,' she said.

Golfers had emerged from the main building and were staring at the burning helicopter. From the look of the mangled wreckage, everybody on board was dead. Several of the golfers had taken out their mobile phones and were videoing the carnage. Unbelievably, a female golfer was taking a selfie with the helicopter burning behind her.

Sally looked around, wondering where to go. The main building was the obvious place to hide and she headed for the entrance.

CHAPTER 96

Hirst took a look over his left shoulder, just in time to see the girl run with Flores into the grounds of the golf club. A shot whined overhead. The three men were spreading out as they fired. It wouldn't be long before they would be able to get shots in from the side and then it would all be over.

'Give me covering fire, I've got to go after Flores,' he said to Alf.

Alf scowled and ducked as another shot went over their heads. 'The shotgun's no good for that.'

Hirst knew the man had a point, so he thrust the HK416 at him. Alf fired two quick shots with his shotgun, then placed it on the roof of the Mercedes and grabbed the Heckler. The three attackers were seeking cover and by the time Alf fired they were all in hiding and keeping their heads down.

Hirst pulled his Glock from its holster, bent double at the waist, and ran along the road towards the golf course.

CHAPTER 97

The Major peered out from behind the wheel of the truck, just in time to see Hirst running towards the golf course. He immediately gave chase, zig-zagging through the parked cars blocking his way.

There was only one shooter left by the Mercedes and he started firing at the Major, but he rushed his aim and the rounds thwacked into vehicles around Gannon, some of them missing him by inches.

The Major continued to run at full pelt, and the shooter turned to follow him. In his haste to take down Gannon, he forgot about Coleman and Reynolds and the two SAS troopers took the opportunity to duck out from behind their cover and fire a volley of shots in his direction. The man dropped down behind the Mercedes, giving the Major a clear run to the entrance of the golf club.

CHAPTER 98

A man in a dark blue suit held up a hand as Sally tried to get into the main golf club building. 'Excuse me, are you a member?' He was a big man, well over six feet tall, with hair that was so uniformly dark brown that it had almost certainly been dyed.

'Look, I need to get inside,' said Sally. She tried to push by him but he was too big to move.

'Don't you dare lay your hands on me,' said the man. He frowned as he saw the gun slung over her shoulder. 'What the hell is that?' he asked.

'Look, we're being chased, we need a place to hide.'

'I'm calling the police,' said the man, pulling a mobile phone from his pocket.

'Do that,' said Sally. 'But in the meantime, let us in.'

The man ignored her and tapped out nine-nine-nine. A bullet whacked into the bricks a few inches from his head and he ducked and cursed. 'What the fuck!'

Sally looked over her shoulder. The bald man was about fifty feet away, holding a gun with both hands. It was a pistol, not the carbine he had been using earlier. He fired again but Sally had already grabbed Flores's arm and was running with him towards the golf course and the shot went wide.

CHAPTER 99

As the Major reached the lane leading to the golf course, he saw Marty Hirst running past the main building. The helicopter was burning in the car park. Dozens of golfers were standing around, many of them videoing the fire with their phones. The Major didn't bother shouting at them to get back; if the fuel tank exploded it would be their own fault.

He gave chase after Hirst. He couldn't see Sally or Flores, but he was sure that Hirst was going after them. 'Marty, wait!' he shouted.

Hirst whirled around, clasped both hands on his gun and fired two shots. The Major ducked to the side, thankful that Hirst only had a handgun and not a Heckler. Hirst started running again and Gannon followed. He was already breathing heavily. He was in pretty good condition but Hirst was almost two decades younger and in better shape and he wasn't sure how long he could keep up the pace.

CHAPTER 100

Sally looked over her shoulder and realised that the bald man wasn't shooting at them, he was firing at a man outside the club house, one of the men who had been firing from the other side of the A40. She didn't know if he was a cop or SAS but he was clearly on her side.

'Come on,' she said, pulling at Flores's arm.

'I can't,' he gasped. He was exhausted, panting like a dog, his face bathed in sweat.

'You have to,' she said. 'If he catches us, it's you he wants to kill, remember.'

Flores held up his bound hands. 'It'd be easier to run if I wasn't tied.'

'I don't have anything to cut them with,' she said. She grabbed his arm and pulled him down a path that led to a footbridge across the river that cut through the golf course. Flores was unsteady on his feet but he managed to jog. Sally kept pulling him, trying to conceal her impatience. Without Flores to slow her down she was sure she was more than capable of outrunning her pursuer. But her job was to protect him and she couldn't do that by running away. They reached the footbridge and Flores grabbed at a rail for support, gasping for breath.

Sally turned her back on him and swung the carbine up. 'Diego, head over the river and then get to those trees,' she said, gesturing at a small copse beyond the golf course. She took aim at the bald man and fired. He threw himself to the side but even so, she knew that her shot had missed him by yards. 'Go!' she shouted.

Flores nodded and started to jog across the bridge. Sally knelt down on one knee to steady her aim and fired again. She couldn't see where the bullet went but it clearly didn't hit the man. He got to his feet and ran to a clump of trees, seeking cover. Sally fired again and this time bark ripped off the tree he was hiding behind, at about head height. She smiled to herself. Her aim was getting better. She took a quick look over her shoulder. Flores was across the bridge and jogging unsteadily towards the copse of trees. She turned back. The man was peering around the tree and pointing his gun at her. She took aim and pulled the trigger. There was a click but no explosion and no recoil. She frowned and pulled the trigger again. Nothing. She was out of bullets. She dropped the gun and turned and ran after Flores.

CHAPTER 101

Hirst saw the woman drop the gun and run. He realised immediately what had happened and sprinted after her. She was fast and she was pulling away from him as she ran over the bridge and towards Flores. Flores was jogging slowly across the grass, his feet dragging as if they were made of lead.

She drew level with Flores and took him by the arm, obviously trying to encourage him to run faster, but the Mexican was clearly exhausted. Hirst began to gain on them. He took a quick look over his shoulder. The man chasing him was some distance away. Hirst had time to do what needed to be done.

He caught up with the girl and Flores. She stepped between him and the Mexican, and put her hands out. 'Keep away!' she shouted.

'Don't be an idiot,' he said, levelling the gun at her. 'Get out of the fucking way!'

'If you want to shoot him, you'll have to shoot me first,' she said.

'Who the hell are you?' asked Hirst.

'My name's Sally. I'm with MI5. And my job is to protect him.'

'He's had dozens of people killed, maybe hundreds,' said Hirst. 'Not just killed. Raped and tortured. You know what the cartel does, right?'

Sally frowned in confusion. 'But you work for the cartel,' she said.

'I don't have any choice,' he said. 'Now get out of the way or I swear to God I will shoot you.' He pointed the gun at her but she stared defiantly back at him.

They both turned as they heard the Major running across the

grass towards them. Hirst took the opportunity to clip Sally around the ear with his Glock and she staggered back. Hirst grabbed Flores around the neck with his left arm and jammed the barrel of the Glock against the man's neck, then swung him around to face the Major. 'Stay the hell where you are or I'll shoot him.'

'That's the plan anyway, isn't it?' said the Major. He had his carbine in front of him but he wasn't aiming it at Hirst.

Hirst pointed the gun at Sally. 'And I'll kill her, too.' Sally was rubbing her head where he had hit her. She looked at her fingers. There was some blood, but not much.

'You don't have to do this, Marty,' said the Major.

'You don't know what you're talking about,' said Hirst.

The Major lowered his carbine and slowly placed it on the ground. 'You need to know that your wife and daughter are okay,' he said as he straightened up.

Hirst's eyes widened.

The Major took out his mobile phone and switched it on. He scrolled through the phone and found the video he had shot of Amanda. He pressed play and held the phone towards Hirst.

Hirst stared at the phone and his face softened as he listened to what his wife was saying. 'How?' he asked the Major.

'We tracked her to a house in London. We went in and got her. She's in Wellington Barracks as we speak. I can take you to see her. And Sophie.'

'They're okay?'

'They're fine. Tired, obviously, after everything they've been through. But they're fine. They want to see you, Marty.'

'They said they were going to kill them. They said they were going to rape them and kill them and make me watch.'

'I know,' said the Major.

Hirst frowned. 'What happened to Javier?'

'He's in custody. We know he was threatening you, Marty. We know you were acting under duress.'

Hirst kept his gun pressed against Flores's throat.

'You don't have to kill Flores now,' said the Major. 'It's over.'

Hirst shook his head. 'It's not over. They know who I am. The cartel will get its revenge. They always do.'

'Think about your wife and daughter,' said Sally. 'Would they want you to be doing this? You know they wouldn't. It's over. Just give us the gun and we can fix this.'

Hirst shook his head vehemently. 'It's unfixable.'

'How did they know about you, Marty?' asked the Major. 'How did they get in touch with you in the first place?'

'I got caught in Colombia. We were doing surveillance operations for the Colombian government, targeting cocaine factories in the jungle. I was captured by a Mexican cartel. They tortured me.' Hirst shuddered at the memory. 'It was nothing like I'd trained for. It was . . . it was horrific. I broke. I told them who I was and what I was doing. I told them everything.'

'And they let you go?'

Tears were welling up in Hirst's eyes. 'They knew where I was, they knew everything about me, they said they weren't going to kill me, but one day they would come for me. They had everything on tape . . . they owned me.'

'And this week they got in touch?'

'The man called Javier. He told me he wanted me to work for him and I told him to fuck off and then he had Amanda and Sophie kidnapped. I had no choice. You understand that, right?'

'I understand. A man has to do whatever he can to protect his wife and children. No one will blame you.'

Hirst smiled ruefully. 'We both know that isn't true. I've killed a lot of people over the past twenty-four hours.'

'You were acting under duress,' said the Major.

'That doesn't make it right,' said Hirst. 'Tell Amanda that I'm sorry and that I love her. Tell Sophie that her dad was thinking of her.'

The Major opened his mouth to shout but he was too late. Hirst released his grip on Flores's neck, took a step back, pressed the barrel of his Glock against his temple and pulled the trigger. The side of his head exploded in a shower of blood and he fell to the ground.

Sally stared at the body in horror as blood soaked into the grass. Flores staggered away and fell to his knees, gasping for breath.

The Major looked down at Hirst and shook his head sadly. 'I'll tell them,' he said quietly.

CHAPTER 102

Giles Pritchard sipped his glass of Evian water, then flashed Sally a smile. 'The Major here tells me that you put up one hell of an impressive performance protecting the DEA's informant,' he said.

Major Gannon was sitting next to her and he nodded his approval. 'She was a fighting machine,' he said. 'We should put her in for SAS selection.'

Sally smiled but didn't say anything.

'You shot down a helicopter?' said Pritchard.

'Tim and I did, between us,' she said quietly.

'And how is your boyfriend?'

Sally was about to correct him and say that Tim wasn't her boyfriend, but she just smiled. 'He's in hospital but the doctor says he can probably go home tomorrow. The bullet went in and out. He was lucky.'

'Give him my best,' said Pritchard. 'The director general has already spoken to the commissioner and he won't have any problems from Professional Standards or any of that nonsense. He might well end up with a commendation.'

'He'll be glad to hear that,' said Sally.

'And you,' said Pritchard. He took another sip of water. 'Well, Diego Flores is on a plane bound for Dallas. The three DEA agents are all alive if not well, but there'll be no lasting damage. I'd be tempted to say that all's well that ends well if it wasn't for the fact that we lost a lot of good men – and women – yesterday. Possibly the worst day in the Service's history.' He looked across at Major Gannon. 'And the Regiment has its losses to deal with, too.'

The Major nodded but didn't say anything.

'It was a mess, right from the start,' said Sally.

'It was,' said Pritchard. 'But we need to move forward, and on that front we need to think about what we do with you. It beggars belief that you were kept back as long as you were, and we need to remedy that. One possibility would be to slot you into Ian Hadley's job. You certainly have the experience to run the footies. Or we could definitely find you something in Technical Operations and Surveillance.'

'I'm flattered, obviously,' said Sally, shifting uncomfortably in her chair.

'I'm sensing there's a "but" coming,' said Pritchard. 'Please don't say that what happened today has put you off the Service.'

'Not at all,' said Sally. 'It's just that the DEA have offered me a job.'

Pritchard frowned. 'In the States?'

Sally shook her head. 'Here in London. Eric Mitchell is moving to Washington and he has recommended me as his replacement. His bosses have agreed in principle.'

Pritchard nodded. 'They do pay well,' he said.

Sally grinned. 'Yes, they do.'

'And it might be to MI5's advantage to have a friendly face working with the Americans,' added Pritchard.

Sally smiled and nodded. 'Absolutely,' she said.

THRILLINGLY GOOD BOOKS
FROM CRIMINALLY
GOOD WRITERS

CRIME FILES BRINGS YOU THE LATEST RELEASES FROM TOP CRIME AND THRILLER AUTHORS.

SIGN UP ONLINE FOR OUR MONTHLY NEWSLETTER AND BE THE FIRST TO KNOW ABOUT OUR COMPETITIONS, NEW BOOKS AND MORE.

VISIT OUR WEBSITE: WWW.CRIMEFILES.CO.UK
LIKE US ON FACEBOOK: FACEBOOK.COM/CRIMEFILES
FOLLOW US ON TWITTER: @CRIMEFILESBOOKS